# THE WINDS OF CHANGE

Following the death of her husband and the loss of a son in WWII, Dottie finds comfort, but little happiness, in the daily routine at her home in small-town Iowa. Then slowly her life begins to change as she confronts her feelings for Al, the husband of her deceased friend. As romance grows, Al encourages Dottie to confront her fears, move outside her comfort zone and take chances. Along the way, Dottie and Al find not just contentment but joy, happiness and purpose.

Gail Kittleson's latest novel, *The Winds of Change*, is the heartwarming story of an older couple who make the most of a second chance. Sidebars include the changing role of women in society and the mistreatment of Japanese immigrants during the war.

The author weaves timeless themes throughout the story. Love outshines hate. Diversity makes us stronger. Good things happen when we put our differences aside and treat each other with kindness and decency. *The Winds of Change* delivers a message of hope and civility sorely needed in the contentious world we live in.

Michael Barr

*In Times Like These* clearly portrays the difficulties for women during WW2. First, there are the challenges of raising food, preserving it, making money stretch, wisely using ration cards and just plain living in fear of the war. But then the overlay of Addie's controlling husband made me instantly empathize with the main character. His verbally abusive and cold treatment of Addie unfortunately is not just a problem from another era. God's provision for her was intriguing. The value of faith, friendship and compassion are evident in this book. I personally enjoyed the food tips and recipes, as well as vivid descriptions of farm life. This may be my favorite book by Gail Kittleson. It is the first in the series, *Women of the Heartland*. Be sure to read the books in order.

Cleo Lampos

This extraordinary story classically captures the mindset of the 1940s. Addie and her friend Kate reflect the voices women hear as they face confusing dilemmas 75 years later—my first read kept me up into the wee hours. I will refer my readers to *In Times Like These*!

Patricia Evans, author of
*The Verbally Abusive Relationship,*
*Controlling People,*
and other books listed at www.VerbalAbuse.com

Wartime brings out the best and the worst in people. I loved the way Addie and Kate, each in her own way, dug down inside to become more than either had ever dreamed. *With Each New Dawn* will inspire you toward resilience and personal growth even as it keeps you riveted with each page turn.

Sonia C. Solomonson, freelance writer and life coach
Way2Grow Coaching

Gail Kittleson introduces us to a small town community, under the strains of World War II. The everyday lives of the town folks unfolding their thoughts and concern for the husbands and brothers fighting for their country. The family and friends dynamics in this story keeps the reader wanting to turn page after page. The author knows how to keep the reader engaged. Looking forward to Ms. Kittleson's next book.

K Currie

Kittleson's writing style fosters instant empathy as her quiet heroine, Addie, struggles through daily living in Iowa during WW2. Readers are introduced to Addie through patriotism, friendship, and self-realization. "I've spent my whole life in fear instead of living each day," highlights Addie's growth in overcoming an emotionally abusive husband. Highest recommendation.

Carolyn Cobb

…the pages almost turned themselves. Great period piece exploring family dynamics and interpersonal relationships as well as the growth of self-esteem and the importance of friendship.

Lisa Lickel

Kittleson deftly writes strong female characters facing heart-breaking tragedies. *Until Then* features two: Marian, caught in the Blitz, and Dorothy, a surgical nurse whose work with the 11th Evacuation Hospital has taken her to North Africa, through Sicily and into France. Their stories intertwine in a narrative that touches then heals the soul. Highly, highly recommended!

Literary Soirée

# Also by Gail Kittleson

*Women of the Heartland Series*

With Each New Dawn
A Purpose True
All for the Cause
Until Then
&
Kiss Me Once Again
*a Women of the Heartland story*


and


A Mystery on Church Street
Land That I Love
Secondhand Sunsets
Catching Up With Daylight

# THE WINDS OF CHANGE

## a novel of second chances

### GAIL KITTLESON

WordCrafts

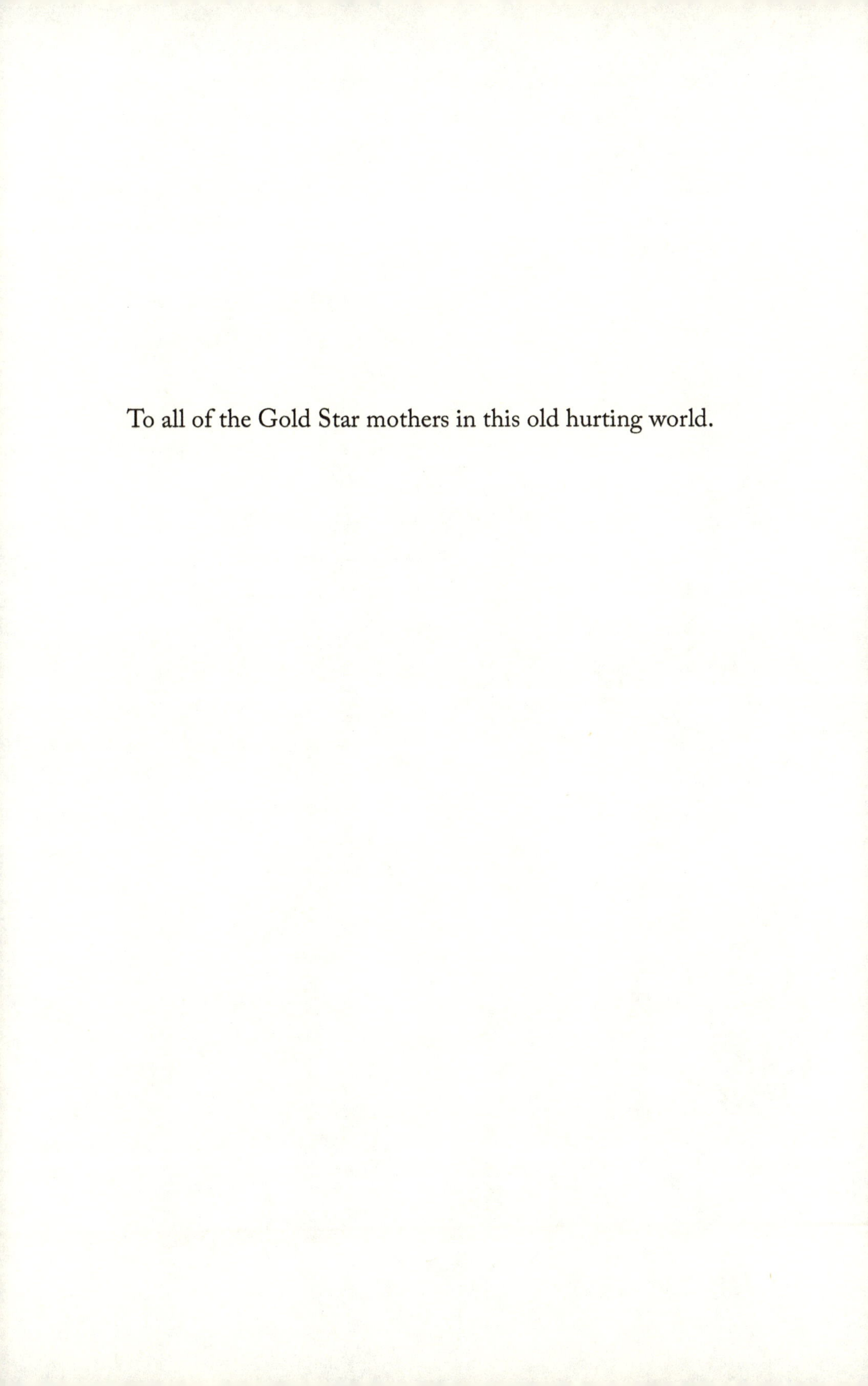

To all of the Gold Star mothers in this old hurting world.

# Chapter One

On certain Sunday mornings, Dottie could step through the door of First Methodist Church without visualizing her husband Owen's casket near the altar rail. But not this Sunday. Memories of two recent funerals assailed her, though there hadn't even been a casket when their son Bill died.

The friendly hum of children and Sunday School teachers spurred her to the basement. Through the serving window, she counted heads and cut sixteen pieces of chocolate cake.

A while later, a chair scraped on the cement floor, and the primary teacher caught Dottie's eye—time to serve the cake. She placed forks on the plates and handed them across the countertop.

"Watch your step, children. Take your time. And remember your manners. What do you tell Mrs. Kyle?"

Fifteen versions of "Thank you, Mrs. Kyle" descended and Dottie gave each child a smile. Ina added her own gratitude before she left.

"What would we do without you, Dottie? You're as faithful as irises in April. Sure you don't need some help?"

"Thanks, but I can manage. And you've got family coming for dinner."

When the basement lay quiet, Dottie boiled water on the stove, filled the dishpan, and went for the broom. But in the corner near the cleaning closet, a slight movement gave her a start.

Who was that small figure clinging to the dank stone wall? Peering closer, Dottie noted frosting on little Sammy Jorgensen's face and dark brown goo spewing from his two front pockets.

Stooping to his height sent a twinge through her bum knee. She let it pass and lowered even more, until she could look into his glinting eyes.

"Sammy, did you want some more cake?" He nodded as she reached for the wastebasket. "Let's get you cleaned up as best we can. Now, pull the insides of your pockets out."

Still as pooled water, Sammy's dark eyes watched her pare some Fels Naptha soap into a small tin bowl of hot water. Then she rubbed the once-white insides of Sammy's Sunday trouser pockets with a damp rag.

"You gonna tell my mommy?"

Dottie wiped crumbs from his mouth and patted his shoulder. "She'll see it, honey. We can't get these stains out, but your mommy loves you, you know that."

Absorbed in her ministrations, Sammy failed to notice Mrs. Jorgensen slip into the kitchen, a sleeping baby in one arm, Sammy's coat draped over the other.

"Sammy? I've been looking for you."

He covered his mouth with both palms.

"What have you done?"

"Mommy, I…Missus Kyle bringed us treats and…"

"From the looks of your shirt, you decided to take some home?"

Sammy's bottom lip curled toward his chin.

"He was trying to help, I think, when I was busy gathering up the dishes." Dottie's words did little to ease the lines on Myra Jorgensen's forehead.

"Look at this floor—cake tracks everywhere. You made more work for Mrs. Kyle, after all the nice things she does for our Sunday school. Tell her you're sorry."

Sammy's whisper penetrated Dottie's heart, and she pulled him close. Warm chocolaty breath tickled her nose.

"It's all right. I once had a little boy who looked a lot like you. Believe me, I found plenty of bugs and baby toads in his pockets." Dottie caught Myra's eyes. "Seems like only yesterday Bill was that size."

The beginning of a smile worked its way across the weary young mother's lips. Dottie helped Sammy into his coat and patted his warm head.

"Come along, then." Myra reached for the little fellow's hand.

"You have a nice afternoon, now."

Sammy gave Dottie a wave and swished toward the door. Stiff pant legs—Myra might add a bit less starch to her hand washing next time.

"That boy never stops. Dottie, some days…"

Dottie patted Myra's arm. "Let me get the door for you. I'd be glad to have Sammy over for a few hours this afternoon so you can take a nap."

"That's so thoughtful, but we're going to a family reunion out at the farm. Gotta hurry home to check on my chicken, frost a cake, and get everything loaded up."

"Ma…maa." Myra's petite bundle let out a wail, but Myra took time to squeeze Dottie's hand.

"I hope you know how much we appreciate your work around here." Her forehead creased. "I don't know how you made it through losing Bill and then Owen, too. You're such a strong woman."

"We do what we have to do. The war was hard on everybody."

Elbows spread wide, Myra called to Sammy. Dottie watched until she had him safely in the automobile, thinking of Cora, her youngest, out in California. Her arms bulged with a baby and a two-year old right now, too—such precious cargo.

Hopefully she wasn't driving around by herself, though. These days, you never knew what young mothers might attempt.

Letting the old wooden door shut behind her, Dottie retraced the stairs to the kitchen. From the very back of the shelf below the sink, she retrieved a two-inch wiry square cut from a large scouring pad. Smelled like it still had a little soap left, so she ran it around the faucet edge and rinsed off the residue before she swept up the crumbs and wet mopped the well-worn linoleum.

The Sunday school room smelled of recently opened crayon boxes, dusty hymnals, and the mothball tinge of Sunday best clothes. She straightened the shelves, pushed child-sized red chairs under the low table, and took one last look around the kitchen before turning off the lights.

The uneven floor, slanted toward a central drain, tripped her up, but she caught herself on the countertop. Something about the sight of a few more red-brown crumbs and the little-boy breath still hovering in the air buckled her knees.

A cry rose from some unearthly place inside her as she sank to the cool floor. "My son and my husband—Dear God, did you have to take them both?"

Her fists pummeled the cracked linoleum's surface. "If only I could see Cora's little ones—oh, why does she have to live so far away?"

Her complaint echoed in the dim eerie quiet. From the shadows, Myra's description mocked her—*Such a strong woman.*

Through it all, she'd set her mind and plowed on, but what choice did she have? At this moment, though, she might not even find the strength to get up off the floor.

An old aluminum pail banged against Dottie's thigh *en route* to the third bedroom on the right. The hallway clock marked each moment. Well, George Hanson would simply have to jiggle his foot on the front porch for a few more minutes.

At least he could go outside in this warm weather instead of tapping his foot in the boarding house dining room. Feather duster in hand, Dottie opened his window to let in the breeze and worked around George's few belongings. A bright circus flyer decorated his desk.

**Ringling Brothers and Barnum Bailey
Combined shows coming to the Hippodrome
Waterloo, Iowa—August 30, 1946**

Over a week ago. If George took the train down to Waterloo that day, she hadn't even noticed. But then, like the other three boarders, he kept to himself, and most days she hardly stuck her head out of the kitchen except to do the washing in the basement.

Back on his closet shelf, something metal caught her eye. She slid his desk chair and climbed atop it, groaning at the impact on her sore knee. But Helene wanted everything dusted thoroughly.

Dottie swept her duster around the engraved tin box, most likely George's money stash. He hired out for farmers during the busy season. That was all she knew about him. She wielded her duster as far back as she could, but without warning, the closet door slammed shut behind her.

She grabbed at the suffocating sensation threatening her throat, but calmed herself enough to fumble for the knob and push open the door. For a moment, she held her moist forehead.

Close to the closet, a desk's solid edge helped her ease to the floor. She took a deep breath, finished her cleaning, and went out into the hallway. No sound from the kitchen where she had left her boss checking the cupboards for supper ingredients.

Good. That meant she had a few minutes alone, because Helene had driven down to the butcher shop.

A kick sent the dirty clothes pile closer to the steps, where Dottie shoved it over the edge with her toe, a method Helene frowned upon. But it saved a trip up the stairs for the cleaning supplies.

The entire bundle splatted on the landing—a perfect pitch. Halfway down, another well-placed kick produced equally successful results. Maybe all those years of watching Bill kick the football had taught her something.

At the bottom of the stairs, Dottie bent to pick up the laundry, but instead of splotched green and white linoleum swirls, a woman's black patent leather shoes greeted her. Shapely legs led to a pair of dimpled knees and a bright flowered dress. Standing tall, Dottie stared into a redhead's flagrant green eyes.

Finally, she sputtered, "Why Bonnie Mae Ingersoll, is that you?"

The lanky girl chawed her gum. Her bemused half-smile rang a bell way back in Dottie's memory.

"Well, I'll be—someone remembered my name." Bonnie Mae scratched the back of her head with long fingernails painted as red as her lips. She looked Dottie up and down. "Fancy meeting you, too. Don't recall your name, though I do remember that amazing coal black hair."

"Dottie. Dottie Kyle—but the coal black has turned to charcoal, I'm afraid."

Bonnie Mae's squint could have meant anything. "Where's Helene? She told me to come at ten."

"Probably buying meat for supper. Would you like to leave her a message?" Dottie's neck spewed heat like the ramshackle building's ancient coal stoker.

Bonnie Mae twirled a strand of flaming hair around her forefinger and cracked her gum. Near her mouth and eyes, telltale age lines marked time's passage—probably twenty years.

"Nope. This is my first day of work. I'll just look around." She flounced her skirt like Maureen O'Hara in *The Hunchback of Notre Dame* and headed into the parlor.

Helene hired Bonnie Mae to work here? A niggling sensation just below Dottie's collarbone warned her to put up her guard.

Whatever it was, she'd have to set the past aside, that's all. Like her mother used to say, "The past is past—it wasn't meant to last." Funny how Mama's advice lived on, even though she passed so many years ago.

The dining room door still swung from Bonnie Mae's passage. Dottie drew back her good leg, launched the laundry down the basement stairs, and flung up a prayer. "You've seen me through a whole lot worse than this. Here we go again."

The screen door fought Dottie. Tired and cold, she wrenched the handle free from its moorings.

"Time to get out the storm windows and doors. Can't put that off any longer."

Her stomach growled, though she'd eaten at the boarding house earlier. A piece of apple cake and some hot cocoa wouldn't hurt on such a cold night. She kicked off her shoes and hung up her coat, crossed the dining room to a kitchen chair, and rubbed her feet.

Fourteen hours of work was too much, but what could she do? Helene wasn't about to clean up the dining room herself.

Bright yellow walls cheered Dottie like an old friend when she switched on the light. The spiffy aluminum cover glided over her cake pan, last year's Christmas gift from her daughter Millie.

Sliding cake pan covers—what would they invent next? A moist cinnamon-apple aroma wafted from the pan. The furnace kicked in, belching warm air through the wide iron grate under the table, inviting her to wiggle her toes.

Over a gas flame, she melded a scoop of chocolate powder into a cup of milk with a wooden spoon. When she glanced up, Owen's dark eyes observed her from his WWI army discharge photo hanging above the fern stand.

At least he saw the latest war end, although he was never the same after the news about Bill. The chocolate bubbled up, and she turned off the burner just as someone banged on the front door.

"At eight thirty? Who could that be?"

When she flipped the switch, the porch light formed a rectangle on the dining room floor. Al Jensen stood there, about as tall and thin as a human being could get. His lips curved into a lopsided grin.

"Don't worry. It's just me."

The tightness in Dottie's neck muscles let go. "Al, what're you doing out this late?"

One toe of his bedroom slippers perched on the threshold. Two distinct worry lines divided his thick, sandy eyebrows. "In the full moon, I noticed some odd puffs from your chimney when I closed the drapes." He held his palms up and shrugged. "Maybe I ought to take a peek."

Dottie stepped back. "All right, but shut the door quick. Terrible cold for October, isn't it?"

"Yeah. You sure got home late tonight." He stumbled on her rubber boot but caught himself on the doorframe. "Trying to kill me?" His chuckle matched the upswing of his low voice, and she relaxed even more.

"Guess so."

He left his slippers and headed for the basement door just off the kitchen. Dottie set her boots in the closet and followed him to the top of the stairs.

"This is awful—gotta clean these steps. Talk about trying to kill someone…"

Her comment traced a gallon paint can, stray brushes, and a few empty canning jars down the side of the stairs. A couple of rags brightened the conglomeration, thrown there the other day when her knee bothered her too much to walk them to the soak pail down by the washer.

Al turned into the furnace room and pulled the light chain. Dottie leaned her forehead on the door. Just like him to notice her chimney.

"Got any new furnace filters?" The long planes of his face jutted around the doorframe in the dim light.

"Look on the top shelf down there."

A few seconds later, he shuffled into view and glanced up at her. Batting at a cobweb, he raised his bony shoulders.

"Nothing? Look on top of Owen's old Army trunk then, behind you." Al bent and touched the trunk, but his left shoulder jerked back as though someone had attacked him from the darkness.

"What is it?"

He didn't answer, and it took him a few seconds to meet her eyes again.

"I've got a filter over home, I think. Brought it from the hardware for Mrs. Grundy but haven't taken it over to her yet."

"Can't this wait till morning?"

He reached the top of the stairway, and Dottie stepped back. The set of his jaw declared it couldn't wait. "Can't be too careful around fire."

Dottie closed the front door behind him. A speck of white beckoned her from her coat pocket in the open closet, and she reached for Cora's letter. How could she have forgotten?

She hurried to the kitchen with it and scanned her younger daughter's distinct lines for news. Good. Everything was going well for her and Dennis, and she'd sent a picture of the children.

"Oh, those little cuties." The photograph of baby Joy in Jeffy's arms captured her, and she barely noticed Al letting himself in again. He tromped downstairs, so she put the letter aside to savor the details later.

Banging and shuffling rose from the cellar. Her cake plate sat on the counter—might as well cut Al some, too. By the time she positioned another plate and cup of hot chocolate at the table, he emerged, cobwebs strung ear to ear and the unrecognizable dusty filter in hand. His brows arched at the late-night snack.

"Smells good. Chilly down there tonight." On his way to the sink to wash up, he handed Dottie the filter, and his knee brushed her dress.

Condensed dust prickled her nose as Dottie set the wire contraption in her frigid back porch. A brutal wind blustered through cracked caulking, and frosty air swirled up her legs. She slammed the door, wiped off her fingers, and nudged her natural wave behind her ears.

There sat Al at her kitchen table, waiting for her. In the distance, from the picture on the wall, Owen watched over all.

# Chapter Two

White steam rose over Dottie's face every time she exhaled. She forced herself out of bed and scuttled in her moccasins across brittle floorboards to turn up the heat. Mustn't let the pipes freeze—what a mess that would make!

Setting the dial at sixty-six degrees, she gave Owen a mental hug for replacing their old coal furnace before he crossed the Great Divide. The harsh wind rattled an eave spout, shuttering a draft down her spine. With his robust constitution, she always thought Owen would outlive her. What else had she been wrong about?

Baggy eyes met her in the mirror. Last night, sleep came only after a struggle. To her left, her stiff white cotton stockings straggled over the towel bar like icicles.

"Be thankful for your job. Gets you out of the house."

Owen would never have agreed to her working like this, and back then it would never have crossed her mind. But a few weeks after his funeral, Helene mentioned she needed help in the boarding house kitchen. The fit seemed perfect, and now two years had gone by.

*Wonder what she'd do if I showed up in a pair of trousers?* The thought produced a chuckle in Dottie. Some women had taken to wearing long pants in winter, but Helene balked. "I run a proper boarding house, mind you, Dorothy Kyle. What if one of the men happened on you bent over cleaning the stairs or taking something out of the oven?"

The four boarders, long past the age of noticing her backside, would have a less dangerous view if she wore pants, Dottie conjectured. But she swallowed her protest. She didn't mind the dress rule, yet hated being called by her given name. She even drummed up the courage to mention this once. But to no avail—Helene did exactly as she pleased.

A cup of steaming tea and a fried egg tucked between two pieces of toast fortified Dottie for the frigid walk. Her wool scarf's fringe tracing her cheeks, she turned the thermostat down ten degrees. The house would be glacial tonight, but at least she didn't have to stoke the fire in that dusty dungeon below the kitchen.

At the end of her sidewalk, she turned north. A light shone from Al's kitchen window, and the living room drapes parted as she walked by. A wave of sympathy swept her. He still hadn't gotten used to Nan being gone, but some wounds only time and love could heal.

Twenty minutes later, Dottie led Bonnie Mae into the pantry, a converted back porch. Helene had painted the door shut and lined the walls with shelves. In spring and fall the space served as a cooler, and in winter, an extra freezer.

"In here you'll find most of our meal supplies."

"Our meals? You eat here?"

"Sometimes, if I'm really hungry."

Dottie faced narrowed cat's eyes. The girl's tone took on a brittle edge. "I have to pay Helene a quarter per meal. That's no fair." Dottie almost expected her to stomp her foot.

"That's what I have to pay, too."

"Oh." Full red lips slid into a sulk.

"We store everything but the dry goods in here."

"I'm not cooking, not on your life. Helene hired me strictly for cleaning and errand-running."

A relieved sigh escaped in spite of Dottie's early morning vow to avoid any show of emotion. So, at least Miss Smart Mouth wouldn't hover around the kitchen.

"On this side, you'll find things we serve to outside dinner guests." Dottie gestured toward boxes of tea, tins of salmon, and preserves.

"You mean she don't give the boarders jam?"

"Not this jam. It's Maudy Akins' finest—a bit too pricey."

"What do you mean?"

Dottie lifted her palm. "That's what Helene says, and she's the boss." She tried to herd Bonnie Mae toward the entrance, but the gum-popping apprentice wouldn't budge.

"So she treats the boarders like second-class citizens?"

Dottie bit her tongue. She didn't agree with everything Helene did, but if you worked for someone, you didn't ask questions. She almost retorted, *Did you learn that fancy language in Chicago?*

But just in time, she bit her tongue. Backed into the small room, her chest filled as though it might explode—she had to get out of here. She met pursed lips and squinty eyes until the younger woman finally backed out of the narrow space. Dottie let out a shaky breath, wrapped up the tour as quickly as possible, and deposited Bonnie Mae beside the wringer-washer.

"Guess you've run one of these before?"

Wrinkles redesigned a freckled nose. "Unfortunately, yes. I can't believe Helene hasn't invested in a newer model with an automatic rotator. This takes forever, and the stirring breaks your back."

"But the clothes come out clean, don't you think?"

"Yeah, but women shouldn't have to do this kind of hard labor anymore, if you ask me." Intense green eyes sparked.

Dottie averted her face from the girl's fiery stare. She could say, *I didn't ask you,* but there was no use tackling that one—no use at all.

A golden Indian summer day surprised rural Iowa after the past week's cold rain. Dottie trimmed her bushes and cleaned up the last garden remnants. About half an hour into her work, she came upon a woolly bear caterpillar.

On two fingers, she lifted the little fellow clinging to his leaf. "I'd better count your stripes." Black bands numbered more than brown on either side of the fuzzy creature's rusty orange middle. "This winter's going to be a bad one."

She settled the caterpillar under the garage window and surveyed her hydrangeas. Mrs. Grundy cut hers in the fall, but Dottie's oldest sister Mildred, who raised her after Mama died, swore springtime was best.

She glanced through the alley toward her elderly back-alley neighbor's house. Sure enough, her hydrangea bushes had shrunk into stubs. "That grandson of hers has no mercy. Could've left at least six inches. Ah well, to each his own."

Once spring came, no one could tell the difference in their pruning techniques, since the plants grew equally tall and bushy. But maybe Mrs. Grundy's produced more flowers—Dottie had never checked, and she wasn't about to.

"Fiddle-faddle. It's all in what your folks taught you."

"What was that?"

Dottie's clippers flew into the air as she jumped half a foot. "Al Jensen—don't sneak up on me like that—you'll be the death of me some day."

Al chuckled and picked up her clippers. "I doubt that. A stairway somewhere will do you in—probably over at the boarding house."

No tart response came to mind, so she grabbed the clippers and clacked them back and forth. "Cleaning your garden, too?"

"Sure am. But I thought I heard you say something about a caterpillar."

Had she muttered her thoughts loud enough for him to hear over in his garden? Dottie scratched her head. Didn't most men lose their hearing with age?

Al stood there, skinny arms akimbo. "Well, did you?"

Dottie gestured toward the window. "Yes. Such a cute little guy, but he's got ten black stripes. Bad sign for a cold, cold winter."

"You're right. Weather vane's been swinging east pretty regular for the past week, too."

Dottie slanted her head toward the vane atop his shed. "How does that one go again?"

"A weather vane that swings to the west proclaims the weather to be best. A weather vane that swings to the east proclaims no good to man or beast." He puffed out his chest like a schoolboy reciting for his teacher.

"Well. Let me know if you see any more sure signs, all right?"

Al's grin spread from jawbone to jawbone. Of course, with such a slender face, it had little space to cover. "Sure."

Dottie went back to her work, and Al headed across the yard. But not a full minute passed before she heard his voice again.

"Your garden always looks so neat and tidy, Dot. Even in winter."

That sounded like a compliment, but she wasn't sure what to do with it. After scanning Al's spaded growing space, she straightened. "Yours, too."

Now, that wasn't exactly true. He left too much to chance with his raspberry patch. He ought to clip them down some. She bent over her day lilies. About eight inches from the ground, according to Mama. She enveloped a few greenish-yellow leaves with her clippers.

*Crunch*—leaf shards fell around her feet. Twenty minutes later, four lilies stood short and sassy, dressed for winter. Because she paid attention to her cutting angle, the foliage even looked pretty now. Orderly and…yes, pretty. She stood back to admire her work.

"Dottie?" Her knee jerked when she leaped in the air again.

"Oh, I'm sorry. Didn't mean to startle you." Long fingers grasped her elbow. "You all right?"

"You've got to stop this, Al. I just wrenched my knee."

"Oh, man." Something dark wavered through his eyes. For an uneasy second, Dottie feared he might try to rub the hurt away. But he gained control, working his mouth like a horse with an uncomfortable bit.

"What I wanted to say was…I mean…" He closed his eyes, pulled his shoulders back, and spit it out. "Want to go fishing?"

"Fishing?"

"Out at Goplerud's pond. They say the fish are biting out there."

"Why, it's been such a long time since I've…"

"That's all right. I'll bring everything, even pack us a little supper." He reddened. "We ought to wait till about five-thirty, when the fish get hungry. And since that's about supper time, I thought…" Pucker lines zigzagged his forehead.

"You and Owen had some good times down at that pond." She stared at the back fence. "While you were gone, Nan and I had some good chats, too."

"Yeah. Too bad they both couldn't have lived longer."

Al shook a nearly comatose fly from his shirtsleeve. Dottie considered what it would be like down at the pond with him. Then her empty living room passed before her eyes—anything would be better than that.

"Well, I suppose…"

"I'll get right on the provisions. Pick you up in the alley about half-past five."

Dottie's head spun as though someone slapped her out of a deep sleep. Going fishing with Al Jensen. Who would have thought it?

"Al?"

He turned on a dime. "What is it, Dot?"

"Just so you don't expect me to take Owen's place…"

"Nope, wouldn't expect you to."

She crimped a wayward hollyhock, stuck a spindly stick where she needed to dig dahlia bulbs, and cleaned her hoe blade before hanging it between two nails pounded into the garage wall.

Out in the sun again, she stretched her arms overhead. It was wonderful to do something you thoroughly enjoyed without having to hurry. What a perfect day—a thread of breeze wove through the back yard, sunshine warmed her, and a cardinal oozed good cheer from the telephone wire.

When the workmen first strung that wire a few years back, she'd resented the way the post marred her view. Now, she hardly noticed. Reluctant to leave the garden's gentle spell, she wandered to the asparagus bed and pulled a wayward weed. Nothing as calming as getting your fingers in the dirt.

Fishing was close to the earth, too. She'd not made time for fishing since…she thought back. Maybe when Cora was a little girl.

Unlike Millie, with no affinity for slimy things, Cora took to fishing right away, snaring the worm and doubling its wriggly body like a professional. Bill did, too. Dottie's chest throbbed as she turned toward the back steps.

Her sigh hung above the flame bush, with its rosy-red profusion of leaves. That's how she'd come to think of Bill, beautiful and bright. Sometimes a good memory came to light, and she'd catch herself smiling right in the middle of mixing a piecrust.

For a moment, he became a little boy again, running to her with a treasure. She still kept a box of those things, way back in her top bureau drawer.

That friendly cardinal intoned his song again. Dottie gave him a wave. She'd better get ready. Al's invitation troubled her, though she didn't know why. Maybe it was that change kept coming and she had no choice but to let it do its work.

She turned toward the porch. Al's clapboard siding reflected sunlight across an expanse of rich grass, still verdant this late in the season. She still had time to run over and make up some excuse. But her heart felt lighter than it had in days. Maybe an outing wouldn't hurt.

Al puttered around for a good long while, till he got antsy. He gathered the poles, filled a can with some pudgy worms, and stuck everything in the back of his 1937 Ford truck.

He patted the old girl on the fender. "Ten years and still hummin' like a youngster."

He took off his boots and went inside stocking-footed—ooh, his feet stunk. Better wash them and put on new socks. What would Nan say, changing socks part way through the day?

But she passed a little over a year ago. Some days when he closed the hardware store, he stopped in at Benson's Market, where old Tibbs lounged near a pot-bellied stove. Never one to refuse socializing while his daughter-in-law worked, Tibbs repeated stories to anyone with ears.

Though Al wearied of the same old tales, listening made more sense than coming home to memories in every corner. By the time he filled the truck with gas, if it needed any, and drove home the long way around, the evening loomed less stark.

He ransacked the cupboards and Frigidaire, and was about to pull out the remains of a bologna ring he boiled last night when the phone jangled. Three shorts and a long.

"Hi Dad, how ya doin'?"

"Good. Fine. You?" His son Charlie, in the southwest corner of Iowa, checked on him every now and then.

"Got the garden all cleaned out?"

"Yeah. Beautiful day, eh?"

"It is. Got the kids out putting the storm windows on. Supposed to hard freeze in northern Iowa Monday night."

Al pictured Charlie's three children out in the fresh air.

"Any more news up there, Dad?

"Uh, the Ingersoll girl's moved back in with Ned."

"Bonnie Mae? You don't say. Don't know if that's good news or bad."

Al's memory danced a jig. Something about Charlie's wife, Marion, getting in a row with that wild-eyed Bonnie Mae years ago, in high school.

"All right then, Dad. Come out and see us sometime. We'd love to have you."

"Thanks, Charlie. Maybe I will." They talked a while longer before Al set the receiver in its cradle. Maybe he could take the train down there sometime. If Nan were still alive, they'd go several times a year, but the thought of going alone weighed him down.

He turned back to the Frigidaire. What had he been doing? Oh, yes, the bologna. He cut some chunks and layered them with rich gold longhorn cheese between thick slices of rye bread.

He placed a few of Henrietta Perry's cookies in a brown paper bag. Though she had ten years on him, she never gave up trying, and made great raisin oatmeal cookies—not as good as Nan's, but close. He took them to the store with him for lunch, but luckily counted four still in the bottom of the box.

The kitchen clock alerted him—time to pick up Dottie. Feet planted in the middle of the pale green linoleum floor, Al bowed his head for a few seconds.

"If only Dottie could like me—she wouldn't have to *love* me the way Nan did—but if we could be more than neighbors..."

A niggle of doubt rendered his "Amen" lame—probably an old fool to even dream Dottie would consider him. He donned his lopsided khaki fishing hat, stained and fingerprinted, swung the grocery bag to his hip, and let himself out the back porch door.

Chapter Three

Porky's Pond, named after its owner's rotund silhouette, lay toward Maple River. Trees extended from the body of water half a mile south, creating an elongated U-shape. Al accelerated down the hill.

A cursory scan encouraged him—not another human being in sight. He turned to Dottie. "We're in luck—best fishing hole in the county all to ourselves."

She seemed a little quieter than usual, but one thing he could count on, she wouldn't scare the fish away. He veered into the woods on a seldom-used lane with tire-high weeds down the middle and cut the engine.

"You hungry yet?"

"A little. I don't think it'll take long to work up an appetite."

"Okay. We'll take the food with us. Just let me know when you're ready to eat."

"You'll hear my stomach." Dottie's easy grin reassured him every-thing would be all right.

She grabbed the fishing poles and bait can. He maneuvered the grocery sack, his tackle box, and two canvas-covered stools.

"I'll come back for the water and pail while you get set up, Al."

"Good. Thanks." His voice sounded jittery. He had to relax. He mustn't let his nerves take over—then she would decline another invitation.

He set up his stool, opened the tackle box and surveyed his options. While he picked a lure and baited his hook, Dottie studied the murky water.

She picked up her stool. "What was Owen's favorite spot?"

"Tried 'em all, but he attracted fish wherever he perched. Kept me on my toes."

She flashed him half a smile, but her eyes didn't fill, as they had for so long. She walked a few steps and settled her stool in the sand. The upward curve of her nose below her dark, arched brows struck Al as particularly perky. It was hard to catch her lately when she wasn't worn out from work.

"Choose your weapon." He held out four poles, but berated himself. Why did he mention weapons, when that might bring up a bad memory about Bill?

But she didn't seem to notice and chose an old bamboo rod he'd kept in his shed forever, most likely inherited from his father. Just like Dottie not to take a newer, shinier one.

He held out the bait can, and she hooked a worm with her forefinger. "Need any lures?"

"Do you think so?"

"Some swear by them, others say fish know artificial when they see it."

"Hmm. Maybe I'll stick with the worm."

Al attached a silvery lure above his worm. You never knew what would work. It all depended on…luck? No, the time of day had a lot to do with success, and the weather. But some people just plain had an uncanny *feel* for fish.

Squiggles marked the water, and a slap sounded. He lowered his voice just above a whisper. "Maybe we came at the right time."

Dottie, already scrunched over her pole, gave no answer. He cast his line far from hers. A bevy of crows announced disgust at the human invasion and flocked away. Serenity fell over the scene.

As always when he came here, knots untied inside Al's gut. He tried not to think of anything in particular. Dot seemed content, so he let her be.

Nan never took to fishing. She didn't like bugs, for one thing. The image of Dottie holding that woolly caterpillar in her palm surfaced. When Charlie and Bill needed a home for an injured squirrel, it ended up at Dottie and Owen's, not with him and Nan.

Once, they found a baby cardinal fallen from its nest, dead by the time Al got home from work.

"We want to take him for show and tell on Monday, but he's gonna stink if we don't keep him cold. Think Mom will let us put him in the Frigidaire?"

Al knew the answer, and so did the boys. "Go ask Dottie."

Sure enough, she let them. He hadn't noticed before, but she had on a pair of Owen's blue and white striped overalls, a red bandana sticking out the back pocket.

She swam in them, for Owen was nothing if not thick and muscular. Dottie…Al peered from under his hat brim…he supposed she was what men called *stacked* at a younger age. Shapely, he'd rather say, and she'd kept her muscles. Probably helped that she worked at Helene's, although he'd rather she didn't.

Helene rankled him. That woman watched her boarders' mail like a hawk. A time or two when he delivered the mail after Owen got sick, he'd reminded her that letters were personal. Her shrewish look made him wish he'd thought better of it. He didn't like the idea of Dottie slaving for a woman like that.

A southwest wind shook the pine branches—good sign. Even as he thought it, Dottie's bobber went under. She reeled her line in a bit and slowly stood. "Oh look, Al—I think I've got one!"

Her tone electrified him. He hightailed it back to the pick-up. Why hadn't he brought the net along in the first place? He felt behind the grimy seat for the long wooden handle, jerked it out, and raced back. Not a moment too soon, for Dottie's shoulders matched her taut line.

"You might have to bring it in…"

"You're doing fine."

He poised, net ready. Energy bounded through his limbs as if he'd snagged the fish himself. His insides tensed as he prayed the line would hold.

In another few seconds, Dottie brought up a glittering bluegill, about as big as they grew. The creature put up a fight, but she forgot all about being quiet.

"Oh my…can't believe I actually caught one!"

"You do most everything pretty well, Dot." Her dark eyes shone. She dipped the bucket into the pond so Al could deposit the fish into its new home.

"Wow—that was quick. We haven't been here long at all." Her fingers already searched the worm can for more bait.

"You hungry yet?"

"Yes, but I don't want to stop. Let's fish a while longer."

A smile split his face. "You betcha, Dot. Sure thing."

Al pulled in his third fish, Dottie her fourth. Her stomach complained, loud enough for him to hear a few feet away.

"Trying to tell me something?"

Dottie rubbed her middle. "Guess so. We can eat fast, can't we?"

"Hooked on fishing?"

"Maybe so." She re-baited her hook and propped her pole. "I'll get the bag."

She rolled a log near him, distributed the sandwiches, cheese, and cookies, grabbed her stool, and plopped down before he could gather his wits.

"You going to bless the food?"

"Sure." He leaned his pole against a stump. "For health and life and daily food, Father in Heaven, we thank Thee. Amen."

By the time he picked up a sandwich, Dottie already chewed a big bite. "Does this ever taste good—you make a fine sandwich, Al."

"Thanks."

She took a second bite and looked up at him. "What?"

"You're quite the fisherman."

"You picked the perfect spot. If the fish are biting, anybody can be quite the fisherman."

"Give yourself a little more credit. Not everyone can bring in a fighting one."

"Aw, my Grandpa taught me that years ago. I was afraid I'd forgotten how, but it came back, I guess." Sunlight broke through low-hanging clouds and framed her dark hair. Out here in the fresh air, she looked younger.

"You're a natural." Al chomped into his sandwich, and Dottie took another.

Across the pond, a loud splash alerted them. Voices wafted over.

"Kids trying to skip rocks. You ever learn to do that, Al?"

"A little. Not many flat enough around here. I got some good practice when I was stationed in France, though."

"Where was that?"

"With the French Army near Saint-Mahiel."

"How old were you?"

"Barely seventeen, but I was so tall, they believed me when I claimed an extra year." Al shook his head. "Don't know what I was thinking."

A leaf floated by, home to some late ladybugs. "Actually, I do know—I was trying hard to please my dad."

"He wanted you to go?"

"Strange, huh? When Charlie enlisted, I would've given anything to take his place, but my Dad wanted me to serve. Probably because he never got to, and someone drilled into his head that you weren't quite a man if you'd never worn a uniform."

"Um." Dottie's forehead furrowed, and Al wondered how much she knew about the war. By the time Owen entered, the worst of the fighting was over, but his decades of mail delivery, no matter what the weather, warranted a medal.

Mellow late-day sunlight profiled barren oaks and maples. Five minutes later, Bill's face appeared in the water, gentle against the glow, tinged orange in the sunset. Mesmerized, Dottie sat motionless.

Al's voice interrupted her reverie. "Sorry Dot. I didn't mean to bring up the war."

His earnest expression touched her. She reached over and patted his wrist. "It's all right."

His eyes dropped to her hand. Cold tingles ran over Dottie's shoulders, but she patted him again. "You're a good friend. I…I just had a visitation from Bill."

"A visitation?"

She drew a shaky breath. "That's what Helene would say, and I don't know what else to call it. I saw his face out there on the water. You ever have that happen?"

"Once or twice, with Nan."

"It was as if Bill floated on the sparkles. He looked so kind and bright-eyed and young—a good way to remember him."

Al's admission evidenced his understanding. The knowledge took some time to settle in Dottie's consciousness. She considered how Owen would have reacted and decided he might have scoffed at her.

Finally, she stirred. "I needed this. Thanks for bringing me." She ate a cookie and unscrewed the water jar's lid. "Care if I drink out of this?"

"What choice do you have? I forgot to pack glasses." His shy grin endeared him.

"But you did great with the food." Dottie wiped away a dribble tracking down her chin. "Well. We'd better get back to the reason we came." She took another cookie. "You make these yourself?"

"No. I can see my way through the basics, but cookies are beyond me." A flush crept above Al's khaki shirt collar. "Henrietta Perry brings me baked goods pretty regular."

"Ah."

"It's criminal, letting her feed me, but she doesn't seem to get the hint." He broke into a wide smile.

"Guess I can't see that it does much harm." She moved her stool a few feet away, not as far as before. She might have added, *Everyone needs to feel they're needed.* Instead, she bent to her pole.

"Want me to help clean our catch?"

"Nope, not unless you really want to. I've developed a system."

"Thanks again, Al. I've discovered a new hobby."

"Want some fish for supper tomorrow night? You working late?"

"No. I mean yes. I'm not working late. And there's nothing I like better than a fish fry."

"Don't bring a thing. We'll eat around six, all right?" He swept his hat in a grand gesture.

"Okay." She took a few steps and turned back. "I still can't believe how many we caught, can you?"

"I'm not too surprised. My Daddy used to quote a little fishing rhyme:

> When the wind is in the north
>> the fish will not go forth.
> When the wind is in the east
>> the fish will bite the least.
> When the wind is in the west
>> the fish will bite the best.
> When the wind is in the south
>> the bait goes in the mouth."

Dottie's laugh tiptoed down Al's backbone. He hadn't heard it in a long while, and before he knew it, he joined in.

"You're brimming with poetry. Let me know the next time your weather vane points in the right direction."

"All right, Dot. Thanks for coming along." She swung around the front fender, and Al followed her progress to the back door.

Dinner with Dottie tomorrow night…Al wanted to lay on the truck horn in triumph. A misty sun turned an outrageous persimmon before dropping over the world's edge. A tune he hadn't whistled for ages barreled from his lips. He couldn't recall all the words, but the title was *I Only Have Eyes for You*, and Nan liked to dance to it.

Normally, he used a sawhorse and plank table out in the driveway, but in the twilight, he brought the fish into the back porch to filet and carried the remains to his burn barrel—couldn't have that river smell when Dottie came over. The sky looked brighter and closer tonight. He whispered thanks toward the heavens.

"Tomorrow, I'll air out the house and clean the floors. I've got a guest coming to dinner—a very special guest." His whistle pealed out again. He simply couldn't help himself.

# Chapter Four

"Now, girls, I want you to deep-clean the whole house by week's end." Helene's bosom ballooned as she sucked in a big breath. "I suppose you saw the notice on the grocery store bulletin board? The Presbyterian Church invited some traveling singers and their wives to town on Saturday night, so I want everything spiffy."

She craned her neck toward Bonnie Mae. "You'll scrub and dust the parlor, dining room, front hall, and the whole upstairs."

"They're going upstairs?"

Helene's lips curled. "It's none of your business, but one couple has rented Number Six, and the others may ask to see the rooms. I want to be ready. These men travel the area regularly, and they draw a big crowd. I bet even some of the Holy Rollers from the Gospel Hall will sneak into the performance."

Helene's sneer encompassed her entire face—squinched eyes and mouth, drawn forehead, and raised chin. "Can't have music in their own church, don't you know, but don't mind slipping in to borrow someone else's."

Bonnie Mae's eyes bugged out, and Dottie shot her a look. If that girl could just keep her mouth shut, she'd be a lot better off.

"Who knows? Maybe the singers will invite some folks over here afterwards. The best advertising is a sparkling house and word of mouth."

"Word of mouth…then you oughta be rich." Bonnie Mae's mutter reached Dottie, and she held her breath. But Helene heard, too.

"What was that?"

"Oh, nothing. I'll get started." Bonnie Mae strolled toward the parlor, her skirt tight against her hips. A blue and white polka-dot scarf kept her brilliant red curls contained. She'd neglected to button the top button of her everyday white blouse, even though Helene told her to earlier.

"Would you want me to make a coffee cake and an extra pot of coffee in case they do invite people in?"

"No. No use wasting ingredients if they don't show up."

Dottie thought how happy the boarders would be for a late night snack or breakfast treat, but held her tongue.

Helene drummed her fingers on the kitchen table. "I'm being nice to that girl, so how does she repay me? Did you catch her smart-mouthed comment?"

Dottie mumbled something about getting to work, and bent to a tottering old pots-and-pans cabinet that had seen better days. She started pulling out specimens, most in need of repair after years of use. She had no desire to get involved in a family fight. Hopefully, Helene would soon go downtown to get her hair done or something.

"Now, Dorothy, I know you have an opinion, but you're too well-behaved to speak. You've surely noticed her mouthy backtalk, haven't you?"

Dottie wracked her brain for a noncommittal comment. "How old is Bonnie Mae, anyway?"

What Helene called her *pancake make-up* deposited tiny globules in her wrinkles as she pondered. Dottie could certainly see where the stuff got its name.

"Why, my sister was—let's see—not even sixteen yet when she had Bonnie. Shameful, don't you know? Felicity's condition, even though Mother hid it, wrecked our once-happy family. Felicity cried all the time. Of course, I didn't understand what was going on. I thought my sister had some dread disease."

So, Bonnie Mae wasn't Helene's younger sister? Dottie couldn't remember Felicity quitting high school.

"How did your mother keep such a secret in a small town like this?"

"You don't recall Felicity down with the whooping cough for part of a winter? Your Millie's about her age—I bet she'd remember."

"Felicity was a few years older, I believe. Those days, I was running after children—I didn't get out much and really didn't know your family at all."

Helene eyed the ceiling. "Running after children—the way women spend their lives!" She harrumphed and smoothed her hairdo.

Dottie followed her upward glance to two patches near the north outer wall where water leaked in during a driving rainstorm. Helene really ought to have someone check the roof.

"That awful birth took place in the room next to me. I still remember Felicity's screams—that girl never had an ounce of self-control, don't you know? Suddenly, we had a baby bawling at night. Daddy couldn't stand to stay in the house evenings—he married old, and the noise and commotion wore on him something terrible. Mama aged overnight, that's the gospel truth. And me—well, nobody paid any attention."

Obviously, Helene needed to pour out her frustrations, and *that* Dottie could handle. She emptied one shelf and started another. Helene took a seat at the table and wagged a painted fingernail in her direction.

"Your Cora and Bonnie Mae are close in age, aren't they?"

"They were several years apart in school."

"From the beginning?"

Dottie tried to remember, and suddenly, it came to her when Bonnie Mae became trouble for little Cora. Mrs. Marias was Cora's teacher, so it must have been second grade. Cora was giggly and bubbling with life when for no particular reason, Bonnie Mae started harassing her. Then Dottie found out that runny-nosed, loud-mouthed snippet terrorized younger girls whenever she had the chance.

"As if being born that way wasn't enough, Bonnie Mae flunked fourth grade, to add to our family's shame."

Ah yes. Now Dottie remembered—a child couldn't repeat a grade without the whole community knowing, and the mark followed them forever. She ran a pail of hot soapy water to clean the shelves.

"Cora must've known her, school being so small. Surely they played together on the playground?"

An uneasy feeling sashayed through Dottie's chest. Why would Helene be so intent on finding a connection? Better to keep her mouth shut on that score, so she asked a question instead.

"Didn't Bonnie Mae live somewhere else for a while?"

"Um hum. Felicity ran off to Nebraska with some tramp, but then she brought Bonnie Mae back. Mama treated her like an only child, a spoiled brat."

A pan lid slipped from Dottie's grasp and clattered to the floor. She set it inside a semi-matching pot, but Helene seemed not to notice. She leaned over her chair to Dottie, on her hands and knees now, purging the lower cupboard with a wet rag.

"Mama sort of lost her mind, don't you know, all on account of that girl. Mama made umpteen trips to the principal's office because of her antics. Once, the pastor even made a special call to our house. I was never so humiliated."

"So…what does Bonnie Mae know about all of this?"

Helene's head bobbled back and forth. "Who knows? And what does it matter?"

Dottie wrung out her rag and reached farther back, like a cow straining under a fence for grass. Mixed scents clung to the old piece of furniture—dust, flour, even a tinge of vinegar. The roomy space, dented and neglected, revealed several attempts at renovation.

A flowered triangle where somebody stripped off old shelf lining tempted her to make this a project and strip off the rest. Seeing flowers when she opened the door would be a good thing on long winter days.

"When Felicity dragged Bonnie Mae off with some boyfriend or other, what a relief for us all. That girl's pranks set Mama up for an early grave, that's what."

An itch began behind Dottie's ear and extended to that unreachable spot between her shoulder blades. Didn't Helene have an appointment this morning? She probably did, but had forgotten.

The sprinkling sound of shattered glass shot from the parlor. Dottie arched out of the cupboard, banging the top of her head against the lowest shelf. Helene's cheeks, already high ruby, glowed.

"Why that…" She started from her chair and turned her heel. She almost slid into the Frigidaire, but grabbed the silver handle and steadied herself. The vein traversing her forehead like Highway Thirty across southern Iowa stuck out even more than usual. So did her wide hazel eyes under beauty salon eyebrows.

What if Helene had a heart attack right here in the kitchen? What if she…? But her employer straightened, soldier-like. "You know what that girl's classmates called her in junior high? B.M, because she raised such a stink all the time."

Thick heels clacked against scarred linoleum. Her skin under her arms shaking, Helene swung the dining room door wide and turned an imperial stare on Dottie, her chin quivering like a turkey's wattle.

"Mind you, Dorothy Kyle, even though you keep your opinions to yourself, I know full well you agree with me—that girl's a hopeless case."

Dottie sat back on the floor. Hopeless? A clear recollection surfaced from Cora's elementary school days, when Bonnie Mae led some taunting schoolgirls in a singsong rhyme:

*Cora Kyle ain't got no style!*

True, Dottie's youngest wore hand-me-downs from Millie, or dresses Dottie sewed from scratch. So did quite a few other girls, but Bonnie Mae was the type to rub it in.

A long-forgotten pronouncement Owen made at the supper table one night came flashing back. "If that little snot don't let up on Cora, I'll go down to the schoolyard and smack her one myself."

Yes, this flashy young woman was the same Bonnie Mae, but still, Dottie wondered, was it fair to label anyone hopeless?

Sweat dripped off the full eyebrows forming a hedge above Al Jensen's eyes. He swiped his brow, but kept scrubbing the kitchen walls. He hadn't intended to go this far, but once he got started, the cleaning bug bit him hard.

"Why did I let the house go for so long? Nan would have something to say if she could see this grease and dust."

He already dumped the scrub pail four times. Now, he climbed down from his stepladder to do it again.

"Most likely, my work is all in vain. Dottie probably won't even come past the kitchen. Bet she'll eat and head home as quick as possible."

But just in case, he scrubbed the dining room and found those walls badly in need of his ministrations, too.

"I'm ashamed of you Albert Jensen, for allowing this mess." His indictment floated through the living room. Would Nan say that?

No, she knew he chastised himself often enough already. He made it around three living room walls before someone knocked at the front door. No one ever came by in the daytime, except when Eva Maloney wandered this far from home. But she never knocked. To her every closed door signaled an invitation. The only other visitor…

From behind the heavy pale green drapery, he peered through the front window. Sure enough, his worst premonition became reality. Henrietta Perry, holding a pie tin-sized box, stood on his front step.

His mouth watered—maybe the pie was raspberry. But he didn't want to get cornered by the most talkative woman he knew, not when Dottie would be home from work in less than two hours.

He plastered himself against the wall and lifted his eyes to where a spider crawled nonchalantly into the corner. Oh man, he'd have to whack it down as soon as Henrietta left.

"Please, let her leave the pie and go on home."

In this pause from his labor, a bad odor reached his nostrils. He lifted his shoulder and cranked his head down. *Phew*—his armpits smelled something awful. He'd better take a shower and change his shirt as soon as he finished that fourth wall.

No, he ought to fry the fish first, so he wouldn't smell like the river when Dottie arrived. Yes, that's exactly what he'd do.

Another knock echoed, sharper than the previous one. He immobilized, as he learned to do decades ago when the enemy stalked. He waited. Waited some more. The knocking ended, but his front door knob turned. Surely Henrietta wouldn't…

"Albert? Albert Jensen, you home?"

The screen door swung open and two feet planted in his entryway. Henrietta's shrill voice filled the room.

"I could've sworn he didn't saunter by to the store today. Where could he be?"

Al prayed hard.

"Albert?" Her volume increased. A long minute passed. "Well. I guess I'll just set this pie here in the entryway where he can find it." Her voice picked up speed. "And then, he'll have to bring me back the pan."

Fabric swished. Al pictured Henrietta depositing the pie ever so gently and turning to go.

"Strange, though. He always walks right past my house whenever he goes anywhere. So odd—I was watching just like always."

The door shut. Al nearly collapsed. He pulled the curtain aside a smidgen. Henrietta swayed down his sidewalk, her prim hat tipped over a bluish hairdo.

His relieved sigh bounced off his rag-tag armchair in the corner beneath Nan's knick-knack shelf. On closer inspection, he noticed thick dust lining her thimble collection.

"Better take them all down and rinse them in the dishpan." Then he smiled. "I have a pie for tonight. A pie fit for a…fit for a wonderful woman like Dottie." He loosened the towel covering. The mellow aroma of sugar and fresh-picked raspberries drifted out, and he gazed at a perfect crust and rich red juice oozing from Henrietta's precise cuts.

He carried the treasure carefully to Nan's Hoosier cupboard and went back to the living room for the pail. When he tossed the dirty water over the back porch railing, late afternoon sun shone down on him bright and clear. Not two rods away, Dottie's east kitchen window glinted.

"Nothing but the best for Dottie. Nothing but the best."

# Chapter Five

"Why, Al. Your house is so clean. Do you always keep it this way?"

"Only for special company." Al passed Dottie a platter profuse with fish and fried potatoes, his ear tips beaming as though he'd plastered them with rouge. "You are special company, you know."

Dottie wasn't quite sure what he meant, but tucked his words away. "You fried these fish to perfection, I'd say."

"Nan taught me to dust them in that flour and cornmeal mixture."

"You took good care of her during her sickness—such a hard time."

His large Adam's apple worked up and down. "Sure was. Wish it hadn't ended the way it did, but…" He lowered his eyes to his plate.

"You did your best for her."

He nodded. "So did you, for Owen." He took a big forkful of potatoes.

Finally, it felt okay to be here, in this room where she and Nan shared so many good talks, so many cups of tea. Dottie could count on one hand the times she'd poked her head in since the day of Nan's funeral, when the whole town descended upon Al, as it had on her when Owen died. Nan's kitchen was nothing without her in it.

Once in a while, Dottie dropped off something she'd baked or a bowl of leftovers. But now that more time had passed, she felt all right.

When she'd consumed far too much, Al took their plates over to the sink. "Got a surprise for dessert."

The pink and grey teapot wallpaper she helped Nan apply one time when the guys were off doing something, probably fishing or hunting, still looked serviceable, though a little worn in spots. At the moment, a teacup perched atop Al's head.

He set a saucer with a steaming cup of tea before her, a cup of coffee at his place, and a bowl of thick cream in the middle of the table. While he busied himself at the counter, Dottie sniffed. Green and full-bodied, exactly the way Nan served tea. Al must have made it earlier and let it steep.

He returned to the table with two massive cuts of dark red pie.

"Raspberry? Don't tell me you made this?"

"You think I'm too dimwitted?" He angled his head like he asked a serious question, and Dottie wasn't sure whether he teased her or not.

"Dim…? Not at all—it's just that you told me you didn't make cookies. Oh, I don't know. Maybe you did make it."

"Naw. You're right. Pie's not my cup of tea. Speaking of cups of tea, is your all right?"

"It's perfect. Thanks, Al." She took a sip, and the mixture of tart and mellow flooded her senses.

"Wasn't that long ago, we had to stretch the coffee and tea for the war effort."

"I don't think we'll ever be quite the same after those years, do you?"

"Nope. I was never the same after the first one, either. Something happens when things turn upside down like that. A person doesn't even know how to talk about it."

For the first time, Dottie considered what it must have been like for him facing a second world war. During the Great War, no one from her family except Owen had to go, and he only served stateside during the last few months.

"So the world has changed around two times in your lifetime."

"Something like that. Makes you think—makes you appreciate things more. I felt that way when Nan and I married—a double gift, since I got Del at the same time." Al ate some pie, but the lines in his forehead didn't budge.

"When Charlie came along, everything took on new meaning all over again. It was like seeing the world through new eyes." He fiddled with his cup handle. "Know what I mean?"

Elbows on the table, Dottie rested her chin on her folded hands. She'd never heard Al talk like this and didn't want him to stop. Had Owen ever spoken about how life changed a person? She couldn't recall a time.

"I felt that way when the children were small—every stick in the path seemed there just for us to discover. Is that what you mean?"

"Yeah. That's it exactly." Al's eyes shone like Bill's used to when he built train stations and firehouses all over the house with his blocks. His intensity drew Dottie to the floor with him, to get acquainted with his make-believe town.

The more Al laid bare his thoughts, she forgot whether or not Owen ever shared such feelings. Incredible warmth enveloped her. She forgot about her pie, too, and about the time until Al glanced at his watch.

"Better finish your pie, young lady." He went to the counter for the teapot and refilled her cup. "Guess I got off on that subject. Sorry."

"Don't be sorry. I haven't talked with anybody like this since…" Since Nan died. Better left unspoken, but it was the truth. Helene had no capacity for such conversation. And Bonnie Mae? No use even considering that.

Al shifted in his chair. "Say, did you hear the cold's swinging back into the state tonight?"

"No. I didn't listen to the radio all day."

"S'posed to be a hard freeze—the real thing. Got any plants you want covered?"

"Oh my. I haven't dug the dahlia bulbs. For goodness sake, how could I have let that job go?"

"Because you work such long hours." His voice carried no accusation, as Owen's would have. No, it was more like…

"Let's get right out there. I'll help you dig them."

"Why, that's so…"

"You can wear my coat, Dot. I'll grab something else." He pulled his wool jacket from its hook and thrust it at her. "Let's see, your dahlias are…"

"On the south side of the house, down a yard or so from the last hydrangea bush. I marked them with sticks."

"I'll get my flashlight. Come on." Dottie meekly followed, aghast that she'd stayed so long. The first star shone above them.

"Meet you at the dahlias." Al veered into his garage, and Dottie streaked toward the south side of her house.

She'd barely found the first marker when he arrived, pail and shovel in hand. "Here, you hold the light and point out the sticks."

Dottie grasped the smooth metal cylinder, aware that the wind whipped up even more by the time Al leaned back, foot still on his shovel. "Think that's about it?"

"Yes. Thanks a lot. I'd have hated to lose these. Started them from my mother's years ago."

"Hmm. You sure we got them all?"

"I think so. Good enough."

"Didn't take long at all. Glad you remembered them, Dot."

There, he did it again—called her what Owen used to. She couldn't decide if she liked it or not. They walked toward her back steps, the artificial light sphere creating a comfortable circle in the night. Al handed her the pail of bulbs.

"You want me to cover that pink rosebush out front with a canvas tarp? You started it from your mother's, too, didn't you?" Concern showed in the shadows undulating across his high forehead.

Why would he remember about her mother's bush? Nan must've told him, but that would have been years ago. "No, that's all right. It's hardy enough."

"You're sure there's nothing else?" He strained forward. Something about his pose, gangly and eager to please, niggled the pit of Dottie's stomach.

"I'm sure, but thank you." Cold air billowed her skirt. "Well, then. Thank you for supper." She started up the steps. "What's the matter with me? I need to help you with dishes."

"Oh, no you don't. You've got an early morning tomorrow. I'll pick up my coat after you get home from work, if you don't mind. Don't want you to catch a chill."

"Okay." She moved toward her back porch steps, but his voice turned her around.

"Thank you for letting me ramble on. You're such a good listener." He gave her a salute and shrank into the chilly night between their two houses.

As if to remind her it meant business, a shaft of wind skittered around the staircase. Winter lurked a blink away—and to think, last evening, they'd sat out fishing. Good old Iowa—you could count on the weather surprising you.

Al bobbed up his back steps and into the back porch.

That niggling, like a fish at a worm, worked at Dottie's insides. Her mind flashed to the boarding house. If only she didn't have to get up so early and go to work. If only… Al's profile appeared in his kitchen window as he moved from table to dishpan and back again. He did so well on his own—even cooked for himself. Could Owen have managed like that if she'd gone first?

A field of stars flooded the sky. Autumn flew by so fast this year. The old pail in her hand overflowed with knobby bulbs that had produced so much gallant color. Just a few short months ago, they produced seedlings that grew strong green stalks and blossomed, but now shrank into dry, spent remnants.

The rich taste of raspberry remained in her mouth. Dottie smoothed her tongue over her teeth and glanced again at Al's kitchen window. It looked as though Henrietta Perry had committed herself to satisfy his sweet tooth.

"Henrietta would spit fire if she knew I enjoyed a piece of her beautiful pie. I sure hope she never finds out."

Unforgiving wind swooshed her chuckle back at her, so she

started up the steps. If Al looked out and saw her dallying, he'd have something to say about her catching a cold. The creaking wooden stairs marked her every step. Winter encroached, and it looked to be a long, cold one.

Chapter Six

"Morning, Dad. There's a pallet out back to unload already. Truck came early."

"I'll get right at it, Del."

Al tackled the first section, full of small wooden boxes laden with screws, nuts, and bolts. He used an iron trolley to haul the heavy containers, lifted them to the floor one by one, and began filling the wooden slots ranged along the right aisle. With great care, he tipped boxes into the correct spaces. The tedious job took until noon, but the full pallet gradually lowered.

When the clock struck twelve, he donned his coat and hat to walk home for lunch. He'd put a couple of pieces of fish in the Frigidaire before he went to bed last night, and plenty of Henrietta's remarkable pie awaited him.

"Mind picking up the mail on your way back?"

"Sure."

Delbert walked out front with him to rearrange snow shovels against the building. He'd always been a hard worker. A thrill of pride ran through Al at the sight of his older son's muscular arms. He looked back as he exited the door, and noticed for the first time that Delbert's scalp showed through his hair on top.

Could he already be going bald? It seemed like only yesterday when Delbert came into his life with Nan. A double blessing, he'd thought at the time. Al's vague memory of Nan's father ran through his mind. Had he been short on hair? They'd only met once before he took to his bed, about to die.

Al touched the top of his own head, cap and all. He still had some hair up there, but never knew how much because Ed down the street trimmed it so short.

Slim traffic crept like sated cockroaches down Main Street. November did that to people, slowed them down and enticed them to hole up like moles. Every year about this time, he'd had to run a hardware ad in the newspaper with some sort of specials to draw people into the store.

He turned into the Post Office. Wallace handed him the mail before he could ask. "Fine sunny day out there."

"It is. Cold but bright."

"You workin' over there today?" Wallace tipped his white head toward the hardware.

"Yeah. Unpacking pallets for Del."

"Good man, Del. Glad for such a quality store in Sternville. Without it, we'd have to drive over to Heston for a hammer or a nail. Wouldn't that be somethin'?

"It would. Thanks, Wally. Have a good afternoon."

Al turned at the town's one stop sign. With such a wide Main Street, a stop sign seemed unnecessary, but the city council approved it last year. Richard Folkers pushed for one—always some new expenditure to raise taxes.

Across the street, a familiar female figure marched toward the grocery store. Henrietta. Al ducked under an awning until she stepped inside.

*Saved again.*

A brilliant idea dawned on him. Right now, while she shopped, he could quick slip the rest of the pie into another container, wash the pan, and hurry to her back door with it and her other box. That way, he could avoid getting embroiled in one of her long conversation about nothing.

By gum, he'd do it. He struck his fist against his hip and loped around the corner toward home. Fifteen minutes later, his evil deed accomplished, he made himself a sandwich—cold fish and Colby cheese. Delbert didn't care how long he took at noontime—he volunteered his time, anyhow.

He pulled out a chair and ran his fingers over the combination salt and pepper shaker Nan had bought when they took the boys to the Ozarks. She'd been so excited about its compact design, and the boys agreed it made a perfect keepsake from their trip.

Seemed like forever ago. He always wanted to take them out west, too, but things hadn't worked out. At least Delbert started buying the store before Nan died, and Charlie was established on his father-in-law's farm down in southwest Iowa by then, too.

He glanced over at Dottie's place. Maybe he'd take advantage of the sunny day, in spite of the cold, and see if he could do anything around her yard.

He didn't want to push her or make her think he was trying to take over, but she worked so hard. He watched her tired progress past his house late in the afternoon. Most days, she looked barely able to take another step.

That Helene, he ought to tell her a thing or two, making a woman Dottie's age work like that. But Dot would never complain. Oh, no. She was quite the trooper.

Silence reigned in the boarding house, except for continual drivel from the dining room radio. Every time Helene switched it off, within minutes, Bonnie Mae turned it back on. At times, Dottie could have sworn she cracked her gum in time with the music.

That wasn't so bad, but songs she and Owen used to dance to over at the Heston Dance Hall made her sad. She'd opt for the quiet of the old house any day, accompanied by bird songs from the open windows three seasons of the year.

Winter had borne down on Sternville the twenty-eighth of October. Only sparrows and a few raucous blue jays braved the cold, and once in a while, a brilliant cardinal. Dottie found herself wondering what possessed the Creator to fashion such a flashy bird, a splash of bright paint on a sullen landscape.

She cut some fresh rendered lard, with its soft, almost-rancid odor, into four cups of flour for piecrust. George had a birthday today, and she'd told him she'd make whatever he wanted for dessert. He'd dropped his eyes, and she had to coax out a reply. Cherry pie it was.

As if answering a personal invitation, flaming red wings flapped against the window. The chirping visitor puffed his feathers. He reminded Dottie of Bonnie Mae. After all, God made her, too, regardless of how Helene stormed about her birth. The girl definitely had a flashy exterior, but so did cardinals. What was so wrong with that?

Deep in her heart, Dottie still held a tiny grudge at Bonnie Mae for taunting Cora. It was harder to forgive wrongs done to your child than to yourself. But when Cora came back from California for Owen's funeral, she and Dennis also attended the all-high school reunion, and she'd had a good talk with Bonnie Mae.

"Mom, I can't believe she married a rich man from Chicago." Cora made no mention of the past, and that was a good thing.

That was the first time Dottie met Dennis. Seemed strange, after he and Cora had been married for a year, but that was the way of war. They'd met when he sailed out of San Diego, and Cora worked in a munitions plant.

One of her letters noted a dreamy sailor fellow. The next one described how he'd asked her out to the USO dance. A few letters later, their baby girl had married that sailor, and after the war, he found a carpentry job right there on the coast.

Too bad Owen never got to meet Dennis, but by the time she took her son-in-law and Cora to the train for the trip back west after Owen's funeral, Dottie was satisfied. Dennis seemed honest, hardworking, and devoted to Cora, the qualities she wanted in a son-in-law.

Now Jeffy, their oldest, would be three years old in February, and the baby, Joy, turned seven months yesterday. It didn't seem right to be missing out on them growing up, but how could she ever get to California?

She sprinkled a quart of canned cherries with a cup and a half of sugar, stirred in a half-cup of flour, and spread the mixture over the bottom crust. She could understand George's choice. She might pick cherry pie too, if somebody asked her favorite, although Henrietta's raspberry melted in her mouth the other night.

*Clunk, clunk, clunk*—that was Bonnie Mae stirring the wash in the rinse water downstairs. Her feistiness had mellowed some as she accepted Helene's way of doing things. Too bad she and that Milt hadn't had children—what would it be like to be Bonnie's age and have only her stepdad and an older sister? Especially when that sister was Helene, her only other living blood relative—Dottie shook her head. Hard luck.

Almost against her will, her heart went out to the girl. For all her brash pronouncements and irritating ways, underneath, she seemed…what was it? Lonely? Dottie pinched the piecrust edges and slit the top with a sharp paring knife. Yes, she decided. Lonely. Too bad Bonnie Mae couldn't find some decent man around here and marry again.

Bonnie Mae clumped up the stairs, a huge basket of towels and sheets in her hands. She dropped the load on the table and started folding.

"What kind is that pie?"

"Cherry."

"Ooh. You don't think Helene would let me have a piece, do you?"

Dottie raised her eyebrows. Bonnie Mae knew better than that. Why did she even ask? Helene kept a sharp eye on her, caught her more than once with her hand in the proverbial cookie jar, and docked her wages. She did the same thing with towels ruined in the wringer. They had to wrench them to pieces to remove them, and Helene charged her each time.

"What do you think?"

"She wouldn't even consider it."

Dottie turned her attention to the second pie. At least the girl had learned to crimp her unsuitable language since she'd started work. "If you have a minute, I can show you how to make a pie."

"Me? I can't cook."

"Anybody can learn."

Red eyebrows scrunched in a dubious slant, but before long, Bonnie Mae rolled out a crust. It wasn't half bad.

"Now, you fold it in half—be gentle, mind you—and place it in the pan. Come over here to the stove, and I'll show you how to make the filling."

"Helene must have extra guests tonight?"

"Yes. Somebody's rented Number Six."

"So—do they ever leave you a tip?"

Dottie guessed they did, but Helene always snatched the coins up quicker than a lightening flash in a sudden summer storm. And when overnight customers vacated a room, she appeared out of nowhere to make a first pass through.

"Well, do they?"

Dottie pressed her lips together. This conversation couldn't lead anywhere good. "Does it matter to you?"

"Sure does. When I clean Number Six or Seven, people sometimes leave as much as a quarter, but Helene says that's for her. Don't that seem odd to you? People pay her at the counter for their night's stay, but they intend tips for the maid, don't you think?"

Dottie agreed, yet hesitated to say so. Nothing positive could come from getting between Helene and her baby sister. But the girl wasn't about to let it go.

"Don't you think that's true?"

"It sounds likely."

"Likely?" Bonnie Mae's voice rose. "'Course it's true, and you know it. Don't worry, I'm not gonna tell Helene anything you say. But we ought to stand together, you and me. You work hard all day long making supper, and if the guests want to say thanks with a little gift, that's only natural."

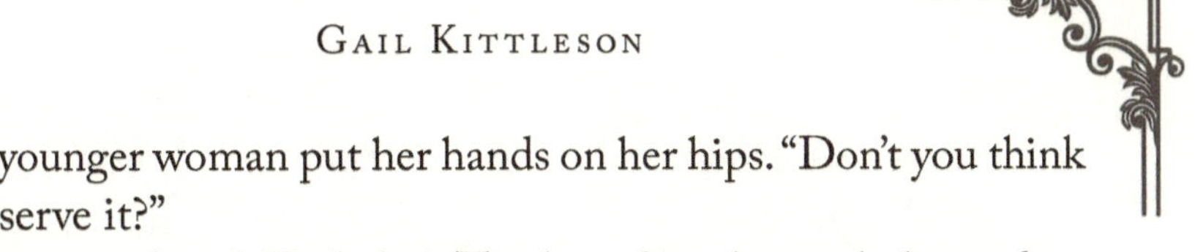

The younger woman put her hands on her hips. "Don't you think you deserve it?"

Dottie pondered. Did she? The boarding house belonged to Helene, along with all its headaches. If a light bulb went out, she had to buy its replacement. If the front steps needed fixed, Helene paid the bill.

"All these years, you've cleaned bathrooms, hauled stuff up and down the stairs, made beds…if people left tips in their rooms, they meant them for you. Helene has no right to them."

Dottie perused the long line of meals she'd made, with a parade of people leaving a few coins beside their plates—maybe a nickel or dime, but once in a while a quarter, or even more rarely, fifty cents. That one gentleman from—where was it—Detroit?

He'd dressed so fine and displayed such perfect manners. He looked her in the eyes after a pot roast meal and told her thank you, that he hadn't eaten such a tasty beef dinner for years. Then he placed two shiny quarters beside his plate. He left another quarter on the bedside table, but Helene swooped it up. Seventy-five cents—why, that was a lot of money.

Bonnie Mae might be right. How much more could she have saved over the past few years with all the tips intended for her? Enough to pay for half a round-trip train ticket to California, maybe.

"You think she does?"

"Does what?"

"Oh, you are so frustrating. Urrggh!" Bonnie Mae twirled her ponytail. "Do you think Helene has any right to your tips, or to mine?"

Dottie took a deep breath. During adult Sunday school class last week, someone talked about forming opinions and standing by them. People not speaking their minds led to the war's terrible destruction, so we'd better learn a lesson from that.

As if coming out of a daze, Dottie turned toward Bonnie Mae, who flapped a sheet in the air to clear the wrinkles. Clear emerald eyes flashed, daring her to express her belief. Cora's dark eyes transfused with Bonnie Mae's for a second, and Dottie heard her younger daughter's excited voice when she landed her first job. She must've been all of fourteen.

"Mom, guess what? Barb hired me down at the café. Some girls make as much as a dollar a day in tips!"

Dottie opened the oven door to check on the pie. She shut the door, blinked at Bonnie Mae, let out a long breath and found her voice. "I guess not. No. Rightfully, I would say she doesn't."

Al shot out his front door when he saw Dottie coming down the street in spite of a miserable sleet and ice shower. "Got something new to share with you—want to come over in half an hour?"

"Oh, Al. Thanks, but I'm so tired tonight, I can't leave the house."

Before he thought it through, he blurted out, "That's all right. I'll bring it over. Maybe in about an hour?"

His eyes, more blue than gray today, shone so sincere as he fell in step, Dottie couldn't turn him down. Really, though, she longed to drop in her armchair and put her feet up.

"Okay, but I'm warning you, I'm worn out. By the way, you're getting soaked."

"So are you." He grinned and held her door open for her. "I don't mind. What I'm bringing over will put a spring in your step. Don't do a thing for supper. Promise?"

Not a hard promise to make. He shut the door behind her. She pulled off her boots and draped her coat and scarf over a dining room chair. A steady drip fell on the floor, but she turned up the heat and collapsed in her armchair. It was all she could do to pull up the ottoman for her feet.

The talk with Bonnie Mae about tips had only foretold the day's stresses. George suffered what looked to be a heart attack. Bonnie Mae found him on the floor of his room and came flying down the back stairs.

"Call Doc Schulz, quick. It's George. He can't even answer me."

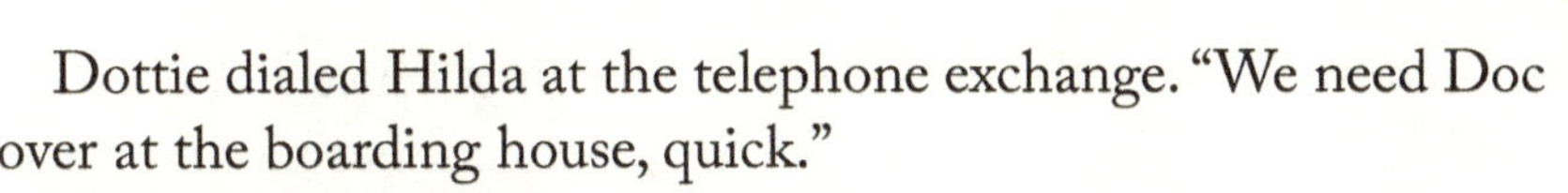

Dottie dialed Hilda at the telephone exchange. "We need Doc over at the boarding house, quick."

"Dottie, is that you?"

"Yes, but I can't talk. Get Doc over here as soon as you can."

"But…"

"No buts—just do it!" Dottie hung up, shaking. She'd raised her voice considerably, something she almost never did. She grabbed a cold cloth and shadowed Bonnie May up the stairs. George's eyelids fluttered when he heard her speak. She placed her palm on his forehead, realizing her utter helplessness.

Close enough to his ear to see hairs and dry wax flakes, she whispered. "Hang on, George. I'll stay right here with you."

Bonnie Mae's eyes went wild. Dottie recognized unfettered fear—the girl needed to get away.

"Go downstairs to watch for Doc and let him in, would you please?"

Thankfully, Hilda got the message across, because in a few minutes, two men with a stretcher followed Bonnie Mae and Doc up the stairs. Dottie moved out of the way and fidgeted with her apron as Doc knelt on the floor beside George.

When he finished his examination, he directed the men to carry George to the ambulance. Dottie ran to the bed for some warm wool blankets.

"You want these on him, don't you? It's freezing out there."

"Yeah. Glad you found him as soon as you did. My guess is his old ticker's acting up. Don't know what we can do, but I'll sure try everything I know. Does he have any next of kin?"

Dottie ransacked her brain. "I've never heard him mention anyone, but maybe Helene has. I'll ask her when she gets back."

"Um." Doc folded his arms over his chest and headed down the stairs. "Thanks."

Dottie gathered up the scatter rug where George had fallen. Signs of drool showed toward one end. She folded it in thirds and carried it downstairs to the top of the basement steps. One kick landed it smack in the middle of the landing. Since Bonnie Mae washed all the linens now, she hadn't practiced that kick for some time, and it released her emotions.

"Help George, Lord. Such a shy, gentle man—please spare his life."

On his birthday, no one had been able to prod his age out of him, and it was only because Helene kept her records that they even knew the day. She wished Helene would hurry back from whatever she was doing—probably shopping. Surely, she would have some information about George's family.

If she didn't, how depressing. What would it be like to live like that, without any family connections? Even though Cora lived so far away, Dottie had Millie and Ren in Cedar Rapids, where they'd moved in '40 to work at Collins Radio. They were so busy, with work and their three children leaving the nest, she didn't see them often. But at least they lived only two hours away.

She went back to her supper preparations, her thoughts far from her work. She made a big macaroni and cheese casserole—George didn't relish the dish, so he wouldn't miss one of his favorites. She got out two jars of green beans, keeping an ear open for the side door's squeak, announcing Helene's return.

Finally, with supper in the oven, the table set, the floor swept and mopped, Helene appeared, arms full of packages, her coat wet from the icy drizzle that blanketed Sternville all afternoon. Dottie helped her out of her coat and told her the news.

"Doc took George to the hospital, thought it might be a heart attack."

"How did…"

"He fell upstairs. Bonnie Mae found him."

"And you called for Doc?" Helene whisked off her plastic rain scarf, revealing a pinkish tone to her hair.

"Yes, right away."

"Hmm…I wonder if that was necessary."

"What?"

"I mean, he's an old man, don't you know? What could they

possibly do for him? We might have just put him to bed and watched him."

"Who would have watched him?"

"Why, we could all have taken turns."

Dottie had no idea how to answer, so she changed the subject. "Doc wanted names of George's next of kin. Do you have a list?"

"Why no. George has no family left."

"You're sure?"

"Of course I'm sure. His only sister died a few years back, leaving no children, and George never married. He came here from Missouri before the war. Worked on farms all over the county over the years, followed the wheat harvest to the Dakotas, but had no one to call his own."

Dottie's heart sank. A sudden awareness of how much her feet ached fell over her like a pall.

"Should we call the hospital to see how he's coming along?"

"Make a long distance call?" Helene's chins trembled. "I should say not!"

"But…don't you want to know if he's all right?"

"In the morning. We'll give Doc Schulz a call at his office. That's plenty soon enough—no use wasting money on long distance." Helene patted her new hair-do and pulled some canned goods from a grocery sack.

Something dark and sinister engulfed Dottie's throat. Words teletyped into her mind like war messages. Helene didn't care one bit about George, except for his rent money. To her, he was just another bundle of cash every month.

Rain spattered against the kitchen window. Helene pulled more things out of her parcels and held up a bright red sweater.

"You think this goes well with my hair color?"

Yesterday, she came home with pink hair—pink and red together, a startling array. The clock relayed a steadiness Dottie needed right now. Her own words surprised her as much as the shock reflected on Helene's made-up face.

"I need to leave a little early tonight, since we don't have any guests."

"Oh, you do, do you?"

Dottie had never made such a request—she wasn't even sure of its origins. "Uh, yes, if you don't mind. Bonnie Mae is still here, so maybe she can help clean up."

"Why didn't you mention this to me earlier, Dorothy?"

"You've been gone all day. How could I?"

"Oh." Helene's widow's peak moved up and down above her forehead wrinkles. "I guess not." She rubbed her thumb and forefinger together. "Well then, go on. I'll do as much as I can, but don't be surprised if I leave most of the cleaning for you to finish in the morning."

She headed for the parlor, propping the door open. "There's no mess upstairs, is there? I surely hope George didn't break anything when he fell."

Dottie stared in disbelief. "No. I brought his rug down to wash, that's all."

Helene whooshed toward the stairs. Heaviness Dottie hadn't experienced in a long, long time descended. She checked the stove to be sure nothing would scorch, stuck her arms into her wool coat sleeves, and tied on her scarf. She yanked her rubber boots over her shoes and trudged out the back door.

Her feet, heavy as oil barrels, led her home like Daisy and Lilly, Papa's old mares. When Al ran up, she accepted his suggestion without question.

Something awful happened today, something earth shattering. It had to do with her hope for the world. Helene's attitude drained her, temporarily, of that hope. How could that woman be so uncaring, so crass?

The old armchair's familiarity held her, soothed her. She dozed off and didn't even hear Al cross the back porch and tap at the kitchen door.

# Chapter Seven

Al let himself into the kitchen, set a pot on the table, and ran back home for a glass pie plate. He slipped off his shoes and set the pie on the granite surface of Dottie's cupboard. Then he went back into the cold porch for a rag and swiped swirls of snow from the linoleum.

"Dottie?"

Poor woman must have fallen asleep. Good for her—she needed rest. He quietly set the table and turned on the gas under her water kettle.

At first when he tiptoed into the dining room, he couldn't see her from the living room archway. Drenched in shadows away from the streetlight, the shadowy space challenged his vision. When he located Dottie folded into her armchair, his heart did a triple beat. He knew she was awfully tired, but maybe—he hunkered down until he heard her clear, regular breathing. A wave of relief flooded him—he quaked at the very idea of losing her. Yes, now that's how he thought of Dottie Kyle, Nan's best friend. He might as well admit it.

He steadied himself with a hand on the plaster archway, mentally reviewing their fishing jaunt. Everything Dottie did that night impressed him, and she'd been constantly on his mind ever since. His heart was all bound up in her.

But did she harbor the same feelings for him? He doubted it. All he could do was pray, wait, and try whatever came into his mind to woo her.

Accustomed to the dim light after a few moments, her simple furnishings caught his attention. They were similar to his, although Nan splashed some turquoise throughout their living room. He liked the way things blended here in Dottie's front room—muted yellows, deep brown, and rose tones met in a quiet way, reflecting her personality.

Careful not to make any noise, he shuttled stocking-footed back to the kitchen to make tea. When he lifted the yellow ceramic teapot from its shelf above the stove, a stained piece of stationery drifted to the stovetop. He couldn't avoid reading the few words in Nan's handwriting.

"To my dearest friend. Thank you, Dottie." Must be a note Nan sent long ago. But Dot had kept it—she had few friends, as far as he knew, unlike Nan, who attracted chatty pals who used to come over often. Yet Nan always turned to Dottie when she was really hurting. No wonder she'd written *my dearest friend.*

A trace of guilt heated Al's neck as he scooped a good-sized spoonful of tea from its white enamelware container. He shouldn't have read the note, although it was too late now. The vision of Dottie asleep two rooms away eased his conscience—she was too kind to take offense at such a small thing.

Maybe he'd drink tea tonight, instead of coffee. She probably didn't have coffee in the house anyway. He took a whiff of the dry black leaves before replacing the lid. He could get used to drinking tea. He would make whatever changes he needed to. His own sigh startled him—better take it easy, not get his hopes up too high.

He tiptoed back into the living room, thankful that this house was far newer than his. At home, every floorboard he touched would squawk. At the precise moment he reached the curved archway, Dottie raised her head.

"Al?" Her voice sounded so sleepy, he wanted to tuck the afghan in around her.

"Yeah. You hungry?"

Her arm stretched out from the chair. "I must've fallen asleep. What time is it, anyway?"

"About six-thirty. I've got a feast for you in the kitchen."

"Really? Good. I don't think I could have cooked anything tonight."

He took a few steps toward her and held out his hand. "Come on. You need some nutrition."

She let him help her up. His heart raced at her touch. He had to get hold of himself—Dot wasn't one for any sort of swooning.

"Sorry. Don't know what came over me—we had a hard afternoon at the house."

"You can tell me all about it if you want to. I've got tea ready for us, too." They moved toward the kitchen's light.

"Tea? You?"

"Yup. I'm converting."

Her eyes widened. "Well, I'll be. Wonders never cease."

"My Gramps used to say bless my buttons, and followed it with 'wonders never cease.'" He pulled out her chair, and she dropped into it. "And Grandma Jensen swore by a good cup of tea for whatever ailed a person."

He poured her a steaming cup and one for himself. Pungent steam laced the air, and though the scent was mild compared to coffee, he found comfort in it, as Dottie seemed to. Then he dished up two bowls of chicken and noodles he nursed all day on the slow back burner. All afternoon, he plotted to share them and his extra bounty with her. And now, the moment had come.

"Chicken and dumplings? Don't tell me you made this yourself?"

"I did. Nan taught me, once she got so sick. She had a craving for it every once in a while, so I had her show me how to make the recipe."

"I didn't realize she craved noodles." Dottie took a bite, aware of his eyes on her. "They taste just like hers."

"She used to say the blend of salty broth and flour soothed her throat."

"Hmm." Talk went by the wayside as they ate the mild, satisfying concoction.

"Her mother used to make noodles, too, when all they had was eggs and hand-ground flour in the house. They satisfied a longing in her, especially salted down and cooked in chicken broth. Know what I mean?"

Dottie nodded. "Now I remember—that's what Nan brought over when we lost Bill." They cleaned their plates in easy silence.

"I have something else for you." He jumped up and brought the pie to the table.

"Another pie? You made it yourself this time?" Dottie pulled off the towel cover and stared at him, her lips turned out like Bill's when he was a little boy. If ever a child looked like his mother, it was that one.

She pinched a tiny piece of crust into her mouth and exclaimed, "No, I don't think so."

"You recognize it?"

"Of course. No other woman in this town makes her piecrust with a tablespoon of vinegar. I'd say Henrietta Perry has struck again."

Heat prickled Al's neck as he sat down. "Guilty as charged. You should be a detective."

"Does she have any idea what you do with all the food she brings you?"

"I suppose she thinks I eat it. And mostly, that's true. I've only shared with you."

He scrutinized Dottie's expression, unsure if her quirked brow showed amusement or disapproval. "You don't mind eating Henrietta's baked goods, do you?"

"No, not exactly. I mean—she's a great cook. But I think she might have a problem with me benefiting from her heartfelt gifts."

Her tone maintained cheer, but those dark eyes spoke of something else going on, something deeper. Al sat down and picked up his fork.

"What happened at the boarding house today?"

"Oh, Al." The tremor in her voice startled him.

Dottie's dimples showed for a moment as she grimaced, but then returned to her normal controlled expression. She would tell him when she was ready. One thing he felt sure about, Dot couldn't be pushed into anything. Obviously, she'd decided to wait until after they finished their pie, which was fine with him.

In a few minutes, a smile lit her eyes. She touched her stomach.

"Oh, my, that pie is so good. Thanks for bringing it over." She glanced at the clock. "I still should be at work, but something upsetting happened today. I left early."

Sounded pretty serious. She stayed late plenty, but never left work early. He tried to keep his voice even. "Upsetting?"

"Not like you might think."

"How might I think?"

She didn't answer for a while. "I guess you know I'm not a crier—I mean, upset like that."

"When you say you're upset, that's enough for me, Dot, tears or no tears."

Her cheeks colored. "Hmm." She tapped her fingers on the table. "I realized something today that bothers me to my toes. Don't know if I can talk about it just yet."

Al worked on the last of his pie. He wanted her to feel free to tell him anything, yet a part of him didn't want to know. If it was bad enough to upset her, it had to be something awful. He almost blurted out the first thing that came into his mind, but thought better of it. Best to err on the side of silence. He refilled their cups and returned to the table.

When he set her cup down, Dottie's face cracked. He blinked hard. What would he do if she did cry?

"Al, you don't owe me anything. Do you really want to hear about my day?"

"I sure do. What are neighbors for?"

Her gulp was loud enough for him to hear clear over in his house. "George Hanson may have had a heart attack today. You know who he is?"

He leaned closer. "He's come into the hardware a few times over the years. Nice fella, really quiet."

"Bonnie Mae found him on the floor up in his room this afternoon. Doc took him to the hospital in Heston. But then Helene chided me for calling Doc, and vowed she wouldn't spend the money for a long-distance call to see how he's doing."

Her first two sentences came out in spurts, like the new electric irons when they were warming up. But the rest of the details exited her mouth in an avalanche. Severe creases formed permanent pleats on her forehead, and he wanted to smooth them away.

"I've had my share of dealings with Helene down at the store, so her penny-pinching attitude doesn't surprise me one bit, but this is one of her boarders. How could she be so hard-hearted?"

He tamped down a rising tide of indignation and glanced at his watch. "You want me to drive you over to Heston to check on George?"

Dottie's jaw dropped. "You would do that?"

"Sure. Visiting hours last till eight-thirty, I think."

"George doesn't have *anybody*, Al, and Helene doesn't care about him at all." Her eyes brimmed. He'd only seen her like that one time, when Owen died. With Bill, she'd kept it all inside, at least in front of him and Nan.

One day, a few weeks after word came about Bill, Owen told him he couldn't stand it if Dottie didn't stop going up to Bill's room. When he confronted her, she responded that she needed to smell Bill's clothes, touch his high school letter jacket, and re-read his last letters. That would be Dottie—grieving in her own quiet way.

"Get your coat."

"But isn't it still sleeting out there?"

"Nope. Stopped before I came over, and I heard the county truck go by to sand the streets."

She glanced around the kitchen as if seeking something, but slid her chair back, and returned from the dining room wearing her coat and scarf. Energy coursed through Al.

"I'll get the truck started while you put on your boots."

Cold wind sent a flurry through the cab, but the engine roared to life. In the darkness, he felt for the blanket he kept behind the seat and nudged it toward Dottie when she sat down. Al jammed his palm hard on the lever that controlled the outside air to be sure the vent was shut tight. In the small space, his elbow touched Dottie's as he turned the wheel to back out.

The old engine purred down Main Street. Good thing he'd given it an overhaul recently—for such a time as this. Businesses on Sternville had locked up for the night. Only Almira's café showed activity, but as they passed, those lights dimmed, too. Al accelerated on the outskirts of town.

"At least no ice is falling, eh?"

Dottie gave him an arched-brow look while she sorted out his words. "Right." She practically shouted over the truck's noise. Talking would be impossible from here on out.

Darkness hid the farmhouses along the gravel road, one he'd traveled often enough during Owen's sickness when Al ran his mail route for him. So far, the moon hadn't risen, so he kept a watchful eye for deer, fox, raccoon, or possum darting from fence lines and groves.

The shoulders looked slick—hopefully they wouldn't meet any traffic from the other direction. He leaned over the wheel, especially when shifting at corners. His hands, so cold they almost stuck to the clammy wheel, fought him. Why hadn't he run home for his gloves? His cold toes and ankles reminded him he left his boots behind, too.

Dottie surely knew how to maintain quiet when a person needed it. Without her beside him on the cracked leather seat, the thick darkness beyond the twin arcs illuminating the road might have struck him as eerie. As it was, resolute calmness filled him. He had a mission to fulfill, like delivering the U.S. Mail those weeks before Owen died. Still, he breathed easier when a few lights flickered in the distance.

"We can already see Heston."

He thought she replied, "Good," but wasn't sure, with the cylinders cranking beneath the hood. An obscure clatter, kind of like a bolt coming loose in the steering column, drew Al's attention out of all the various sounds issuing from under the hood.

He'd better check on that tomorrow. For now, he basked in the reality of being this close to Dottie for an extended time, and the blessed responsibility of getting her where she wanted to go.

The county seat of Heston edged a curve of the Maple River, the town's lights creating an S punctuated by tall oak groves, low undergrowth, and a wide swatch of pines. Through towering tree trunks, the river shimmered in the background. The night beauty beckoned Dottie. She hadn't been out like this after supper for a long time.

She tried to remember when—maybe last year on Christmas Eve when Millie and her brood drove up to spend a couple of days and they all went to the late candlelight service. Those three grandchildren had grown up so fast—at thirteen, Alice was developing into a young woman already. Walking home from church, the two of them linked arms and Alice commented on a sky blazing with stars.

"Do you think Grandpa Owen can see us?"

Dottie hadn't known how to answer. "Maybe—do you think so?"

"Yeah. He was a Christmas sort of guy." Her words stuck with Dottie for a long time. She supposed Alice meant Owen's fun-loving, cheerful nature—of course, the grandchildren only saw him on holidays.

Only one lone star peered down at them tonight, and she wished for more. Maybe by the time they came home, the haze would rise, and the heavens could strut their stuff.

When her heartbeat calmed after a few miles, she noticed a patch of brown below her feet. What was that? Then it hit her— it was the gravel road, seen through an odd-shaped hole in the floorboard—she recalled it from that fishing trip she and Al took. No wonder the cab was so cold.

Al hunched over the steering wheel, his lean profile intense in the dashboard's dim light. He looked like Ichabod Crane, from a story she'd read the children ages ago. After a while, he reached for a knob and yanked on it.

"The heater works, but it takes a while. Sorry." He yelled the message above the engine's loud hum.

"It's fine." Her reply never reached him, she was pretty sure.

She really hadn't spent that much time in vehicles. Her dad, not much of a forward thinker, rebelled against the new automobile craze in her youth. He never did switch over from draft horses to a mechanized tractor.

By the time another farmer rented the land and allowed for some innovation, she lived with Mildred, but she'd inherited her dad's penchant for judging that they had enough, whatever they did have. When something new came along, she always eyed it with suspicion, like the kitchen faucet. Owen saw to it they got one, but she'd been perfectly happy with the pump sitting atop the counter. It wasn't until after the change that she embraced the helpful convenience, wondering why she'd resisted it for so long.

Al turned off to the south, and several more stars appeared. She could have sworn one of them winked at her, and she took a longer look out the window. She'd have to find reasons to come outside at night more often. If she weren't so blamed tired after work, she'd take an evening walk like she always used to, unless the weather was truly terrible.

Good for the digestion. Mildred used to say that about her evening walks. Dottie let out a long sigh—seeing the stars reminded her that all was right with the world, even when things got out of hand.

Another source of awe seeped through her. Al had taken up George's cause as soon as he heard about the heart attack. He offered his time, his pick-up, and his gasoline, although he barely knew the boarder. She tilted her head to glimpse him through the corner of her eye, and the sight of him so intent on reaching their destination touched her heart. Al Jensen was a good man—a very good man.

A house or two came into view and then a whole street full. Al maneuvered the vehicle through town as though he made this trip every day. Now, heat gushed from the dashboard. The warm barrage brought feeling back to Dottie's feet.

At a stop sign, Al turned her way. "Sorry it's so cold. But the road wasn't icy—I'm mighty glad for that."

Dottie eased her grip on the door handle as a large white building came into view. "Yes." She left it at a one-word reply, but she wanted to say, "Al, you have nothing to apologize for—I'm so grateful—I can hardly believe you drove me over here."

He let her out at the hospital entrance. "I'll park and meet you inside."

An air of unreality enveloped her. She hadn't traveled to Heston for years. And to her knowledge, she hadn't ever been inside the new hospital. Her first two babies entered this world at home, with Old Doc Schulz, the present doctor's father, attending. He still lived in a small cottage behind his son, but rarely helped with anything medical anymore.

By the time Cora came along, Owen drove her to Heston for the birth. But back then, an enormous square white house on Third Street housed the hospital. Yes, 607 Third. How could she ever forget? She'd been so far along in her delivery that Owen had to carry her up to the second floor, and young Doctor Schulz arrived after the fact.

Actually, she'd been relieved—such a young man, who hadn't married or had children yet, embarrassed her. They might just as well have stayed at home and saved the ten dollars.

She stretched her neck at the new brick hospital building rising before her like a palace. With no reason to come to Heston, she hadn't even viewed it from the street before. Soon after Owen died,

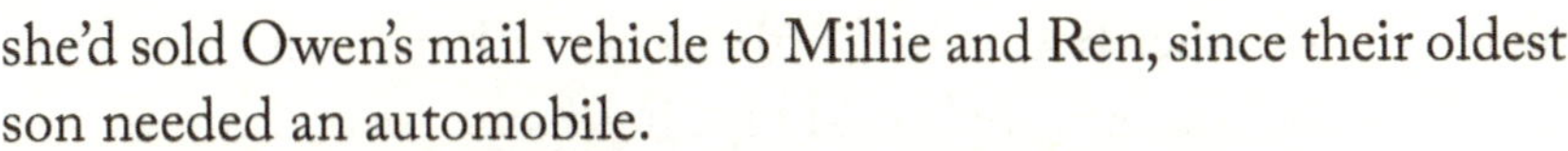

she'd sold Owen's mail vehicle to Millie and Ren, since their oldest son needed an automobile.

"Are you sure, Mom? You could learn to drive, you know."

"Me? Whatever would I do that for?"

Millie shrugged and held out the money. "Don't limit yourself—if you got your license, you could come down and visit us now and then."

But Dottie watched Millie drive off, confident that everything she needed she could find in Sternville. To be anywhere else, even to be here now, visiting someone at the hospital, seemed peculiar. She walked up the cement steps, her chest tight, and pulled on the heavy wooden door.

That old stifling feeling almost overcame her in the entryway, but a few deep breaths gave her strength to open the next set of doors and slip inside. She clutched her purse handle and leaned against the wall. Everything would be all right—Al would be here any second. When he joined her, she gave him a smile and gladly followed his lead.

He stopped at the desk and a nurse asked who they came to see.

"George Hanson, please."

She pointed down the hall. "Room fifty-four. Mr. Hanson is stable enough for visitors."

"So he's not...uh..."

Al put Dottie's worst worry into words. "He might be able to come home?"

"Let me look at his chart." A stern-nosed, middle-aged nurse surveyed a clipboard hanging on the wall. "The doctor brought him in for observation. He hasn't made any final diagnosis, as far as I can see. Mind you, visiting hours end at eight-thirty."

Outside George's door, Al stepped back. "You want to go in by yourself?"

Dottie shook her head. She'd cleaned George's room for three years and cooked his meals every day except Sundays, but couldn't say she knew him well. She always attempted to chat with him about the weather, but he had little to say. When he did, he called her "Missus," though she'd told him her name several times.

The white room startled her. Sheets, walls, blankets, table—everything as white as new potatoes in spring. A bare light bulb above his head rendered George's paleness even more pronounced. Three or four other men occupied beds farther along the wall. At least the room was large—Dottie's breath came easier.

Al slipped to the corner and switched off the light nearest George's bed. Through the door, the hallway's large bulb cast plenty of brightness.

Dottie turned to him. "That's much better. He couldn't open his eyes if he wanted to, with that thing shining in his face."

George's hand jerked when she touched it. She leaned closer. "George, can you hear me?"

"Wha—Missus, is that you?"

"Yes. We drove over to see how you were doing."

He rubbed his ear. "You came all the way over here to see me?"

"Yes. This is Al Jensen, my neighbor. He brought me."

"What time is it?"

Al studied his watch. "A quarter to eight." He held out his hand. "I remember meeting you in the hardware store a few times, George. Glad you're at the boarding house, to keep an eye on this young woman while she works."

George licked his white lips. "She's a good girl. Treats everybody the same." He coughed, and lifted a white handkerchief to his mouth.

"Is there anything we could bring you—anything you need?"

"Not that I can think of. No, they feed me fine. 'Course, not like what she serves up." He waved his right hand toward Dottie and coughed again.

"I don't expect so."

Dottie's mind veered to Helene. She would be glad to know George would be returning, or at least for his monthly payment. She put such thoughts aside. George sounded hoarse and dry.

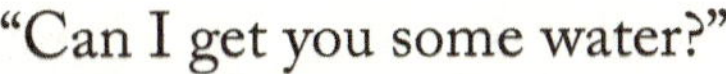

"Can I get you some water?"

"That would be—" He broke into another spasm.

In the hall, Dottie found another nurse, younger and pleasant. "Do you have a glass? George in room fifty-four needs a drink."

"Sure. Glad you came to see him. You're his only visitor so far."

"He has no family that we know of."

"So you are friends?"

"I work where he lives. I hated to think of him being all alone here."

"Thanks so much for coming. Visits like yours can make all the difference to heart attack patients, Ma'am."

"So he did have a heart attack?"

"Probably."

When Dottie returned, George eagerly drank the entire glass.

"Here, let me refill that." Al grabbed the glass and left the room. Dottie tipped her head close to George's face, with a splendid view of his right ear. A sudden temptation almost overcame her—she wanted to twist the end of the sheet into his water glass and wash out the gritty wax.

"The house won't be the same until you come back."

"Hah. Nobody'd even miss me."

"I would."

George didn't answer, but his glinting eyes revealed more than words. This man was built thick, like Owen, with a wide face, wide nose, and large ear lobes. Thick was the only word Dottie could think of to describe him.

She tried not to stare at his wrists, more muscle than bone. These were thresher's wrists, hay-baling hands, with fingers strong and sinewy. A line from an old rhyme her Mama used to repeat went through her mind: *The smith, a mighty man was he, with large and sinewy hands.*

From the other side of the bed, Al handed George a fresh glass of water. Bony as a willow sapling in the cold of winter, he made quite a contrast to the patient, but his eyes, bright with compassion, turned George's head his way.

"There you go. After we're gone, don't hesitate to ask for more. You need lots of water. That's what those nurses get paid for."

George hid his emotions in his glass. The older nurse came in.

"Mr. Hanson, it's time for your medications. I need to check your vitals, too."

Al looked to Dottie. She gave a little nod of agreement that they ought to leave.

"We'll be going then, George. I hope you feel better. But we'll be back tomorrow night, and we'll try to think of something to bring you. You like to read?"

Dottie turned to Al, questioning. She wasn't sure George could read.

"Some. Maybe a newspaper…"

"All right. Good night then." Al patted his arm and walked around the bed.

Dottie touched George's hand again and witnessed the closest thing to a real smile from him since she'd worked at the boarding house. Even the cherry pie she made for his birthday produced less facial reaction.

# Chapter Eight

"If I had my way, I'd find a new boarder. Don't know if we can count on old George any more." Helene swung her coat around like Greta Garbo, waltzed down the back stairs, and slammed the door behind her.

"She makes me so mad!" Bonnie Mae stamped her foot on the linoleum. Dottie had a mind to tell her if she had enough time to stand around and fume, then maybe she had time to scrub the floor. But she understood the girl's feelings.

"Don't it bother you? Can't you see how unfair it is?"

Helene's pronouncement rang in Dottie's ears as she scrubbed the sink with the corner of a pad she brought from home. It was hard enough to hear her say that, but she wished Bonnie Mae hadn't been in the kitchen at the time. That girl just couldn't let anything go, and churning things around in her mind caused more problems.

Fifteen minutes later, as Bonnie Mae folded clothes at the table, Helene walked in again. "Here's George's mail, with a bill from Dr. Schulz, I'm thinking. Don't know how he'll be able to pay it, what with all this time he's missed working out at the Miller's farm. You know he does their chores when Heinie has to be gone some days with his seed corn business." She flipped the bill onto the table, walked over to the sink, and gave a shrug. "But then, that's not my problem."

When Dottie looked up from peeling carrots, Helene faced her with the frazzled scouring pad in her hand. "Dorothy, what's this? Have you been wasting money on scouring pads?"

"Not your money, Helene. I bought that myself."

"Tch, tch. Waste not, want not."

Bonnie Mae launched a sizzling look over Helene's head toward Dottie. Her narrowed eyes, set teeth, and jutting jaw declared she would careen into a rage about thirty seconds after Helene left for the beauty parlor.

Dottie's estimate was accurate. The trouble was, so were Bonnie Mae's sentiments.

"What's she going to do, throw him out if he can't pay his rent? I don't know how a woman so *unjust* stays in business. She could offer him a little help, couldn't she? After all, he's paid her a lot of rent money over the years. Wouldn't you think she'd extend some human kindness to him now?"

It was one of those times when Dottie felt something way down inside her, like those geysers she'd heard folks describe out in Yellowstone National Park. The pressure built and built until it had to let loose. But she couldn't let go yet—what might happen then?

Bonnie Mae pounded up the stairs with the folded laundry, leaving Dottie with the flak from her outburst. Pieces of it scattered all over the kitchen like broken china shards. No matter what Dottie put her hand to, the bare, unpleasant facts stared her in the face. An undeniable reality grew inside her as she mulled over both women's pronouncements.

Hard to believe those two came from the same family—blood relatives. How could they see life in such opposite ways? Their perspectives were so at odds—Helene churchgoing and proper, and Bonnie Mae as cynical as her gum cracks. And yet, the younger woman truly cared about a lonely man like George Hanson, while Helene lacked even the pretense of concern.

No doubt about it. This time, Dottie had no choice but to side with Bonnie Mae. She scooped three cups of flour into a yeast mixture for a double batch of bread. Little by little, soft dough formed under her fingers. She liked working the pliable texture.

Of course, she didn't always agree with the cleaning girl's

tempestuous conclusions, but this time, her words found their way into Dottie's insides. She'd gotten to know George so much better over the past two weeks, and Al thought a lot of him.

On the way home from the hospital that first night, her heart had almost overflowed with gratitude. "Al, I'll never forget you doing this for me." At first, he didn't hear her, so she repeated her words a few levels louder. His response touched her.

"He needed a visit—you were right, he's a lonely man. Did you notice how hard he grabbed my hand just before we left?"

Dottie had.

During the rest of the ride home, she kept her eyes on the firmament, as the Psalms called it. After the all-day storm and misty evening, the stars shone so bright, she might have rolled down her window and touched them with the tip of her index finger. It felt good to be riding beside Al, good to have taken the right action, visiting George.

So many times, she thought about doing something, but even when she knew it would be right, she held back. What was that about? Thank goodness, neither of her girls followed in her footsteps—both Millie and Cora spoke up when they needed to, and every time, Dottie was proud of them.

She pressed her head into the seat and allowed her shoulders to sag. It seemed awfully good to be proud of herself tonight. Of course, without Al, she would never even have thought of going to visit George.

Now, her bread batch molded under her hands—the fourth time she turned the wad of dough over, its elasticity responded to her ministrations. Only a couple more minutes, and she'd plop it into the bowl she'd already greased. The oven, turned off from the noontime meal but still warm, waited to help the dough rise.

Her thoughts turned back to George—and Al. The afternoon after their first trip to the Heston Hospital, Al stood at her back door five minutes when she got home from work. She hardly had time to take off her coat and light the burner under her kettle.

"Shall we go see George a little earlier tonight? I gathered some magazines and several newspapers for him to read. Thought maybe he could use a toothbrush and a washcloth, too. That hospital doesn't offer anything but a bed. Do you think he'd be offended if we added them to a basket of cookies and candy?"

His kindness floored Dottie. How could one man be so thoughtful? "Why, I don't know. If he found them amongst the other things, maybe not…"

Al angled his head, waiting for her to say more. His eyes revealed genuine concern, as if he'd known George Hanson all his life.

"Give me a few minutes, all right? I'll see what I can add to your basket. You've already put in cookies?"

Al's smile came easily now. "My *source* brought me two dozen more today—thought I might as well share them with George. Spread the pleasure, you know?"

Dottie chuckled. "You definitely are all about that."

He took a step toward her, his fingers edging around the cap in his hands. "Uh…I thought afterwards we might stop by that little diner in Heston we passed last night." His Adam's apple pulsed. "For supper."

The tips of his ears flamed scarlet. "I thought it would take less time that way—we wouldn't have to cook."

"Why, I suppose so. Let me get my…"

"My treat. I'll pick you up in fifteen minutes, all right?"

Dottie observed the wide spread between his shoulders as he headed into the porch. Then he turned toward her again. "George reminds me of my dad's brother Arthur—the kind of man who doesn't say much, but holds a lot inside. I like him."

Through the window, she watched Al cross the crisp, frosted lawn. Thoughts pummeled her mind like racing horses. He liked George, and he liked helping people. She noticed a lilt in his walk that she didn't recall. And he went to all the trouble of putting things in a basket…

When the kettle burbled, she poured some steaming water over a scoop of tea. Fifteen minutes. Enough time for that cup she'd been longing for all afternoon, and to find something to add to Al's gift. In the back porch, she chose her three best apples and a couple of pears she'd picked green and wrapped in brown paper to ripen.

If she'd known ahead of time, she could've stopped at the grocery store for a banana. Well, maybe they'd go over again tomorrow—she stopped herself. Al had used *we*—something about what *we* put in the basket. She glanced out the window toward his house and sat down to her tea. She couldn't corral her unruly thoughts—they kept trailing back to the night before like mischievous children.

Now, with the dough rising in the oven over a bowl of hot water, Dottie pulled out a bag of turnips and washed them. She relived the closeness she felt with Al when they walked into George's room and found him sitting up in a chair. The way George's eyes lighted warmed her heart, and she knew instinctively that Al sensed it, too.

And what was *it*? Maybe joy? The joy Pastor Langley mentioned last Sunday—the kind that came from giving? He always meandered to the theme of giving around Thanksgiving Day, but this year, his sermons sank deeper, maybe because she'd moved to a better place.

The ache in her chest whenever she passed Owen's picture, or something else reminded her of him, had let up. When she arrived home at night, she no longer lingered at the thermostat, but wondered what interesting adventure the evening would bring.

She pared enough turnips and potatoes for supper and checked the dough—time to punch it down. She liked the sound of air escaping, and the *blurp* the soft ball made when she gave it a pat. She turned the growing mass over and covered it with a dishtowel before sliding it back into the oven.

Downstairs, Bonnie Mae still slammed things around, but Dottie ignored the extra noise. If that's how she worked out her anger, so be it, as long as she got her work done. In the dining room, she checked the table for supper—oh, Bonnie Mae had forgotten the napkins.

Well, the poor girl trekked up and down both sets of stairs fifteen times a day. Forgetting napkins was a small thing. Dottie pulled out a drawer and carefully set one under each fork, noticing how precisely Bonnie Mae ironed and folded them. She was such a good worker, even if Helene didn't notice.

Somehow, that hospital visit altered things in Dottie's mind—the good side of things showed up more. Maybe it was George's exclamation over the basket and the newspapers, such small offerings. She'd never seen him so enlivened.

"This'll keep me busy for a few days. And cookies! Did you make these, Dottie?"

She hated to tell him she hadn't, but Al took over and explained that a lady pursued him with enticements from her kitchen. George guffawed so heartily, Dottie feared he might endanger his health. Al talked with him so easily, she only added a comment here and there.

And then the café—things had changed for her there, too. She studied the menu like a waif entering a rich uncle's mansion for the first time. What should she order? The California hamburger sounded tasty, and french fries—did she dare? A time or two, Cora brought some home from her high school restaurant job. How long had it been since she'd tasted their salty goodness?

Al grinned at her over his menu. "Order whatever you want—the hardware's paying. I hardly ever do anything like this, so it's about time." He smoothed the plastic-covered menu with his finger. "I think I'll have the tenderloin sandwich—if I remember right, they're the size of a dinner plate, with fries to boot."

"I'll have that, too." She ate every French fry, but even with her good appetite, she couldn't finish the tenderloin. The waitress wrapped half of her sandwich in a brown paper bag, and today at noon, Dottie enjoyed it all over again.

She took a last look at the boarding house dining room, all ready for the meal, and sat down at the kitchen table. For once, nothing pressing came to mind. Bonnie Mae tramped up the steps, and, through the window, some sparrows twittered. Interesting how these recent good memories could lighten one's frame of mind. Now, she didn't get so upset with Bonnie Mae. And another thing—she could see that girl's viewpoint as well as Helene's.

Helene's opinions, like the idea of throwing George out if he couldn't pay, troubled her more and more. A solid determination grew inside her, even as Bonnie Mae shot her a fierce look passing through the kitchen.

"Bonnie Mae?"

"Yeah?"

"You're right. I agree with you one hundred percent."

The younger woman dropped her clothesbasket, pulled out a chair and faced Dottie, mouth agape and eyes round as pancakes. For once, her tongue failed her.

"I mean it, honey. I'm resolved not to let anything happen that would keep George from living here. At his age, where would he go?"

Bonnie Mae beamed and banged her fist so hard, the table bounced. "Attaway, Dottie!"

"Every man deserves a place to call home, even if it isn't a real home." Dottie almost added more of her sentiments. *Even if it's owned by a ruthless woman who cares more for her beauty shop trips and snazzy outfits than a fellow human's well-being.*

But she controlled her tongue. Her proclamation had already thrown Bonnie Mae into a state of shock.

By Tuesday night, George looked ten times better. Al took him a book about the history of trains, since he'd shown an interest in the miniature one that circled the interior of the hardware store, about eight feet up the wall. On their last visit, Al explained how that train ended up where it was, endlessly tooting its way around the store.

The story revolved around Del and little Charlie. Al's delight at pleasing his boys became obvious as he described building the tall shelf and lifting the tracks and train cars piece by piece like a fire brigade from Charlie to Del, then up the ladder to himself. Dottie could feel Charlie's exuberance when the last car found its place, and Al flipped the ON switch he installed under the cash register where the boys could reach it at will.

On the visit before that, he brought a floor lamp, so George wouldn't have to endure that piercing ceiling light. Dumbstruck at the sight of Al walking in with the lamp in his fist, George fumbled for words.

Now, Dottie and Al sat on either side of his bed while George thumbed through the train book, stopping at every picture. "Rode the best of 'em and the worst of 'em, too. Lived like a hobo for a while, when work got hard to find. Covered most of Missouri and southern Iowa in boxcars, I'd say."

"You ate out over open fires?"

"Another fella and I buddied up, so it wasn't that bad. Lotsa beans and bacon, sometimes biscuits and gravy, not so different from following the harvest out in Dakota."

"Ever pass through Rolla?"

"Sure enough, more than once. Sleepy little town. You got people there?"

Al nodded. "Let's see—my father's cousin once removed—her daughter married a Rolla man. Now that I think of it, he worked the railroad. Yes, I do believe that's right."

"Don't recollect the name of that one engineer down around there—he knew who we was, knew the train was our only hope of finding work. He was awful good to us."

The exchange fascinated Dottie. Who knew, that engineer might have been Al's relative. The world grew smaller by the day.

Before they left, George shook hands with Al. "Doc says I can go home on Thursday. Looks like I'll get to ride a train again."

"The train to Sternville? I don't think so—I'll be over to pick you up. What time can you leave?"

"Around noon, I guess. But I can take the—"

"Nope." Al set his jaw, giving his reply an air of finality. "My old truck needs to be driven more. This'll give me somewhere to go, and besides, I need to pick up this lamp." He patted the brass pole with his long, slender fingers. "I'll be here at eleven thirty, in case they let you out early."

George lowered his eyes. "I don't know how to thank you folks. Couldn't believe it when you toted that big lamp in here the other day." He gestured toward his basket of goodies. "Them cookies is awful, awful good, too." He smacked his lips.

"Is there anything I can do for you at the house?"

George stroked his chin, glancing at Dottie in shy snitches and snatches. "I s'pect some bills might be comin' in. Got money stored away—in a can way back on the closet shelf, on the right. Would you mind checking my mail?"

"I did overhear Helene say a bill came from Doc Schulz. Shall I bring your money over tomorrow?"

"If you don't mind, would you go ahead and pay him? Just count out what's needed and put the receipt in the can. I hate to be beholdin' to any man. Don't like the feelin'."

Dottie and Al exchanged a look, since she'd told him about Helene's comment on the way over. Al jammed his hand into his pocket and tapped his foot on the floor.

"I won't forget. I'll drop the money by Doc's after the noon meal tomorrow."

"Appreciate it. Maybe someday I can do somethin' for you."

"You never know, George. We all need each other in this tough old world."

Al picked up his hat. "I suppose we'd better mosey back home. This woman's got a job to get up for in the morning."

The arched hallway's lights hurt Dottie's eyes, and the acrid scent of ether drifted from somewhere down the corridor. What would it be like to be a nurse here? Her mind catapulted to Bill. She knew no details, only that he was buried overseas. Maybe he died in a makeshift hospital. Mustn't think about that right now—speculation did no good.

Al opened the door for her, and in the darker entryway, she composed herself. With him beside her, this narrow room didn't bother her so much, and after the first night, she waited on the steps so they could walk through it together.

He was right—she needed her sleep so she could get up and work tomorrow morning. The truth of his words hung heavy over her. She'd sensed God's guidance three years ago when Helene asked her if she'd be interested in working at the boarding house. But with such a bold, brassy winter, her body reacted more and more like an old bear, wanting less each day to traipse to work.

They drove toward Main Street, and Al turned toward her. "Want to stop and get something to eat?"

"Maybe not tonight, thanks. It's getting awfully late." Chugging along between fields of frozen cornstalks that glittered in the headlights, she knew she'd miss these trips. Freezing air rose from the hole in the floor, and her longing to stay home tomorrow increased with every mile.

Sequestered by the engine's roar, she thought how things had altered since Bonnie Mae came. For one thing, she rarely had to maneuver her recalcitrant knee up and down the stairs any more. And an understanding had grown between them. She had come to like that girl, at least most of the time.

Just went to show how you could learn from a person, even if you started out on the wrong foot. But Bonnie Mae's forthrightness had broadened her perspective on Helene, too. The more Dottie studied the tip situation, the more she knew the girl was right as rain.

Should she keep working for a woman so set on increasing her profits, even at a loss to her employees? Didn't silence imply approval of Helene's tactics? Not one to upset the applecart, Dottie wished her discomfort would vanish, but she knew better. The simplest solution would be to quit her job—that would take her out of the picture.

But might that be a cowardly choice? She would still know what was going on, and it would trouble her. Besides, she would lose contact with George. And then there was getting up every morning—what would she do with all her time?

Al slowed for a corner, and in the brief interlude of quiet, revealed his thoughts. "Once George gets home, I'm going to visit him, Dot. Maybe he likes to fish. Or maybe he'd enjoy going to a high school basketball game. You think so?"

"What? Sorry, I was thinking about something." He repeated his questions, and she paid more attention. There was no use trying to analyze all her conflicting feelings about her job right now, anyway. If God guided her to it in the first place, couldn't He as easily guide her away?

As for the question of how to use her time, a longing thrummed inside her as Al's trusty truck roared home. If she could—if there were some way—she would visit Cora in California. With those two sweet little grandchildren, she'd never have to worry about having something to do.

But even the thought of stepping into a train sent shivers through her. Visiting Cora would mean riding clear across this huge country. She'd gotten used to Al's truck cab, true, but he sat right here beside her. Stay inside a train for several days and nights? She shook her head. Impossible.

# Chapter Nine

Helene huffed into the kitchen. "George is back. Looks like he's found himself a friend, too. Al Jensen's out there in the parlor with him, acting as if they're old pals."

"That's all right, isn't it? I'll take them some coffee."

"Oh, I don't think so, Dottie."

"Why not?"

"If George gets in the habit of bringing folks here, who knows who he might haul home next? I don't want every Tom, Dick, and Harry sitting in my parlor. Why, the next thing you know, that crazy old Eva Maloney who runs wild through town will find her way in here."

Bonnie Mae jerked her head up. "I must not have heard you right. I thought you wanted to attract customers. Remember—word of mouth is the best advertising?"

Helene pointed her chin at the clock, high above the window overlooking the back yard. "I didn't mean just any kind of customers. Surely even you know that."

"There's nothing wrong with Al Jensen—couldn't find a more upstanding member of this community. You're just too stingy to offer a decent man a cup of coffee."

Electric current surged through Dottie. She wanted to add, "She's right, Helene. Al Jensen isn't just *any* kind of customer— he's a solid citizen. Besides, this is George's home. He ought to be able to invite a friend over if he wants to."

Helene glared at Bonnie Mae. "Well, I never! You are the most obnoxious person I've ever known."

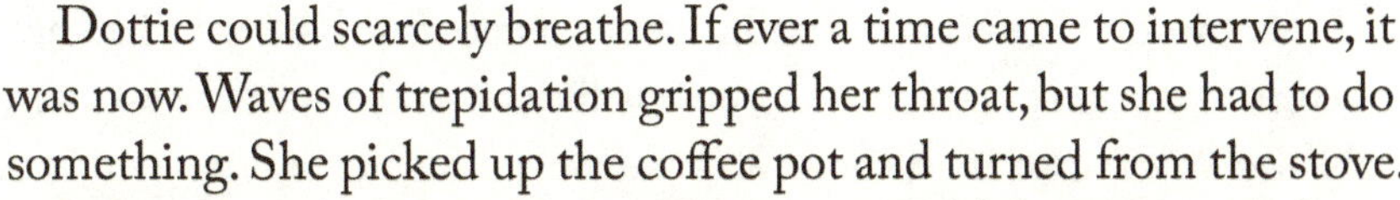

Dottie could scarcely breathe. If ever a time came to intervene, it was now. Waves of trepidation gripped her throat, but she had to do something. She picked up the coffee pot and turned from the stove.

"Now, Bonnie Mae, I know Helene wouldn't really mind me taking coffee in there, if she thinks this thing through. We keep a pot perking all day long, and it probably costs less than a penny a cup. We throw the extra out after supper, and you know how she hates waste.

"A man like Al Jensen, a bachelor, and a hungry one at that, might decide to start coming over here a few nights a week for supper. Better to eat with a friend than alone at home or in a restaurant. Wouldn't that be good for business?"

She filled two cups with coffee. "Right, Helene? Waste not, want not is what you always say."

"I do? Yes, I suppose I have repeated that a time or two." The owner's fleshy chin shook like the lemon Jello Dottie made for supper awhile earlier, although Helene eschewed such an expense. Knowing that Helene would be gone tonight and tomorrow, and rarely looked into the Frigidaire, Dottie whipped up the salad early this morning. She shredded in three carrots and added a can of pineapple rings, since George liked it that way.

With the two cups in hand, she cranked her neck around as she passed Bonnie Mae and Helene. The older woman struggled for words, but Bonnie Mae twisted her lips to the side and lifted her shoulders. For once, she aimed a considerable tide of respect in Dottie's direction.

"And don't forget, Mr. Mosely's going to deliver the coal sometime later this afternoon." Helene's starched dark blue blouse and a new crème-colored suit belied the bitter cold outdoors. She put on her coat and hat, but Dottie knew she waited for confirmation.

"I'll go down and open up the chute for him when I see him in the alley."

"You can pay him out of the household account. The weather has been so cold these days, buying coal is like paying a fulltime worker."

"I'll take care of it." Dottie kept her eyes on her potato peeling.

Tonight, Helene expected three outside guests. With the regular boarders, that made six, and Helene was going to eat here too. "That's why I wore this new suit—what do you think?" She twirled in a circle, but had to grab the chair back to keep from tottering over on high heels that looked new, too.

"It's fine."

"I look great in this shade of blue, Dorothy, don't you think? And the pearls…they're real, don't you know? I thought they added just the right touch."

In no mood to support Helene's fashion habit, Dottie gave a curt nod. She felt like saying, "Look at me—how many times have you seen this same dress in the past week? Do I look like the kind of person who'd be the least bit interested in fashion?"

Her boss put on her rubber boots and walked outside. Dottie got out the ingredients for mashed potatoes. She could never make too many—every single bite always disappeared, no matter how large the bowl. Even Helene didn't know her secret recipe: she added a little chicken bouillon with the warm milk and melted butter. The mellow bouillon caused the other flavors to blend in a pleasing way.

People raved over the dish, and no one ever guessed its secret ingredient. Dottie didn't even remember where she'd learned the technique…maybe from Nan.

Al's whistle burbled from the parlor, where he and George played an afternoon round of checkers. She recognized the tune, a snappy song Cora used to hum when she came home from work. Something about eyes…having eyes for someone.

Ever since that day he brought George home from the hospital, Al stopped in after the noonday meal, as the boarders scraped back their chairs. A simple checker game transformed into a tournament, since the men's evenly matched rivalry attracted the other boarders to cheer for one or the other.

Then, of course, each boarder had to challenge Al, and thus the Sternville boarding house tournament began. Helene wavered around the room's edge like a hovering dragonfly during the first afternoons, making sure no roughhousing occurred, but as time passed, she tempered her disapproval.

Bonnie Mae, on the other hand, whisked through the kitchen from the basement time after time throughout the afternoon, a smile intruding on her freckles. The games energized her, Dottie figured, and she felt the same way. She would hate to think of going back to the lonesome old house's peculiar creaks and groans for company.

Al started bringing home-baked treats, too, which the men loved, but it was his winning smile that did the trick. One day when Dottie helped Bonnie Mae nest some linen tablecloths and napkins into the deep bureau drawers, they caught Helene tasting a cookie.

Dottie couldn't help herself. "Why Helene—stealing cookies from these poor, hungry men?"

Helene's wattle waddled, and her cheeks flushed mercilessly. After she left the room, Al voiced an idea to the other men. "You know, someday I could bring along the lady who baked these wonderful morsels. Would you like to meet her?"

Two of them grinned, and George gave an eager nod. "Well, then. I'll give it a try." Al winked at Dottie, mischief in his eyes.

Back in the kitchen, she studied his strategy. Would he set George up to meet Henrietta? She couldn't even imagine starchy Henrietta coming over here, but what if she did succumb to Al's persuasion? What could it hurt? Helene might raise her fake eyebrows, but then, she did that anyway. She might see Henrietta as fashion competition, even though Henrietta's idea of style extended back into the twenties.

The more Dottie thought about it, the more certain of Al's motives she became. Wouldn't it be nice for these men to have a little social life? Most of them had lived alone most of their lives and had few connections in town. Why shouldn't they enjoy others' company more? Why not engineer some excitement for them?

Behind the scenes, maybe she could help lay the groundwork. She would ask him about it as they walked home together. This, like the checker games, had become a new daily ritual. It seemed normal to meet Al when she rounded the boarding house to the front sidewalk after she navigated the back steps.

Often, they walked in companionable silence, but once in a while Dottie let go, and Al absorbed whatever injustices Helene had foisted upon the world that day. She gave him an earful, as Owen would say.

Today, Al met her at the corner, and half a block from the boarding house he confirmed Dottie's speculations. "What do you think Henrietta would say if I told her I shared her latest cookie batch with the men? I could tell her they could use a little perking up over here.

"But how could I ask her to come over without having it look like I…" He paused. "Like I was…uh…wanted her to…uh…spend time with me?"

"So that's *not* why you want her to come?"

"Of course not, Dot!" Al jerked toward her, his forehead scrunched in disbelief. She snickered. It was fun to catch him unawares. "That's exactly what I don't want her to think—I just don't know how to make it happen."

"Hmm…" They walked quietly for a while, a few cars passing, but most people in town had already gone home from work. Al slowed his long stride to accommodate her aching feet, without making the change obvious. At least it wasn't sleeting or snowing today. Still, he could cover this five blocks in one-fourth the time if he wanted to.

After they crossed the street, a solution to his conundrum occurred to Dottie. "I might have it. What if somebody else asked Henrietta to come over? They could say her cookies have gained fame, and that the men want to meet her. If I know Henrietta, that might ignite her curiosity." Dottie bit her lower lip. "Now, I shouldn't have allowed that out of my mouth—wasn't the Christian thing to say."

Al laughed, one of those infrequent, deep, rumbly sounds that came from the belly. "I'm not so sure about that, Dot. You spoke the truth, plain and simple. You know that verse about truth setting us free?" They walked a few paces before he slanted his head, his hand to his chin.

"I like that about you. You see to the center of things, and so often put into words the real meat of an issue. Maybe that's why, when something disturbed Nan, she always felt better after spending time with you."

He faced Dottie head-on. "You know that's a gift, don't you? You're a quiet woman, and you don't jump to conclusions. You think about things more than you talk about them. But when you do say something, it makes sense and gives people something to think about."

She supposed he was right. Maybe it even counted as a compliment—at least the quiet part. After a day with Helene around the house more than usual and Bonnie Mae frolicking her way through the kitchen singing jazzy radio songs, quiet sounded mighty good.

But lately, she wondered about some of the unplanned words that came out of her mouth. Being around Bonnie Mae had something to do with that, she figured. That girl did too little to stem her own word flow, but maybe her example had a good effect.

Up till now, Dottie always followed one simple principle. "If you can't say something good about somebody, say nothing at all." That was the household rule, and the punishment for maligning others was severe—Dad's razor strap on your backside. Mildred probably saved her from that a few times.

But maybe she had finally found middle ground, a healthy mix between saying too much and not saying enough.

Al saw her to her door. "So, about half an hour? My house tonight?"

"Okay." Since their fishing excursion, eating together every night seemed the natural thing to do. Al brought a huge pot of soup over yesterday, and tonight, she looked forward to eating the leftovers.

She'd take along some rolls she'd made last weekend, and that would be that.

She went inside to scrub off the day's grime in a sink full of hot water. She leaned over, but stopped midway as she caught her reflection in the mirror. The gleam in her eye stunned her, and that rosy hue on her cheeks, even though she was bone tired. November's crazy up-and-down weather played a trick, warming up in the afternoons this week so she could walk home without her gloves and scarf—maybe that produced the glow.

But it was more than that. Staring at the light in her own eyes, a word formed in her mind.

*Joy.*

A shiver swept her. With Thanksgiving just around the corner, she hadn't even thought about Christmas carols yet—*Joy to the World* was her favorite, and motivated Cora's middle name since she was a December baby.

What shone in her eyes reminded her of a Yuletide feeling, warm and fulfilling—a church full of candles held by hopeful folks, and coming home to more lights on the tree. When little Sammy brought her a flower one Sunday and hugged her tight, she felt warm and alive again—this was that kind of feeling.

Thanks to Al, she'd become involved in bringing a little happiness into some lives. She hadn't done that for a long time, and it felt awfully good.

It wasn't until they finished the soup and sipped their tea that Al brought up Henrietta again. He fingered his upper lip as though something important occurred to him.

"I've been thinking about it, Dot. You're right—somebody else should tell Henrietta about the boarders and the cookies, emphasizing how much George appreciates them. She should hear in a roundabout way how they helped cheer him up in the hospital, maybe even speeded his recovery."

"Do you have somebody in mind?"

"I do." He picked up his cup, turned it around, and set it down again. "I have no idea if this person will see it the same way I do, or if she'll agree, but I definitely do have somebody in mind."

Maybe he would have Delbert's wife, Edie, bring up the subject—she worked with Henrietta on the Sunday school committee. Or his niece—Alma had such a winsome way with prim, snarly folks like Henrietta.

A smile wiggled along his lips. "Can you guess?"

"Edie?"

"Nope. Has to be somebody a little older. Henrietta looks down on youth."

"Alma?

Al shook his head, and the glimmer in his eyes told her there was no use prolonging this discussion.

"I don't know—tell me."

"All right, I will. It's you. I think you're possibly the only person who could convince Henrietta to come to the boarding house."

Dottie drew back from those penetrating grey-blues. What on earth could he mean?

But Al's voice took on urgency. "You're the only one except Bonnie Mae who's witnessed what those cookies did for George—and your connection with the boarding house—Henrietta can't question that. If you told her about George's health problems and how I shared some of her cookies with him, she would never suspect anything amiss."

Dottie let go a "Hmm…" She'd never been high class enough to fit into Henrietta Perry's circle. Oh, they got along when they needed to, but Henrietta looked down on her, she could tell. She was only a farmer's daughter, while Henrietta's father had owned the bank.

But there sat Al, his face expectant. She wouldn't want to disappoint him after all he had done for her, and for George.

"Why, I don't know. I rarely even see Henrietta."

He pressed his right fist into his left palm. "Wouldn't that be something, if Henrietta and George caught on?"

"Caught on?"

"Yeah. Henrietta's lonely, and so is George—what if they showed an interest in each other?" His grin reminded Dottie of Bill's one time when he succeeded in playing a joke on Owen.

"Al Jensen—you're matchmaking. What would Nan say?"

He studied the ceiling. "Nan? Maybe she'd say it was a gas." His self-effacing grin told Dottie he didn't really think so. The pat he gave her hand was reassuring.

"Now, don't feel pressured to do this, all right? If you don't want to, something else will work out. I'm sure it will."

Dottie finished her tea. "I'll sleep on it."

"Great idea. A good night's sleep can do wonders."

Dottie walked home slowly, surveying an incredibly bright bank of stars cascading through the heavens. *Such a glorious display, Al should—*

She stood stock still halfway across her back yard. Normally she would have thought, *if only Owen could see this with me*, but instead, she'd thought of Al.

What was happening to her? Here she was, considering a rather underhanded way of relieving her neighbor of Henrietta's advances, and possibly even paving the way for a romance between George and Henrietta. And now this—circumstances seemed bent on complicating her life.

Right before her eyes, a star scuttled downward. A falling star— didn't Millie and Cora used to make wishes on falling stars? If she could, what would she wish? All this time she'd been wishing Owen back, but that sort of wishing did no good. Her desires had no power over life and death, or over much else, either.

She could wish for Helene to revise her attitude toward Bonnie Mae, or Bonnie Mae to find an honest man who wanted to settle down and who would provide well for her. She could wish for peace on earth.

But what if she had the chance to wish for something about *her* life? The concept, fresh and intriguing, struck her imagination.

Tingles ranged her shoulders as she stared at the point where the star fell, and she realized what she wanted most of all—strange she'd even had to think about it. She wanted to see Cora and her little ones in the worst way. She leaned her head back to behold the full, glittering expanse above her, and held her arms wide.

Even though darkness had fallen, she turned a slow circle to be sure no one was watching. Then she did it. She wished to see Cora and her babies.

# Chapter Ten

"Why Henrietta, imagine meeting you here."

"Yes. I'm hardly ever ill, but today my gall bladder got me down."

"You have gall bladder trouble?"

"Sometimes, yes. Doc gives me these little miracle-working pink pills. And you?"

"Oh." Dottie's heart thumped. She had prayed last night as she got into bed, asking for a sign like the Lord sent Gideon. She didn't press for three, like that unlikely saint of old—just one would do.

Now, she stood near the clearest sign she could have received. She never met Henrietta anywhere except church, and hadn't been inside Doc Schulz's office in such a long time—maybe four years? Yet the one time she entered, here sat Henrietta.

She cleared her throat. "Uh, well—hasn't the weather been nice the past two days? Thanksgiving will be here already next week."

"Are you avoiding my question, Dottie? I divulged the purpose of my visit, now you must, too."

Ordinarily, she would have stiff-armed Henrietta at such a brazen dig for information about private matters, but not this time. "I'm paying a bill for one of the boarders, actually, a very, very nice man. He's been sick and asked me to bring his payment over here. Such an honorable, upright gentleman."

She couldn't believe how easy this was—why, she practically gushed about George, when she would have guessed she didn't even know how. Better yet, her comment had an obvious effect.

Henrietta's eyes bulged below high arched brows. "And who might this fine man be?"

"His name is George Hanson. He's become good friends with Al Jensen, my neighbor."

"Of course Al's your neighbor. Don't you think I know where he lives?"

Dottie almost choked on the spittle in her throat, but produced a loud ahem. "Oh, sure. Everyone does, how could I be so foolish?"

She took one of the upholstered chairs near the door. "As I was saying, Al and George have become good friends. It started when Doc hospitalized George, and Al took him some of your cookies. Now, they've started playing checkers at the boarding house in the afternoons.

"George simply loves your cookies, Henrietta. So do the other men at the house. Best cookies they've ever tasted, they insist."

Henrietta eyed her askance, but her low-slung brim couldn't hide the upturn of her lips. "Well."

Was that all she would say? Dottie hadn't counted on Henrietta being dumbstruck, but the well-dressed matron clenched and unclenched her fingers in silence.

Dottie fidgeted with her purse handle, wondering what to do. Should she plunge in and say something else, or leave well enough alone? Would saying something else lessen the effect of what she'd already disclosed? Heat made clear progression from her neck into her cheeks.

But Henrietta Perry was never stumped for long. "You say they play in the afternoons?"

"That's right."

"But, for a man like Al—isn't going to the boarding house a bit—you know what I mean—below his standing?"

"Below…? Whatever do you mean, Henrietta?"

The older woman pursed her petulant lips so tightly, Dottie was sure they would squeak out a "pip." But evidently, her lips were used to pursing. Henrietta slid a delicate gloved hand along her skirt edge. "I mean, that boarding house—isn't a place like that mostly for indigents? And Al Jensen—why, he's a respected businessman."

Dottie's mind jumped to indigestion. Then she realized Henrietta referred to tramps.

"Indigents? Absolutely not! Helene would never let an *indigent* into her boarding house—you should know that! And George Hanson, an indigent? Oh my goodness, no. He has made a decent living by the sweat of his brow his entire life. He simply has no wife or children, so he lives at the house."

Her face fired with the knowledge that she left out the period George lived as a hobo. But couldn't a man be an upstanding hobo? She might as well go all the way.

"George has had a wide variety of experience. You'd marvel at his stories, I know you would."

Henrietta's eyebrows met her hat brim. "But the boarding house… It isn't…uh…*clean* there, is it?"

That got Dottie's dander up. "Are you saying Helene runs an unsanitary place?" She drew her chest up. "Or implying I'm an unfit worker?"

Henrietta's hands flew to her mouth. "Oh, my. No, no, not at all. It's just that I've heard…"

"What? Tell me one thing you've heard."

"Well, Helene hired that no-account Bonnie Mae Ingersoll, just your everyday run-around…"

"Is that a problem?"

"Not exactly, but with her past, I can't help but wonder…"

"What do you know about her past?"

Henrietta glanced around on every side. "Don't you know about that, Dottie? My, my! That girl was…" She stuck her neck out and peered around the empty waiting room again. Her voice resumed its surreptitious hiss. "She was an *illegitimate baby*."

"Yes, but how can anyone fault *her* for that? I would say she had nothing to do with the circumstances of her birth, wouldn't you?"

"I—er—well, yes. But…"

"But what?"

"It does say a great deal about her origins."

"My Mama taught me not to judge, as the Bible instructs us. But you teach a Bible study group—maybe you know better. Have you read something contrary to that teaching?"

Henrietta' face turned close to purple, and she squirmed like a fish fighting for its life. But fire still stirred in Dottie, as if a long-stoked furnace had suddenly been fanned into flame.

"I can testify that Bonnie Mae is a good worker, and very clean. And she's a fast learner—did you ever think maybe she wasn't taught how to do things quite like the rest of us?"

Henrietta's eyelids performed a nervous flutter, but she remained quiet, so Dottie continued. "Hiring her was one of the best decisions Helene has made since I've worked at the boarding house."

Henrietta sucked in her breath and ducked her face under the shade of her hat brim. Luckily for her, rustling issued from the bowels of the office, and a short, chubby, cherub-faced nurse, swished into the waiting room. She wore a severely starched nurse's cap and a bumpy white uniform, belted at the waist.

Not a speck showed on her pearly white nurse's shoes. A yellow-orange pin decorated her lapel, an almost perfect match to the color of her permanent-waved hair—and her eyebrows.

"Why hello, ladies. And how are you both today? Doctor is just getting in from a long house call, but he will be ready for you in a few minutes, if you'll tell me which one of you came first."

Dottie forgot all about her unreliable knee and shot out of her chair. "I only need to pay a bill, Ma'am, for George Hanson over at the boarding house. He already paid one last week, but this came in the mail today, and he instructed me to pay the Doctor immediately. He doesn't want to be in debt to any man, not even for a day."

She pulled herself to her full height. Out of the corner of her eye, she glimpsed Henrietta putting a thoughtful finger to her temple.

"Of course he doesn't. Do tell him thank you, won't you Dottie? I hope he's feeling better by now."

"He is. He's developing a lively social life and enjoying every minute of it. I'm not at all surprised Doc could see what a solid man he is."

"Ah, yes, Doctor has an intuitive gift." She scribbled something and handed a paper to Dottie. "You may take him his receipt. Thank you, and give him our best regards."

"Good day, then." Dottie gave the slightest turn toward Henrietta. "And to you, too, Mrs. Perry."

"The weather forecast says tomorrow will turn colder again, with ice. Sure is nice to enjoy this warmth, though." Al accidentally bumped Dottie's foot as they stepped onto a curb two blocks from home. "Sorry."

She flitted her hand in the air. "Yes. We have to take warmth when we can get it. How did the checker playing go today?"

"Good. Bert Smith forged ahead of me, though. Seems he's had even more practice than George. Going to have to fight to maintain my lead. You must've had a busy afternoon?"

"Yes, Helene's having what she calls *special guests* tomorrow night. Someone from out of town, she says, looking at buying a business."

"Which one?"

"I don't know. She's all hush-hush about it, as if the FBI were involved. But she did emphasize using the thickest cream in the gravy, and put in an order for an extra afternoon milk delivery, including more cream for whipping, so I'm wondering if it might be the Creamery. Harvey's been talking about retiring."

"Hmm. That's a logical guess." Al veered off the sidewalk to avoid a hell-bent-for-leather canine.

Dottie's secret bubbled inside her. She felt like a little girl again, holding a handpicked bunch of flowers behind her back for her Mama or Mildred. She held out the smallest hint of the news she'd waited all afternoon to share with Al.

"And then, I had to make a delivery for George between cleaning

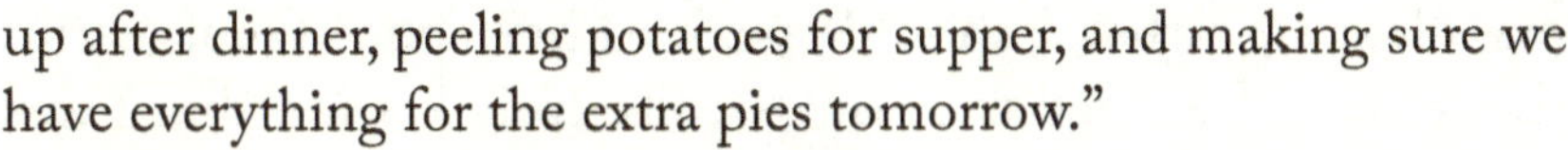

up after dinner, peeling potatoes for supper, and making sure we have everything for the extra pies tomorrow.”

“Oh?”

“Mmmhmm. Doc told him not to walk over a block at a time this week, but he got another bill in the mail today. He wanted it paid right away, so I took the money over to Doc’s office.”

“Hmm…that was nice of you.”

“It was good to get out of the house in the middle of the day.” She paused. “By the way, I met someone quite interesting in the waiting room.”

“Really? Who was that?”

“A woman. Someone you know quite well.”

Al’s right eyebrow formed a V. “Come on. You know I don’t do well with puzzles.”

But ever since she stood up to Henrietta a few hours earlier, just like Gideon facing his enemies, Dottie had felt extra pleased with herself. Now, she sensed her comical bent emerging, something that didn’t happen very often. She feared she might burst into laughter and spoil the surprise.

“You will with this one. This woman wears white gloves, even in November. Her stocking seams are so straight you could measure with them. Her eyes are a flinty sort of blue…”

“Betsy Sievers?”

“No—does Betty have eyes like that?”

“Not exactly, but I did notice she’s got those straight seams…”

“You did? Interesting.”

Al’s prominent cheekbones reddened.

“One more hint. Only one, mind you, Mr. Jensen.”

“All right. Give it to me.”

“She excels at baking, and she’s a lonely woman on the prowl. Oops, I guess that was two.”

“Henrietta? You saw Henrietta?”

“I did. I was careful not to hurry into anything, because I prayed for guidance. Last night, I put out a fleece—asked for one clear sign that I should speak to her about George and the cookies. I wanted to know—really, truly know—that I was meant to do this."

Al looked off into the distance for a few seconds, then back at her. "You took this task really seriously, I see."

"Of course I did. I *never* see Henrietta except at church, but when I walked into the waiting room, there she sat."

"Let me guess. Her gall bladder?"

"How did you know?"

"Trust me. I know more about that woman's gall bladder than I do about my own. Henrietta never gives away her baked goods without exacting a price, and I've paid that price far too many times." He peered into her eyes. "So now you know you're supposed to talk to her?"

"No." Dottie smiled at Al's upheld palms. She'd better put him out of his misery. "Now I *have* talked with her." She rolled her shoulders back as they stopped at the corner of their street.

His voice rose with interest. "You did? How did it go?"

"Pretty well, I think. I'm a little disappointed she didn't show up at the house today, though. I could tell when I left that she was thinking it over."

"You could?" Al touched her elbow as a car whizzed by. He steered her across the street.

"Yes, once she got it straight that the boarding house is not a place of ill repute." Dottie forgot all about how much her feet hurt tonight, and that her knee acted like a balky mule. The expressions on Al's face during this conversation were priceless.

"She told you that?"

"That and more. So I laid it on fairly thick about George being so honorable, wanting to pay Doc right away and all. Henrietta has strange ideas about the house—she thinks it's dirty. And she has a bad picture of Bonnie Mae, too. But you—she thinks you're a respectable gentleman."

Al ran his fingers through his hair. "Heaven help us. Oh Dottie, if this works, I tell you, I'll be indebted to you for life. To be free of Henrietta would be a mighty gift."

"But then your supply of baked goods would dry up."

"Oh, I'm not worried about that. I have a back-up plan."

"What sort of plan?"

They approached her door. Al scooted ahead and held it open for her with a grandiose gesture. "That's my secret. I'll be over in about an hour. You don't mind eating beef and dumplings tonight, do you?"

"You know that coal guy?" Bonnie Mae cracked her gum, but with a different rhythm than normal.

"Coal guy?"

"The one who made the delivery the other day."

"Oh, Tom Mosely?"

"Yeah."

Dottie examined the younger woman's face. Something important rolled around in that red head, that was for sure. Bonnie, with her flamboyant ways, rarely asked a question in such a serious tone.

"I do know him. Not well, but I think everyone in town recognizes his name, because his wife, Darlene, died last winter of pneumonia. Left him with three children seven and under."

"Wow, quite a brood. Is he a likeable guy?"

"Likeable? I've never heard him cross Helene in all the years he's delivered here."

"Well, that says something. You mean, she's never commanded him to, *Waste not, want not?*"

"No, but she's certainly given him ample opportunity to react, always peering over his shoulder and doubting the number of gallons he writes on the slip. But he knows how to practice self-control."

Bonnie Mae hung around longer than she might have. The timer dinged for her to check the whites soaking in bleach water, but she frittered with some pancake batter left on the side of the griddle while Dottie dried the last of the dishes.

Maybe she could add a little more to what she'd already expressed. "Never heard Helene utter a nasty word about Tom, either. That says even more."

"Hmm." Bonnie Mae picked up a bed sheet to fold. Her face flamed, although she tried to mask it by billowing the sheet in front of her.

"Here, let me help you fold that. Sheets go so much better with two people."

They worked in silence until Bonnie Mae reached the bottom of the clothesbasket. "You know when he'll be back?"

"Usually once a month. Doesn't he deliver to your place?"

"I'll have to check. Know anything else about him?"

"No. Well, let me see. I believe he goes to the Presbyterian Church, and he lives on a fair-sized acreage at the east end of town."

"The east side?"

"You know, out past the hatchery and the Gordon's big white house—a couple houses down from there, with yellow shutters, I think."

"Yeah?" Bonnie Mae paused at the back window on her way to the basement, as if she might see Tom out there, making a delivery.

# Chapter Eleven

Dottie cleaned up the table, hoping Al would arrive before she got deep into food preparation for another big supper. When Helene showed her face in the kitchen this morning, she announced that last night's guests had signed a contract to buy the Creamery. Now they would stay at the boarding house while searching for a home.

Twirling a long string of gaudy beads between the two peaks made by the new Maidenform brassiere she'd bragged about purchasing the day before, Helene looked extra pleased with herself. All Dottie knew was that the couple had good appetites—big ones. She had three pies to make today instead of two, beef roast with mashed potatoes, fresh rolls, a large Jello salad, and scalloped corn for eight. This time, Helene herself suggested the Jello, so Dottie knew she was out to impress.

"You won't need to stay through the meal, Dorothy, since you came extra early this morning. Just expect more than the normal workload tomorrow."

The four boarders went straight to the parlor every day after dinner now, eager for more tournament action with Al. Dottie immersed herself in flour and lard, creamed corn, and crushed saltines. The harder she worked, the less she thought about what went on in the dining room. Late in the afternoon, she tidied up the kitchen and put on her wraps.

When she stepped out the back door to go home, he waited for her on the bottom step. The look in his eyes made her heart lurch.

Al grabbed her by the shoulders, his long fingers penetrating her wool coat's thick shoulder pads. A jittery sensation edged along her backbone.

An odd light showed in his eyes. Something must have happened this afternoon.

"Dottie, you're a wonder, do you know that? Henrietta came this afternoon, and started talking to George like nobody's business. It took him a while to get over his shock, but after a while, they started chatting like old friends." He led the way around the house and onto the front sidewalk.

"If you say so, I believe it."

"I tried to slip into the kitchen to tell you, but she and George parked right in front of the swinging door. I thought about going upstairs and down the back way, but figured Helene wouldn't have appreciated that."

He squeezed her shoulders again. "How can I thank you?"

"It was your idea. I only opened my mouth when the Gideon sign showed me I had no choice."

"You ought to take more credit. You were brave. You made a decision, and good came of it. I'm proud of you." He helped her down the last step and steered her toward home.

Proud of her…Al? He kept hold of her elbow as if he owned her arm.

Dottie didn't know what to make of his statement. Parents were proud of their children for earning good grades or doing what was right. But she couldn't quite conceive of Al being proud of her. He must have sensed her dilemma.

"You're not the type to confront people, and that's a good quality. But this time, you let loose—stepped beyond what you'd normally consider doing. I don't often do that myself, so I know how much courage it takes."

The *I'm proud of you* part of Al's admission still swarmed her mind. "Courage?"

"Yes, courage. People don't realize how much of it they have until they use it. Everyone thinks it only counts in battle, but everyday courage like what you showed inspires me."

She had no idea what to say. Which, as Mama used to say, indicated the perfect time to say nothing.

Al gestured like an orator behind a podium. "Most of all, I'm excited for George. If he and Henrietta keep hitting it off, who knows what might happen? Wouldn't it burn Helene if George ended up living in the oldest, most respectable house in town?"

Dottie chuckled. "You're a born matchmaker, Al. I never would have pictured you this way."

"Me neither. But it's kind of fun, don't you think?"

Dottie pulled her collar up against a brisk breeze. Before they got to Third Street, sleety rain slashed at their faces. "The only thing is, George would have to hear about Henrietta's gallbladder till he's in the grave."

Al laughed out loud. A few minutes farther on, he motioned to the right. "Turn in here."

*Here* turned out to be Almira's Café. Dottie pushed back her dripping hair. "I must look a sight."

Al grinned, a raindrop balanced on the tip of his nose. "Me too, but who cares? How about I treat you to a California hamburger? Otherwise, it's dumplings for the third night in a row."

"You're going to go broke, Al Jensen."

"Nope. Del owes me for a lot of hours at the store. Even though I've only been working mornings the past couple of weeks, I rack up the hours. Besides, we've got something to celebrate."

"Del pays you?" She could have sworn Al told her he volunteered at the hardware.

He made a Stan Laurel face. "No, but it sounded good. Del's still making monthly payments on the store, though, and will be for a good long time."

He helped her with her coat. "What a sudden storm. Hope it lets up by the time we're ready to go." He handed her a menu from behind the chrome napkin holder.

"Dottie?"

"What?"

"I meant it. I'm indebted to you. What's something you would really, really like? Somewhere you'd like to go, maybe?"

The falling star and her wish to see Cora and the children flashed through Dottie's mind. That scene out in the starry back yard replayed, her hands raised to the heavens and her heart open to surprises. But she tore her eyes away from Al's to stare at the menu.

Putting out a Gideon's fleece for divine guidance was one thing, but wishing on a falling star was an entirely different matter. And admitting to Al what she had done? Not on your life.

"Mom? How's it going there?"

"Cora—it's so good to hear from you. I'm fine. How are the children?" Dottie jammed the earpiece against her ear and hunched into a kitchen chair. A quiver went through her at the sound of her baby's voice.

"Fat and sassy. I'm going to hold Jeffy up to the phone. I taught him to say, *Grandma.*"

Amidst intermittent crackles, a garbled emission came through. The backs of Dottie's eyes sparked. Her hands itched to hold that little guy.

"Dennis and I want you to come out for Christmas. We would help with the fare."

"Come out? You mean take the train?"

"Yes. Would you? Millie would pick you up and drive you to the station."

"Why, I don't know. I haven't ridden the train, ever. Not even to see Millie, honey."

"But you could. It's safe, and the fare isn't…"

Dottie half-listened to all the details, but her mind veered along a dark channel. Ride the train all the way to California? She shuddered. Why, she couldn't do that—what would Owen say?

"I don't know. I want to see you and the children more than anything, but…"

"Maybe you could find a friend to come along. Dennis fixed up the attic above the garage, and we have room for you right in the house. You'll think about it, won't you, Mom? Please?"

"I'll try."

"You'll try to think about it?"

Loud crackles filled the line, so Dottie could barely make out Cora's words.

"Yes. I'll think about it." Her volume increased, but all she got for her effort was louder crackling. She yelled into the phone, but the static only grew worse. Finally, she hung up.

Her head spun. Take the train to California? She would do just about anything for her girls, but boarding a train alone for that long journey was too much to ask. She simply couldn't consider it.

Yet the catch in Cora's voice tugged at her. So did little Jeffy's greeting—what she heard of it. The picture Cora sent in her last letter showed a Sammy look-alike, and the "Gamma" Jeffy murmured into the receiver tore at her heart. For the rest of the evening, she pondered, visualizing a little house along the coast, with Cora alone all day long while Dennis worked. But what she couldn't visualize was boarding a train.

What would the fare cost? How long would the trip take? She had about $2,000 saved up, but even finding out all the information she'd need in order to decide boggled her mind. Maybe she ought to give Millie a call—that girl knew how to do anything she set her mind to. But Millie had an important job at Collins Radio and her husband and three children to think about.

All night long, Dottie tossed and turned. Cora's offer to help with the fare bothered her the most. No, she wouldn't let them. Why, of course not. If she went, she'd pay her own way. She got up for a drink of water and noticed Al's light still on. There was something comforting about knowing he couldn't sleep, either.

Bonnie Mae had done something different to her hair. Dottie noticed it right away. This morning, she looked more like a dignified, grown-up woman than an awkward, scatterbrained high school girl. Her gum cracking greatly diminished, too. Dottie thought about asking her how her Sunday had been, but decided to wait. With Bonnie Mae, nothing stayed secret for long.

Today, Helene helped things along. "So, Missy. You weren't in church yesterday. What was that about?"

"About? Oh, nothing. Maybe I just got weary of the same old sermon, same old songs. Needed a little variety in my life."

Helene honed in on her, moving around the table like a thunderhead. "What are you talking about? Pastor Diers told a very interesting story yesterday—a true one."

"Oh, goody." Bonnie Mae went about her folding. Helene harrumphed.

"You watch your mouth. It behooves us to put ourselves under the teaching of our designated shepherd." Bonnie Mae sneered, and Helene left the room in a huff.

The exchange gave Dottie ample time to examine the hairdo change. Instead of coercing her wild locks into a chokehold at the back of her head, Bonnie Mae let them fall to the sides a little more, framing her face. Maybe she even snipped her thick shaft of curls some. A connection went through the back of Dottie's mind—hadn't Bonnie Mae asked her about some man recently? But she couldn't remember who it was.

Helene stormed back in, a stack of silverware in her hands. Behind her, the door swung back and forth as if it took on her ire. Her throat clearing filled the room, and she zeroed in on Bonnie Mae, her voice razor sharp.

"You don't know what's good for you. You are too smart-mouthed for your own good. You bite the hand that feeds you, and some day you'll be sorry. How would you like it if I fired you?"

"I'd like it a lot, actually." Somehow, Bonnie Mae managed to mumble so Dottie heard her but Helene didn't. Dottie held her breath. Getting herself fired was the last thing Bonnie Mae needed. Visions of tramping up and down the stairs with the laundry basket fluttered before Dottie.

"What did you say?"

"Oh nothing. Well, gotta get these linens upstairs. Wouldn't want to keep the boys waiting."

Helene's chin trembled so much it seemed in danger of falling off. "What do you think of *that*, Dottie? I am so tempted to write her off."

"What do you mean, write her off?"

"I only hired her because of a deathbed promise I made to mother, and I'm tired of putting up with her smartness. I don't know how long I can keep this up. There's only so much a person can take, don't you know?" Helene dumped the silverware on the table. "By the way, this all needs to be polished."

Dottie thought back to the way things were before Bonnie Mae came. Basically, she did both of their jobs for the same wage. She wouldn't want to go back to that situation. Besides, what would Bonnie Mae do if Helene threw her out? It wasn't as if Sternville grew by leaps and bounds these days like bigger towns, with new businesses requiring new workers.

"Now, you wouldn't want to do anything rash, Helene. You have to admit, she's learned her job well, and her work makes a big difference around here."

"If I had to pay her myself, it'd be different. I would fire her in an instant. As it is, I just cut into her inheritance. The man she calls her stepfather certainly won't provide for her."

"Calls her stepfather?"

"Mama died when Bonnie Mae was ten. Felicity came back to town a few months before that. Brought this man named Ned back with her—don't know if they ever married or not. Didn't make much difference to her one way or the other.

"For some reason, he decided to stay on. And for some even stranger reason, he took to that flighty little redhead. He bought the house he still lives in, started working for the feed mill, and acted like he wanted to be regular people."

Dottie folded a cup of sugar slowly into some whipped cream, gradually, cautiously—the secret of successful meringue. But her stomach jittered. Something about Helene's description of Ned bothered her. What did she mean, regular people? Helene and Henrietta Perry seemed to think a lot alike.

Helene's fingers trembled as she poured herself a cup of strong black coffee and sat down at the table. The beautician had gone a bit too far this morning, creating a greenish-blue sheen for her new hairstyle.

"That lasted about six months for my wild sister." Helene spewed the word sister like spittle. "She couldn't stand having a child around, for one thing, even her *own* child. But when she left, Ned stuck with it here. And he stuck with Bonnie Mae, too, until she lit out with that numbskull from Chicago. Like mother, like daughter."

"Have you ever heard from Felicity?" Dottie leaned her bad knee against the old cupboard while she cranked the mixer into a frenzy through the meringue mixture.

"No. I asked Ned a while ago, and he had the same opinion. I wouldn't be surprised if she died in a back alley somewhere."

"So Bonnie Mae only spent six months of her life with her real mother? Does she know your mother wasn't…?" The meringue stiffened so well, Dottie felt a surge of satisfaction.

"I told you—I don't know what she knows, and I'm beyond caring. When Felicity's birthing screams woke me in the night all those years ago, I vowed I'd never get myself into such a fix, and I surely haven't. A couple of men tried, but I batted them away. No marriage for me, I vowed—not until all possibility of *that* happening was long past."

Downstairs, the washer swished back and forth, back and forth, creating a vibration through the countertop. Helene drank her cup dry and drummed her sharp fingernails on the table. After coaxing the meringue into graceful, peaked snowdrifts over her warm lemon pudding, Dottie slipped the pie into the oven and refilled Helene's cup.

"Felicity took in every scruffy tomcat that prowled around. Broke Mama and Daddy's hearts, and I wanted no part of it. Through those early years, Mama sent Bonnie Mae along with her a couple of times, but our peace was short-lived. Felicity always brought her back, bawling and more selfish than ever. Now, wouldn't you say it's unfair that I'm stuck with the consequences of my sister's sinful life?"

Dottie's sympathies went out to both Helene and Bonnie Mae, but for different reasons. Helene couldn't forget the past and embrace her last family connection, but it was sadder still for the younger woman. She only needed a fair chance.

Helene sputtered her next words. "I *knew* you wouldn't voice an opinion, Dorothy. But it *is* unfair. It's un*just*! So maybe I'll just forget about that vow I made to Mama. Maybe the next time that girl shoots off her mouth, I'll tell her it's over. Tell her to find herself a job wherever she can. I've taken all I'm going to take."

Dottie opened the oven door a smidgen to peek at the pie, eased it shut, and in that moment when she removed herself from Helene's tirade, she recalled who Bonnie Mae asked her about the other day: Tom Mosely, the coal man. And she'd mentioned that Tom attended the Presbyterian Church. She would bet all the pots and pans in this room that's where Bonnie Mae went yesterday morning.

"Helene, how do you know Ned won't provide anything for Bonnie Mae? Does he have other children?"

"He might—some men spawn kids all over the place like tadpoles, sometimes they don't even know they're theirs. I can't tell for sure what he'll do. But it would serve that smart mouth right to be cut out. She doesn't deserve a darn thing from anyone. Spoiled rotten is what she is."

Dottie filled her mixing bowl with warm water, thankful for the timer's steady *tick-tick-tick*. The back of Helene's head glowed with a peculiar aura, like a pre-dawn moon, and her flushed countenance revealed her unabated anger. But if her boss expected another comment from her, she'd have to be disappointed. What could she say, when Helene's every other word dripped with self-pity?

Helene plopped her cup down beside the sink and wandered off somewhere, but the force of her fury remained, like scum on a long-used pan. Helene *let* Bonnie Mae make her miserable—that was the truth of it. How did you go about helping someone get rid of such a hindrance to her own happiness?

# Chapter Twelve

A cardinal lighted at the kitchen window for a few seconds, peering up at her as if seeking information. She touched his bright feathers through the glass and drank in the mellow aroma of lemon pudding filling the room. Interesting how you could lace sour lemon juice with sugar to create a pleasing taste and smell.

The timer went off, and Dottie pulled out the most perfectly browned meringue ever. She wished Al would stop in so she could show him.

She cleaned up the counter and started on the dishes, scanning the yard's bare branches for that winged harbinger of cheer—no sign of his bright scarlet, but she did glimpse a man's long overcoat and straw hat crossing the back yard. Eva. For her age, that woman had incredible energy—she never seemed to sit still. Poor Ily, having to wonder where her mother had gone every day, search her out, and apologize to people all the time.

Eva barreled straight for the other side of the yard as if she saw her prospector husband Helmut resurrected there, and he'd just struck gold. But when she arrived, she threw up her arms and walked away dejected toward the back door.

Dottie dried her hands and hurried down the stairs. She motioned for Eva to come, and pulled her in out of the weather.

"You're freezing, honey. Want a cup of coffee?"

"Drank it black, Helmut did. So thick it sat in drops on his whiskers."

"Come on in—warm up your hands. Didn't you bring any gloves today?"

"Hawkers—that's what they were. Heartless hawkers, them what stole the nuggets. But they paid—oh, they paid dearly." Eva leaned against the door, wagging her head back and forth. "But I paid the biggest price. Oh, my." She raised her eyes. "Forget your name, young lady, but I'd best be off, help the sheriff, now that's a praisable thing."

Before Dottie could gather her thoughts to cajole her to stay, she was gone, her shoulders jerking in their own private dance.

"Umm…must be awful to live like that, with your thoughts playing tricks on you all the time. At least Eva had her chance at adventure, though—that's what Bonnie Mae says." She pulled the door tight and went back to her dishwashing. "Too bad she couldn't have stayed out in the mountains after Helmut died—too bad she can't find any peace."

She set her mind to her task, but Eva's flighty form stayed with her. Her chance at adventure—yes, she had that, and her memories from those days of panning gold with Helmut. Most people called her crazy, but once in a while, she stopped long enough to let Dottie look into her eyes as they chatted, and a couple of times her ramblings made sense.

Suds rose in the dishpan. Dottie tried to put Eva's plight out of her mind—some things, you truly couldn't make better. She washed the cups and glasses first, like Mildred taught her years ago. If she kept up with the dishes during the day, they didn't loom so overwhelming later on. One thing for sure—Helene would never come in and find her at loose ends.

Al manhandled a twenty-two pound turkey up the back steps into his porch, glad for the cold weather's return since his Frigidaire would never hold the massive bird. He hadn't thought ahead about Thanksgiving, except to assume he'd go over to Delbert and Edie's like always, but this morning, Del reported Edie and their youngest son down with a severe case of the flu.

Dottie's kitchen light still shone, and the way its rays filtered across the grass between their houses gave Al an inspiration. Or maybe it was staring at the edible monster Frank O'Brien handed him a few minutes ago.

He hadn't recognized the old farm truck idling up the alley, but happened to be looking out his kitchen window at the time. He waited until the tires crunched on the bunched-up frozen snow and ice in his driveway. When big brown rattling fenders came abreast of his back steps, he ran out to see who would be paying him a visit this late in the evening.

Frank doffed his hat. "Thought this was your place. Had an abundance of turkeys this year—sold a passel of 'em, but this one needed to be butchered, too. So heavy she could hardly walk. The Missus thought to bring her to you. After all, you was so faithful to bring us word from Anthony, over there."

He gestured in the general direction of the Atlantic Ocean. Al hadn't spoken much with Frank over the years, just a few times when he'd waited at the mailbox for a letter from their son, fighting in France and Belgium. But those chats bonded them. The same thing happened with several other folks along the route.

That was about the time Delbert bought the store. Owen took sick and asked Al if he wouldn't take over the mail route for him till he recovered. And so it was that Al delivered the mail north of town until they found a suitable replacement.

"Why, thank you. I can't imagine you'd think of me, Frank."

"Course we did. Maybe you don't know how the Missus watched for you those last days o' the war. Stood at the window and waited for your truck every day…yep, every single day." Frank pushed his tattered cap back. He could have launched into Anthony's trials at the Battle of the Bulge, but drew his shoulders back instead.

"Cook the old bird up. If you've a mind, take some over t' Owen's widow. Sure sorry he had to go and die so young—best mailman our neck of the woods ever had." Frank shifted his engine into reverse and backed away.

Now, Al patted the turkey, sitting in a big brown cardboard hardware box, and located a couple of clean, tattered towels to moisten and tuck around its bulging breast. Something pulled him to look behind him, out the window again. There stood Dottie on her porch. He couldn't see what she was doing, but she still had on her work dress.

Why not run over and ask her what to do with the turkey? Maybe the boarding house could use it on Thursday. He grabbed for his coat, and an idea hit him that sent a surge of energy through his chest.

"Helene's leaving, so I could help her prepare a mountain of a feast for George and the others. We could have an old fashioned Thanksgiving for them." Al's whisper wafted through the icy porch. He stood there another half minute, then made his decision.

He flew across the yard. By the time he mounted the steps, though, Dottie had turned off her light and shut the door to the kitchen. Through the window, he could see her near the stove, probably making a last cup of tea.

He stepped into the porch to the telephone's jangle. Behind him, a gale raged. The weatherman predicted exactly that—amazing how fast storms pressed down from the northwest. Al counted the longs and shorts coming from the wall-mounted oak telephone. Yes, that was Dottie's number.

He didn't intend to eavesdrop, but a shiver took him. Probably Hilda down at the exchange, lonely for someone to talk with. It didn't make any sense to go back home now.

"Why Cora, it's you!"

Dottie's voice pulsed. Torn between paying attention and putting his hands over his ears, Al wavered at the door.

"I'm so glad you called back again. Maybe we'll have a better connection this time." Silence for a few seconds.

"You're *what*? Oh, Cora—so soon?"

"Five months already? And you've been sick—but you had such an easy time with the other two. I wonder what—

"Have I what? I'm sorry, it's so hard to hear with this crackling on the line. Must be bad weather between here and there.

"What? The Rocky Mountains…mmmhmm. Yes, I have thought about the train. I just don't see how—" Dottie's end became unearthly quiet. Her frame bent over the receiver. He wanted to rush into the kitchen and put his arm around her shoulders.

"You what? But sweetie, I'm not sure at all…" Dismay entered her voice.

"Hello? Cora, are you still there? Oh this confounded telephone—the lines must have crossed or something."

A loud click led to a screech as Dottie drew a chair across the floor. Al glanced toward the table where she held her head in her hands over a cup of tea. He stomped his feet a couple of times and knocked on the door.

Her face curved toward him. Did her eyes show delight or irritation? Most of the time he could read Dot, he thought, but from the looks of her pained expression, things might be more complicated tonight.

She rushed to open the door. "Al—am I ever glad to see you. How did you know I needed you right now? Sit down, please."

She poured a cup of tea for him, but the sensation that filled him at her words warmed him deeper than any steaming drink.

"Bonnie Mae, I have some special work for you this afternoon. I know I'm not your boss, but this job is made for you."

"Made for me? Right…" Bonnie Mae dragged out the "i," bringing her hand from her mop to the table.

"You trust me, don't you?"

"Um…so far, anyway."

"All right. I appreciate how you've helped me in the kitchen this morning. With Thanksgiving tomorrow, and Helene going off to Minneapolis, I'm going to share a secret with you. Al Jensen came into a twenty-pound turkey, and we're going to make the stuffing later this afternoon."

"Do we get to eat some?"

"Absolutely—as much as you want, tomorrow at dinnertime. It's for all of us—the boarders, you, me, Al, and whoever else you might want to invite."

"You mean it?"

"I do. And that leads me to the job I have in mind for you. About four o'clock, we expect a special coal delivery, since we've used up almost a whole load already this month. I have a lot more baking to do, but someone needs to watch for the truck and open the hopper. I'll be busy rolling out biscuits for supper about that time."

Bonnie Mae arched a brow. "That's the job?"

Dottie nodded. "And while you're waiting, I want you to help with the pies. Think you can handle that?"

The younger woman grinned. "Start teaching."

"First, I have a list of errands—fetching from the larder, the pantry, the fruit cellar." Dottie handed her a scrap of paper, "Oh, and by the way—please don't mention our Thanksgiving feast to Helene, if she should happen to stop in before she leaves.

Bonnie rolled her eyes. "Under no condition, sister." She whacked Dottie's shoulder and bounded away.

"That girl's going to be all right. I hope she invites Tom Mosely and his children over for tomorrow." Dottie creaked the old cupboard door wide. With Helene on her way out of town, she could almost feel her heart expand.

"I hope they fall in love." She raised her voice again. "I really hope they do."

Ingredients for yeast rolls, pumpkin and apple pie covered the kitchen. When Bonnie Mae returned with an armload of containers, Dottie busied her peeling and slicing apples.

"Keep a sharp eye on the pumpkin in the oven. Poke it with a fork in about twenty minutes. When the peeling's soft, take it out and scrape the insides through the sieve into my biggest mixing bowl. Use this potato masher to work it down as smooth as you can."

She stirred up a batch of yeast dough and kneaded it. About that time, clanking sounded from out in the back yard. Bonnie

Mae slammed her bowl of peelings on the table, her eyes blazing. "Be right back."

From her vantage point, Dottie thought Mr. Mosely's hat leaned awfully close to that bushy red hair. Bonnie ran back inside and down the basement stairs. Scraping ensued as she opened the hopper, and then her feet thumped up the stairs and back outside. Long after the coal lay safely in the basement, she and Tom lingered beside the truck.

Dottie set the dough to rise and rolled out a triple batch of pastry. In a big bowl, she mixed eggs, milk, sugar, and spices to add to the pumpkin once it cooled. Afternoon light weakened. Still, Bonnie Mae and Tom talked.

Finally, Bonnie Mae charged through the back door. "You're sure you don't mind if Tom and his children come over tomorrow?"

"Don't mind at all. In fact, I sure hope they do. We could use some young people to spice things up around here."

The smile on the girl's face was worth all the effort Dottie made this afternoon—all she would do this evening and in the morning, too. When Bonnie Mae dashed back in, her cheeks glowed.

"He's coming! They're all coming." She whirled Dottie around the kitchen.

"All right. We'll have enough folks for a real feast! Finish up those apples now, and mix in a cup of sugar and one-fourth cup flour before you put them into the crust. Oh, and a sprinkling of cinnamon."

Bonnie Mae's step contained a new bustle, but for once, she kept her thoughts to herself. Dottie respected that.

With the apple pies in the oven, Bonnie Mae set the table for tomorrow, as special as she could make it. The whistling that came from the dining room left no doubt about her excitement.

Describing the afternoon to Al when he slipped into the kitchen gave Dottie great enjoyment. It was almost as if her own family were coming home for the holiday.

"Didn't you call me a matchmaker not long ago? Seems to me

you've got some skill in that area, too." Al put a hand on her shoulder as she formed the rolls after punching down the dough for the last time.

"Mind if I grab a bite here? I'll stay and help as long as you need me."

"Sure. There's some cold beef in the Frigidaire. Heat it up and take some in to the men, only they'll have to eat somewhere besides the dining room table. Tell them I'm so busy getting ready for tomorrow, I forgot to make supper, and remind them not to mention this to Helene."

"You don't need to worry. We all watched her back down the driveway a long time ago. The men are looking forward to tomorrow more than you know. Shall I take out some milk too, and bread?"

"Yes. Whatever you can find to fill them up—there's a bowl of leftover goulash in there, too. Why don't you have them eat in here?"

Al hauled in a couple of extra chairs, and the men crowded around the table. Dottie liked having them so close, jostling back and forth. She even liked the smell of them—lye soap and muscles latent under plaid flannel shirts.

Al took over as host, cleaned up the table, and set to washing dishes, with George wiping. The kitchen took on a festive air, not much different from when Owen and the children helped with Thanksgiving preparations years ago.

Dottie and Bonnie Mae snacked on the go, and that girl plunged into the work with gusto. Midway through the evening, she turned to Dottie. "Care if I invite Ned, too? He's got nobody to spend Thanksgiving with."

"Sure, bring him along—I don't believe I've ever met him."

# Chapter Thirteen

So it was that the four boarders, Bonnie Mae and Tom, his three children, and Ned gathered at noon on Thanksgiving Day. Al and Dottie presided over the group like proud grandparents. When Dottie passed his house at five a.m., Al joined her. The turkey, basted in its own juices since six, couldn't have tasted better.

Bonnie Mae bounced into the kitchen early that morning and learned more about producing a good meal than she had in her entire life. Aromas of roasting turkey, gravy, fresh-baked rolls, and pie billowed out of the kitchen into the rest of the house.

When Tom arrived, Bonnie Mae brought him and the children in to meet the cook and her chief assistant. Al even donned a crisp green cobbler's apron for the workout, complete with appropriate utensils popped into its pockets.

Once Tom's youngsters each had a job carrying things into the dining room, they relaxed. Their laughter added more than Dottie could say. She lost the forlornness she'd felt when Millie called from Cedar Rapids two weeks ago to say they wouldn't be driving up this year.

Crowded into the dining room were people who had little or no family, all in one place, enjoying the day. Dottie viewed the gathering through misty eyes. Once or twice, she thought of Cora needing her so much, especially since she expected another baby now. Five months along, tired and feeling sick, with two energetic little ones to care for—how would she ever manage? But she forced herself to put that image aside for the time being.

Al seemed to sense what was going on. Twice during the morning, he patted her arm. She'd probably told him too much when he came over after Cora called, but what was done was done. Her frustrations about the impossible train trip tumbled out, and he hardly gave a peep. He simply listened.

She appreciated that most of all—he didn't try to patch up her woes or make suggestions. He simply sat there and listened with such a sympathetic look that her heart went out to him. Before the evening ended, they delved into the plans for this dinner, so she went to bed with a lighter heart.

Because of Al's patience in listening to her, she'd been able to sleep. Otherwise, she would have spent the night worrying about Cora, traveling an endless circle of wanting to help yet seeing no way. Today, all it took was that pat from him to remind her that things would be just fine. That was what he'd told her before he left for his house the night before.

"I have a feeling it'll all work out, Dot." Such a brief statement, but the resolution and confidence in Al's eyes calmed her. His words prompted her to remember what she already knew—the best thing she could do for Cora was pray.

But today, she could attend to these fine folks, and attend to them she did. When they'd passed and re-passed the main course, she jogged Bonnie Mae's shoulder. "Come with me. You can whip the cream."

Emerald eyes sparkled like a little girl's on Christmas morning. Bonnie Mae followed Dottie's instructions to the letter, and the cream cooperated. The result was something to behold, sitting up on the pies like snow fluffed and frozen in place.

"Thanks for teaching me, Dottie." Bonnie Mae's eyes turned heathery.

"The more you know about cooking, the better. I know my girls—"

She stopped herself. No use adding to Bonnie Mae's hurt. Obviously, Felicity taught her daughter nothing about functioning in a kitchen. But neither her grandmother nor Helene had taken time to help her, either.

Bonnie Mae proudly carried the luscious creation to the dining room, where Al proposed a coffee and hot chocolate toast. He raised his cup and surveyed the diners.

"One thing I'm thankful for this year is having met you men—I've had a gay old time matching my wits with yours at checkers. May I propose a round robin tournament this afternoon—everyone included?"

"Women and children, too?"

Al caught Dottie's eyes. "Absolutely. No one left out. But first, you put your feet up, and we're going to do the dishes."

Bonnie Mae joined in. "Good idea. I'll put everything away."

George and Al took over the dishpan. Sitting in the parlor surrounded by Tom's children, Dottie finally stopped sputtering. Ned and Bert joined them, and she learned about the importance of greasing engine valves. In no time at all, the tournament began.

At five-thirty, weary guests hovered around the last players left standing—or sitting—Ned and George. Everyone awaited one final brilliant move. Bonnie Mae took Tom's two youngest to make turkey sandwiches for supper, but his teenaged son wedged a stool between Ned and George, as close as he could get to the game.

Al stood like a grand marshal, ready to award first prize. George's last play astounded them all into applause. Ned shook George's hand and raised it in victory.

Al made the pronouncement: "Behold the winner of the first Thanksgiving Day tournament in Happiness Haven."

"Happiness Haven?" Ned raised the question, though he had been quiet much of the day.

"Yes, I christen this place anew. Why not? Today, it's been a haven for all of us." Al bowed in several directions. "Thanks to each and every one of you. This was the finest Thanksgiving I've had in a long time." He turned toward Ned. "You ought to start coming over here for our afternoon games. We'll have to hustle to keep up with you."

Ned's wide smile answered for him. Bonnie Mae swished through the kitchen door with a huge tray of food. Tom's daughters followed with coffee and milk.

Tom reached for the tray, and everyone dived in again.

"I don't know about you, but I've eaten far too much. How about we all take a walk?" Dottie liked Al's suggestion, and George, Bert, and another boarder joined them in a promenade down Main Street and back as dusk eased into twilight. Back at the house, Tom and Bonnie Mae left with the children, but not before the younger woman wrapped her arms around Dottie. Her eyes brimmed.

"Thank you so much. I can come back and help with dishes…" An unvoiced communication passed between them. If Dottie had to put it into words, she would say it spoke of love and respect.

"Thank you for offering, but Al and George will handle them, I suspect. You go on and have a good evening."

An hour later, with the dining room cleared and set to rights by the boarders and Ned, George helped Al with the dishes. Dottie scrubbed the kitchen counter and table clean. George's bulk somehow managed to fit into the nook near the dishpan. Beside Al's Stan Laurel, he looked even larger.

The two men ribbed each other, leading to frequent outbursts of laughter. Dottie searched out containers for all the leftovers, not an easy task. For the dressing, she had to resort to an empty roaster that dared her to fetch it from the top of the cupboard.

She pulled open the bottom door, stepped up on the shelf, and stretched her arm as far as she could. All of a sudden, a warm hand supported her lower back. She looked into Al's eyes.

"That's quite a reach for you. One of these days, you're going to hurt yourself."

That got her ire up, maybe because George was watching. But he joined in, too.

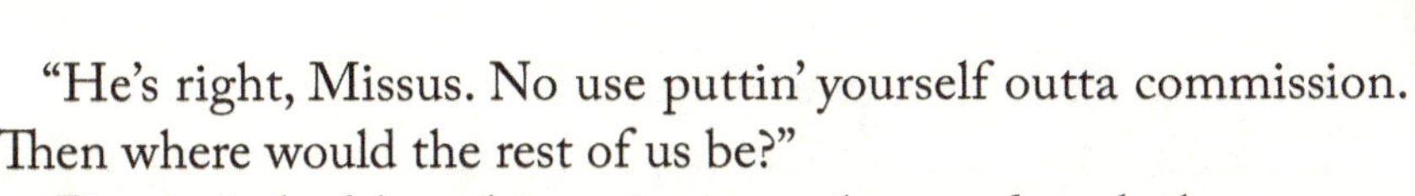

"He's right, Missus. No use puttin' yourself outta commission. Then where would the rest of us be?"

Dottie jerked her shirtwaist into place and took the roaster from Al. He noticed everything, and saw that she needed help. He was right, but for a moment, she had visions of Owen, when he'd taken to the house during his last months. It seemed to her that he watched her every move. She'd actually felt relieved when he lost the strength to follow her into the kitchen.

She spooned in great wads of sage dressing. When she finished storing everything, the porch resembled a circus vendor's tent, piled with wares from end to end.

With the dishes almost done, she brought the mop pail from the closet, but Ned took it from her. His no-nonsense look told her not to argue.

"Here, let me do that. You take a rest. Best turkey I ever ate." His nose, splotched in variegated shades of brown and red, shone like a beacon. "Especially that stuffing—reminds me of my mother's."

George looped his fourth soaked dishtowel over the basement doorknob and took a fresh one to dry the last two remaining pans. "Me, too. That was some dinner you cooked, Missus. Some fine dinner."

"My pleasure to cook for such good eaters. Happy Thanksgiving."

In the dining room, Bert engaged a boarder in another round of checkers. With George's promise to check the lamps and lock the doors, Al guided Dottie into her coat and out the front door.

"Today was a success, wouldn't you say?"

"Yes, a great success. Remember, it was your idea. And your turkey."

"But you cooked the massive thing. Oh—that wonderful stuffing—sage, onion, chicken broth, but what was the other taste? You mixed in some other ingredient."

"Cook's secret. But it sounds like George and Ned's Mama's knew it, too."

"Mine didn't—and she called it stuffing."

"Dressing, stuffing—same thing, no matter what you call it."

"Right, and the best part is, there's some left for tomorrow!"

Dottie chuckled. "You'll be ready for more by then?"

"Sure will." Her shuffle told him her feet hurt more than usual. "Let's stop by my house and soak your feet."

"Soak…?"

"That's what helped Nan when her feet hurt so much. Hot water with a little hand soap scraped in."

"All right, but at my house. That way, I won't have to walk home later."

Al grinned. "You've got a point." He walked her to her door. Her gait on the stairs made him wince. "I need some supplies. Sit in your armchair and wait."

Dottie saluted. "Yes, Sir!"

Al muttered to himself on the way to his back door. "Dot's a strong woman, but this day really was too much for her." He hurried up the porch steps. "She works far too hard. I wonder if she has to, or just doesn't want to be at home all day long?"

Owen left Dottie his pension, but Al had no idea how much that amounted to. Crossing the porch, he tipped his head to study clouds closing in. The weatherman predicted snow in the next few days. He could feel the change in the air. He turned his doorknob, glad he didn't have to settle into this cold house yet.

Dottie's heart swelled with weary satisfaction as she turned the thermostat dial. Good memories of Thanksgivings past flooded in, with the children at home and a much smaller turkey than she'd cooked today, but always with a spirit of gratitude. Those had been good years.

For a fleeting moment, three faces, Millie, Bill and Cora, glowed around the dining room table, Owen at the head. When Millie called to say they wouldn't be able to make the trip up this year, she hadn't been too surprised, since Millie and Ren both worked fulltime, even after the war.

But her heart would have been heavy today without Al's boarding house idea. Why hadn't Al's youngest, Charlie, driven his family home for Thanksgiving? Seemed like he had every other year for as long as she could recall.

"Nothing stays the same." Her whisper echoed against the walls as pain zinged the soles of her feet. She leaned against the entryway threshold to take off her boots and scuttled toward her beckoning armchair on slanted ankles. She used to work just as hard, but her feet never hurt like this. The cold weather didn't help any—or maybe it was time to face what her body proclaimed—she'd turned old.

She dropped her coat and hat on the brown velvet sofa, raised in some places, bare in others from decades of hard use. The old matching stuffed armchair received her as if waiting for her. She groaned as the cushions conformed to her back. Ah…nothing like your favorite chair.

The front door squeaked. Al tapped on it and pushed it open. "I'm in the living room."

She waved him in as spokes of pain shot up the backs of her legs. Shin splints raised insistent voices in the front. How did she get into such a fix?

Al rested a grocery bag on the sofa, took off his wraps, and eyed her. "Hurting pretty bad, aren't you?"

Those perceptive gray-blue eyes didn't wait for an answer. He whisked his pail into the kitchen, rattled it around and let the water run while it heated. Dottie leaned over, rolled her white stockings down to her ankles, pulled them off and tossed them to the side. She closed her eyes, knowing whatever Al had in mind, it would be fine.

Recollections of the way he took care of Nan in her last days floated to the surface. Dottie had been willing to do whatever she could for her dear friend, but she really didn't need much at all.

"Just brew some tea and sit with me," Nan would say. "Al's a peach—he takes care of everything."

Dottie drifted off until he knelt before her and lifted her feet, one by one, into hot water. He smoothed his fingertips over them, easing into a firmer hold.

"Old Doc showed me how to do this when Nan's legs gave her such fits. He used to work with Army horses, you know. Something about the nerves—what you do to your feet can affect other parts of you, he said."

Dottie had never heard of such a thing, but the sharp leg slashes she'd tried to ignore since about noon took on a life of their own. She didn't care how his treatment worked, only that it did.

Her trusty chair invited her to sink in deeper. Al's fingers traced her heel down to her toe tips, eased along her arch, massaging with a gentle touch. A soothing current rimmed her neck and shoulders as he continued to knead the bottoms of her feet with increasing pressure.

Her sinuses let loose when he rubbed the tops and ends of her toes—she'd never experienced the like. She fished in her pocket for her hankie and blew her nose.

Head bent with intensity, Al tackled her other foot. Dottie's wrists flopped outward on the chair arms. She must look like an old hen ready to stew, her legs stuck out and her arms like rubber. But she didn't care at all. She willed him to rub harder under her arches. As if he could read her mind, he increased his thumb pressure.

She felt herself slipping away. He didn't say a word, but continued to massage as Dottie faded.

# Chapter Fourteen

The taut lines of Dottie's face relaxed, and her fine foot bones melded under his touch. Sitting at her feet brought to mind Nan's troubles before she left this earth. Good thing Doc taught him this technique to ease her pain. But mainly, Dottie filled his mind.

He changed his position to stop a cramp in his thigh, and viewed her from a slightly different angle. Such a good woman—she'd given fully of herself today, working nonstop to satisfy everyone.

Pies, fresh rolls, heaps of mashed potatoes, tawny gravy as smooth as glass, that massive turkey, so moist and succulent, cranberries with walnuts and raisins, and her dressing—yes, he could call it that instead of stuffing. He had trouble finding words for the unique taste. What was that secret ingredient?

"Ooh…" His unintended verbalization fell short of her ears. He peered closer in the dim light. Why, she'd fallen asleep. That was a good thing, and not just for her—it gave him time to study her high forehead and the curve of her cheekbones.

Every nook and cranny revealed strength. A very strong woman—larger-boned than Nan and solid, but Dottie kept herself shapely.

Her ankles cracked and popped, the bones sharp and delicate in his palms. He massaged around and above them a few inches, keeping an eye on her face in case she showed signs of discomfort. But her eyelids never twitched.

When the water turned tepid, he tiptoed to the bathroom for a towel, removed her left foot from the water, fluffed the skin dry, and placed her heel on the scatter rug. She didn't budge. He repeated the movements with her right foot and carried the water out the back door, splashing it across the snow-covered yard.

Moonlight pervaded the sky. A long breath of cold night air enervated him. His fingers still tingled from the texture of Dot's skin. He pictured her asleep: quiet and trusting—trusting him.

His prayer ascended like an updraft. "What should I do?"

What he'd known in his heart for weeks settled there in a new way, converting from knowledge into desire and determination. He paused longer, the pail's cold enamel harsh against his hand, Dottie's back steps solid under his shoes.

The world around him kept changing. Didn't somebody once say, "Nothing is as sure as change?"

Delbert was doing so well, with the increasing need for paint, nails, and ladders for a few new houses going up in town. Farmers, too, seemed to be catching a second wind after the war years. No doubt the hardware would continue to thrive, and Del could manage just fine without his help.

He scanned the heavens one more time, for more succinct instructions that might be written there. A tremor scooted through him. Still, he waited. Finally, back in the kitchen, he brewed a pot of tea, set a cup on the end table beside Dottie's chair, and gathered his coat and hat.

Eyes fixed on him from the shadows—he felt rather than saw them. "You're leaving?"

"Feeling better?"

Her soft voice prickled the back of his neck. "Yes, thanks to you. You're a miracle worker, Albert Jensen."

Suddenly shy, he heard his reply as if from someone else standing beside him. "Anything else I can do?"

"Drink some tea with me."

He set down his wraps and returned to the kitchen for a cup. Perched on the end of the couch nearest Dottie, he relished the easy hush that settled over them. When they both finished their tea, he stood again.

"Let me help you up, Dot. You fed a multitude today, made a lot of people happy. You deserve a good night's rest."

She accepted his help, rose from the chair and leaned on his arm moving down the narrow hallway. At her bedroom door, Al stopped. She turned against his shoulder, her dark eyes gentle.

"My body's wearing out. I could never have done what I did today without you."

He wanted to pull her close. The sight of her full lips so near sent an even stronger longing through him. He searched her eyes, so deeply tired. He ought not take advantage of that to steal a kiss, no matter how long he'd waited. She tottered toward her bed and sat down.

His voice croaked. "I'll refill your cup—you can drink tea in bed for once."

"Thanks, Al. What would I do without you?"

He hurried to the living room for her cup and poured in steaming water from the kettle, mulling her words. Could she possibly mean that she needed him? His hand shook as he placed the cup on her nightstand.

"You've had one long day. How about I go over and make breakfast with George in the morning? Did you have any idea he was a cook at one time?"

"Sure didn't. But now that he told us, I can picture him dishing up beans and steak over a North Dakota campfire. Feeding harvest workers—who would have thought it?"

"Helene's not due back till Sunday, is she? Why don't you let us take care of the breakfasts till then?"

Something in Dottie's face shifted. She rolled her lips in. "All right, I will, but only because it's you. Only because I'd trust you with my life."

Now, he was the one to swallow. Emotion drained his face, like hands wringing out a mop. His knees went weak. Such warmth filled the space between the two of them, it almost became a separate presence.

"All right. Don't you worry about a thing. Sleep as long as you can. We'll clean up the kitchen and cook leftovers for dinner. You never know, if you stay away long enough, maybe Bonnie Mae will take the opportunity to show what you've taught her."

He backed away, step by step. Dottie gave him a bleary smile and a feeble wave. "Thank you. Lock the doors, will you please?"

He could barely breathe. "I will."

Happiness followed him home. He was weary, too—exhausted, actually, but the tiredness intertwined with a deep fulfillment he couldn't deny. Dottie had actually breathed those magic words, *I'd trust you with my life.* With every pace across the back yard, he clung to them. If the grass weren't so frosty slick, he might even turn a cartwheel.

When his hand touched the doorknob and he let himself into the kitchen, a dreamy aura accompanied him. Suddenly, his kitchen seemed even more small and lonely. His impulse, to race back over to Dottie's and declare himself gave him pause. No, that would be foolhardy. She would never go for such an impulsive action.

She needed her rest. She'd been working so hard these past two days, and she bore worry for Cora, expecting another baby with those two sweet little urchins already. But the other night, Dottie made it clear she couldn't face that long trip clear across the country alone.

He could understand how the vast expanse between here and California loomed too large for her to conquer. To him, it spoke of adventure, but he'd crossed the Atlantic and traipsed around another continent, albeit thirty years ago. Taking a trip to the West Coast piqued only anticipation in him.

In spite of her fear, Dottie couldn't hide her longing to go. Her expression after Cora's phone call, alight with anxiety and desire, came back afresh and tore at his heart. It simply wasn't right. A woman like Dot ought to be able to see her grandchildren.

He dropped his coat on a chair and sank at his kitchen table, reaching for a pencil and notepad. Then he raced to the bookshelf for his old United States atlas. All the desires that burgeoned in him since that first fishing excursion with Dottie came to the fore. If he was honest, he wanted nothing more than to spend the rest of his life with Dottie Kyle. *Dottie Jensen*—yes, that's what he wanted, for her to share his name till death do they part.

Everything coalesced as he spread the map out on the kitchen table. How much time and money would it take to get a marriage license, buy Dottie a wedding ring and get train tickets to San Diego?

Something else careened through his mind—he could sell this house, and… His imagination whirled. He felt like a young man again, challenged, hopeful, energetic, and positive. Even the pink teapot wallpaper backing the stove seemed to cheer him.

His breath came in spurts, but logic calmed him down. The one thing he had no power to do was sway Dottie's feelings. No use trying. Either she loved him or she didn't. Tonight, he thought he'd seen something more in her eyes—something lasting. And she trusted him. Wasn't love another word for trust in action?

Yet he wouldn't know for sure until he launched the all-important question. He jumped up and paced the house. A question like that for a woman like Dottie—he must tread ever so carefully and bide his time. No hurrying such a thing.

Owen's face entered his mind. How many times had they fished down at the pond together, taken all the kids sledding, made cider from the apple trees in their back yards? Would Owen mind if he pursued marriage with Dot?

He circled through the archway connecting the kitchen with the dining room for the fourth time. If the tables were turned, would he mind if Owen wanted to marry Nan?

He paused to stretch his neck. His quandary ricocheted off the dark walls, and perspiration crept down his temples, in spite of the cold draft through the old rooms. Across the way, Dottie's bedroom light went out.

No. He didn't think he would mind, if he were dead and gone. He would only want his Nan to be cared for and loved. No, he would far rather have her settled with Owen than to live out her days alone. Finally, he set his little alarm clock for six o'clock and went to bed.

After a few topsy-turvy hours, Al raced to the boarding house. George was already up and had coffee boiling. Al cracked a dozen eggs into a bowl. The back door slammed, and he peeked into the porch.

Bonnie Mae, eyes flashing like lightning bugs in a summer cornfield, loped up the steps. She flung her coat onto a hook and took the next set of steps to the kitchen in one bound. Snowflakes still peppered her wild curls. "Where's Dottie?"

"I told her to take the morning off. If I know her, she'll be in pretty soon, but her feet hurt so bad last night, I told her George and I could handle breakfast."

Bonnie Mae ripped off a strip of George's first pancake. "Yummm…looks like you did. Glad Dottie agreed to stay home. That woman works harder than anybody I've ever known."

She mumbled something about "Helene…that old battle-axe" under her breath and started down the basement stairs. Al scraped one of those new-fangled little wiry sponge things over a frying pan and rinsed off the area—shiny as new. Amazing what you could find in a hardware store these days.

"That girl could run the whole show here, if Helene would let her."

"You think so?"

"Well, maybe not the kitchen, but she don't let any ants or dust make a home upstairs, that's for sure. When I hear her clatter up the stairs with her dust mop and pail, I clear out quick."

Bonnie Mae brought up a gigantic load of clothes to fold. Al and George kept talking as she matched sheet corners together and smoothed out wrinkles.

"You hang all those downstairs to dry?"

"Yup, until it warms up. The lines strung down there could kill an unsuspecting person. Lop off their heads."

An uncomfortable squiggle ran down Al's spine, as always happened at the mention of gore. Ever since he'd left those horrible trenches, although thirty years had passed, he couldn't manage phrases like *lop off their heads* very well.

"Tom Mosely's children were so well behaved yesterday. It was fun having some younger folk around."

Color rose in Bonnie Mae's cheeks until they almost matched her hair. She grabbed another sheet and hid her face in it. Dottie was right—wedding bells would be ringing for her sooner rather than later.

Dottie had told him a few details about the tension between Helene and Bonnie Mae, but he couldn't understand it. Why would an older woman like Helene turn against her one remaining relative?

He remembered how he loved to jiggle his own babies on his knee. Even under the worst of circumstances, when a baby came into Helene's childhood home, how could she not love the tiny thing? Something was just plain missing from that woman. He tried to recall if she'd always been this way—age was a funny thing. It could turn people sour or sweet, the way he saw it.

Dottie was a case in point—Bill's death could have made her bitter, but it didn't. He couldn't say that for some other people in the community. He shied away every time he happened to see Madge Lenard on the street because the loss of her nephew had become her focal point. The same was true with Orville Blake, whose younger brother died in the Pacific.

He couldn't blame them and was more than grateful Charlie managed to come home in one piece. If he hadn't, he'd likely be every bit as befuddled as old Mrs. Maloney.

In the dining room, the men gathered at their places when Al carried in scrambled eggs and a platter of pancakes and bacon heaped on a platter. George brought a steaming bowl of oatmeal, and Al fetched the coffee.

He sat down with the men and turned his attention back to George. "So you cooked for threshers? How many at a time?"

"Sure did. Threshed some days and cooked some days—twenty-five to thirty-five hearty men, I'd say. Whatever the boss needed, I did. Ever been out west?"

"Not much. Always wanted to travel, especially beyond the Missouri, but the hardware store held me here. Nan and I planned some trips once our son took over, but the war started, and then she got so sick…"

The back door creaked open, and Al recognized Dottie's footfall. His heartbeat quickened as she entered the room, flushed but looking refreshed.

"Good morning. Looks like you're doing just fine."

"Fair to middlin', Missus. Nobody's complaining, but then, there's not much a cook can do to destroy flapjacks n' bacon, long as they're flooded with butter n' syrup." George gave her a grin and rose to carry the dishes to the kitchen.

"Well, you're a professional at dishwashing. I may never let you out of that job."

"Okay by me. I kinda like it. Gets the grime out from under a fella's fingernails."

Dottie's lips contorted. She glanced Al's way, and for a moment, he expected her to say something, but she went into the kitchen for her apron instead. He took a pile of plates to the dishpan.

Bonnie Mae appeared from the basement and patted Dottie's shoulder. "You have a good sleep, Dottie?"

"I did. I have a neighbor who ought to be a doctor. He helped me relax like I never have before."

The same warmth that wafted over Al last night flooded his chest. At the same time, shyness struck him, and heat poured into his face. This remarkable woman certainly expressed a lot—or hinted a lot—with her big, beautiful brown eyes.

# Chapter Fifteen

"I say we make chocolate chip cookies."

"You can't be serious. Helene would never allow me to buy one of those expensive bags of chips." Dottie couldn't believe Bonnie Mae's audacity. She scrubbed harder on a pile of dirty potatoes.

"Morsels, you mean? I'll chip in half." Bonnie Mae giggled at her pun.

"Out of your wages? Now, that would be a waste of hard-earned cash, and you know it."

"All right then. I'll get George and the others to each donate a nickel, and bake them all by myself. After all, it's Saturday."

Dottie turned her head. "So?"

"Well, it's the start of the Christmas season. We should make merry."

Dottie shrugged. The idea itself wasn't half bad, but making those cookies would be such an unsanctioned luxury.

"I picked up the lard free this morning at the rendering works. Elmer sent Helene a message that he feels like Christmas today. What's the difference between making those cookies, if I can round up the cash, and baking gingerbread—same amount of ingredients, right?"

Dottie calculated. "Just about, except for the morsels."

"Well, then." Bonnie Mae headed into the dining room tournament, an all-out war of Five Hundred. Through the open door, bids drifted into the kitchen.

"Two hearts—good ones."

"Good ones, eh? Well, I've got good spades, and since you've forced me, I'll bid three."

"Three spades? I'll raise that heart bid to three."

The bidding stopped at Al. During a long pause, his tension floated all the way to Dottie. If he didn't raise the spade bid, he would disappoint his partner, but she could tell from his hesitation that he didn't have the card power to do it. Playing Five Hundred revealed a lot about a person—Owen, for instance, would never let a bid go by, even if he and his partner went in the hole over it.

"Sorry, Bert. I don't have the cards to bid four—I'll have to pass." Bert groaned, but Dottie could imagine George, who'd bid three hearts, grinning wildly as he gathered in the five-card blind. A sudden recollection overwhelmed her—something Owen remarked years ago one morning after they'd played Five Hundred with Nan and Al.

"Al doesn't have that killer instinct, you know? If he did, we would have won over you women hands down last night."

At the time, Owen's perspective seemingly rendered Al less manly, but now Dottie knew differently. Owen's analysis was true— the tenderness in Al Jensen ran way down. She couldn't imagine him *doing whatever it took* to win a hand of cards, as Owen would. But that tendency didn't make Al less of a man. It only meant that he understood some things were more important than winning.

The men concentrated on this life-and-death round. Dottie bet they didn't even notice Bonnie Mae approach the card table.

"You men hungry for chocolate chip cookies?"

"Never had 'em, but they sure do sound good." George was the first to answer.

"They melt in your mouth. If everybody contributes a nickel or a dime, Dottie says I can buy the chips."

Dottie crossed the kitchen, held the door open a smidgen and peeked through. Al's head jerked in her direction. "So Helene would be against this? While the cat's away, the mice will play, eh?" He dug into his pocket. "I'll put in a dime. How many cookies do I get for that?"

Bonnie Mae held out her hungry palm. "A batch makes about sixty. Divide that by six—you'll have enough for a stomach ache."

"Sounds good by me." George's pocket change jingled into Bonnie Mae's hand, and the other men doled coins out, too.

She dashed back to the kitchen in victory. "See? It's worth it to them."

"All right then, go on down to the store. Do you have the recipe in your head?"

"It's on the package."

"Um. I'll keep working at supper."

A frivolous air filled the kitchen when Bonnie Mae raced in ten minutes later. For a girl who hung her head when she started working here, she certainly held it high since the day before Thanksgiving.

She got out a big mixing bowl and set to work. But a minute later, she brought the chip package over to Dottie. "What does it mean to cream the butter and sugar?"

"Put the sugar in the bowl and then the butter. Mix them until they're smooth—creamy, I guess."

A few questions later, Bonnie Mae slid a pan of cookies into the oven, and in fifteen minutes, pulled out some rich-smelling treats. She transferred them to a big platter and headed into the living room. *Oohs* and *ahhs* caressed the air.

Up to her elbows in soapy scrub water, Dottie wrung out her rag and attacked the baseboard of the kitchen. She had to smile at Bonnie Mae's success. What harm did a little luxury do once in a while? After all, the war ended more than a year ago, even though Helene still lived as if they were under enforced rationing. Except, of course, for her beauty parlor splurges and now, her trip all the way to Minneapolis.

During the war, she couldn't have driven up there. Getting enough sugar and flour to feed these men posed a challenge in itself. Dottie gave thanks she hadn't worked here the whole time—making do for boarders would have been tougher than scrimping at home.

Bonnie Mae danced back in with the platter. "Go ahead. You're gonna love these."

"Give me a minute. I still have work to do around here, you know."

Bonnie Mae grinned, and a silent communication passed between them. She'd realized Dottie was joking. A month ago, she would have taken that comment personally.

She was right about loving the cookies. Eating one of the soft circles was like biting into a rich, chocolate and caramel candy bar, only better. The hot chocolate melted on Dottie's teeth. Dottie filled a couple of teacups and motioned Bonnie Mae to the table. She picked up another cookie.

"How'd you learn about these?"

"In Chicago. A woman from Massachusetts stayed at the same place Milt and I did. She knew a lady who worked in a restaurant out there. One day she cut up pieces of chocolate into her cookie dough—or maybe they got in there by accident—I forget the details. Word of these cookies spread far and wide. Eventually, she traded the recipe for a lifetime supply of chocolate."

"You don't say. Do you know her name?"

"Ruby something...or was it Eleanora? Quite the inventor, huh?"

Bonnie Mae munched her third cookie. "Anyway, that woman in our building brought us some cookies that Christmas. Nicest gift we had that year."

Bonnie Mae never mentioned her time away from Sternville, so Dottie ventured a question. "How long did you live out there?"

"Too long. I got spoiled, although Helene believes I was already spoiled before I left."

Dottie declined to comment.

"Well, anyway, that's the past. The future looks better every day. Never thought I'd say I wouldn't mind living in this town the rest of my life." Bonnie Mae fiddled with the edge of the oilcloth.

"You and Tom getting along?"

Cheeks bright, Bonnie nodded. "Real well."

Dottie reached across the table and tapped the back of her hand.

"I'm so glad for you. Those children need a Mama, and you'd make a fine one."

"You think so? I don't know—never pictured myself like that."

"Well you'd better start—seems like my picture of myself changes every day, in ways I never imagined." Bonnie Mae leaned forward—she was really listening. "Those children aren't going away, and I saw how Tom looks at you. Children bring you a lifetime of pleasure, mark my words."

"Helene would have a fit."

"Yes, but that's what she does no matter what. She might as well have one over something good for once."

"I didn't know about you at first, I'll admit. But you've turned out okay, Dottie."

"Thanks. At least, I think that's a compliment."

"It is. I would imagine Helene's talked to you some about me." Bonnie peered at her, but Dottie kept a blank face. "That's all right—I don't want to know what she said. I could probably repeat it right now, anyway, without hearing. I'm no-good. I'm spoiled. I'm foolish. I've got a big, sassy mouth. I was trouble from the moment I was born. That about it?"

Dottie gave nothing away.

"I *was* foolish to take up with that confounded Milt. But his sweet-talkin' got to me—I itched for adventure and believed every word he said. After Mama died, Helene pretended she didn't have a little sister. Our older sister Felicity was as fickle as gas pains, and..."

A warning light went off inside Dottie. She sat up straighter. Had Bonnie Mae just called Felicity her sister? She stirred a little honey into her tea.

"I suppose that happens more often to young girls in big cities— you don't know a man's family, so you have to judge everything by what he says. People can put on airs, and lying comes easily to some folks."

"That's for sure. Milt was a prime example. But I never did get it until the end, when he took up with a high school girl right in front of me." Her brow puckered, as if reliving that awful time. She took a deep breath and a sip of tea. "Helene probably calls me stupid, too, and I have to say, I sure was, back then."

"But you've learned from all that, haven't you?"

Bonnie Mae took another cookie. "I sure have."

"If you're learning, you're not stupid. Most people can't stand back and see their mistakes, Bonnie Mae—that's a real plus. And sometimes we do get second chances."

"Do you believe in them?"

"I do." Al's attention to her aching feet and the tender moments they shared Thanksgiving night passed through Dottie's mind. "Without second chances, where would any of us be?"

"Even people like Helene? You think she'll get a second chance at being happy?"

Dottie drew a breath. "Maybe we have to be open to see our second chances. But some people find their happiness in being miserable, to my way of thinking."

"You're right—she does enjoy being upset." Bonnie Mae's eyes took on a faraway look. "Wonder if Felicity ever got another chance. Or if Ned has had an opportunity for one, but didn't take it."

"You mean in romance?"

"Yeah."

"Ned seems like a good man. I never knew Felicity, but she's the sort of woman I could never understand." Bonnie Mae jumped up to refill their teacups. She took the kettle back to the stove, and Dottie assumed she'd stopped paying attention. "To leave again after…now, that's something I can't fathom. She gave up so much."

"What do you mean?"

Dottie reached for her second cookie. Bonnie Mae sure had been right about this recipe—it had a soothing effect, and drinking tea in the middle of the afternoon was a forbidden treat. She tried to analyze what Felicity might have been thinking the last time she left town.

"To leave again, once she came back here when your Grandma died. To have seen what a wonderful girl you were, and then to…"

She almost choked at the painful way Bonnie Mae's face twisted. "My Grandma? What a wonderful girl I was…?"

"Er, yes…why I…" Dottie had never felt so bumble-headed. She'd known better than to let the conversation stay on Felicity for long. How could she possibly dig herself out of this? She swiped at her forehead and diverted her eyes, but it was no use. One look at Bonnie Mae's face told her not to even try.

"Mama was…" The girl shook her red curls as if to clear her head. "Are you saying Mama was actually my grandmother?"

The clock on the wall ticked so slowly Dottie could scarcely breathe. She grabbed the edge of the table. "Oh my. I've spoken out of turn, dear. I didn't mean…"

Bonnie Mae rose in slow motion, her eye color like the low, scraggly boughs of a pine forest on a cloudy day. Dottie bit her lip, and a coppery taste filled her mouth. If only she could take back her words.

"Mama—she wasn't my mother?" Bonnie Mae jerked sideways, half standing. Dottie wished those eyes would veer away from hers. The girl's voice turned thoughtful.

"She always told me to call Helene *Auntie* on account of her being so much older, even though she was my sister." Bonnie Mae stumbled against the table leg. "But Helene always *seemed* like an aunt, not a sister—know what I mean? Something never fit quite right."

The weight of the world crushed down on Dottie. Her eyes smarted. "Honey, didn't you know why she let Felicity take you with her those times?"

Bonnie Mae's tone took on a lifeless edge. "No. Felicity was a wild one, that's for sure. I don't remember much from those trips, except they always involved men. One named Harry, and one named Percival. There was another. I don't even recall his name, but he was mean to Felicity."

Dottie hung on every word. Oh, why had she allowed a little tea and some savory cookies to addle her brain so?

"Mama's illness made it hard for her to take care of me, so everyone decided I should go live with Felicity for a while. Then when Mama—Grandma—died, Helene maintained my only rightful place was with Felicity and Ned. But nobody ever…"

She ran her tongue back and forth over her teeth and reared up from her chair. Back and forth, she paced the floor. "I wanted a daddy real bad, so when we came back here that last time, I started calling Ned my stepfather."

Dottie pressed her palms into the sides of her chair. What had she done? She ought never to have left her normal mode, keeping her words few and far between. She kneaded her throat with cold fingers.

Bonnie Mae flopped her arms against her sides. "I always wondered about Felicity—our eyes looked so much alike. There's still a picture of her in the house, you know, and when I look at it, I feel…"

She halted square with Dottie's chair. "But she never uttered a word—not even good-bye. How could she have been my mother?"

"I don't know—I can't understand that, because you're a fine girl, and you've grown into a beautiful woman." Dottie's voice came out hoarse. "Maybe…maybe she was so young when you were born and it seemed best to…"

"Lie to me?" The girl's voice strained, as though she suffered a bad sore throat. "So that's how it was! I'd been living a lie way before I ever met up with Milt. I've lived a lie from the moment I was born, and Helene kept it up—she could've told me when Mama—when Grandma died. She could have said, I really *am* your aunt, and Felicity is your moth—"

Her face paled, even her freckles. "She could have told me when Milt left me, too, and I had nowhere else to go but here. And all this time…" She ran her fingers through her hair.

Dottie reached for her forearm, fumbling for words. An angry rush wracked her abdomen. Didn't a person have the right to know their origins? Why didn't Helene tell her the truth?

"Are you…are you all right? I'm so sorry…"

"All right?" Bonnie Mae flung back her hair, startled out of its pins. "I'm as all right as rain. I'm going for a long, long walk. Maybe things will fall into place in my head. But you…" She pulled on her coat and scarf and turned back.

Dottie quailed. Bonnie Mae might never forgive her. Closer, the flushed young woman squatted before her and touched her cheek. Chocolate cookie aroma laced her breath.

"You've got nothing to be sorry about, Dottie Kyle. You're the first person who's ever looked me in the eye and told me the truth. Even if you did it accidentally."

Dottie sat at the table after the outside door banged shut. The touch of Bonnie Mae's fingertips remained on her skin.

She took a deep breath. She needed to finish making supper. That roaster full of leftover turkey and gravy bubbled in the oven now, and she needed to peel potatoes. Reheat yesterday's corn. Cut the leftover pie. But she felt glued to her chair. The clock's faithful *tick-tock* reminded her of the passage of time.

Her comments about second chances swirled in her head like wayward tumbleweeds. She did believe in them, especially for Bonnie Mae. If that poor girl could only get past this shock, she'd be okay. No wonder she ended up the way she had. At her age, she surely deserved another opportunity for marriage and family.

Dottie walked through the dining room corner into the parlor. The men were so involved in another game, they didn't even notice. She found an angle where she could see Bonnie Mae's retreating form hurrying along the sidewalk toward Main Street.

"Please help her find peace, and give her a second chance with Tom."

Al's laughter joined the other men's as they ended a round of cards. He was such a gentleman, to spend all this time with George and the others—so unselfish, so caring.

His serious expression in the dim light of the back hallway last night might have given her a start if she hadn't been so weary. Once he left, she got into her flannel nightgown, climbed into bed, and lay there thinking about their satisfying day and that look on his face. Except for when he teased her, she'd begun to know what he was about to say by the look in his eyes.

But last night, she couldn't fathom what his expression said. She hoped it had something to do with second chances.

Bonnie Mae's figure disappeared around a corner. Dottie returned to the kitchen and fished a paring knife out of the drawer. Maybe she'd make George another bowl of his favorite Jello salad, since yesterday's disappeared with the first passing. Leaning down to gather potatoes from the vegetable bin, she caught the heady scent of chocolate chips.

Al's laughter wafted through the closed swinging door. Dottie pictured Bonnie Mae walking out her newfound discovery. Her heart thumped in rhythm with that sweet girl's spritely step, though she couldn't see her right now.

The men guffawed again, and Al explained something to the others—she could tell by the rhythm of his sentences. Praying for Bonnie Mae was easy, much easier than putting her own longings into words.

Jensen's Hardware geared up for Christmas. Delbert ordered a case of Daisy Red Ryder BB guns, and hung a yellow and red poster featuring Red Ryder himself. The first time Al saw the bright tag board message in the window, he stepped back. Under a white cowboy hat, Red Ryder pointed his forefinger at the reader like Uncle Sam.

"I'll help you get a DAISY for Christmas. Send coupon below for your free Christmas kit." A prominently displayed Winchester boasted carbine action. Underneath, another enticement wooed young would-be buyers. *Only $2.99, a big box of BBs included.*

But the gun itself cost way more than that. Al rubbed his chin. So many hard-working families couldn't come up with that kind of money, with or without help from Red Ryder. Good thing his grandsons had grown too old for such. Back in his day, his dad gave him a real gun when he turned twelve, and taught him to bag squirrels and rabbits to help feed the family. But for Christmas? They enjoyed Grandpa Jensen's gift of a crate of apples, with maybe a few oranges thrown in.

Al rarely interfered with Del's decisions at the hardware, but these toys seemed wasteful. He'd ventured his opinion a few days earlier. "You sure you want to tempt hard-working folks like this?"

Del's curt answer left no room for argument. "Dad, the company's already sold almost a million guns this year. Think of it—a million! We might as well get in on the rage. Why shouldn't we, when other merchants all over the nation sell them? And we only have to pay shipping from Michigan."

Al moseyed back to the new electric iron display. On the market for about ten years before the war, irons were in such short supply from '40 to '44 that he'd hardly stocked any. The newer streamlined models were much lighter. He lifted one to compare with Nan's old one.

Delbert's order might be right on track—maybe fifteen women in Sternville would ask for one of these for Christmas. But Al couldn't imagine such a thing.

Other years, he'd been eager to see the store's proceeds at the end of December. But this season, his mind often wandered when he came in to help Delbert. He was getting downright fuzzy headed, thinking about Dottie's dilemma—how to see Cora and those grandbabies. And his own puzzle, how to win her heart, left him bewildered.

Dottie wasn't the kind of woman who could be *won*—not like *winning* that round of checkers last week. He couldn't strategize his way through this. There was no impressing her, no wooing, flattering, or pursuing. She would have to want his companionship, and for that to happen, she'd have to realize she needed him—she'd have to feel lonely.

Trouble was, he didn't know that she did. Except for that night after Cora's phone call, she'd never admitted as much, and she seemed to handle things well on her own.

Love for him would have to grow in her on its own—he felt utterly helpless. He looked down, realized he put a cardboard display together backwards, and threw up his hands. Nothing he disliked more than wasting time, and that's exactly what he'd done.

He wandered the quiet aisles of tools—shovels, rakes, hammers, saws, thermometers, rain gages, and a plethora of other inventions that used to interest him. Now, they swam before him, insignificant. But one memory encouraged him: Dottie declared she trusted him the other night. That had to mean something. Surely it did.

He straightened a row of detergent boxes in the cleaning aisle. Maybe he'd outrun his usefulness here. With the afternoon games at the boarding house, he hadn't volunteered to work as often, and Del rarely called with an emergency. Maybe he was getting too old for this.

He'd even had trouble concentrating at checkers and Five Hundred lately. To lose track of trump during a game, when victory depended on remembering, had given him several embarrassing moments. Once, Bert's stare almost bored a hole in him after a blooper like that.

Dottie had so much sympathy for him on the way home, he'd been tempted to go ahead and explain what was wrong with his head. But at the last minute, he stopped. What would she think, him begging for sympathy?

He circled back to the iron display and ran his hand over a new model's smooth aluminum surface. Would Dottie like one of these for Christmas? No, she'd say he wasted good money, her old one worked just fine.

He opened the front door for some air. Truth be told, the weather had turned miserable. This morning, the thermometer between his inside window and the storm window registered fifteen degrees above. Out in the wind, it was probably zero or lower.

Icicles as long as yardsticks gaped from the rolled-back canvas awning above him. "Better knock some of them off—one could kill somebody if it landed on their head."

He grabbed a pitchfork, picked them off one by one, and shoveled them into the gutter. Old Manny Burrows ought to be along one of these days to scrape the streets and haul the extra snow and ice to the mound at the end of Main Street.

Al thought back to when he'd proposed to Nan. He'd been nervous then, too, but they'd corresponded through the war. Her letters gave him hope and something to come home for—he'd looked forward to seeing Del, too. He would never forget that magic moment when he raced up her folks' cement steps and she stood there waiting for him with Del in her arms.

He whirled them around like a toy doll, and didn't recall thinking she might refuse him. But Dottie seemed to do fine without him. He might as well face it—the heartthrob of young love had long since passed both of them by.

"I'm glad I didn't ask Dottie yet. But how can I possibly know the right time?"

Something thumped him on the back. He whirled around to see Ily's mother grab a shovel and set to work on the ice layered over the curb. His first impulse was to stop her, but he stood there for a minute to watch. Under her battered straw hat, Eva's face seemed serene—maybe having something to do helped calm her mind.

Keeping his hands occupied did the same thing for him when he was nervous—at least, it used to. Instead of stopping Eva, he patted her shoulder. "Thanks, Eva. You do a real fine job."

The battered straw hat lifted and fell in acknowledgment, but Eva attacked an ice wedge thicker than the shovel handle. Back inside, Del opened more newly delivered crates. Al took the mis-assembled box to the back room and tore it apart in disgust. A five-year old could've figured that out.

"Guess I'll go now." He grabbed his boots and coat.

Del hardly looked up. Outside, a chill wind peppered Al's face with dry snow. Maybe he was presumptuous, thinking Dottie would even consider a proposal from him. But if he didn't ask, he'd never know.

# Chapter Sixteen

For a day and night, Al pondered. He puttered about in his garage after supper, even though snow blew in under the door, nasty cold drafts nagged him, and the bleak single light bulb sent forth little encouragement. He did some cleaning, generating a stack of stuff for the junk man.

Proposing to Nan had been easy, but this was different. Waiting for the proper time was essential, and he'd been doubly glad for his self-control a few hours earlier, walking home with Dottie. She burst into all the latest news concerning Helene and Bonnie Mae—he loved it when she let go like that.

But what a conundrum—he couldn't make heads or tails of it. A fine girl like Bonnie Mae rejected by her own mother, and not knowing who she really was till now? He searched his memory, but couldn't recall Felicity at all. Must've been after Del graduated, when Charlie was still in elementary school.

Hearing details about Dottie's embarrassing slip gave him hope— she felt comfortable enough to share them with him. Her sharp intake of breath as she diverted to another topic drew him in.

"And that's not the half of it. You'll never believe what's happened with Helene. In Minneapolis last summer, she ran across an old beau."

"Helene?"

"Mmmhmm. They've been writing each other, and he drove down here to visit her in October. I never saw him, so she must not have brought him to the house. Sounds as if he's about to ask her to marry him, and if he does, she says she'll sell the boarding house to the highest bidder and leave town."

"Helene?" Al's mind stuck on her name. She seemed too old for a marriage proposal, too short, too full of herself, too…too fleshy in the chin. But then again, he was considering the same action on the other side of the ripe old age of fifty. His fingers flew to his own chin, which left something to be desired.

"I don't know what it would mean for Bonnie Mae. We never know what might happen, do we?" Dottie's dark eyes flooded with light, and Al attempted to take in her meaning.

"Guess not."

They had discussed the situation more during supper, and now, he scrounged around the garage to temper his restlessness, adding two more rusty tin cans to his pile. He reached to turn off the light, but a low shelf caught his eye, and he rustled his hand way back along its depths. Something cold and hard, but still pliable, lay next to the stone foundation. What could that be?

He tugged the awkward object out from the shadows, but dropped it on the earthen floor as soon as he realized what it was—a boot. But not just any boot. He'd sloshed through French muck in this one more than he cared to remember. A rash of goose bumps covered him. So he hadn't thrown them out—he thought sure he had.

He scraped around for the mate, but it must've gotten caught back there between the shelf and the wall. Al's jaws ached as he touched the crusty old leather, its toe so tipped up with wear and age that he doubted he could even get his foot inside. He sat back on his haunches, eyes closed, balancing the boot in his hands. His breath came hard, and he couldn't seem to think.

A whirr of noise and confusion unfolded inside his head and took his breath away. He bowed his forehead on the boot's brittle surface and fought for breath. Finally, he shook his head like a mad dog and shoved the boot back on the shelf. He'd deal with it next spring—find the other one and throw them both out.

On the sidewalk to the back porch, a sparkling winter night cleared his mind. He was alive, right here and right now, unlike so many in his unit who'd never come back. And a stone's throw away lived a woman he longed for. A plan took shape. What if he took Dottie out for supper on Saturday night? And what if he talked to Friedrich Messerschmidt about a ring tomorrow morning?

Fred would have to vow silence, but Al figured he could trust him after all that man went through during the past decade. The jeweler suffered a peculiar dishonor, hidden away here on the Midwest's backside. As a result, he'd changed his name to Fred.

How was he to know a German engineer would design a killer fighter plane bearing his family name? But Al overheard a comment one day in the store linking Friedrich to the plane.

"Can that be a mere coincidence? I think not! Maybe that technological German genius was Friedrich's cousin, don't you know?"

From '39 to the war's end, some folks literally crossed the street near Friedrich's jewelry and china store. Some of their sons or grandsons piloted Spitfires against those wicked Messerschmidts, or gunned them down. What a mockery, that name above the doorway right here in their hometown—they forgot they'd known this good man since he emigrated in '22.

Some people even took the long route to the grocery store, although Friedrich scraped off the name in '41, replacing it with *Fine China and Jewelry*. Somehow, he survived the war, and his jewelry business recovered, with engagements increasing right after the war.

"I'll go down there first thing in the morning." Having made the momentous choice, Al hurried into the house

He hadn't slept well for a few nights, but tonight he drifted off right away out of sheer exhaustion. Sometime before dawn, he heard fire crackling, and horrific screaming. He jerked out of bed in a cold sweat. What…where was he? Then he realized he'd dreamed of the Great War again.

Sweat poured off his head. Oh no—not again. He thought he'd

grown out of those nightmares—must've been that blasted boot that triggered this. He got up and paced, glancing over toward Dottie's a hundred times. He didn't want her to have to put up with what Nan had those first years of their marriage, although Nan never complained.

Back in bed, he willed himself to sleep another couple of hours. In the morning, his plan jelled as he gulped a cup of hot coffee. Despite his nerves, he would proceed. He would woo Dottie with dinner and a proposal. The calendar pinned above his kitchen counter mocked him. November twenty-ninth—no time to waste.

He wasn't in the habit of making spur-of-the-moment decisions, but had realized his purpose for over a month, actually longer than that. That night out at the fishing hole had done it for him. It was high time to voice his intentions, come what may. He couldn't go on like this.

He turned left on Main Street instead of heading toward the hardware. Fred's sign, shiny in the sun's early glow, drew him. He pressed his nose into the cold front window like a small boy. Prices didn't show out here in the glittery display, of course. He'd have to go in if he were serious.

"Am I serious?" He whispered the question out loud, creating an oval smudge on the spotless window. He rubbed it off with his coat sleeve. "Sorry, Friedrich."

Dottie's dark, warm eyes rose before him. A tight-drawn wire of hunger for her stretched through him. He remembered the feel of her feet in his hands. Yes, he was serious. It was now or never.

He opened the door and made the plunge. "Nice to see you, Friedrich. I need your help."

Friedrich's friendly smile proclaimed his delight to oblige.

The last sound Dottie ever thought she'd hear out of Bonnie Mae was a sob. But a gut-wrenching one filled the room like the aroma of a pie almost ready to take out of the oven. Dottie thought back to the thirties, when Millie lost her best friend to encephalitis. She sat with her for hours, holding her, rocking her. When dawn broke, Millie's tears finally wore out.

Nothing quite so dramatic with Cora, but she'd had her moments, too. The night before she left for California with her two girlfriends, to work in a munitions factory out there, Dottie soothed her tears, too. But those salty drops mixed with Cora's anticipation at joining in the war effort.

Dottie entertained more doubt and fear than Cora did, even though one of the girls' uncles wrote them to come out and vowed to watch over them. They would stay right in his house, working the shift opposite him, with his wife. But for Dottie, his reassurances fell flat.

Still, Cora convinced her, against her better judgment. "I'll be totally safe, Mom. I'm old enough to do my bit for victory. Don't worry, now."

Owen sided with their daughter. It was time to let her make her own decisions, he said. But for Dottie, it wasn't that easy—moving to California could mean Cora would never come back. It could mean she would never see that child again.

The war set things in motion that couldn't be held back. Dottie never did feel quite at peace with her baby going, but what could she do? People scattered in all directions. Even grown men and women set out for destinations they'd never have dreamed of apart from the war demand. A mother had to swallow her objections and get along as best she could with what was handed her.

But to hear this independent, hard-talking, wild-thinking redhead's violent sobs almost broke Dottie's heart. Bonnie Mae buried her face at the kitchen table, her shoulders racked with the effort of breathing.

After a good fifteen minutes, Dottie felt she needed to say something besides, "There, there." She licked her lips and sought words.

"You've been through hard things before, and you've survived. You'll survive this, too."

"No. I won't."

The week's occurrences rambled through Dottie's consciousness. Helene netted a marriage proposal. That boggled the mind, as Al's reaction confirmed. Her fiancé, a successful Minneapolis merchant, amassed holdings far and wide. Their honeymoon would take place on an ocean liner and in Europe. Helene already put her house—Bonnie Mae's birthplace and childhood home—up for sale and had a solid offer.

Dottie gritted her teeth. If Helene's suitor had as much money as she claimed, why not deed the house to Bonnie Mae? And why say no to the girl's innocent request to walk through it one last time? Sheer meanness, that's what it was. Helene had no room in her heart for anyone but herself.

Dottie told Bonnie Mae as much a few minutes earlier. "I pity the man she's marrying. Whatever they have in common, it can't be love. Helene isn't capable of that. You'll be better off without her around."

But right after dinner, Bonnie Mae got up her courage to confront Helene about the truth of her birth, sending the older woman into a fit. She actually struck the girl for daring to speak the truth—red marks still burned across Bonnie Mae's jaw when she came running to Dottie.

Dottie could barely contain her fury—worse, she couldn't understand Helene's anger. What had Bonnie Mae done wrong? She had half a notion to trot upstairs, where Helene prepared a guest room, and confront her head-on. Slapping someone in the face equaled saying they weren't worthy to breathe, and Bonnie Mae certainly didn't deserve that kind of treatment.

Because she'd experienced slaps like that from her own father, Dottie knew the girl's humiliation. Those times seldom came to mind anymore, but today they returned with a vengeance. She pulled Bonnie Mae to the table and let her cry, wishing Al would hurry and come over.

A few minutes later, he stuck his head in before the checker game, and Dottie sent him a silent, urgent plea. Thankfully, he comprehended and took a chair. He put his hand on the weeping girl's shoulder.

"Bonnie Mae, what could we do to help you?"

"Nobody can help me. My own people want nothing to do with me. I'm beyond help."

"What about Ned? What does he say?"

"He says it's none of his business, and not to worry. I'll inherit his house and his car, isn't that enough?" She mumbled all of this with her head buried in her arms. Dottie wished she'd look up, so Al could see those marks.

He worked his lips. All Dottie could think was that Ned's comment was true. Bonnie Mae would inherit as much as she had when Owen died—that ought to see her through. But Bonnie Mae could see only the minus side of the ledger right now.

If Al would say something, it might help. Instead, he fished in his pocket. "Here, use this handkerchief." Practical Al. But it did the trick—Bonnie Mae raised her head.

Al's gasp made Bonnie Mae's eyes widen. "What? That woman laid hands on you?"

Bonnie Mae ran her finger along her jaw. Al's fist tightened against his thigh. Then he slipped into a thoughtful state, his cheek muscles dancing the Virginia reel.

After Bonnie Mae blew her nose, Al still kept silent. Finally Dottie glanced at the clock and straightened her back against the chair rungs.

"Ned may have a point, don't you think?"

"What?" Bonnie Mae shrieked as if Dottie threatened her with a butcher knife.

"Well, inheriting a house and a car…that's not so bad. When my husband died, that's exactly what I inherited, and I thought I was lucky."

Bonnie Mae's lips turned down so low, they almost met her chin. "You think I'm out to get more than I deserve, don't you?"

"No, I don't. I wish Helene would see the error of her ways and give you what's rightfully yours—your grandmother's house. But think, Bonnie Mae. Can you imagine her doing that? No, she's too selfish and greedy. It's not your fault at all that she blames you for things you can't help, but Helene's set in her ways. She's not about to change. I can't see that butting your head against a stone wall will do any good, can you?"

Bonnie Mae calmed down some, and Al's eyes sparked. Dottie willed him to help her out, but when he didn't, she continued. The words spewed forth like a flushing fire hydrant.

"Why distress yourself so? It's only money, and money, as you can see from Helene's pitiful life—isn't all that matters. It can't make your days rich and full. Only love can."

Bonnie sank back in her chair. Al's eyes shone—with what? Dottie wasn't sure, but right now, getting Bonnie Mae back into shape was all that mattered. Tom had invited her to his place for the first time tonight, and she couldn't go like this.

"You have so much going for you. You're bright and attractive and a hard worker. Those are all things to be valued, as much or more than an inheritance. You might look at them *as* your inheritance, Bonnie Mae."

She took a deep breath—she wasn't used to pontificating. Al's jaw went slack, and he seemed to have no intent of rescuing her..

"Helene's shortsightedness makes a statement about her, not about you. Use what you have already—isn't that what Teddy Roosevelt once said? *Do what you can with what you have, where you are.* Inheriting your Grandma's house wouldn't add a thing to the wonderful girl you are."

Al shifted his weight and straightened in his chair. But he seemed overcome by some strange silence.

"You've attracted a wonderful man's attention. Tom already owns his house and has a steady job, even some savings, I'd wager, after all these years at the coal company. You'll have a good life together, if you put your mind to it. When you inherit Ned's house, you can rent it out or use the proceeds to put the children through college—give them what Helene could have given you if she'd had any sense at all."

Al blinked as though coming to life. Dottie could not abide any more. What was wrong with him? He always came up with something. She faced him. "What do you say, Al?"

Bonnie Mae turned toward him too. He rubbed his forehead as if waking from sleep. "I say I've never heard a better suggestion. Go for what's coming your way with Tom. Enjoy your life. So many folks miss happiness by their own choice."

He rested his gaze on Dottie for a moment. "Dottie's right. Walk away from Helene and the past. That's what her life can teach you—she clings to yesterday, and it makes her miserable. But you can choose to be happy from here on out."

Bonnie Mae gnawed her fingernail. A clank sounded from the back yard and she jumped six inches high. "That's Tom. He's delivering across the street today."

Bonnie Mae leaned toward Dottie. "I—you're right, of course. It's just the unfairness that gets me. You do see that, don't you?"

"I do. But expecting Helene, or life in general, to be fair gets you nowhere. You can spend your whole life fighting for fairness. But if you look at what's right before your eyes, it's a wealth untold."

"Tom's over there right now."

"Yes, and probably hoping you'll come out." She pulled Bonnie Mae from her chair. Bonnie Mae buttoned her coat as Al reappeared, looking a little pale. Maybe he was catching a cold.

The redhead turned back to give Dottie a strong embrace before she left the house. "Thank you, Dottie. You're a wonderful woman, you know?"

Dottie shrugged. "Just a woman, honey. But I have learned a few things along the way."

Al's eyes flared too brightly—something mysterious stirred in their depths. One part of Dottie wanted to know what went on in his mind while another didn't.

# Chapter Seventeen

"I wish you well, Helene." Dottie followed Helene to the front door, grasping three handwritten pages of instructions about what needed to be done before she returned from her latest Minneapolis trip.

"I was about to leave town, but came back to make sure you keep a close eye on that girl." Helene's voice grated on *that girl*, and a chilly breeze riffled the papers in Dottie's hand. "Mind you, don't go soft on her. She'll take advantage of you. I'm the one still paying her—so I hold you responsible."

Dottie reacted without thinking. "But you're not paying her, remember? It's your mother's money, from Bonnie Mae's inheritance."

Helene's nose bunched up. "So, you've learned some sass from her? I thought better of you, Dorothy."

In that moment, Dottie saw a slight physical resemblance between Bonnie Mae and Helene. The slant of their jawlines matched, but the likeness stopped there.

"Besides, it's none of your business." The older woman swished out onto the wide front porch, seams crisp black against her pudgy calves. She clicked to the steps and started down, her burgundy felt hat brim swaying in the wind.

A bevy of emotions fought inside Dottie, but what she wanted to yell, she whispered. "I thought better of you, too. And I've made it my business, because I *care* about your niece. On top of that, I don't like being called Dorothy."

She closed the door and picked up a feather duster. She couldn't

153

recall when she felt so let down by someone. Helene would never know how much her behavior disappointed people. But the good side was, she'd be gone for several days.

Rose and purple diamonds from the leaded window spread their cheery hues over the room's northeast corner. "A thing of beauty is a joy forever." Dottie didn't know where that quote originated, but it brought her an odd comfort.

There might be nothing lovely about Helene's character, but here in her boarding house, beauty still existed. "And I'm going to take a minute to enjoy it."

On the brushed velvet settee, the reflected color moved over Dottie's faded green housedress and calico apron. She held out her legs to study its effect on her plain white stockings, and decided she liked that better. Her worn right heel frowned up at her—she really ought to buy a new pair of shoes as much as she was on her feet.

She took her time dusting, picking up objects here and there to notice their shapes. A pottery teapot, a ceramic vase, a platter that reminded her of her grandmother—carnival glass, she thought it was called. Grandma Pitman had a couple of odd pieces on her cupboard shelf. Dottie set the table with care, using the linen napkins, though no special guests would be here.

"Special, my foot," she sputtered to the dining room's placid furnishings. The Creamery buyers had found a house, and yesterday, Al explained which one—Helene's. She'd even let them take over the upstairs as she packed away her things for her move to Minneapolis.

George and the other boarders deserved linen napkins just as much as those wealthy people. Her boss didn't see it that way, but Dottie didn't care.

She went into the kitchen to light the oven for the pies. She'd waited, to be certain they would still be warm to serve after dinner. Al promised he'd come over to eat before their afternoon game, too, so she decided to sit right up to the table with the men. And she set a place for Bonnie Mae. Why not? That girl worked so hard—why should she only eat in here on Thanksgiving?

After Dottie opened the oven door and lit a match, she smelled something amiss. She blew out the match, but it was too late. The oven's dark interior filled with flames, and a violent whoosh rattled her ears like one of those bottle rockets Bill and Owen used to send up on the Fourth of July.

A distinct tang ringed her tongue as she flew backwards against the table leg. A sharp pain knifed through her ribs. That was the last thing she remembered.

"Al, stop it. You're pawing the floor like a nervous horse." Old Doc Schulz waved his fingers behind his back. "Go on, now—give me some room. I'm doin' the best I can."

Al sucked in his breath. A nervous horse? Old Doc picked his comparison well—a nervous horse shied without due cause. Of all the days for the doctor to be out of town—Dottie deserved better care than an elderly man could give her. Al dropped his head into his hands. In the process, he forgot about the hacksaw he still carried from the hardware, and it clattered to the floor.

Doc's white mustache shook at the ends, along with his pointed finger. "Get that thing out of here. You're not helping at all."

"It'll be all right." Bonnie Mae's voice, as soft as Al had ever heard it, trembled. She'd proven herself a hero today, racing from the basement when she heard the boom and summoning Doc.

Now, her fingers pressed into Al's elbow, guiding him into the dining room. "Sit down. I'll bring you a cup of coffee." She went into the kitchen, and Al fiddled with the table setting.

The pre-dinner scenario went through his brain. Bonnie Mae alerted George, who carried Dottie to the sofa, while she called Doc. Then she sent George down to the hardware store. When he burst through the door, Al looked up from his project behind the counter.

"Can't wait for afternoon to beat me at checkers?" Al's attempt at joking faded as the other man's blanched face neared. "What's wrong?"

"It's Dot. She was lighting that old oven, and—"The two of them tore down the street, but Old Doc, in his dark red '36 coupe, beat them. Panting for breath, in chatter completely unlike him, George filled Al in on all the details as they mounted the front steps.

Now, Al fingered the pale rose fringe of the tablecloth. At the sight of Dottie lying on the parlor couch, his heart lurched out of control. He squeezed the dense fabric into a ball. He didn't care, any more, if the whole world knew the truth.

He shunted into the corner, where he could still view Dottie's hand dangling on the floor. He'd never felt so useless.

"Probably suffered some shock from the blast. But she'll come to. I'm sure of it."

He trusted Old Doc—they'd navigated all the ins and outs of Nan's illness together. His son gave her the choice, "When it comes to the way you're suffering, Mrs. Jensen, my father knows far better than I how to help."

Nan chose Old Doc. As faithful as a man could get, he sat with her every single day during those final two weeks—as often as their pastor. But this was different. Al's breath gurgled in his throat. He thought he might be sick.

"Oh God, let Dot be all right. Please, won't you?" He let go the cloth, leaving wrinkles Helene would really appreciate. Palms hard against his hipbones, he paced around the dining room table six times. On the window ledge, a few sad-looking brown sparrows gathered in the cold.

Bonnie Mae handed him some coffee. Her calmness seemed out of place—out of proportion to what had happened. "Now, Al, drink some. I'm sure…"

Some rustling came from the other room, and Al tiptoed to the living room archway. A few seconds later, Dottie's foot twitched and Doc held up one finger.

"How many fingers do you see, Dottie?"

Al barely heard her wobbly response, but it was enough. Bonnie Mae's face lighted with a smile. She lifted two fingers in his direction—V for victory. He let out a long breath. Dottie would be all right.

In the kitchen, George worked with the oven. He'd slung the back door wide to release the gassy odor, and the room was freezing.

"She was all set to bake them pies." George's huge hand gestured toward two beautiful creations on the table. "Musta been somethin' with the pilot light. Contraption peers to be worn out—Helene oughta buy a new one."

"Right. But she could care less about this old house, and she probably won't be that concerned when she hears what happened." Fire raced through Al's abdomen. His acid response shocked him.

George got the oven going, put the pies in, and looked Al full in the face. "You look a little sick. Gonna make it?"

Al let out a long sigh. Oily black soot covered the wall next to the stove. The whole room could have blown up, and Dot might have been killed. He fell against the coats lined on their hooks. Perspiration ran down his temples.

George put his hand on his shoulder. "Sure you're all right?"

He nodded. "Thanks for coming down to tell me, George. I need to walk around a while. If Dottie gets up, tell her I'll be back."

"Sure thing."

Bunches of scarlet berries on a bush near the property's edge drew his attention. How did the birds know to save them until winter? Everything took on new life—the hydrant, its short black pump handle ready for action, the grungy underside of a heavy iron gas tank at the corner of the lot.

He attempted to bring order to his thoughts. The freezing air should have set him to rights, yet something under his breastbone hurt. He looked down at his plaid flannel everyday work shirt, as if the blue and gray pattern would tell him what he needed to know.

He glanced back at the house and walked around the block, chiding himself for not wearing his coat. But he didn't want to go back to the store for it, either. Nothing seemed simple anymore.

A few feet away, inside that monstrous house, Dottie might have died a little while ago.

He imagined she would go right back into that dangerous kitchen and set to work. She'd serve them all dinner and wash the dishes afterwards, as if nothing happened. Maybe Bonnie and Doc would force her to rest a bit, but he doubted she would abide that for long.

The more he thought, the more solid his conclusion became. Dottie needed someone to take care of her, someone who knew her well and valued her far beyond her ability to cook wonderful dinners. On his third trip around the block, clarity finally came. The ring, ordered from Chicago, would be in on Friday's train, Friedrich said.

Al's shoulders shook like bulrushes in a strong wind. He hurried toward the store for his coat as fast as his long legs would move. When he ascended the front stairs of the boarding house again, the aroma of Dottie's triple berry pie drew him in.

<h1 style="text-align:center">Chapter Eighteen</h1>

Late Tuesday afternoon, bad news wended its way to the board-ing house kitchen through George. He often stopped in to offer a hand when Helene was out of town.

"You know that Eva who runs the streets? She got hit out on the Heston road, by a freight truck headed toward Waterloo. The driver felt mighty bad—he thought it was almost like she ran into the cab on purpose."

South of Heston and northeast of Waterloo, a family-run dinner and dance place had sprung up. Al overheard someone talking about it at the hardware—a little expensive, they said, but a nice atmosphere and great steak dinners for a dollar and fifty cents, drink and dessert included.

Dottie would never go for anything fancy, or approve of him spending too much money. On the other hand, he wanted her to feel special when he asked for her hand. Even thinking of that yielded a cold sweat on his forehead—what if he did this all wrong and drove her away?

He broached the dinner invitation with great care, walking her home late Wednesday afternoon. She hadn't even taken the whole afternoon off yesterday, and her step told him she was dragging. He didn't say much until he saw their houses down the block. Then, he tried to keep his voice casual.

"Say, you wouldn't want to run down a ways beyond Heston late

Friday afternoon, would you? Del has a few things for me to pick up at an implement place, and I thought…"

"Farther than Heston?"

"Not too much…maybe ten more miles."

She looked him full in the face, and the sun hit her hair just right to create a glow around her waves. Al felt that little muscle in his cheek working, but tamped down his impatience. Finally, Dottie agreed.

"If you need to do any shopping, we could look around a little too—that is, if you want to."

"Shopping?" She frowned. A look he didn't recognize crossed her face. Aw, that was the wrong thing to say—Dottie wasn't one to spend valuable time on such a frivolous activity.

"We don't have to—I thought I'd mention it just in case, with Christmas coming and all."

"I'll need to send a Christmas box out to Cora. She called again last night—breaks my heart to think of her so worn out, with three months left to go. But maybe I could find something for the little ones, and for the new baby."

"Yes, and something for Cora too—would she need a nice robe? I heard Edie say Black's Department Store has a sale on those, and we can ship everything for you from the hardware."

"Oh, would you, Al? Wrapping gifts and getting them sent off— just the thought of all that wears me out."

He thanked his lucky stars for Cora being in California, for Dottie being willing to go along, for her thinking of something she needed, and for the sky above them staying in place. He guarded his tongue meticulously until Friday afternoon when he picked her up outside the boarding house. Helene had taken off again, and Dottie had dinner all ready. Bonnie Mae and George agreed to handle the cleanup.

Sunlight sparkled on frosted corn stalks, like skinny legs bent at the knee all along the road. Dottie exhibited an exceptionally happy mood, and Al reveled in her comments as he steered the pick-up down Highway 218.

"No more gravel roads for us. Glad the highway department extended this route in '34. Owen had to use the old road to fetch the mail from Waterloo when the mail truck couldn't make the trip during spring thaws. I was so glad when they paved it."

"Me, too."

Snow-covered fields glittered, but Al kept his attention on the wheel. As usual, Dottie didn't seem to mind the quiet. But around the curve west of Charles City, she spoke again.

"Wonder what makes the sumac and flame bushes stay red when the other leaves all fall off the branches?"

"I've wondered that, too. And look over there—those pin-oaks still have their leaves."

"They shed in spring, that much I know. Owen's dad had one on the farm. Awfully slow growing, but they're built to last."

"How's it going with Helene these days? Has she made any move to replace that stove?"

"No."

"What did she say when she heard about the explosion?'

"Not much. I've finally realized how differently she thinks. You know, Al, I thought she'd be nicer to Bonnie Mae, with the good fortune that's come into her life."

"Did you?"

"Owen always called me an optimist. I don't know about that, but I do like to believe the best about people."

"But Helene hasn't changed?"

"Not at all. Even with Bonnie Mae so upset, Helene threatened to fire her again. When the boarding house sells, what will happen to that girl?"

"George mentioned something about that during our card game today. He's taken a real liking to Bonnie Mae, and Tom, too."

"Not to Henrietta?"

Al slapped his knee and hee-hawed. The truck veered off the concrete for a second, and his blood pulsed in his ear. "She's left off coming this past week. Hasn't brought anything over to my house, either. Maybe she's given up. I don't know what happened between her and George. He's as tight-lipped as a rosebud about it."

"A rosebud?"

"Yeah. Before it blooms, you know. You couldn't coax a blossom out of it for love nor money."

They were quiet again until he turned into a driveway leading to the implement building. "Want to come in? I'll just be a minute."

"No, I'm fine."

Al supervised the men loading the boxes into the bed. When he went back in for the receipt, he spied some small yellow and green toy tractors above the counter.

"How much are those?"

"A dollar apiece."

A dollar—quite a lot for a little boy he didn't even know, but if all went as he hoped, Jeffy might one day become his grandson. An itch started at the base of his neck. He pulled out his wallet.

"I'll take one."

"All right. Made by Fred Ertl over by Dubuque. Pretty detailed, ain't they?"

Who would ever think to make miniature tractors? He tucked the toy into his coat pocket with a sense of accomplishment. Dottie would be so pleased…he hoped.

Twenty minutes later, he steered through Waterloo streets until he saw the Black's Department Store sign. "Want to try Blacks?"

Dottie didn't answer. He found a parking space and turned the motor off. Tension rode the air of the cab. "Dottie? You ready to shop?"

She gripped the door handle. "I don't know, Al. I appreciate that you drove all the way into the city, but I'm not much for big, crowded places."

"Would you rather just shop for Cora back in town at the Wearwithall?"

She turned her face toward the window.

He reached for her hand. "Hey, that's all right. I didn't realize…" He thought how Nan loved trips to the big city, how she lit up inside Black's massive department store, with grand piano music filling the air and so much to choose from in each aisle. But now that he thought about it, he'd never heard Dottie mention shopping.

"Of course you wouldn't. I don't know why, but I'd rather do almost anything than go inside one of those big stores. So many folks milling about, so much…"

"Well, then, we'll just turn right around and find that restaurant. Oh, I forgot—I found a small gift for Jeffy at the implement." He pulled the tractor out of his pocket and plunked it in Dottie's hand. He didn't know what to make of the arch of her brows and her wide eyes, so he waited, hoping he hadn't done something she'd think foolhardy.

But she gave him a bright smile. "Why, Al. He'll surely like this a lot. His daddy came from a farm, and he's told Jeffy all about tractors. How much—?"

"Don't mention it, Dot. I'd be happy if you'd put it in with whatever else you find for him." She smoothed her fingertips over the tiny turning wheels, and he heaved an inward sigh of relief. Maybe things would still be all right.

The road curved north some distance out of town, and they soon came upon the restaurant. He felt Dottie stiffen against the seat as he turned into the gravel drive.

"An eating place way out here in the country? Seems odd, doesn't it?"

"Oh, I don't know—people do things differently these days. Someone at the store told Del they have great food. Worth a try, don't you think?"

A male waiter led them to their seats, something new for Al, and he imagined for Dottie, too. The young man brought water with ice, and fresh cloth napkins.

"Ice in the water, in December?'

For some reason, Dottie sure noticed every little thing tonight. The waiter returned with menus, and she read each word.

"What does *au gratin* mean?"

"I think it has to do with cheese. Potatoes with cheese."

"Mmm. Sounds nice for a change. Did you see tonight's special? Liver and onions. I haven't had that for a long time. Sounds good, and it's only fifty cents."

"Now, Dottie, order whatever you like. That man in the store told me the steak is real good."

She surveyed the menu again, but he could tell from the way her eyes narrowed that she wouldn't go for the most expensive meal listed. When the waiter came, she ordered the liver, so he did, too.

"You were telling me how George and the others were upset with Helene?"

"Yes. Especially after they saw what she did about that oven."

"I didn't realize…What did she do?"

"Nothing! That's the point. The men agreed that Helene doesn't deserve you."

"The truth is, I've had thoughts of quitting, Al."

Her admission smacked him right in the gut. He searched her face, but she revealed no emotion. "You have? Because of the stove?"

"Because of everything. Bonnie Mae—the way Helene's gotten worse, and now the place is going to be sold—and of course, my aching feet. But I…"

Her unfinished statement hung between them. Al wasn't sure he wanted to ask her any more. A spring of hope spurted within him. She was already thinking of giving up her job. That might bode well for his plans.

Chapter Nineteen

"A one-and-a-two-and-a—" The band struck up a tune in the next room.

"A real band? Wow, this is quite the establishment you've discovered. Cora and Dennis would like it—they used to go dancing all the time."

The waiter brought two steaming plates of meat swimming in onions, mashed potatoes, gravy, and two side dishes: corn and a Jello salad. Dottie touched the parsley sprig on the rim of her plate.

"What a nice meal, Al. Thank you. I'm really sorry you drove all the way into downtown Waterloo. On the way, I kept thinking maybe I could overcome whatever it is that bothers me, but I didn't manage very well."

"It's nothing, Dot. I don't have a big hankering to go shopping either. It was worth the drive, though, to see that enormous Christmas tree in the park, don't you think? Did you ever see so many lights?"

She shook her head and settled her napkin in her lap. He prayed over the food and opened his eyes to see her gaze fixed on him. "I appreciate you doing that."

His heart swelled. Her eyes seemed so intense tonight, almost black. He ate a few bites and opened the familiar boarding house topic.

"George and Bert are thinking about going together to buy the boarding house. Can you believe that? They might be able to get it all worked out. George even offered to do some of the kitchen work—make breakfasts and such.

"Bert would put in extra each month so it'd be fair—guess he has quite a sum saved up. And George mentioned they should raise your wages, and Bonnie Mae's."

"Oh, my. New bosses—Bonnie Mae will flip over that."

"They even discussed co-filing a will down at Larson's. Since neither of them has family, the boarding house would go to Bonnie Mae at the time of the last man's death."

Dottie beamed, but a few seconds later, her frown took over. She balanced her fork between her fingers. "They think Helene would agree to all this?"

Al rubbed his jaw line. "She told Chuck Larson she doesn't care what happens to the house. As long as she gets her money, she's happy. Well, not *happy*…you know what I mean—and she won't know about the will till both men pass."

"So George and Bert dreamed all this up, went down to the law firm and talked with Mr. Larson?" Her quizzical look sent a quiver through him. He could see her attempting to picture George and Bert in Chuck Larson's office. It wasn't working.

He filled his mouth with potatoes and gravy. Why did he start the conversation flowing in this direction, anyway?

"You had something to do with it, didn't you? You spoke with the lawyer." It was not a question, so he avoided it. But by the way Dottie's lips pursed, he knew she was onto him.

Over their plates, she touched his hand. "You started putting all this together that day Bonnie Mae cried so hard in the kitchen. You began thinking it through then, didn't you?"

Her touch ignited all sorts of sensations. As for her statements, she was right on the money. She knew him too well, knew the way his mind worked, just like Nan.

"You're such a good man. You'll make sure everything turns out A-OK for everyone."

"And you're teaching Bonnie Mae your cooking tricks. That must be quite the challenge." To his relief, Dottie accepted the change in topic.

"Hasn't she changed from when she started to work? She's a fast learner, and motivated—doubly so with Tom at her door nearly every night. But don't change the subject on me, Al Jensen."

He tackled the meat spread on his plate. Somehow, he'd have to launch his proposal, but he didn't know how. He'd eaten about half of his food when Dottie gave him the perfect opening. At first, he couldn't believe his ears. Maybe the background music had distorted his hearing. He thought she said, "I do think I'll quit working, maybe next week."

He managed to swallow a mouthful of liver and onions. But then his tongue stuck to the roof of his mouth. He drank a few sips of coffee. His taste buds, once so enraptured with this meal, went dull. He put down his fork.

"Dottie." Her name rasped from deep in his throat. He tried again, his heart pounding at the scrunch in her brow.

"What is it? Are you all right?"

He clutched his chest. He'd decided about two o'clock today, when he was getting nervous about tonight, to ask for a sign from heaven, like Dottie did about speaking to Henrietta. Earlier in the meal, the first time she talked about quitting, something jabbed him inside, but he'd passed up that opportunity. Now the heavens rained down another. She was going to quit her job next week—this had to be his sign.

"Al, don't do this to me. Are you having a heart attack? Does it matter that much to you if I stop working? You could still go over to the boarding house for your games, you know."

He burst out laughing—the tension was too much. "No, no. I'm glad you're quitting. But I have something to ask you. I hate to spoil our meal, but…"

"Well then. Go ahead." Her voice resembled Porky's pond on a cool summer evening, smooth and unflappable. She set her fork down. He would have given half his life savings to know what she was thinking.

He cleared his throat, but almost choked again. Good grief. He was a grown man—why couldn't this be easier?

"Ahem. You remember, you told me you'd really like to go see Cora—stay a while out there to help her out?"

"Yes."

"And you mentioned they have an extra room above their garage, in case you'd bring along a friend?"

Her chin moved up the slightest bit, but those burnished eyes stayed steady. Her dark wave, shimmering with silver highlights, fell onto her forehead. He wanted to push it back for her, wanted to smooth his fingers over her cheek. His heart almost erupted at how pretty she looked.

"I've always wanted to travel west. Never got the chance. So I thought if you'd have me, this could be my opportunity. We could, as they say, kill two birds with one stone." Her frown deepened, but he stumbled on. "You wouldn't have to travel alone, and we'd get to see a whale of a lot of country on the way."

She picked up her fork and took a bite of potatoes…and another. Al thought he might choke. "Dottie? What do you think of the idea?"

"When would we leave?"

"Sometime before Christmas. That'd be up to you. I can go any time, but figured you'd want to get there before the twenty-fifth."

"On the train?"

He stared at her, mute. His brain gave out on him.

"On the train?"

"Yes."

Her eyebrows lifted above brown-black pools that held him in a vice. "And how would we…?" He discerned her meaning by the angle of her head.

"Oh. That. Well, we could do it one of two ways."

She poised her fork over the solid square of Jello on her plate.

"We could get separate sleeping compartments."

She might have been frozen to her side of the booth. She didn't even blink.

A boulder clogged Al's windpipe. Other diners' voices suddenly seemed too loud to bear.

"The other possibility…" He closed his eyes, reached into his breast pocket, and pulled out a small blue velvet box.

"The other possibility is if you would…ah…consent to be my wife."

Before the words departed his mouth, he kicked himself to Chicago and back. That wasn't how he meant to say it. This wasn't the proper time, but he hadn't considered how the boarding house conversation might lead to this point.

Something pulled at the edges of Dottie's lips. He couldn't tell if it was a smile or a frown. His heart stopped, and the box, still in his trembling fingers, shook. If only she would put him out of his misery.

She stared at the box for an impossible amount of time. Finally, her reply came, low and quiet. "You mean, you would do this for the convenience of the trip?"

"Oh no! For heaven's sakes, Dot! No, no. I would do it because—" He peered to each side of their booth and leaned forward. She leaned closer, too. He tried to modulate his voice between a whisper and a quiet, normal tone. "I would do it because I love you and want to marry you. I've known it for a long time, but…" She still didn't blink. Now, he lost all control. Words gushed from his mouth.

"I didn't know how to ask you—couldn't figure out the right time. And now, I've…I ordered the ring a week ago, but…" He held the box out and slowly, agonizingly slowly, she tucked her chin and put down her fork. Then, she took the box in her fingers like a fishing worm, looking from it to him.

"You've thought this through?"

"Of course. I mean…yes. A thousand times, at least, like I do everything." He held up sweaty palms. "You know me. Al the analyst." His chuckle sounded limp. Her expression told him nothing, nothing at all. The gusher broke again, and he started spewing details.

"Today I prayed for a sign, like you did. And the other day, I almost destroyed a store display. Del asked what was wrong with me. I've been so preoccupied…"

"Preoccupied?" The tilt of her head made him dizzy.

"I can't think of anything but you. I'm like a love-sick eighteen-year-old, Dot."

Her lips parted ever so slightly. Something he couldn't read crossed her face. It was all he could do to hold his seat. Had he told her he loved her? Had he included everything he should have?

A wall of trepidation fell on him. He ought to have gotten down on his knees, but that would embarrass her to death, here in this public spot. In the long minute that passed as Dottie held the box without opening the lid, he knew the irrevocable truth. He would die if her answer was no.

The cup of tea she'd made as soon as she walked into the kitchen did exactly what Dottie hoped it would. She settled deeper into her armchair and decided against turning on the radio. She'd forgotten the program schedule during the past few months, even though she used to listen regularly.

The prattle took the edge off the eerie quietness that haunted this house at night since Owen passed. But lately she'd been so busy, and so dog tired by the time she got home, she didn't have the energy to listen.

Tonight though, her mind refused to wander familiar channels. Instead, it exploded with sparring emotions. Or was that her heart? Anyway, the tea—scalding, yet soothing—kept her in a level place.

She fumbled with the afghan she'd made years ago. She ought to throw that thing out, but it still did its job, tattered or not. The crocheting showed gaping holes in places but had seen her through so much. She'd literally worn it for days after Bill died. She draped its smooth wool over one shoulder, her other hand wrapped around her cup.

"Oh, Lord. What am I supposed to do now? I feel so…"

She stared at the living room's tan walls. She and Owen purchased this house for $829 from Sears and Roebuck as soon as they saved up that much money after he came home from the war. The postmaster offered him the mail delivery job right away, so it didn't take long.

The entire house arrived by mail order. Somewhere in those boxes in the attic, she still had the bill of sale, along with all their other records dating back thirty years.

After the war, they'd both lived with their parents for six months. She cleaned houses and ironed for people, saving every penny. The look on Owen's face when she pulled $372 from an envelope to add to their stash would stay with her forever.

He wore the same expression when she stood beside him to break ground for the house with the shovel she still used for garden work. Those were the days—nothing seemed too difficult to tackle. Together, they would conquer whatever crossed their path.

Here, they built their family, and she'd planned on living in this house till they moved her to the cemetery. But now, in just one evening, change reared its head. But was it the ugly head she always expected?

She tried to expand her mind to take in all the possibilities. Cora had opened the door with her urging to come to California, but the trip seemed impossible. Yet now, because of Al, maybe she could manage. Who would have thought their old neighbor would become such a good friend? But this was about far more than friendship. He'd proposed marriage.

His statements ran through her consciousness like a radio broadcast. They could go to California together. He would stay in the room above the garage. Or, they could get married and travel as man and wife on the train—*on the train*. Those three words rumbled inside her head like the chugga-chugga-choo-choo book Bill had so loved her to read as a toddler.

Everything melded into confusion. Get married, travel on the train, see Cora and those grandbabies. Most of it she wanted—except the train part. But taken together, the whole proposition stunned her.

Al turned awfully quiet on the way home, and so did she. Every time she thought of something to say, her next thought was how he might take it the wrong way. Besides, she'd have to shout over the engine noise. When he walked her to the back door, his eyes flared like lonely road markers in the evening shadows.

"Thank you for the lovely dinner…" Her profession of gratitude wilted in the frigid air.

"Good night then, Dottie." He slunk away, a shadow of himself. Her heart went out to him, his long face so woebegone. She wanted to call him back and hug him, but then she might say something she'd wish she hadn't. This was no time to make rash promises.

She reminded herself he'd had lots of time to think this through. She'd had inklings, but there in the restaurant, the full scope of an enormous transformation sprang up before her. She could marry Al Jensen and go off to California.

Henrietta Perry would cackle about her impulsive behavior. After church she'd gather her minions and discuss Al and Dottie forward and backward, inside and out. Dottie drew the afghan closer as December's wind shook the eave spouts. She'd forgotten to turn up the thermostat, but now that she was settled, had no desire to move.

From Henrietta's whiny tones, now even more familiar as she turned her charms on George in the boarding house dining room, Dottie's focus returned to Al's face. She'd touched his jawline when he parked behind his house.

"Al, you are so dear to me." He shrank back. The movement told her he knew she couldn't be pushed, and acknowledged he had no claim on her.

But truth be told, she'd wanted him to take her in his arms and tell her she didn't have to make this decision, that he'd make it for her. Yet something kept her from saying that out loud, and his downcast, wounded expression only made things worse.

Her sigh split the cold room's air. She cranked her sore neck right and left against her heavy flannel nightgown collar, willing the stiffness to leave of its own volition. That drew her attention to the pain in her shoulders. If Al were here…

"But Al isn't here," she whispered. That reminded her of him alone in his house. And she sat alone in hers, thirty feet away. He must have become terribly lonely to enter Messerschmidt's jewelry store and buy a diamond ring.

She needed no diamond, that was sure, but Al loved her. That part she remembered, though the rest of the evening blurred.

She closed her eyes—he actually bought her a ring. Where was that little box, anyway? Had she put it in her coat pocket?

Like a vast, slow-moving wave, terror swept her. Al had been so befuddled, and the tension so uncomfortable, they'd both played with their food until he suggested they get on home. He'd acted the perfect gentleman, of course, but his voice wavered from an unearthly place, and his hands felt like ice when he helped her with her coat.

Dottie struggled out from under the afghan. She'd better go check that coat pocket. But when she plunged her hand into the nubby lining, she found nothing. A suffocating sensation struck her throat.

"What have I done? That ring must have cost him a small fortune, and I've—" She combed through every terse blade of conversation on the ride home. What had she done with her fingers all that time?

Gripped the door handle, that's what—she had not been holding the box.

She knew what she had to do. It was past nine, and she was in her nightclothes, but she would never go to sleep with this on her conscience.

# Chapter Twenty

W hat if she'd left that darn ring on the restaurant table? What if the waiter made off with it? Male waiters—she'd never heard of such a thing. If Al lost all that money, she could never live with herself.

She buttoned her coat, tied on her shoes, turned on the porch light, and cranked the doorknob. It got cantankerous when the temperatures dropped in the night. Finally, the door gave way, and Dottie made her way down the back steps. Was this how Eva had felt, easing out of Ily and Don's house at all times of the night?

The cold hit Dottie's legs with a difference she couldn't specify—something about the amount of moisture—probably that next storm coming through from North Dakota. Her faded pink and white nightgown billowed under her coat, leaving room for icy air to attack behind her knees.

Halfway toward Al's truck, she stopped. A star-spangled sky drew her eyes upward. From up there, this world must look miniature. She'd witnessed that in some of the photos airplane pilots took during the war. *LIFE* magazine displayed one she'd seen at the boarding house one day. Helene kept a stack of old issues in the wooden magazine holder. In those pictures from high in the sky, earthly objects appeared like ants in a colony.

Unique warmth coursed through her, although arctic wind seeped through her coat, right into her bones. She'd better hurry up. She gathered her senses and set her course again, straight to Al's truck. She mustn't jump to the worst conclusion. She'd visited the end of the world a time or two, and this wasn't it.

The doors did not open quietly—the whole neighborhood would hear. An old calico cat on the prowl rounded the front tire, and Dottie clapped her hands together. "Shoo. Shoo now."

Over at Mrs. Grundy's, all lay dark and quiet. Al still had a light on, no surprise there. Dottie wagered that about now, he was thinking he'd done everything all wrong tonight. For the guy who came up with such perfect solutions to other folks' dilemmas, he displayed such a fragile side.

If only she could have given him a clearer answer, but she just couldn't. Not right there in that restaurant, anyway, and not in the confined space of the scruffy truck cab on the drive home.

Hoping for the soft touch of velvet, she wallowed around on the seat with her bare hand. But only cold, crevassed leather met her fingertips. Then she remembered the hole in the floor. What if, in the worst of scenarios, she'd let go of the box, and it had fallen through? Her face scorched at the possibility. At the same time, her limbs pulsed in the icy air. Visions of retracing their route—that long, long trip—flashed through her imagination.

She bent down to explore the floor grit, waving her palms in circles. No velvet. The wind shot up her nightgown onto her thighs. Leaning on the door, she forced it open wider, resulting in an even louder squawk. Might as well butcher chickens out here, with all the noise she was making.

Only one thing left to do—climb in and search the driver's side. She *had* to find that ring and contorted her body every which way to reach the most remote spots. But even as her heart raced with the effort, a dull truth throbbed through her. The ring wasn't here. It wasn't in her coat pockets, either, although she checked again.

Al's light still shone, a beacon in the darkness. She carefully shut the door, stared at his back porch, and trudged around the hood toward the other side of the truck. Another loud noise split the silent night when she shut the door after a second fruitless search.

Just as she raised her torso in defeat, Al's porch light illuminated. His head poked from the door, sticking out of his pajama top like a giraffe's. He peered toward his truck, focused, and found her. She wanted to shrivel into an insignificant bump in the frozen driveway.

"Who's out there? Dottie? That you? What in the world are you doing?"

The backs of her eyes flamed, even as cold air nipped at the fronts. How could she tell him? Her mind flashed to the cemetery—to the day of Bill's funeral, then the day of Owen's. She bit the insides of her cheeks. She'd done harder things. She had no choice.

His boots crunched step by step toward her. She glanced up at the stars. Despite the despair that wedged in her chest, this wasn't the end of the world—no, not at all. A lot of money might be lost, but put in perspective, things could be so much worse. Somehow, she would pay Al back every penny.

His tortured eyes didn't help her much. It was obvious he wouldn't sleep a wink this night. "Dottie? What's up?"

She put on a stoic face, resigned to her fate. "I'm afraid I might have—I might have done something terrible, Al."

His eyes widened. He touched her hand. "Why, Dot, you're freezing. Come inside for a minute and warm up."

She trudged up the steps behind him and into his porch, each movement stone against stone as she willed her legs to work, a criminal on the gallows climb. Al gestured to a chair and she sat down.

"Now, what is the matter?"

His already pale skin whitened to the color of fresh snow. "Whatever it is, you can tell me. You know that, don't you?" The tender force of his gaze almost dropped her to the floor.

Steam flowed from his coffee pot on the stove, with an aroma so pungent she knew he'd put in twice the normal amount. Made a pot to see him through the night, no doubt. He'd turned on the radio in the next room, too. A love song from the war wafted into the kitchen. The unforgettable Glenn Miller and his Army Air Force Band—great sound, and a genuine Iowa hero's heart, to boot.

Snatches of the lyrics came to her—something about the sky

having millions of stars, but the singer having eyes for only one special person. Why, that was the same song Cora used to yodel around the house.

"Dottie, answer me. What's the matter?"

Furrows cut into Al's forehead. His caring touched her so deeply, she almost wept. Here he was, thinking of her, after she'd made him a pauper in one fell swoop.

"Al, I…"

He waited a reasonable time. "What is it?" His foot tapped the floor in staccato. He chewed his thumbnail, something he never did. She wanted to comfort him somehow, yet her news would do anything but that. She knew she should spit it out, but he'd probably have a stroke, and she'd be responsible.

She closed her eyes. Pressed the back of her hand against her nose. Moisture tugged at the corner of her left eye. No, not that. She couldn't fall apart and make this even worse.

"The ring—I can't…"

"The ring?" His tone sounded hollow, like an old eaten-out log.

"I can't *find* it."

He seemed stunned, as though she'd slapped him. "You never even looked at it anyway." His mumble hit her like a shout. Two strides took him to Nan's Grandma's Hoosier cupboard.

"Here it is." The dullness in his tone matched that in his eyes. He set the box on the table and dropped into his chair, staring at the floor. That pesky tear rolled down her cheek.

"Oh." Her hand slapped against her coat buttons. "I was so worried when I couldn't…"

"Well, it's right here, so you can go on home now. Get some sleep."

The muscles around his mouth puckered, tightened, puckered again. He wouldn't meet her eyes.

Dottie sat down and reached for his hand. "Al, I…" She had no idea what she intended to say, but in that split second, the gray mass of befuddlement left her. Everything came together, and she marveled at her slowness of heart.

Of course, she loved Al. She had all along. What woman wouldn't love a man who rubbed her feet and helped her in the kitchen? Nothing stood between them but a minor misunderstanding.

"No, Dottie. It's all my fault. I was an old fool, that's all. We can be friends still, can't we? I don't know what I'll do if you can't bring yourself to…"

He stared at the tablecloth, faded from years of use. Against the dusky pink teapot wallpaper that framed his face, he looked faded too, and shrunken into himself.

"I hope so. I mean, how could I marry somebody who wasn't a friend?"

He took forever to digest what she'd said, took forever to raise his eyes. Her heart pulsed up the front of her neck while she waited. Her shoulders tingled. But she deserved the long wait, she told herself, for putting him through this.

"Marry?"

"Well, you asked me to marry you, didn't you?"

He nodded, dumbstruck.

"I want to. That is, I want to marry you, Al.

A visible shiver spliced him. His prominent Adam's apple bulged. "You do?"

"Of course I do. You're the finest man I know. Unless you've changed your mind, you love me, and you've shown me in so many ways. You're smart and kind and…"

His whole face crumbled. Then he was on his skinny knees beside her, his long arms wound around her shoulders, and she thought she'd never breathe quite the same way again.

He pulled back. "You don't have to, you know. I can still see you to California. I know how bad you want to go. I shouldn't have put everything together like a store display. I wasn't thinking right—these last few days, I've been so worried. I should've told you a little bit at a time."

"I admit, it was pretty overwhelming, but I think I want the entire package, Al Jensen, my dear, dear friend. I do. I want it all.

I just needed a little time to think it over." She swiped at her eyes as he stood and pulled her up.

"You mean it, Dot? You really *want* to marry me?"

"Are you withdrawing your proposal, Mr. Jensen?"

"No—no, I would never do that. But…"

"One thing you ought to know about me by now. I don't say things if I don't mean them. I do want to marry you, if you'll still have me."

Her last "do" muffled as he drew her closer, so close their lips touched. Wild tingles racked her, burned her teeth and the insides of her ears. The rush of emotion gave her goose bumps—the sensation she had placed on a shelf in the back of her mind years ago, never to be brought out again.

"Al…"

He loosened his hold and thrust back his head so he could look into her eyes. "What is it?" The start of a smile played with the right corner of his lips. An undeniable desire urged her finger to the spot.

"I love you, too, by the way."

"Seems like I don't know what's real anymore, the world moves so fast." Dottie brushed her wave back from her eyes.

Millie glanced around her living room. "I know what you mean, Mom. Look at the kids—they're almost grown up, and it happened so fast. Now you and Al are getting married." She shook her head. "And you're off to California. On top of that, Cora's expecting her third baby. The last time I saw her, she was still a baby herself."

Dottie exhaled a long breath and loosened her belt. Her daughter's new sofa cushioned her so well, she might never get out of her position. Millie outdid herself on dinner—fried chicken and homemade biscuits, potatoes and thick gravy, scalloped corn and the best homemade tomato relish Dottie had eaten in a long while. She even splurged on Oreo cookies and ice cream for dessert, a treat Dottie would never have purchased.

She studied Millie's face from the side for a minute. She'd never say it to her, but she could see her own mother's profile there, because the skin under Millie's chin had started to sag a little.

"I ate so much—that was a perfect dinner."

"Well, I don't go all out very often any more, with everyone traveling in so many directions. Some nights, when I work late, Alice cooks supper."

"Hmm…good experience for her. She's turning into a woman already."

"Seems like she's grown up overnight. She wants to attend Iowa State to be a home economics teacher. I'm betting she'll see it through."

Dottie's first granddaughter had already hugged her good-bye before she left for the Christmas program practice a couple of blocks away. Dottie gave herself a silent chiding. She ought to have found a way to come here more often since Owen died, but the trip down to Cedar Rapids seemed way too far when she thought of making it all alone.

But she'd missed out on Alice growing up, and that was a shame. Now, though, she wouldn't repeat her mistake. No, she would get on that train bound for California, come what may.

Her lower leg jerked. Suddenly, with her bloated stomach, she felt as though she couldn't sit in the same position for one more minute. "Want to take a walk?"

Millie leaped up. "Sure. I'll show you where I work." She led the way through the dining room, where the men discussed the World Series.

"How'd you like Yogi Berra pinch hitting that homer? I was sitting right here listening that night." Millie's husband Ren drummed his knuckles on the table. "You root for the Yankees or the Dodgers, Al?"

"Guess I didn't pay that much attention this year, with so much going…" Al held out his hand as Dottie walked past. She wasn't sure, but the day Yogi made history might have been the day Al

took her fishing—the day he realized for certain he couldn't live without her.

She twined her fingers with his, and her cheeks heated like a stoked furnace. "We'll be back in a little while."

He looked at his watch and gave a gentle tug on her hand. "Probably ought to leave by four, don't you think?"

She wanted to smooth the thinning spot on the crown of his head. Worry lines crossed his forehead as she unlocked her fingers from his. But her voice failed her at a sudden rush of feeling for him.

"Oh, Al, don't worry. I'll bring her back." Millie's chuckle tickled Dottie's ears. It was so good to hear her daughter's laugh—at least that was one thing that stayed the same about people. At the same time, she knew it would be a long time before she'd see Millie again.

She swallowed down a lump rising in her throat. Getting married, traveling to California, even the trip today to see Millie and Ren and the grandchildren overwhelmed her. She felt dizzy. Maybe she'd taken on too much too quickly, or else she simply wasn't meant to travel.

Millie helped her with her coat and linked arms once they started down the sidewalk. "That Al's a worrywart, isn't he?"

Dottie stiffened—Al? She hadn't thought of him that way. "He's only wanting us to get back safely, before that snowstorm blows in from the Dakotas."

"What storm?"

"Why, the one they forecast on KGLO out of Mason City. It'll be a big one, they say, and should hit sometime this evening."

"Hmm…"

"Al's quite a thinker, Millie. I've been amazed at how he plans ahead and figures things out before we have to deal with them— like this winter he noticed my chimney smoking and put in a new filter before I was even aware of it."

Millie's hair swept Dottie's shoulder. "That's good, Mom. I'm glad you'll have someone to take care of you—Al will fit right into Dad's shoes."

181

Dottie bristled. Al Jensen take Owen's place? No, it wasn't like that at all. In fact, Al and Owen were opposites. The more she got to know Al, the more she wondered how the two men could have been such good friends all those years.

## Chapter Twenty-one

"This was the last street in town when we first moved in." Millie gestured ahead along the street.

"Really? It's grown that much? Guess it's been so long since your dad and I drove down here, I've forgotten."

Dottie focused on the new section of houses burgeoning all around them. So many brand new homes, all of them pretty much the same, covered acres of what used to be fertile Iowa fields.

How long could this growth continue—wouldn't a day come when the city had to stop spreading into the farmland? But change rode the wind. Dottie could sense it, not only in her life, but all across the United States, and mostly because of the war.

Several city blocks later, Millie guided her around a corner and across a wide street toward an imposing stone building, pulled some keys from her pocket, and fitted one into a heavy steel door.

"I'll show you where I spend my days."

"Didn't you used to drive out to the plant?"

"Yeah, but I moved in here a couple of years ago."

Granite—or was it marble? Dottie wouldn't know the difference, but the smooth, chiseled rock filled the inside of the building. She hadn't visualized Millie dressing up each day and working in such a fancy place. Early on, she'd assembled radios in the factory, and that picture still lived in Dottie's mind—Millie in long pants, her hair hidden in a man's cap, helping with the war effort.

Her daughter's sensible heels clicked down a long hallway, and Dottie's thoughts returned to Millie's comment about Al. He would take Owen's place? Something about that settled wrong in her stomach, but she swallowed it.

How would Millie know? She'd never lost a husband. For that matter, since she and Ren married at seventeen, she'd never had to live alone. Well, she could think what she would—it didn't matter, at least not enough to spoil this precious time together. Dottie pressed her irritation into a distant recess of her mind, where it belonged.

"My cubbyhole is right down here, Mom." Millie unlocked a wide door with glass almost to the edges and led the way across some sort of thick, newfangled carpet to a huge oak desk sitting in a corner. There was even a green plant beside the window.

"So this is where you work? Doesn't look much like a cubbyhole to me."

Millie rounded the desk and pointed to a framed wall certificate.

Mrs. Ren Stanley
Director of Marketing

"You're the Director?"

Millie grinned. "I got promoted because of the war, Mom. If we hadn't lost so many men, I wouldn't be in this office."

She gestured toward a row of egg-carton indentations along the hall visible through a wide inter-office window. A shiny pipeline rode the wall from about three feet above Millie's desk through a hole, extending as far as Dottie could see along the row of desks stuck into the small cubicles.

"The staff and I use that to send notes back and forth. Cuts down on congestion." Millie reached almost to the floor. "The returns come to me down here."

Dottie eyed a few metal canisters with screw-on lids stacked across the side of the desk. So, Millie put messages in those and sent them down the pipeline—what would they think of next?

As if reading her mind, Millie added, "Forced air pushes the canisters along, kind of like vacuum cleaner suction."

"When did all this come about?"

"Oh, about a year ago."

"And they let you keep this position even after the war?"

"They is *me*, Mom. I'm the director." She chuckled, but no one could have missed the gleam in her eyes. Her oldest child had climbed the ranks to become so successful at only thirty-four. The war certainly did bring an avalanche of change.

"You never told me that when you called. You make me proud."

"Thanks. I'm proud of you, too. You have a whole new life opening up before you, and you're moving right into it." Millie locked her office door and turned to Dottie. "And of course I didn't tell you—I'm put together just like you."

Millie led the way to another room with a couple of soft chairs, a round table, a brand new refrigerator with no compressor unit on top, even a sink and cupboards. "Here's where we eat lunch—do you like it?"

"I do—looks so handy."

"I figured on miserable winter days, why not have a place for the staff to go during breaks—and my boss agreed. It's fun to get ideas and see them put into practice. We're alike that way, Mom."

"What do you mean?"

"You're the one who helped me with that prize-winning cake recipe for the county fair—don't you remember?"

"I did?" Maybe she and Millie were more alike than Dottie thought—maybe that was why Millie married so young—she'd needed to be out of the house, managing her own life.

When Dottie peeked over the railing, the building's floors swirled below her. Tomorrow, workers would mass through the doorway in a busy whirlwind—it made her weary to imagine it.

She guessed Millie was right—if she worked here and got a big promotion, she wouldn't toot her own horn either. Maybe that was one reason she missed Bill so much—he was wired more like Owen, needing someone to listen to all his ideas. Both of her girls inherited her quieter nature.

"Be right back." Millie disappeared down the hall, and Dottie reflected on the coming week. On Thursday, she and Al would go to the courthouse for their marriage license. On Saturday afternoon, they would say their vows in a quiet ceremony with Reverend Langley and his wife, Marie, as witnesses.

And then—her thoughts jumped forward to the train bound for California. She had to face it. Though she knew there was no other way to see Cora, the idea made her light-headed. She steadied her hand on the wooden bannister.

"Over here, Mom—look what we've installed." Dottie approached some shiny doors as Millie pushed a button. Metal latticework appeared in a hole in the wall. "Come on in, let's take a ride."

In response to her daughter's obvious excitement, Dottie stepped over the inch-wide cut in the floor. "This is my favorite new con-traption—you'll love it." The latticework closed, and then the shiny steel. Dottie fell back against the wall.

"Mom, you all right?" Millie found the button and pushed it again. Light flooded the enclosure.

"Let me…let me out." It was all Dottie could manage.

Millie punched a button, the door slid open, and she guided her mother to a bench.

"Lower your head—your hands are like ice." Millie rubbed her back for a minute. "I didn't know you—they have a name for this, you know—claustrophobia. I'll run and get you a glass of water. Be right back."

Dottie gritted her teeth until the swirling sickness faded. A photograph on the wall of a tall man shaking hands with a woman caught Dottie's eye and she perused it closer.

The shapely slant of the woman's hat brought Dottie's older sister Mildred to mind. She used to wear a dark brown one shaped like that, with a red runner on the brim.

The sudden memory transported her to a day Mildred took her shopping in Mason City—probably her first time in a store. It should have been a red-letter day, a happy memory.

"There's a sale today, Dottie. For sure, you need some new shoes and a coat, and we'll see what else when we get there." Inside

Damon's Department Store, a sea of ladies in wool coats unfolded around them. But somehow Dottie became separated from her sister—she could hear Mildred calling her name, but couldn't find her. And then, she no longer heard her name. Panic tightened her chest.

Squashed by perfumed, chattering ladies, she found herself closed in a stuffy space that squeaked and moved. Worse, she stood at the edge of the gaggle of women and could see walls passing by, darkness below, and a light high above them. Finally, the motion ground to a halt, with much shrieking of gears. Dottie tried to ask for help, even tugged at a woman's sleeve, but her voice refused to work.

Arms reached for her when the doors slid open—Mildred's arms—but she could barely make her way to her sister, and didn't breathe easy again until they reached home that night. The expected joy of being treated to new clothes vanished in that fear-ridden ten minutes.

Strange how this long-ago scene would come to her now, but she emerged from it with her fingers to her throat, that same old suffocating feeling riding the base of her neck.

"Here, Mom. Are you feeling better?"

"I'm sorry."

"Nothing to apologize for." Millie sat beside her and patted her shoulder. Some folks can't handle elevators, that's all."

"Oh, Millie—I'm so afraid—what if this happens when Al and I go to board the train?"

"The train? You don't need to worry about that. It's got windows. As long as you can see out, you'll be fine."

Frosty breath circled above her in early morning semi-darkness. Dottie stretched and stared at her bedroom's four ceiling corners. Even in the recent minus zero temperatures, a moth had somehow survived to flit from one side of the room to the other. A ray of light from the window caught a cobweb floating in the northeast corner—spiders ate moths, so that made sense.

Her mind returned to the present. Had she actually accepted a marriage proposal from Al Jensen a week ago tonight, or had she dreamed he took her to that fancy place for supper? Her fingertips grazed her cheeks, instantly hot with the memory.

As if to prove her memory right, she breathed the words out loud. "It's true. He did ask, and I agreed."

She scanned the bureau for the self-same box—she hadn't started to wear the ring all the time, but tried it on every morning. She crossed the cold floorboards in her bare feet. Thick velvet caressed her fingers, and a shiver rambled down her spine. Yes, the box was real. She opened the lid to stare at the glinting diamond.

"Al loves me." The words, floating on air so cold she could see her breath, warmed her all over in spite of the drafts rising from the floor. She repeated them, just for the delight of their cadence. "Al Jensen loves me."

She closed the box and grabbed her pale green chenille bath-robe from its hook, slipped on her worn leather moccasins, and entered the hallway. Putting those slippers on brought Cora to mind. One Christmas during her high school years, she'd given them to Dottie.

"Mom, you need something for the mornings. It's not good to walk around barefoot on this cold wood."

Dottie took her observation to heart, and the moccasins became her ready companion in winter. She traced her finger over her three children's graduation portraits along the short hallway, stopping at Cora's engaging blue eyes.

"We're coming to California to see you, honey. Al and I will be there before Christmas. I can hardly wait to hug you and your little ones." Through thin glass, she patted Cora's pert nose with her fingertip before she walked into the front room to turn up the thermostat.

The east window showed no sign of life from Al's house as she flipped on the gas burner under her already full water kettle. He slept fitfully, anyway—Nan had mentioned that years ago.

"When we're in bed, his legs jerk and sometimes he shouts 'No, no!' It's like he's reliving something terrible."

Getting up the nerve to propose to her and planning this trip had to take their toll. She hoped he could stay in bed a little longer this morning.

"Al's way smarter than me, that's for sure. But thinking things through so thoroughly causes him an undo amount of distress. If he hadn't jumped to conclusions when I didn't give him an instant answer last Friday night…"

From his driveway, the chrome of his truck flashed as a vehicle passed through the alley, and Dottie let forth a chuckle. "If he hadn't been so upset that I would turn him down, that scene with me standing on my head, trying to find the ring, would have been downright funny."

She spread a handful of loose black tea in the bottom of her teapot. Might as well get dressed while she waited.

Close to the bathroom sink, waiting for the faucet's icy blast to heat, she eyed her reflection, which told her plenty, even though she didn't turn on the light. She was no spring chicken, but a new glimmer flickered in her eyes.

A hot, wet washcloth rubbed clear her head. She drew the terry fabric over the back of her neck and under her arms, relishing extra time, since Bonnie Mae and George had taken over cooking breakfast. And that meant, of course, Helene was gone again—amazing how much more pleasant life became without her.

Her work dress eased from its hanger over the bathtub where she hung it each night. But the buttons defied their stretched-out holes—good thing she could cover her bosom with a full apron at work in case a button popped. She'd better round up some decent clothes and a suitcase for the trip.

The kettle whistled her back to the kitchen, where she leaned over to breathe in some steam. Only today, tomorrow, and Wednesday left to work at the boarding house—three days, and short ones, at that. With Helene gone, Bonnie Mae developed new confidence in the kitchen and planned to prepare the noon meal if Dottie would come at eleven to check on her.

*Tap. Tap-tap. Tap-tap-tap.* Did Al even realize he used the same rhythm each time he came to the back door?

"Dottie? You up?"

She waved him in, glad to recognize his step on the shadowy side of dawn. He approached slowly, and she turned toward his luminous eyes.

"Why Al, I thought maybe you'd be able to sleep a little longer today."

His long arms took her in. "I'd rather hug you than sleep any day."

Millie might think Al a bit on the nervous side, but his warmth enveloped Dottie like the shawl she wore to church services in springtime.

# Chapter Twenty-two

*Smack!* Al ran into the back of Henry Olson's delivery truck at about eight o'clock. He'd been considering Dottie's fear of crowds, wondering how to prepare her for the busy Fort Madison train depot. But even more, he puzzled over what held her back. Why couldn't she enjoy shopping in a big department store like most other women?

The *thunk* of the truck's grill shook the cab. The larger truck's bed, complete with chicken feathers and their stuffy smell, hulked over his hood like a vulture's beak. Too shocked to utter a syllable, he loosed himself from under the steering wheel and raced around the front.

If there was no damage to Henry's vehicle, he could quietly back down the alley without causing a stir. But it was not to be. Del emerged from the back door of the hardware, and for a moment, seemed much taller than the day before. His forehead swam with question wrinkles.

"Dad? How'd you manage to hit the one vehicle anywhere near here?"

Al shrugged his shoulders. "Lucky shot, I guess. I'll take care of this with Henry."

"You sure?" Only a yard away, Del paused. "You all right? You've been in another world lately."

Al startled as the hatchery door banged. "Oh…that. I've had a lot on my mind, Del. Have I told you I'm getting married?"

"Married?" Del hunkered down, his neck elongated like a flying goose. "Who to?"

So the town gossip brigade hadn't reached his son's ears yet. But then, Del kept to himself. He'd inherited Nan's family's chunkiness, and paired with her first husband's height and brooding nature, the first impression he made warded off most folks. Nan always predicted Delbert would go far, but would have to work alone.

Henry's balding head bounced around his truck fender, so Al lowered his voice.

"You know her pretty well, Son." He waited for the gears inside Del's mind to move. "Our old neighbor."

"Dottie?"

"Yep."

"Dottie Kyle?"

"The very one."

"When?"

"Saturday. But keep it to yourself." As if he needed to tell his quiet, lumbering son to keep a secret. Al chuckled at Del's awestruck expression and turned toward Henry.

"Morning, Henry. Guess there's a first time for everything, eh? How many years have we avoided each other in this alley?"

"About thirty, I'd say." They shook hands and Henry bent to survey the back of his truck. "Heard the crash clear inside the hatchery, but don't look like much damage to me…this old girl's got plenty of dents already. Can't run a delivery truck without 'em. Looks as though your hood took the impact. We'll write it off to friendship, shall we?"

"All right. Thanks." Over Henry's sparse hair, sprouting from his scalp like a spring sorghum planting, Al surveyed his firstborn's rugged face. Del still stood in the alley, dumbstruck, continuing to grapple with the idea of a new stepmother.

Del and Henry went their separate ways, and Al backed from under the delivery truck without incident. He needed gas, anyway. Maybe he'd drive on down to Benson's and fill up the tank. By the time he parked beside the pump, nothing had fallen off the front, so he let his thoughts retrace their familiar route to Dottie.

The storm closed in on Sternville like a tornado, whirling and swirling from its first moment. No easy free fall of downy, gigantic flakes, creating a winter wonderland. From its onset, wild wind wracked Al's old house and shook its brittle wooden structure. Hail-like clatter heckled the windows, so he pulled down the shades and shut the heavy drapes to hinder the draft.

"Glad I re-caulked all the windows last fall. Glad I put in that new insulation along the roofline where it used to leak. Glad…" He felt along the bottom of the front door.

"Should have bought one of those rubber flaps for this." He tucked an old rag rug from the back corner of the closet underneath the opening. "Gotta remember, she's an old, old house. Always in need of something."

Seemed like his life pared down to two piles, things he wished he would have done and those accomplishments he took pride in. And it seemed that many in both piles revolved around this house. Dottie's tight siding caught his eye as he passed through the kitchen *en route* to stoke the furnace.

Unlike Dottie's husband—no, her former husband, no…first husband—aw, Al didn't know how to think of Owen any more. His fishing buddy—that sounded best. Anyway, unlike Owen, he hadn't gone for a new furnace, what with this old limestone basement crumbling on its foundations. He ran a fingernail along the chalky stone, green with some sort of musty growth.

Getting a massive steel furnace down here would require knocking out a wall and replacing it, and they would have had to tear apart and reassemble the furnace, so he took Del's advice and stuck with his coal stoker. He didn't like making trips into this dank, freezing hole, didn't like the coal dust, didn't like…he could go on and on. But the stoker did its job without complaint.

The heavy iron door scraped open, and Al scooped in a mound of coal large enough to last all day. He'd observed the innovations—automatic loading shoots to feed the fire, timers, things like that. But most of them required cutting through the aged limestone, which might not take well to being disturbed.

The alternative, rebuilding the basement walls, would cost a fortune—probably upwards of a thousand dollars. Some things were better left alone.

Two generations ago, his grandfather laid these stones—that was something, wasn't it? Behind him, the furnace belched flames. He chuckled at Del's intense reaction to his announcement yesterday in the alley. It brought to mind the shocked look on Del's face the first time he heard the explosion in the furnace. He never quite got used to it, either, so he and Charlie avoided the basement from late October through May.

At the top of the stairs, Al swung the door shut behind him. Those days were long gone now. Del's oldest son, grown and gone, boasted a grandbaby on the way. His son would be a grandfather soon. And Charlie's youngest turned ten last summer. Al wandered through the rooms, wondering what to do with his time today, since he'd already half-packed for the trip and Del didn't need him right now.

The house shook again, a rag doll in a mongrel's teeth, and he gripped the window frame. By Sunday, he and Dottie would have tied the knot, and they hadn't even discussed where they'd live.

Might not hurt to go over there and check on things, although her house was far more fit for a storm than his. He pulled on his coat and his black rubber boots, letting the zippers hang open, stuck his denim cap with its red flannel earflaps over his head, and headed across the back yard.

"What do you think about where we'll live, Al?" Dottie smiled at him over her teacup, sending tremors through him head to toe. He'd been wondering how to bring up the subject.

"I've given that some thought lately."

"I figured so. If you compare our two houses…"

"Yours wins hands down."

"You think so?"

"It's in far better shape. Owen was good about making improvements—this house has a new furnace, tighter construction, and far thicker insulation in the attic."

"That may be true, but you must have some feelings for your place. Didn't your grandfather build it from scratch?"

"He did. But the back porch sways something awful, the wind blusters right through the dining room floorboards. It'd cost a lot to fix it up. If I started on one thing, like reinforcing the foundation, ten more would pop up. It's an old, old house."

Dottie stirred a little cinnamon into her tea and breathed in the scent. Her expression mellow, she leaned back in her chair and made a steeple of her fingers. Her eyes twinkled. Al liked her this way, without the pressure of working at the boarding house the entire day. Of course, he'd liked her the other way, too. The silence built, but like something good, and Al felt the knots in his shoulders stretch out a bit.

"Are you saying you'd be willing to live in my drafty old barn, Dot?"

That wonderful dimple appeared in her left cheek. "I'm saying that drafty old barn holds a lot of your family history. Why, your father was born in that house. And you can't deny the oak flooring is second to none in town."

"Nope. But it's curving more and more. You probably haven't noticed, but the living room floor is cattywampus. We'd have to bring some hefty machinery to straighten it out—stretch it somehow. That would cost a fortune."

"Still, your dad was born right in the downstairs bedroom. Isn't that right?"

"That's a fact, and his eight brothers and sisters. Can't believe they're all gone now—even Dad's baby brother, Uncle Sam."

"I remember his wife—Myrna, wasn't that her name? She and Sam took in Howard and Lizzy Froy when they lost their parents in that flood over in eastern Iowa. Kindest couple in town."

Al reached over to squeeze her hand. He was about to compliment her on her great memory when the front door burst open, and she scrambled from her chair.

"Dottie, is Al here?" Two sets of boots thunked in, and male figures swathed in heavy coats and hats met them in the dining room. Why, it was George and a younger fellow—one of the Bell brothers. The storm had laced them in white head to foot.

George's hair stood on end when he took off his stocking cap. "You've gotta come right away, Al. There's a fire over at the school." Al grabbed hold of a chair back, a fire of his own roaring through his gut.

Dottie ran to the kitchen for his coat and boots. He put them on in a couple of hops, and as the men retraced their steps, he looked into Dot's eyes, since she'd stepped right in front of him.

"Your face is too white, Al. What is it?"

He closed his eyes for a moment. His sigh quivered from the depths, but this was no time to give in to the onslaught inside him.

"Pray, will you please? It's almost ten, and they hadn't called school off yet for the storm when I came over here."

The lines of her face froze in comprehension. "Be careful."

He leaped into the back of the car, and George twisted in the front seat. "I'm not on the department, but it'll be all right if I help, won't it?"

"Sure." Al's hands shook so violently, he had trouble getting his gloves on, but the warmth of Dottie's hand on his shoulder and the feel of her lips on his cheek still lingered. He clung to those sensations as Nigel Bell accelerated into whatever lay ahead.

"We have to keep those sparks from dropping on the Byerly's roof. The wind's in exactly the wrong direction." Henry Olson, smelling like chicken feed and feathers, edged up to Al.

Heston's volunteers had already arrived—that was a good thing, since the Sternville pump truck could only handle so much, and between loads, the fire might move at will. Al's heart beat so wildly he wasn't sure he'd be the best man for on-the-line work.

Del, perspiration draining down his temples into his fire coat, waved him over.

"Keep the older guys from doing anything foolhardy, Dad."

He hurried back to his position on the hose line, his comment grinding in the pit of Al's stomach. *Old guys?* Why, Del had been only a youngster when the newspaper office burned, and it was the old guys who saved the day.

No use fanning that flame with real flames surging from the east side of the schoolhouse. Harm Byerly's place and Ruth McPherson's could use whoever else wasn't on the fire line.

"You're right. Henry, George, let's do something about Harm's roof." Henry lit out and soon returned back with three more men.

"Let's open those two front windows and wet down the porch shingles—the water'll turn to ice, but that's better than dry shingles."

Nobody argued, so he led the way. Mabel opened the door and shooed them all inside. "Don't know why things like this have to happen on such awful cold days."

"We need to wet down your front porch roof. That all right with you?"

"Do whatever you need to." She opened her mouth, shut it, and tears sprang into her eyes. "You think our houses might be in danger?"

"Better to be prepared. We need some pails."

"In the basement, this way." George followed Al down the stairs. "Mabel, where's Harm's toolbox?"

"Down there, too."

George wrapped the ungainly hose around his shoulder and hurried up the stairs while Al searched for pails. Mabel met him in the kitchen, her scrub mop in hand.

"Sorry about the mess."

"It's all right. Gives me something to do."

Men pounded, and muttered at the front windows. "Caulked shut."

Al dropped the pails and ran to a side bedroom to look out. A spark burst into flame on the porch roof. He scampered back into the hallway and yelled. "Knock 'em out—a spark's already caught out there."

Glass shattered. Mabel appeared in the doorway. "You broke—?"

"Flames are catching on your roof already."

She swayed. Al caught her elbow. "Don't worry. Del has plenty of glass down at the hardware. Maybe you should go on downstairs for a while."

Her lips pursed. "I'm okay. Pay me no mind."

"Your children?"

"They all went to school—I imagine the teachers herded them into the west side when the fire started."

Al raced into the bathroom, where George had the nozzle hooked up to the bathtub faucet. He guided the ungainly thing down the hall.

"Good work. Go ahead, I'll turn the faucet on." Water sprayed when Al turned the knobs, so he tightened the nozzle. The sizzle of water on hot shingles sent a shiver through him.

He'd better check the bedrooms—how many children did Mabel and Harm have? This old house, built around the same time as his, contained simple furniture—beds and dressers handed down over the generations—memories and whatnot.

Another spark shot up not three feet away from the first, and the men sprayed it down. Al concentrated on breathing. He wiped his forehead, surprised at how wet it was, and flashed back to a time long ago and far away—a time he'd tried hard to wipe from his memory. He clenched his teeth against the recollection and kept his eyes off the schoolhouse. It was all he could do to remain standing.

"Keep up the pressure, Henry!" George's animated voice brought him back. He stuffed down his emotions. They'd better check Ruth's roof—she'd be terrified by now.

# Chapter Twenty-three

Dottie hated to do it, but she rang one long ring on the telephone to summon Hilda. The operator's breathless response hinted she'd been dying for a call.

"Got any word on the fire yet, Hilda?"

"It's still raging. Elmira Peterson stopped in here on her way from there, Dottie, and it's awful, purely awful. They got all the children out—the flames are confined to the east end, so far, so that would be the elementary. First, second, and third grades on the first floor, and on the second, the fourth, fifth and sixth. But there's smoke everywhere. Oh my. I've got a grandson in fifth, you know, Val's his name, and—"

"Yes, I know, Hilda. But I wondered how many fire trucks have come—any from out of town?"

Several rings vibrated in the background.

"Why of course. Heston and a couple from Mason City, even. Can you believe that? It's a massive conflagration. I don't recall a fire this big in…maybe twenty years, and I heard, too, that some men are over wetting down the roofs of nearby houses—"

"Thank you. You'd better answer your other calls."

An image of Al wielding a fire hose and climbing a ladder straight up the side of the schoolhouse gave Dottie a sick feeling. She hung up and grabbed her coat. She couldn't stay here when he might be in danger. Besides, there must be something she could do. She called down the basement stairs.

"Bonnie Mae? Would you mind coming up here?"

Bright red hair flashed around the landing corner. "What's up?"

"I finished browning the chicken fried steak and set it on the back burner to simmer. The potatoes are almost ready to mash—think you can handle dinner? I want to go over and check on the fire."

"Sure. I've got everything under control." Bonnie Mae brushed back her unruly flock of curls. "You don't need to come back, Dottie. The weather's so awful, and Helene won't be back till tomorrow."

"You'll call me if you need me?"

"You bet. Be careful out there."

The temperature must have warmed the slightest bit, because freezing rain pelted when Dottie stepped out. By the time she reached the west end of the schoolhouse on Sixth Street, she sloshed through a mountain of icy slush. Before she could make out anything more than indistinct figures on the Byerly's roof, something told her Al was involved.

The knowledge seeped through her, as had a similar kind of knowing the week before Doc Schulz diagnosed Owen's condition as terminal. That was a long time ago, and she hadn't sensed that kind of thing since. Rounding the corner, she faced Ruth McPherson's house. A hatchet broke through one of the windows situated above Ruth's front porch, and the chopper wore a brown coat just like Al's.

Dottie splashed close enough now to recognize the men on the Byerly's roof. One looked like Mr. Crowley from the meat shop, and Henry Olson leaned halfway out the window. She moved down Ruth's sidewalk, and there Al was, halfway through a broken-out window, manning a garden hose that added water to waves of ice pouring from the sky. She banged on the door and it opened.

"Ruth, you here?"

The tiny older woman stood with a blanket around her shoulders, staring out the front room window. "You all right?" Dottie pushed the door farther.

"Oh, Dottie. Is that really you?"

Dottie put her arm around Ruth's slight, childlike frame. "You doing okay?"

"I am." But Ruth's voice shook like the telephone wires outside the house.

"Let's brew some coffee for the workers."

The elderly woman perked up and threw her blanket onto an armchair.

"Should've thought of it myself. I've got cookies in the back porch, baked ahead for Christmas. She bustled toward her tiny kitchen set at the back of the house.

"Those poor men out in this miserable weather, and here I stand, doing nothing. Scared to death and doing nothing…"

In no time at all, Dottie carried hot coffee and a tray full of cookies upstairs. She made two trips, maneuvering carefully with all sorts of wild scraping and calling overhead.

George saw her first. "Why Missus!" He ducked his head. "You've brought us coffee—just like at the boarding house!" He filled his big paw with several cookies and grabbed a cup of coffee.

"Could you—would you mind handing a cup out to Al? It's so cold out there." George dutifully reached a cup out the window.

"Anything else I can do?"

"Can't think of anything." He scratched his head. "Oh—Al mentioned something a while ago. A good rope, he said."

"I'll find one. Be back as soon as I can."

Dottie hurried down the stairs and asked Ruth.

"There's a strong one out in the carriage house." Dottie slipped and slid behind the house, forced the door open, and rummaged through odds and ends. Finally, she found a rope, dragged it across the yard, hauled it up the back steps, and dropped the cumbersome thing just inside the door.

"Let me give you a hand getting it up the stairs." They grappled it to the second floor.

Just then, Al's leg came through the window opening. "Ah— exactly what I was coming in for. You're a lifesaver, Dot."

His jaw, set like stone, lent a peculiar slant to his face. He held her eyes for only a second as she dragged the monstrosity toward him, but in that brief interlude, she knew something wasn't right. She couldn't put her finger on it, but his eyes revealed a distantness she'd never seen—something almost tortured.

Al knew he was the last man, because he'd counted. Waited and counted in the penetrating cold that convulsed the old firehouse. Through the air vent low on the storage room door, steam rose from the concrete floor. Like dry ice, deceptive—cold enough to burn you, yet steaming.

He slunk into this back corner before the rest of the men brought in the pump truck, but still shivered in spite of his coat and gloves. His thighs trembled like an old, old man's…like his father's when he took to his bed for the final time. Al's soul felt the same way, as needy as a newborn.

Voices drained away as men headed home. He waited a few more minutes before he ventured out. He hadn't wanted Del to see him this way. Now, he caught a glimpse of himself in the still-wet side of the pump truck. Ghostly.

He had to get hold of himself, calm down his erratic heartbeat and the sense that things could never be right again.

"You've got the best woman in the world waiting for you. Only a few blocks away, she's cooking up something good for supper."

The thought of Dottie waiting for him to come home bathed him like a benediction. What a lovely word—home. He breathed it aloud.

That word had kept him alive in the trenches, alive through carrying out inconceivable missions. Knowing Nan waited for him held him together over there. Made it possible for him to catch a little sleep now and then, to keep trudging when they moved, to keep sane when they didn't.

He rounded the fire truck three times, aware only of the shuffle of his boots. And then, from a blackened stick of lumber that somehow managed to land on the truck, he caught another whiff of that awful smell—smoke out of control. Plastered against the side of the truck, he swayed.

"Help me—help me. Make it go away!" His plea rose hollow in the crisp air.

Minutes later, a key scratched in the doorknob, and he jerked his head every which way, seeking a place to hide. But it was too late. Rubber galoshes swished toward the pump truck. Al sucked in his breath. He'd know that heavy tread anywhere.

He filled his lungs and stepped from the shadows as Del approached.

"I thought everyone was gone. I came back for some…" Del stopped a foot away, his forehead bunched up like when he was a little boy aghast that his pet rabbit escaped during the night. Al gave thanks for the few high windows letting in minimal light.

"What're you doing here, Dad?"

"Just making sure everything…" Al mumbled something he knew Del couldn't make out. "Just making sure."

By the time he walked home, the throb in his head released a bit. Dottie met him at the corner. "Come over for supper after you get cleaned up, Al. You look like you could use a good meal."

He turned off at his sidewalk. "Yeah, it's been a long day. I'll be over."

He seemed the same as always now, but exhausted. And no wonder—he'd worked like a twenty year-old for hours up on that bitterly cold roof. Dottie hoped he wouldn't catch a terrible cold.

He turned before he shut the door, and she waved. His fingers barely rose in response, and worry tightened gnarly tendons around her heart.

She defied the bad thoughts. If she let one take her mind, soon she'd have Al down with pneumonia, their wedding and the trip to see Cora postponed. No. She wouldn't allow those imaginatings to fill her mind.

Food—that was what Al needed. After all, he hadn't eaten anything but cookies since breakfast. Let's see, what did she have in the house? Since he'd begun taking charge of supper, her supplies had run low. But she hadn't emptied the potato and onion sacks, she knew for sure.

In the Frigidaire's miniscule freezer, white-wrapped packages of meat stood in a row. Rump roast. Perfect. She unwrapped it on her granite countertop next to the stove. Nothing so tender as pressure-cooked beef. But she also liked the crusty texture that oven roasting created.

Well, she'd mix and match—twenty minutes in the cooker and then a half hour in her roaster in a hot oven. That would heat up the kitchen for Al, too. His face looked sunken in with cold. Nearly four-thirty, plenty of time. She ran a cup of water in the bottom of the cooker and lit the back burner.

Millie gave her that cooker for Christmas in 1940, the last Bill spent with them. A year later, he'd already enlisted with his best friend Ron and couldn't get leave once the Japanese struck Pearl Harbor.

Dottie twisted on the lid and set the pressure gage. By the next year, Ron was already buried overseas, and the army reported Bill missing in some godforsaken part of Africa. Algeria? No, that wasn't it.

But one scene, she could never forget. In the dead of winter, officers arrived with Bill's dog tags. After they left, Owen couldn't stop talking about him, but one day in spring, she'd put the tags into her keepsake box on their closet shelf. After that, Owen quieted down.

She steered her mind back to that Christmas, a wonderful place to stop. Delivering the mail, Owen found a fine fir tree out in a ditch, brought it home to set up in the living room, and set to work. But the tree wouldn't cooperate. Owen fumed and fussed. Finally, he stalked to the shed, came back with a couple

of spikes, and pounded them right into the floor, where Dottie's armchair sat now.

His fury became the family joke that Christmas, with everybody razzing him about his impatience. Millie, Ren, and the children came. Everyone cracked walnuts, strung dried cherries from last summer's crop, and attended the Christmas Eve service. Dottie glanced down the church pew, completely filled with her loved ones, and peace filled her. She remembered lying in bed later, basking in the delight of having all three children under their roof again.

Now, she filled a bowl with potatoes and onions, securing the porch door against a nasty air current. She still recalled opening her new pressure cooker that year.

Millie hadn't been able to contain herself—"Mom, you're going to love this! You can cook meat in a fraction of the normal time, and you can't imagine how tender it gets. Last year at the New York World's Fair, the National Pressure Cooker Company introduced this very cooker."

Dottie forgot what Cora gave her—maybe her bedroom moccasins. Owen—well, he'd never gotten into the habit of gift giving, but enjoyed watching the grandchildren open their presents. Bill gave the best gift of all—being here.

The phone rang, and Dottie counted the rings. It would be just like Hilda to call to discuss the day's events. By now, she would know that Dottie spent time with Ruth, and seek details she might have missed. Dottie sighed—at least no one had been hurt, although the Byerly's house suffered smoke damage.

"Hello? Oh, Cora—I'm so glad to hear your voice. I was going to call you tonight."

"Are you coming, Mom?" Her voice sounded different—weaker.

"We are. I have some news for you. Honey, Al Jensen and I are getting married on Saturday. And then we're coming out to see you."

"Millie called me Sunday night about you and Al. I'm surprised, but so happy for you."

"I know—I was pretty shocked myself. But it seems like this was meant to be."

"Did you buy your tickets yet? I sure hope not."

"No, we plan to go down to Heston on Thursday for our marriage license, but a storm blew in, and there's more coming. "And then… well, you don't want to know all that."

"But I do. Tell me everything."

Nine times out of ten, the line filled with static, so Dottie had to hang up before the conversation finished. She'd better say the important things first.

"I will, but what did you mean about the tickets?"

"Remember, I told you Dennis and I were buying your ticket? We sent it to you three days ago—you leave on the seventeenth. That means you should be here by the nineteenth or twentieth, depending on whether you stay over anyplace or not."

"Stay over?"

"It'll be a long trip for you, so we bought the stay-over option. You can stop overnight somewhere if you want to. You'll be on the Super Chief, quite a fancy train. You may even see some movie stars, Mom, and they serve gourmet meals."

"Oh Cora, that was so thoughtful, but I want to pay you for it. We'll wait to buy Al's ticket until mine comes."

"Mom, you coming out here is worth far more than that ticket. We can't wait to see you. And someone wants to say hello." A burble met Dottie's ear.

"Was that little Jeffrey?"

"Yes. Jeffy Owen, we've started calling him. He's built just like Dad, low to the ground and powerful, but with your dark coloring."

Dottie eyed the Jensen's Hardware calendar hanging above her dishpan. Today was Pearl Harbor day—six years. "Why, Cora. In just ten days, we'll be on our way."

"And married. Millie told me Al looked a little pale. As I recall, he wasn't the bravest sort."

"Oh, really?" What did her girls remember about Al, anyway?

A veteran of the Great War, not brave? Maybe they compared Owen's bravado with Al's more retiring nature.

The usual *tap* and *tap-tap* sounded from the back door. Dottie motioned Al in and mouthed *Cora* to him. He quietly shed his coat.

"That's the other thing that happened today, Cora. There was a fire at the school, and Al led a group of men to wet down Ruth McPherson's and Harm Byerly's front porch roofs. They saved both houses."

Al's face reddened, but she gave him a grin. He sidled over and wrapped an arm around her waist.

"That's great—tell him I'm proud of him, will you, Mom?"

"Sure enough. He can't wait to meet the children, either."

"Good—they can be a handful. We'll have everything ready for…" Cora's voice trembled. But static made its loud entrance, and after a couple more tries, Dottie hung up the phone and turned into Al's embrace.

"Cora says to tell you she's proud of you. So am I, Mr. Jensen. You're a mighty brave man."

He held her at arms' length, his eyes veiled. A parade of colors ran through his eyes, and she pulled him close. Whatever troubled him showed again. His tone had resignation in it, and distance.

"I'm glad it's over and no one got hurt." The scents of his hand soap and aftershave wafted to her. He'd combed every hair just right, even after such a tiring day.

"Me, too." She rubbed his shoulders.

"Guess what? Cora and Dennis already sent my ticket, with an option to stay over somewhere along the way if we want to see the sights."

"You don't say?"

"And she thinks it's good we're getting married. Millie told her before I did."

Al pulled something from his back pocket. When he met her eyes this time, that unreadable look fled, replaced by his usual good-natured sparkle.

"I sent for more information, and this came in the mail today. Perfect timing." He tossed a gold envelope on the table. "I thought nothing could be more exciting than planning our trip, Dot. But now"—he drew her close again—"I'd say just *thinking* about that stopover wins the prize."

"Hey, I thought you were worn out."

"Not that worn out, sweetie." He lowered his voice like Valentino in a love scene, and Dottie couldn't keep from giggling. Whatever it was that bothered him so much—something to do with the fire—fled. She melted as he kissed her soundly. Across the room, steam hissed from the pressure cooker.

"Al, I have to put the pressure regulator on the cooker."

The regulator danced on its stem. *Sss…sss…* She freed herself, but it wasn't easy.

"Now I need to peel the potatoes—I should have had them cooking already, but this day has been so upside down."

He followed her to the sink. "The phone rang, and I—" He kissed the back of her neck.

"Come on. You must be starving." She handed him a knife. Here she was, a grown woman—a grandmother, making eyes like a schoolgirl with her first beau—Millie and Cora would never believe it.

"Start peeling. I'll skin the onions."

Al obeyed, but shot her a hungry sideways glance.

# Chapter Twenty-four

By Thursday morning, snow piled so high Dottie could hardly see the street from the attic window. The clearing crew passed twice yesterday, but more inches fell during the night. Would they even be able to drive to Heston today? She went up to the attic to find a suitcase.

She'd never needed one before. When she moved here with Owen, they brought everything in his father's old truck, in boxes or right in her dresser and bureau. In fact, the only suitcase packing that ever happened in this house took place in the children's rooms. She'd washed and ironed, delivered and watched, but never packed.

Normally, she avoided the dusty half-attic adjacent to Bill's old room. Owen spent more time in there than she did, baiting and killing mice or bats. The door creaked open into close air swimming with cobwebs. Dottie used to clean this space every couple of years, but since Bill's death, she hadn't had the heart.

Maybe there wasn't even a suitcase in here—she should have brought a flashlight. Maybe Cora took every suitable container when she moved to California.

"You home?"

She reversed her direction and waited until her feet left the last step. No use yelling when you could speak in a normal voice. "I'm up here—I'll be right down." Then she went back up and waited till her eyes adjusted to the closed-in space. Along the wall lay exactly what she needed—a straw-colored thick cardboard case with an intact handle at the top. That ought to do.

By the time she navigated the steps and deposited the case near the bathroom sink where she could wipe it down, Dottie's breath came in gasps. She huffed around the corner into the kitchen, where Al stood on the mat, snow up to his trouser knees.

"Boy, oh boy—what a storm! I thought for sure it'd stop during the night, but it's coming down even heavier. The mayor's getting desperate—called in farmers to help with snow removal."

"Really?"

He flicked wet flakes from his eyebrows, looking more excited about the historic snowfall than distressed about their chances of getting their marriage license.

"Have you eaten breakfast?"

"I sure haven't, and shoveling that heavy, wet stuff creates quite the appetite."

"I can take care of that." Dottie rinsed her hands and wiped them on her apron.

"I'll do your front walk again while you cook, is that a deal?"

"Deal, but here—have some hot tea before you go out again." Her questions about being able to say their vows on Saturday stuck in her throat. Up till now, Al had shown more enthusiasm than she had, but suddenly, she realized how much she wanted the moment to arrive. Her train ticket came two days ago, and time was growing short.

He left his empty cup on the table and before long, metal rasped against cement out front. Dottie fried six strips of bacon and toasted four pieces of bread. The steady racket of the toaster followed her into the dining room, where she could watch Al shovel. For such a thin fellow, he had a huge food capacity, like Owen. But more and more, she saw the differences between those two.

Yesterday, the *Sternville Recorder* ran a photo of Al on Ruth McPherson's roof, but he shrank from the display. "Wish they'd have gotten a picture of all of us—George worked like a fool all day long."

Owen would have basked in that small-town glory, making an

appearance at several stops around town the next morning. Actually, he would have been the one to bring the paper home.

"Lookee here, Dot!" She imagined him holding it out to her, a wide grin on his face. "I made the front page!" With Al, it was the other way around. Ruth sent her granddaughter over with a copy of the paper, and Dottie showed it to Al.

"To each his own." The toaster fell silent, so she flipped the toast, set the monitor to medium, and stirred oatmeal into boiling water. When it thickened, she added a big dollop of applesauce and let it bubble for half a minute, then stirred in raisins and thick cream.

The Frigidaire offered up a carton of eggs from Harley Blackstone's farm, delivered fresh every Friday morning. Dottie fried six of them. That ought be about right, if she ate one. By the time Al clattered through the back porch, leaving his boots and coat there, she had the table set, and had worked up an appetite.

"Bring your coat in by the stove so it'll be nice and dry when you go out again."

She helped him drape everything over a wooden bench and a couple of chair backs. He washed his hands and pulled up to the table, reached for her hand and said grace. At the end, he added, "And we give thanks for what's coming on Saturday."

Now, why did he do that? He knew as well as she that the road to Heston might not be cleared before afternoon, and without their license, Saturday's ceremony couldn't take place. Had the cold addled his brain? But Al dug into his food like he'd never before seen a breakfast.

Well, she wasn't about to ask him. "Did you see anybody out there this morning?"

"Yeah, met Friedrich at the corner with his shovel. Such a hard time his wife's having, and in the middle of this awful weather, too."

"She's no better? I'd better take them some chicken soup. Thought I'd make a batch anyway. Does that sound good to you?"

Deep into his second helping of everything, Al nodded. His eyes held a certain glimmer Dottie couldn't place. Something stewed in his head, she was pretty sure. All part of a new relationship, familiarizing yourself with a person's ins and outs. She and Al knew each other fairly well, she thought, but on the brink of matrimony, new things kept popping up to surprise her.

"Saw Ned, too. Bonnie Mae's doing fine down at the boarding house, tuckered out at night without you there."

"Well."

"Well, what?"

"That makes me want to run down there and help her out."

Alarm flickered across his brow, and Dottie spread the suspense over a slice of toast and a few bites of oatmeal. "But not enough to do it, especially on my first full day away."

Al's shoulders loosened. Satisfaction swept her. He really wanted her at home, just where she wanted to be.

Chicken soup was almost too easy to make. And no matter how cute those cherub-faced "Campbell kids" looked on the poster down at the grocery, Dottie prided herself in never forking over twenty-four cents for a can.

Henrietta Perry met her in that aisle last fall, and for once, they agreed about something. Leaning to grab a bag of cornmeal situated near the soup display, Henrietta's nose almost grazed the tip of her hat.

Her tone rose with her torso. "These piddly cans of soup for over twenty cents apiece? Who has the money for it?"

Dottie responded with an "um" as she often did with Henrietta's blatant pronouncements. That gave her a chance to carry on, and Dottie time to formulate a noncommittal reply.

"My father would roll over in his grave if I spent two hard earned dimes for a can of soup that wasn't even homemade. Like I said, who would do that?"

"Someone must, or how could stores continue to stock them?"

"*Humph*. If I had my way, these shelves would be swept clean. Who knows what those factories put into these cans?"

"Right. Well, I need to keep moving, Henrietta."

Dottie might have issued wholehearted agreement, since she'd heard stories about what people had found in cans of vegetables, but to concur with Henrietta would invite a sermon multiplied.

She scooped a cooked fryer from its broth and turned the burner way down. The meat fell right off the bone, so she cut it into bite-sized pieces, the resulting mound enough for the Messerschmidts' supper, hers and Al's, plus some for a potpie tomorrow. Friday. The potpie and leftover soup would last through Saturday—their wedding day.

Like green tomatoes picked before the first hard frost and kept in brown paper bags to ripen, she tucked her questions away. In due time, she'd learned; Al would let her know what he was thinking. She concentrated on chopping onions, celery, and carrots, and when they bubbled away in her savory broth, started to clean up the kitchen.

Then she thought of baking powder biscuits to go along with the soup. Yes, that's what she'd make. It only took a few minutes to stir them up, but in Dottie's opinion, the secret lay in letting the dough sit for a while before baking them. No use trying to hurry bread, even something as simple as baking powder biscuits.

Al didn't show up around noon, so she tided herself over with a sliced apple and a piece of toast. And tea, of course, fresh hot tea. If only Helene had allowed her to drink tea once in a while, the boarding house days would have gone smoother. Dottie chuckled aloud—she bet Bonnie Mae helped herself to as many cups as she wanted, with Helene off in Minneapolis or scooting around the world with her new husband.

Her elbow on the table beside her plate, she leaned her chin on her hand and began talking to herself. "Wonder how long it'll be till wedding bells ring for Bonnie Mae and Tom? That girl changed overnight when she discovered him, or he discovered her. Love's a wonderful thing that way."

That made her think of Al again, but weariness struck. When would she ever catch up on her rest, after those harried days at Helene's beck and call? Must be because of her age. Her energy wasn't what it used to be. She filled the dishpan with dirty utensils and tasted the soup. Her eyes grew heavier. She'd sit down in her armchair for a few minutes before she baked the biscuits, all lined up in crisscross rows on her cookie sheet.

Yes, that's what she'd do, lie down for a little while. Then, while the biscuits baked, she'd add her secret concoction to the soup, and Friedrich would remark on it when he returned her pan. "Berta loved the taste—something special you put in there, eh?"

She hadn't told a soul the ingredient, and with good reason. As a member of her congregation in good standing, what would people say if they knew she added a bit of Owen's brandy—only a bit, mind you—to the thickening flour she stirred in just before serving the soup?

"Confound it all!" Dottie struggled out of her chair at Al's tapping. When she finally untangled herself from her scraggly afghan, he stood under the archway between her living and dining rooms, a mysterious grin on his face.

"Took a little nap? Good for you, Dot. It's about time."

She twitched her shoulders and pawed the floor with her heels, attempting to free herself from the armchair's clutches. Al grinned and offered his hand. "Those new chairs down at the furniture store would be a lot easier to get out of."

"But they cost so much, and a person couldn't go to sleep in them without being knocked out first."

He laughed, the sound so light that it brought the marriage license conundrum back into her thoughts. That was the last thing she remembered thinking about before she fell asleep.

"You're in a jovial mood, Al Jensen."

"Indeed I am, Dorothy Kyle. After all, I'm getting married in

precisely…" He lifted his wristwatch. "Two days, give or take a few minutes."

"Oh my! It's three o'clock already?"

"Three-thirty, Madam."

"The soup…"

"I stirred it on the way in. Looks lovely, and smells even better. Like you."

She blinked and touched her wayward hair. "Oh, I bet."

"I tell you no lies. Tasted it, too, and you did yourself proud. The Messerschmidts will love it, and so will I. That is, if I'm invited to supper."

"Of course you are. Al, what's going on?"

"You don't like it when I'm so happy?"

"Yes, but…" She heard the sputter in her voice and stopped. He would let her know, like he always did.

"Oh, by the way, I picked up the mail." He meandered over to the couch, pulled her down, and plopped a couple of letters in her lap.

One return address was Heston—the courthouse. A squiggle of fear raced through her. Had she forgotten to pay the property taxes or something? Every January, she wrote the year's payment days on the calendar.

With her fingernail, she creased the envelope top, slit it open and unfolded a paper about the size of Cora's graduation certificate. She took a moment to prepare herself for bad news.

"Albert Roy Jensen…Dorothy Marie…state of Iowa…" She looked Al's way. His lips couldn't hold still—he seemed about to burst. "What…how did you manage this?"

He covered her knee with his big hand. "Remember the other day, the Heston Fire Department helped us out?" Mischief crawled from the corners of his lips to his eyes.

"Yes."

"Well, Arnold Smith, the county recorder, and I have had some dealings through the years, and…" He cocked his head. "Let's just say he owed me one. It occurred to me that with the temperature drop and more snow predicted, we might not make it over to the courthouse today, so I signed my name on a piece of paper and gave Arthur our license fee. He thought one of your signatures from your tax records would work, and…"

Dottie topped his hand with hers. "He sent our marriage license. Al, you are a wonder. In the middle of all that chaos and confusion, you remembered. You thought way ahead. You're a living wonder."

He stood and held out his hands to pull her to her feet. "You are, too, Dot. The way you calmed Ruth down—she was beside herself with worry, but you got her busy doing what she could." He drew her close, and she basked in his nearness.

"Why don't you bake those biscuits, and I'll help you deliver everything to Friedrich and Berta? We won't get away without sitting a spell. And then we'll come back here and…how about a game of checkers tonight?"

Full of chicken soup and feeling sleepy, Dottie let Al dry the dishes. With the kitchen back in order, she got a second wind. "You mentioned checkers?"

"I did, but maybe I have a better idea. What if we look over the trip information?"

"Fine. I know you'll beat me at checkers anyway, with all the practice you've been getting."

"Possibly." Al reached for the packet from the back of the table. "Come sit in the living room."

He spread out pictures of a Pullman car, a dining area, and the bright gold cover of the railroad timetables book with the Santa Fe logo at the top. The bottom half boasted men on horseback, cowboys or soldiers riding horses along a ridgeline along a deep canyon.

Indians watched their progress from an even higher escarpment, and between the two, mountain peaks rose in the distance. At the bottom sprawled: *For interesting facts about points along the Santa Fe, just ask for the folder "Along Your Way."*

"Guess I should have ordered that, too." Al's eyes sparkled, and Dottie knew he already had. He pulled the flyer from behind him like a magician.

"You know I've never wanted to make this trip, but your excitement is getting to me."

"Good. I want you to enjoy every minute."

"That's a mighty tall order, I'd say."

"And I say seek and ye shall find. How can you not enjoy real, live mountains and valleys? We'll have views that take our breath away…I think we might even see the Grand Canyon, Dot. Never dreamed I'd actually make it out there."

"You didn't?"

"I've always wanted to. After Nan's funeral, Charlie thought I should get away for a while. 'Dad, why don't you go on a trip? It would do you good.' Del was just getting going at the store then, so I told myself it wouldn't be right to leave yet. You know how it is when you want something, but you don't make the effort to make your dream come true?"

"I expect that describes me wanting to see Cora and the children. But the distance, and the foreignness of everything between here and there scared me." Dottie smoothed one of the flyer's folds. "Still does."

"For me, it was not wanting to tackle something like that alone. Guess I learned way back that things go better with someone by my side. We'll be all right doing it together, don't you think?" His steady breath wisped against her ear.

She wasn't sure how to reply. That moment of panic outside Black's in Waterloo flashed through her consciousness. Hopefully, that feeling, like she was trapped inside her own skin, wouldn't come again on the train, now that she realized its origins. But she hesitated to make any predictions she couldn't fulfill.

"I think so, but just the other day, you saw me…" Heat welled up her neck. "I have to admit I'm looking forward to the journey's end."

They sat in the quiet for a while. Then Al asked her something she'd wondered about, too. "If Owen had lived, do you think you'd have visited Cora by now?"

She wove her fingers through his. "I'm not sure. He got to be quite the homebody, like me, his last couple of years. Losing Bill did something to him."

Al leaned his shoulder into hers. "Well, you're not a homebody any more, dearie. Starting Tuesday, you'll be a world traveler."

Dottie pressed her palm against her collarbone to hold down her fears. She'd believe it once they'd been aboard the train for a few hours.

# Chapter Twenty-five

Saturday dawned cold and clear. Al couldn't sleep, so he rounded a six-block expanse after re-shoveling all the sidewalks. What a week this had been, with the fire and this huge snowstorm. Details from those impossible hours spent on Ruth's roof swirled in his head. He tamped down his anxiety on that day, but since then, he had to squelch it again when he went to bed, and often throughout the night.

He wouldn't allow such ruminations to spoil this occasion, for today, Dot would become his wife. Though she didn't share his excitement about the trip, they would manage just fine. He was sure of it. The sense that all would be well billowed within him—all *would* be well.

Thankful the snow finally stopped, he surveyed Sternville's orderly rows of houses, except for the mess in Harm's yard. You could tell something went awry there not long ago by the pile of debris stashed beside the front porch. Snowdrifts softened it, but still, it was a mess.

He'd never been in that house before the fire. The spurt of energy that filled him that day lurked somewhere down inside—amazing what a body could do when a situation called for immediate action. That inner spurt saved him more than once during the war, and gave him his second chance at life, the chance so many men missed. Now, he was getting another second chance, with Dot.

Still, he'd rather not have that sort of energy surge again if he had a choice. He slowed his pace to calculate the distance from the school's charred bricks to Harm's porch. Could live embers really travel that far?

But he'd even heard the hiss when they hit the shingles. The red bricks on the east end of the school were charred—that whole side would have to be rebuilt.

"We have to accept it, Dad. Some things we can't get to the bottom of."

His tone, so flat and final, ignited Al's desire to trace the wires, follow the clues—but he let go of it. After all, he had other things to think about, and Del had become the unofficial fire chief. But how could he accept not figuring out how the fire started? That puzzled him. He had half a notion to check through the rubble himself, but Del declared the investigation closed.

In the spring, Del could count on a solid order of wood, nails, and paint from the hardware, that was for sure. Probably would take the whole summer to refurbish the building.

Situated a couple of blocks away, the Catholic Church steeple caught Al's eye above several rooftops. At least the Catholic school was large enough to temporarily house the elementary classes. Some Protestant parents weren't happy with the arrangement, but what could they do? Father Plenheim seemed pleasant enough when he came into the hardware to buy extra light bulbs and kerosene heaters.

Al wiped his forehead under his plaid flannel hat lining. "Whew—so glad that snow turned to sleet. Might not have made it otherwise."

In that momentary pause, he saw it. He shook his head, strained toward Harm's house, and waited until the thin dark grey plume ascended again.

A wad of recognition stuck in his throat. Could fire smolder that long, or was his imagination, after a sleepless night, playing tricks on him? He stood still until he counted three more funnels of…yes, it had to be smoke. What else could it be?

He raced around the back of the house and banged on the door with all his might. His heartbeat pulsed in his ears, like thunder or the roar of…No, he wouldn't think about that.

Harm, still in his long johns, opened the door, razor in hand. "You okay, Al? We've got the flu here—couldn't sleep anyway. I keep thinking I smell smoke. Get up six times a night to check. Mabel thinks I've lost my mind."

"Harm, get your boots on quick and come out to the front."

It took only one dark puff to spur Harm into action. "I'll call Central…Hilda's at work this early, ain't she?"

"Yeah, or somebody else is. I'll run and rev up the motor. Your family—if they need a place to stay, send 'em over to my house. Back door's open."

Harm, a large-boned man, ran along the side of the house through snow crunchy with ice and whizzed around the back faster than Al had ever seen him move. Al sprinted kitty-cornered through the Spurgeon's and Wilson's back yards. Huffing and puffing, he rounded the corner and grabbed his set of hardware keys, fumbling for the one to the garage where they kept the fire equipment.

They'd had a few humdingers over the years, but always spread far enough apart that they never developed a workable system. Whoever got there first took charge. In no mind to direct this operation, Al had little choice until somebody else got here.

He cranked open the wide door, his pulse buzzing in his ears. Moist, cold air hit him like a wall. The old boiler kept the building just warm enough so the pipes wouldn't freeze.

A gassy smell met his nostrils when he leaped onto the high truck seat and pumped the accelerator. The weary engine didn't want to roll over. He tried again, hoping somebody had thought to refill the pump tank after the showdown at the school. At least the truck had fuel. Now, if he could only avoid flooding the temperamental thing.

"Come on, come *on!*" The window steamed over, and he wiped it with his coat sleeve.

The cold motor rebelled, but Al kept trying until he thought he'd flooded it. Since he left Harm's, a cloud of unreality enveloped him. He felt as though he inhabited one of those old silent picture shows.

But then tires screeched somewhere—word had gotten to somebody, and a vehicle would pull up any second. In another half-second the fire whistle blew. *Finally.* Al breathed a bit deeper.

About the time the motor finally coughed to life, Del's long stride came into view, and behind him Ben Matthews. Del's face looked as unbelieving as it had when Al told him about marrying Dottie.

"Smoke's coming from Byerly's house. Harm saw it too, and put in the call. Hope that pump truck is filled and ready to go."

Del gaped at him for a couple of seconds, and Al remembered how difficult mornings had always been for his older son. He muttered to the steering wheel. "Come on, Del. I know we just had a big fire, but this is the real thing. Get moving."

Ben grabbed Del, and they scrambled for their coats. Two more men entered, and Ben told them to fill the pump truck. Del and Ben boarded the back. The truck swayed from the building, Al's foot riding the clutch. They careened into the street with the siren squawking in the cold instead of shrieking its usual whistle.

Old Hank Wendt's ancient albatross, a cross between a Model T and a farm truck, cruised into their path from the west. Hank, on his usual morning run to town, veered all over the streets.

Al stomped on the brake, and Hank, a crazed look in his eyes, cranked his steering wheel to the right. A few more men arrived, and Ben and Del directed them to the Byerly house while Al concentrated on keeping the truck from stalling.

Sleepy Sternville hadn't had its coffee yet, though a few shades had been pulled up along the way. That breathless sensation he always experienced just before a summer thunderstorm almost overcame Al, but he maneuvered onto the school street. He parked the truck close to the hydrant, but at the best angle for the hoses to reach the front of the house.

Let Del and Ben manhandle those hoses. He would check to

make sure the children had left the house. That's all that mattered—get everyone out of there before something blew. The furnace, most likely—Harm hadn't updated his, either.

Everything was quiet, so he assumed Harm got the kids out, but checked the bedrooms anyway, the bathroom and attic, every downstairs room, and the basement. He looked around again, for safety's sake, before he emerged with the all clear. Ben and Del manned the hose, sending powerful spray toward billowing smoke.

The resulting sizzle took Al's breath away. His heart pitched into his throat, his eyes stung, but he couldn't crumple to his knees. Not here, not now.

"We can say our vows tomorrow just as well." Dottie stood arms akimbo at the kitchen table as Al ate everything she set before him. Two bowls of chicken soup, a ham sandwich, four buttered biscuits swimming in honey, and glass after glass of milk.

"We have an hour to get ready, and today's the day. No use putting it off."

"But you're frozen through."

"Your soup's taking care of that. Besides, Harm and Mabel need a place to stay, and this way…" He gave her a mischievous grin and worked his brows up and down. "Everything will be legitimate, and the town won't be able to talk."

"They'll still talk—you know that." Dottie piled dishes for the dishpan, shaking her head. "To think of that poor family, with all those children asleep right beside a smoldering fire the past few days. They could all have been…"

She thought through the morning again. "You don't usually take morning walks, do you, Al?"

"My walk down to the store is the closest thing I've taken in years. But this morning, I couldn't sleep, and walking seemed the best medicine." He scanned her profile with glinting eyes and reached for her waist.

He couldn't sleep—was he having second thoughts? But he refused to put off saying their vows. She hated that she couldn't read his eyes, especially when that startled look hovered there, the same one he'd had on the day of the school fire. And some other time—when had that been?

Maybe that night he'd come over to check the furnace filter. Later, he'd mumbled that a person couldn't be too careful with fire.

"For heaven's sake, Al. You're worn out. Really, we don't…" Dottie started to name several good reasons to put the ceremony off till tomorrow, but he stuck out his chin.

"I don't know about you, but I've waited plenty long enough."

With milk all over his involuntary mustache, he looked so funny. She put her arm around his neck, and he pulled her close.

"You're not trying to chicken out on me, now are you?"

"No. It's taken me a little longer, maybe, but I'm looking forward to this as much as you."

"You'd better be, doll. It's not too often a man my age fights a fire and gets married the same day." He shook his head, and that odd cloudiness left his eyes. "I'm headed next door for my clothes. The next time I see you, you'd better be ready to go to the church."

The clock ticked away—exactly one hour. Dottie tidied the kitchen and looked around. When she came home, she would be Al's wife. It didn't seem possible.

In the bedroom, she lifted her new rose dress from its hanger. Millie surprised her with it when they got back from seeing her office on Sunday. One of the newer styles, she said, although Dottie wouldn't have known the difference.

And she brought home three sizes of a lovely black pair of shoes so Dottie could try them on. One fit perfectly.

"The store let you do that?"

"I told them you don't like to shop, and they didn't want to miss a sale." Millie grinned. "There's always a way to get things done." She reached into a shopping bag. "And here's a new package of hosiery, the silkiest I've found."

Now, Dottie wished Mille and Ren could have driven up for the ceremony. "No use wishing—at least we spent Sunday together."

She perched on the edge of the bed, carefully fitted her fingers into the end of the left stocking and drew the softness up her leg, then her right foot. The fine silk eased over her thighs, reminding her she was a woman—a woman getting married. If she had any doubts that Al meant to be joined with her in every way, she certainly didn't after this week of kisses.

Now that the hour drew near, she felt a longing for him she could hardly contain. Tonight, he would sleep right here in this bed. She snapped her garters shut and smoothed the new dress over her slip. When had she felt such softness against her skin?

"I'll wear this on our arrival day in California, too."

The mirror proclaimed her ready—excited, alive, even younger. It was one of those *pinch me* days—to prove it was real. She dug in her purse for a lipstick.

"Wow. You look so…you look real fine, Dot."

She reached to tweak Al's white collar and tie. "And you, Mr. Jensen—is that a new tie you're wearing?"

"It is. I have to say I didn't pick it out, though. Fred brought it by yesterday, since he knew about this before anyone else. You know— the ring and all. He wanted me to have something new to wear."

"He has good taste, I'd say."

"You would, eh?"

She rested her head on his arm, so like a child it caught him by surprise. Her skin, so smooth and clear, her eyes so brown and tender—he needed to be near her, that was all he knew, and God had seen fit to bring them together. The significance of this moment almost paralyzed him with emotion.

Her dimple tempted him too much, so he landed a kiss right there, then a longer one on her lips. A tremor passed through him. Put off getting married? No, not even till tomorrow.

"You sure you want to go through with this, Al?"

His eyes blurred. "As sure as I've ever been of anything." He almost added that he didn't think he could survive another night alone.

"We catch the Atchison, Topeka, and Santa Fe in Fort Madison, Dot. I drew out the route on this map, big enough so we can see where we are at a glance as we go along."

"When did you make this?" Dottie nestled as close to Al as possible. Twenty-four hours they'd been married. She kept reminding herself she wasn't dreaming. Pastor Langley really had pronounced them man and wife.

"Between firefighting and getting ready for our wedding." He gave her a lazy smile and stroked her knee through her bathrobe, a delicate garment Cora sent her for a wedding gift, along with a matching nightgown and her train ticket. She added a note that Millie and Ren sent money to help pay for the tickets.

By the time Dottie opened the girls' gifts, she hardly needed to go shopping anymore. Wearing the new clothing made her feel like a young bride, starting out all over again.

At the wedding, Mrs. Langley exclaimed, "Why Dottie, you look like a million dollars!"

Now, she started planning. If Cora felt up to it, they could shop for Christmas presents in California, instead of having to pack them. She'd started folding things into that old suitcase, but it was Sunday night already, with only tomorrow left to find another decent dress for the trip.

All of a sudden, how she looked mattered—she wanted Al proud to stand beside her. When Mrs. Langley made her million-dollar comment, he scurried to her side.

"Doesn't she? I feel like I must be robbing the cradle."

She gave him a look, but inside, she felt younger. On the trip, she'd have to wash things out at night, but could she do that in the train? The flyer showed small washrooms shared with others, but where would she hang her stockings overnight?

Maybe it would be good, after all, to stay over at some point. Maybe she'd buy some wild Mexican print at a street market like the ones those dancing women flaunted in the flyer. A flush spread to her cheeks at the idea.

Al pointed to the extreme southeast corner of Iowa. "Del offered to drive us down there, and found someone to work at the hardware for the day. The train leaves at one-thirty, so we'll have to take off about eight o'clock."

"I should pack a lunch, then?"

"Sounds good. I hope we have a little time to look around. If I'm not mistaken, this station is where I met the troop train in '17. Bet the town has changed so much I won't recognize a thing." He focused on the flyer again. "I think we start out on the Ak-Sar-Ben Zephyr—know what that means?"

"No, what?"

"Nothing. It's Nebraska spelled backwards. Some yokel had a brilliant idea."

"Must have been an Army man—they're always making up abbreviations. Owen had to translate Bill's first letters for me."

"I know what you mean. Anyway, one train runs east to Burlington in the daytime, and west to Lincoln at night." He read some more. "No, wait. Sorry. We start out on the Advance Flyer operated by the Chicago, Burlington, and Quincy Line, switch in…" His enthusiasm vibrated to Dottie, in spite of her fears.

"Want to read the menu? Says here 'food fit for a king.'"

Eat on the train? How could anyone eat while they were moving? Al's voice pulsed with the thrill of adventure.

"Dot, if I'm reading this right, we go through Dodge City, where that famous shootout—"

Someone banged on the back door, and he went to answer it. Snitches of conversation traveled through the dining room. "Pipe busted. Flooded the kitchen. Could we get some help from Delbert…"

"Sure thing. I'll call him, and he'll meet you down at the hardware, Harm." She could picture Al patting Harm's shoulder. "Don't think a thing about it."

The back door banged shut, and the telephone's gears ground as Al rang Central. "No, Hilda, not exactly a big emergency. Just get Del for me, will you?"

Dottie pushed back into the cushions. Hilda would never change. But she did control herself during the fires, at least. Al's voice sounded so steady as he explained things to Del. His whole kitchen was flooded, yet he stayed calm.

"Harm's headed to the hardware right now. Nope, I'm not going over." Al returned scratching his head. "What next? A pipe burst in the kitchen. Harm patched it up, but he's afraid it won't last long—bound to happen, I suppose, with so many more people in there all of a sudden."

"That makes me think, we haven't ever finished talking about which house…"

"No, but I've been thinking, why don't I sell mine to Harm—he doesn't know if it'd be worth the cost to rebuild."

"Sell your house? I was thinking the same thing about this one."

"This is nowhere near big enough for Mabel and Harm's clan. I know about the family history next door, but…" A faraway look entered Al's eyes. "When memories fill every corner, it's a mix of good and bad. Time to leave the past behind."

"Are you sure?"

"So sure, I mentioned it to Harm today after church. He and Mabel talked it over this afternoon, and he just told me over the phone they're planning on buying it. I had no idea it would happen that fast—I was going to tell you about it this afternoon." He tapped the back of her hand. "Why? Don't you like having me here?"

Dottie snuggled in under his arm. The way he tightened it around her assured her he'd gotten her message.

She looked up to see his smile. "Did you see Henrietta's face today in church?"

"I did, and she kept her distance. I feel sorry for her—all those cookies and pies she brought you, Al. She must have had her hopes up."

"She just needed something to do. Hopefully, she'll get a hankering to take some to the boarding house, where they're really needed." He glanced at the pale yellow drapes. "D'I ever tell you about that one day last fall when she walked right in with a pie? I'd been cleaning, and hid behind the drapes."

"Did she see you?"

"Nah. It was pretty shadowy. But she stood there for a couple of minutes. She carried on quite a conversation all by herself... couldn't understand why I wasn't home, since she hadn't seen me walk by her house on my way downtown."

"You just waited for her to leave?"

"What else could I do? It was the day of our first real date...the first time I invited you over after our little fishing trip. I had to clean the house, and if Henrietta started talking about her gallbladder, I'd never have finished."

Al lifted Dottie's chin. "I was mighty serious about you way back then, Dot. Mighty, mighty serious."

# Chapter Twenty-six

Dottie and Al sank into kitchen chairs for some tea amidst piles of boxes. They'd moved Al's tools into her shed. Her attic held a few more things, but most of the furniture stayed put next door. Del asked for a couple of pieces, and agreed to store Nan's Hoosier cupboard for Charlie and his wife.

"Sure glad Harm agreed to buy the rest." Al's tiredness gave way to a lighthearted sensation—it felt good to be rid of all that stuff. "If anybody told me a week ago about the fires, selling my house, and moving in such a short time, I'd have thought they just flipped their lid."

"You and Harm signed the contract?"

"Signed, sealed, and about to be delivered. Shorty pushed the paperwork through at the bank—lowered his standards this one time if we kept it quiet. Harm promised the down payment by Friday, and he'll pay fifteen dollars a month for the next five years—won't hurt us to have regular money coming in."

One word stayed with Dottie—*us*. She wouldn't have to worry about money any longer.

"You never did get to go shopping, Dot. Do you have what you need?"

"I found just the thing at the Wearwithall this morning, but I feel like we must be forgetting something."

Al gave her a grin. "I'll run down to the bank for some cash. We're married, and we've got our tickets. That's all we need, sweetie pie."

Al left the bank with two hundred dollars cash and steered toward home. But the Benson Market sign reminded him of old Tibbs—he hadn't felt the need to stop in lately. Maybe he'd take a minute to say hello.

His beard moving with every tobacco chew, Tibbs manned his stool beside the crackling stove. The sharp tang of pickled herring wafted from the cooler. Filled shelves offered an assortment of foodstuffs and automobile necessities.

"I'll be jiggered—Albert Jensen. I started checkin' the obituaries, you hain't stopped in for so long!"

Al expected ribbing, but maybe his newly married status hadn't reached the Market yet. "I've been busy—Christmas season. Took Dottie down to see Millie and Ren last Sunday."

"To Burlington?"

"No, Cedar Rapids."

"Oh, yeah. It's the Coulter girl what lives down by the river. How's Millie and hers doin'?"

"Fine." Al waited to be quizzed, but Tibbs changed the subject.

"D'I ever tell you me and Millie's Grandpa—that'd be Dottie's Pa—went coon huntin' over by Heston?"

"Only twenty times." Tibbs' daughter-in-law Janet threw her jibe, but Tibbs paid no attention.

"That old fella was a mean one. Beat his dog when he couldn't tree a coon, and that's the truth. This was 'bout the time your daddy built the hardware."

Al's ears perked up. Tibbs filed away family tales to fit whoever walked in. But he didn't recall hearing anything about Dottie's family.

"Not a good man?"

"Low-down. That night he wanted a coon, one way or t'other, 'cause they'd like to starve the next day, if he didn't scare up somethin'."

Al ransacked his slim knowledge of Dottie's childhood. Owen mentioned her father's failed farming ventures, a line of older brothers and sisters, her Mama dying young.

Tibbs spat in the general direction of a brass spittoon, but squiggles hit dry floorboards all around. Others hissed against the iron stove. Al jerked at the sound, but tamped down his reaction—he'd been doing fine. Being with Dottie was what he'd needed.

"Them was hard times. D'I ever tell you about my daddy bein' a Holy Roller?"

Al shook his head. "Don't believe so."

"He was one, true enough. Tried to make his works match his religion, he did. When I got home after hunting, I told Daddy what Dottie's Pa said, and wouldn't you know it? Daddy got the generosity in him, and we hauled a ham out to their shack right then and there."

"Wasn't it about ten miles?"

"That it was, and danged cold—worst winter I recall. Daddy said, 'That ornery Colwell thrashes his kids regular, for no reason— they're too scared to set foot in the store. Cute as a bug's ear, that little one is. Can't let 'em go without food. No sirree.'

"We skulked through the pasture, only a moon sliver above us. Hung that ham on a nail right over the doorway, with a gunnysack of two loaves of bread and a pound of butter so's they'd bat Colwell in the face next morning."

Tibbs sucked his few remaining teeth. Al took a step back, just in case.

"Wonder if that beatin' kept the hound from puttin' up a fuss? Daddy made me vow to never mention what we done to a living soul—it was his good works."

Several things about the story amazed Al, not the least that Tibbs kept their good deed quiet. "Did Colwell ever mention it?"

"Many a time. Swore things turned around for him that day, and the crops got better that summer, and they had an easier winter next time around. 'Course, the banks went haywire, and everything

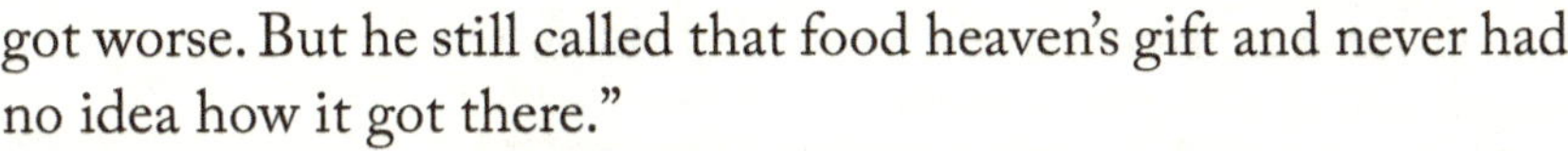

got worse. But he still called that food heaven's gift and never had no idea how it got there."

He resettled on his stool. "Yup. My Daddy believed the kind of fear that men like Colwell put into their young'uns lasts forever. You gotta love it out—no other way."

A couple of farmers walked in, and Tibbs waved them over. Al listened a few minutes longer but faded from the growing crowd as the workday ended. He made his way home to Dottie's house—home, and organized his boxes around in the shed.

One of Tibb's father's statements from long ago thrummed through his brain, over and over. "He thrashes them kids regular."

The kitchen light beckoned, and he visualized Dottie, getting ready though the trip scared her to the bone. She truly was a wonder, growing up like that, but still raising three strong children.

Now, he carried Tibbs' advice with him—to help her overcome her father's legacy, he was more than willing to love those fears right out of her.

Dottie recognized Bonnie Mae's voice first, then George's. The distinct bang of spoons on pan lids jolted her fully from sleep. She shook Al's shoulder. "Someone's here."

He jerked upright. "Wha…?"

The babble of singing, shouting and clacking increased.

Al drew back the drape. "Why, they're here to chivaree us. There's Ned—even Bert Smith's out there."

"Oh, no."

"Might as well get your robe on. They're not going away."

Dottie's Big Ben alarm clock never lied—it was midnight. At least Al had gotten a few hours of solid sleep. She found her moccasins and followed him to the front door, where the jabbering mob now congregated.

"Ready for this?"

Ready or not, here they came. Folks drifted in, bringing frosty air with them. Boots and coats piled the entryway like a rubbish heap.

Bonnie Mae, with a boarding house lid and wooden spoon in her hands, grinned from ear to ear.

"Is this your idea?" Green eyes glinted. George and Ned nodded their heads.

Henry Olson stepped up. "Congratulations." He held out an envelope. "Figured you could use a little extra, so we went together…"

Dottie hung onto Al's hand, thankful she didn't have to say anything.

"Why, you sure didn't need to…" Al leaned toward her. "Dottie and I thank you. Find yourselves some seats. We'll get some coffee going."

Bonnie Mae bustled George and Ned toward the kitchen, each with a big box in their hands. "We brought some food, hope you don't mind."

"No, of course not." Dottie started to follow, but the redhead gave her curls a firm shake. "You stay out here and talk to people. We've got the kitchen covered."

Two hours later, the last guest left. Dottie collapsed against Al as he opened the envelope. "Don't know when I've been this bamboozled."

"Me neither. And to think they put together fifty dollars—maybe I'll splurge on a cowboy hat. What about you?"

"Come on, let's dream about what to spend it on."

But she kept going over their friends' faces—even the Langleys joined the group. And Bonnie Mae instigated it—how that girl had changed.

Before she left, Bonnie Mae whispered, "Tom would be here, but the children need their sleep."

Dottie whispered back, "Let us know how your plans develop, okay?"

If freckles could beam, Bonnie Mae's did.

At the last gas station before Fort Madison, Del filled up his 1940 Oldsmobile. Sunlight saturated the back seat. Last night's festivities left Dottie sleepy. It would have helped if she could follow the men's conversation above the motor's loud hum. She got in on the beginning, but then only snitches wafted her way.

"I heard they stopped production of this model at 200,000 for the war effort."

"Sure am glad I took the plunge and bought early. This hydra-matic drive is the real thing, even though it cost fifty-seven dollars extra. Besides, I like the four forward speeds and no clutch."

"Did you know the Army used it on their tanks—both the M5 Stuart and the M24 Chaffee?"

"Nope, hadn't heard that. I suppose the car manufacturers…" Del stopped the truck for a noisy cargo train yet continued talking, but the noise and watching the passing cars gave Dottie a sick feeling. She gave up on keeping track of their exchange and closed her eyes. The rumbling of the train was the last she remembered when she woke up. The railroad crossing had long ago disappeared, and Al and Del still chatted away in the front seat.

Now wide-awake, she touched her new dress. Yesterday, she studied Brenda's racks down at the Wearwithall. Thankfully, Gladys stayed behind the counter, giving her time to get used to the idea of shopping again. Against the far wall, a pretty tulip print stood out to Dottie. She lifted it from the rack and turned it around.

"Go ahead—try it on if you'd like. "It's sanforized—pre-shrunk cotton, and only one percent shrinkage in the rayon. After you wash it, it'll fit the same as it does today." Gladys gestured toward a small door in the back right corner.

Dottie decided to take the plunge. In the dressing room, she quickly took off her dress and made the switch. The button-up front had a blousy effect, with plenty of room. Wide lapels flattened against her collarbones. Al enjoyed flowers, and it would require less ironing than plain cotton. Red and yellow tulips against a sky blue and white background appealed to her in this smudgy, gray-white season.

Guilt assailed her, since that beautiful new Sunday dress from Millie already graced her closet. But she couldn't wear it all the way to California. And her other dresses had hung there for years, most of them threadbare or faded.

"It won't hurt you to buy some nice clothes, Mom." Millie pressed an envelope into Dottie's palm when she hugged her good-bye.

"The dress and shoes are for Christmas—this is your wedding gift. Wish we could come, but our company Christmas party's been planned for months, and I'm in charge."

Dottie waited till she got home to open the letter, which turned out to be an expensive card—Millie sacrificed a quarter for it, and placed two ten-dollar bills inside.

But she brought along only one bill today, determined to return home with change for the trip, or to treat Cora to something new.

The three-quarter-length sleeves felt smooth between her fingers, and the dress would go nicely with Al's blue shirt. Maybe they'd have somebody take a picture with his Brownie camera for a memento.

The sign above the rack proclaimed SALE DRESSES, yet the tag still read S7.98, a hefty investment. But when Dottie viewed her profile in the three-way mirror, Gladys said, "Whoowhee, Dottie Kyle—I mean Jensen—you look spiffy!" She peered at the ticket. "Oh, this dress is also Spunblend—Montgomery Ward's fabric."

Alvina Flugge entered the store about that time. Her eyes bugged out when she spied Dottie. So…she must have heard, too.

Turning to see if the skirt fell straight, Dottie concentrated on her image.

Gladys adjusted darts in the bodice and murmured in Dottie's ear. "I'm so glad for you. If I'd known, I'd have brought you a little gift, but I'd like to take another 25% off for you today, if you'll accept."

Twenty-five percent? Why, that was two whole dollars—the

price suddenly dipped to $5.98. She'd almost decided to make the purchase anyway, but the offer sealed the deal.

"I hear you and Al are going out to see Cora. I bet you can hardly wait."

"We leave tomorrow—I'm jittery about it—but now, at least I've got what I need. Thank you for the discount."

"A pair of slacks would be comfortable on such a long trip."

"No, I think I'm too old for such things."

"*Phfft*…there's no such thing, Dottie. Want to try on a pair? You've got a good figure for them." Brenda folded the new dress into a white cardboard box lined with tissue paper and figured the bill.

"We do have a sale on hosiery and women's pants this week."

"Millie already gave me a brand-new pair."

"But surely, you'll need more than one, getting in and out of train cars and going up and down steps…"

Yes, she might. What would she do if all of a sudden, a run started in one leg? Gladys waved toward a display featuring some silky nylons.

Alvina sidled up to the counter. "Mind if I check out, Dottie? I've got to get over to the Ladies Aid meeting to plan the Sunday-after-Christmas potluck."

"No, go right ahead."

Alvina placed a pair of nylons on the counter. "Remember how hard it was to find these during the war? My sister's niece out in New York paid eight dollars for a pair one time. Can you believe that?"

"Yes, I sold out of them. A soldier came in one day—wounded and sent home to Heston. He'd met an English girl and wanted to send her some. Guess it was even harder to find stockings there.

"He drove over, all red-faced, and asked for a pair—I only had one, and he scooped it up."

"Whatever happened to him?"

"He moved to England after the war, found a job, and married that girl—she wouldn't leave her mother."

Visions of that run for the whole world to see convinced Dottie to add another purchase. After all, she'd have spent that much anyway, without the discount. All-in-all, for someone who avoided shopping, Dottie thought she'd done rather well with her purchases, and this morning when she put on the new dress, the mirror declared its approval.

Now, three hours later, Del stopped at a gas station and got out to talk with the serviceman. Al reached over the seat. "Want to get out for a few minutes while Del fills up? We made great time." His fingers skimmed her hem. "Is this a new dress? Sure like these bright colors on you."

His eyes revealed something Dottie didn't recall seeing for a long time. She got out to stretch her legs and use the restroom. When she returned to the car, that look still hovered in Al's eyes, and the second time she saw it, she put a name to it—pride and pleasure.

# Chapter Twenty-seven

Al closed the grocery bag. "Thanks for bringing us, Del. Your reward is more cookies to eat on the way home." They shook hands.

"Thanks for helping with things while we're gone, too." Dottie shifted her purse. "If you could have Edie stop by and water my fern in the north window?"

"All right. Have a good trip, and give us a call when you get there." Del reached into his pocket. "Want some extra quarters for the pay phones?"

"Thanks, but I brought a few dollars' worth. Oh, here,"—Al held out a five dollar bill—"take this for the gas. Don't know how we'd have gotten down here otherwise."

"All aboard! Car number three. Step right up, folks."

"No, Dad, you keep that. With that flu lasting so long, we haven't bought Christmas gifts. Consider this yours, all right?"

"Okay. I left a few things at the store for you and the family. Say hello to Edie and the boys, and have a merry Christmas."

"All aboard!"

Dottie bit her bottom lip. Her grip on her purse handle would have choked a strong man to death.

*Better get her in quickly before she changes her mind.* Al picked up the small case, grabbed Dottie's elbow and took a step, but she didn't move.

"Come along, Dot. Time to get on."

She swallowed. "Al, I'm…"

He saw a little girl with red marks on her legs from her own father's hand and stood as close to her as possible. Finally, she raised her chin—he'd seen that look before, in battle—eyes too wide, skin too white, teeth clenched. For half a second, he wondered if the trip was worth what she had to go through.

But he pecked her cheek and whispered, "We'll be together the whole time. I can't wait to see the U.S. with you beside me. Just keep your mind on little Jeffy Owen and that sweet baby girl."

Her breath came in uneven spikes. She took a step, faltered, and sought his face again. He squeezed her elbow and spoke right into her ear.

"You'll be all right, Dot. You can do this." She swiped at her eyes, but moved with him toward the door. One step up…two. That was all he could have asked.

The constant rumble and movement bothered Dottie less each hour, and she loved meeting folks from all over the country. A young couple from Pennsylvania, the Kerns, shared their dinner table. The wife fascinated her with images of their 150-year-old home near Boston.

But her husband, unlike most returned soldiers, needed to talk.

"Bodies piled up—skin and bones waiting for the furnaces." An involuntary shudder took him. "Rooms full of flea-bitten clothes, rats crawling all over jewelry and silver pieces, treasures prisoners brought with them not knowing they faced certain death."

He bowed his head. "Never smelled anything so awful." Dottie's focus moved from his face to Al's—she didn't know which one harbored more distress. Al looked a lot like he had the night he'd proposed—his color faded, and his jaw tightened more with each word the man said. At the word *furnace*, he cringed.

Mrs. Kern patted her husband's arm. "Leave those memories across the ocean, Benjamin, where they belong."

The man stared out the window at brown and grey Nebraska countryside. "Those were my people—I can't stop thinking of them, no matter how I try."

Al made a fist and stretched his fingers, back and forth, again and again, staring at the back of his hand like some foreign object.

"I need to…I'm…some fresh air." His voice didn't sound right. He gave Dottie a glance she couldn't interpret and staggered toward the back of the car.

"Hang on, man. In about five minutes, I have to set the switches. It's against regulation, but I'll let you stand on the deck while I work."

His head between his knees, Al slumped nearby. Any other time, he'd revel in the chance to visit the brakeman's cupola in the observation car. Trains had fascinated him since he was a teenager. But he didn't even remember how he got here. The last he remembered, he'd grasped the car door, trying to push it open, and a swarthy man approached.

"I'll have you know, they just delivered this fancy new yellow-painted one in June—used to be red. The yellow's supposed to attract rich customers, they say." The brakeman shrugged. "Maybe it'll work." He smelled of oil and grease, dirt and sweat.

"You're not the first—plenty of fellas fresh from the war spent time back here—just needed a little outside air. Something about long hours closed up like this brings out the worst in a man. Nothin' to be ashamed of—who knows what all they saw. You're too old for that, though?"

If he expected an answer, he would be disappointed. It was all Al could do to hang onto his dinner. He couldn't figure why the man brought him up here, except that the air was cooler, even with the windows shut tight. He pressed his back against solid steel and let the cold quench the wildness running through him.

What about Dottie? He'd vowed to take care of her, but now he'd left her with that fellow and his wife. Hopefully, he'd stop rehashing the war and Dottie would find her way back to their sleeping compartment. He had to get back soon, but not yet—the mention of fresh air hung between him and the brakeman like a promise. Once he got a whiff of it, he'd be all right—he knew he would.

The car swayed as the train slowed. His rescuer jabbed his shoulder. "Here we go. Stay with me."

He gave the order like a senior officer. The back door opened. The first whoosh of air startled Al, mixed with dusty rail yard exhaust, screeches, and clanks. The brakeman's face came close to his. "Stand right here. You leave and I lose my job, hear?"

"I…won't…leave." Cool night air widened Al's windpipe. He straightened against the outer wall, aware of the switchyard's lights studding the night. He looked up to a velvet sky, unchanged, reliable. The crash of railcars connecting and disconnecting, the exchange of workers' voices surrounded him. He breathed again, deeper.

Nothing had changed—the world still went on. Trains came and went, people carried out their jobs as always. If that Kern fellow hadn't talked about those bodies, he'd have been all right. But the thought of—no, he mustn't dwell on what that man saw—especially furnaces. He had enough fire in his own memories—such old recollections—why did they persist?

But none of it mattered now—Dottie mattered, that was all. Al arched his neck and stretched. The love of a good woman waited for him up ahead—he was a lucky man.

Boots on steel stairs, human scents that kept him together during the past half hour, the brakeman's rough glove on his hand. Brown eyes, real dark, like Dot's, close and sincere. White around the temples—must be about his age.

"Better now?"

"Better. Thanks."

"Great War?"

Al nodded. "Yeah—infantry." The man deserved at least that much.

"Umm." A heavy hand clapped him on the shoulder. "Me, too."

The train lurched, waking Dottie. Al must have slipped into bed sometime during the night. Now, he drew her close. The shadows in their compartment obscured his face, but something flickered through his eyes.

"You're all right?"

He didn't answer, and Dottie didn't repeat her question. She dozed, but he fidgeted the rest of the night, called out a couple of times, and looked haggard by noon.

"Good meatloaf."

"Yes, with a tang I can't trace, too. I can hardly believe I haven't cooked for two days, Al."

"Woman of leisure." His grin belied the dark circles under his eyes.

"Why don't you take a nap? I'm doing just fine—maybe I'll sit in the viewing section for a while."

When he agreed, she knew whatever he'd experienced last night was no passing trouble. Her thoughts flitted back to Monday when she returned from the Wearwithall. Del carried Al's Army trunk into the kitchen, but the catch broke loose. Some papers fell out, along with a thick envelope.

Al scooped them up, but the envelope escaped, and a purple ribbon attached to a gold heart-shaped medal landed on the floor. Dottie held it out to him, but he shrank away, his voice as gruff as she'd ever heard it.

"Throw that back in the trunk." He thrashed in bed throughout that night, too.

Hopefully he slept now. Maybe he reacted to traveling more than he let on—strange, because she was doing all right now. She walked through the next car and found a young woman sitting alone.

"Do you mind if I join you?" The girl gestured for her to sit.

"I'm Dottie—Dottie Jensen, from Iowa."

"Kimiko Tagashi. I go to school in Chicago—Bible school." Dottie leaned in to hear her quiet voice.

"You're going home for Christmas?"

The girl nodded.

"Your parents live on the coast?"

They chatted for a few minutes before Kimiko opened her book to study. The murmur of voices in the car lulled Dottie into a dreamy state. Could she really be sitting in a train, having just met a Japanese woman? With the steady roll of the car, her mind traveled to Millie and her family getting ready for Christmas and then back to Al, as always.

She marveled at his patience with her—there in the Fort Madison station, she'd been so reluctant to set foot on the first step. But with her hand in his, she'd found the strength. What would she do without him? Seemed impossible she'd lived so close to him since Owen passed, yet so unaware of his kind spirit.

She didn't deserve him, that's all. Why, he thought of her all the time—and he'd put aside everything for this trip. What could she ever give him in return for all he'd done for her? Kimiko took out a spiral notebook, and Dottie couldn't help noticing the page she turned to, labeled "Internment." Just then, the girl looked up.

"Oh, sorry—I noticed your title—what does that mean?"

"Internment?" Kimiko's voice lowered even more than normal. She glanced behind them. "You want to know about this?"

"I'm not sure I've heard that word before."

"After Pearl Harbor, the police sent people like my parents away from their homes. They believed we might have something to do with the attacks."

The first thing Dottie thought of was Bonnie Mae. She would be furious about this. Next, she thought of the way Sternville people had treated Friedrich and Berta during the war. It happened almost overnight, after somebody made a comment here, another one there. Even at church, people argued about patronizing the jewelry store.

She patted the young woman's arm. "I'm so glad the war is over—I've always wanted to meet someone from Japan Were you born there?"

"No, Ma'am, near Los Angeles. My parents left Japan in 1910."

"You're visiting them now?"

"It's been three full years—when I left, they were interned at Polston. The authorities let me go back to college because my administrator vouched for me. Now…" Again, she surveyed behind the viewing seat she and Dottie shared. "They live farther inland from Los Angeles now, where my father found work on a farm."

"Has he always been a farmer?"

Kimiko dropped her eyes. Dottie could barely hear her response. "He was a fisherman, like his father and grandfather before him, but…" She stared out the window for a full minute. "Some people lost everything when they returned from the camps—that's how it was for my parents."

"They lost your home?"

Kimiko nodded. "Everything, Mrs. Jensen."

Dottie didn't know what to say. They each lapsed into their own thoughts as mile after mile of rocky landscape flew by. Dottie repeated her new name to herself. Dottie Jensen. Mrs. Albert Jensen. She flashed back to the weariness in Al's face at dinner. Hopefully, he was sound asleep.

Their trip was half over, but even now, only the scenes passing by as they moved steadily westward convinced her she wouldn't soon wake from a good dream. Soon, she would see Cora. Soon, she would hold Jeffy and Joy in her arms.

Sometime later, she caught Kimiko's eye. "Do you have brothers and sisters?"

"Yes, one brother—and one who died in the war. In Tunisia."

A jolt like electricity hit Dottie. "Tunisia?" That was it—that was where Bill died. "My son died there, too—in '42."

"I'm so sorry. That was when my brother died. Do you know anything more?"

"It was a battle at a Pass. I should have it memorized…"

"The Kasserine Pass?"

Dottie held her throat. She could only nod.

"Why, Mrs. Jensen, what if your son and my brother knew each other?"

Dottie pictured Bill and a young Japanese man who looked a lot like Kimiko on the same mission. Maybe he hadn't died alone—maybe someone else was right beside him.

She covered Kimiko's slim hand with hers. "I think they would have been friends."

The door opened, and a couple of people shuttered through the car. After a while, Dottie leaned toward Kimiko. "Dear, where is your other brother?"

"I'm not certain. He studied law at Berkeley when the injunction came—the authorities took him to a different camp from the one we stayed in—Manzanar, I think. We lost contact. I heard he went back to finish school. He was almost through his second year when…"

Her jaw worked, and Dottie marveled at her lovely complexion. "We haven't seen him since then. I'm praying we can all be together now."

"I didn't realize people were pulled away from their homes like that. A town near us back in Iowa kept German prisoners of war, but…"The girl's expression told her anything she might say could cause more pain.

Driving through Algona, not that far west of Sternville, Mrs. Grundy's son had spied a German work crew out in a field. But Kimiko and her family were *Americans*.

"My parents taught us to forgive and forget, but I doubt I'll ever forget that camp. My father became so upset, I thought he might die."

Her voice became a whisper. "Some men did, and many went back to Japan when they had the chance. The authorities passed laws to keep us from going back to our home and confiscated our property—everything my parents worked so hard to earn."

Dottie swallowed. Al probably knew about these camps—it seemed he knew what that Mr. Kern was talking about last night, too. She would ask him later.

The war years tumbled through her memory. At the news of Bill's death, she withdrew, even from listening to the radio. Cora, in her junior year of high school, carried on with her activities, but many nights, Dottie heard her crying in her room. Sometimes she went in, and they held each other. But except for their little household, she shut out the world—her mind seemed wrapped in cotton.

Even at Cora's graduation a year and a half later, Dottie saw Bill walking among the robed students. When it was over, Cora swore she saw him sitting between Dottie and Millie, applauding for her.

Not long after that, Cora begged to go to California. The war droned on, but Dottie lost the heart to care. Then Owen lost so much weight and became sick. After he died, when Helene appeared with the offer of work, Dottie accepted like a greedy mongrel at the cats' dish.

But she'd never been forced from her home or made to live in a camp like a criminal. Now, her sympathy welled for this slight girl who had lost so much.

"I'm sorry you had to go through all that. So very sorry…it wasn't right at all."

Kimiko waved good night, and Dottie set out for the sleeper. Talking this through with Al would help.

# Chapter Twenty-eight

"Winona, Flagstaff, Seligman, Kingman…we might have stayed over in any one of these places. I hope you don't mind not using that stayover option, Al?" Dottie took a sip of her water. "It's just that the closer we get to Cora, the more I hate wasting any time getting there to help her."

Al, his mouth full of what the menu called refried beans, made no reply for a moment. Then he reached across the table for Dottie's hand.

"It's all right. We can always stop some other time when we're traveling. As it is, we've seen more than I ever could have imagined. Actually, I have the same urge as you—we need to get there as soon as we possibly can."

As the sun sank and the sights disappeared, they lingered over dishes of ice cream. What wonderful food they'd enjoyed, and Al—what a wonderful husband—none of her intuitions seemed to bother him.

"Better sleep tonight. Tomorrow's the big day." One last glance out the window showed a mileage sign for Needles, California. Dottie dozed off thinking about how a town like that got its name. For once, Al seemed to fall asleep easily, and so did she. When she woke, he'd already slipped away without waking her. By the time she dressed, he came to find her.

"We're close to Santa Monica, Dot."

"Isn't that where we take one of those electric buses to Los Angeles?"

"That's right. California's a glory, honey. Come and see."

"Can't believe I slept so long."

"You'll need it, with those little ones waiting for their Grandma." He dug into their bag and passed her some toast and a boiled egg he'd saved from breakfast. "I'll go find you a cup of tea. By now, they're headed to meet us. Bet Cora's excited."

A shiver ran through Dottie, but his hand on her arm steadied her. She could hardly wait to see Cora and the children. But Cora's voice sounded strained last night on the phone.

At least there'd been no static, but a person's tone revealed so much. Dottie would bet her last boarding house pay that Cora had troubles.

"Something bothering you?"

"Not that I can explain right now. I didn't like the tremble in Cora's voice."

The conductor called their stop. "Can you manage my jacket and these two bags? I'll run straight for our baggage so we don't miss the bus."

"Whatever it's like, we'll face it together, all right?" They left the train, and he issued instructions. "Stay right here, now. I'll come back for you."

He clutched her hand for a brief moment before running off. Chills ran over Dottie's shoulders in spite of the warm day, in spite of knowing for certain Al would be back. She stared at the crowd on the platform. No one even carried a coat—it felt as warm as July outside.

Her jitters decreased when Al dragged their suitcases over, and within half an hour they boarded a streetcar. Its battered green fenders almost dragged the street, and a sign on the front announced Union Station. A single headlight centered below the front window. From the roof, a black cable connected to a line running down the track.

Despite that old suffocating sensation threatening, Dottie steeled herself to board. She'd come too far to falter on the very last leg of their journey, and Cora waited at the other end.

Al sheltered her with his arm. "Look around us, Dot. Doesn't seem that different from Iowa in summertime, do you think?"

Deep green fields stretched in every direction—was that onions she saw, a whole field of them? Roadside stalls of fruit and bright flowers, and white cottages with children at play drifted by. Dottie found herself back in that restaurant on the way to Waterloo, when Al asked her to marry him. He stumbled over his words, and volunteered to chaperone her on this trip before professing his love or producing her engagement ring.

But every move he made that night bespoke sincerity. He truly did love her—she'd never felt it more than at this moment. Even though the streetcar tilted precariously around corners, he never let go of her elbow.

Still, she couldn't shake what seemed like a premonition. Did it concern Al, or Cora and the children—Dottie couldn't tell. Though she bade it vanish, a few seconds later, it returned, as real as the intriguing scenes on both sides. And then the car screeched to a stop near a mass of people waiting near a small wooden platform. Dottie swallowed her gut reaction to flee and searched for Cora.

She couldn't find her in the crowd—what if no one came to pick them up? Finally, a child's cry rose above the faces, and Dottie's heart raced double time—was that the voice she'd heard over the telephone?

At the platform's far edge, a little boy a head above the crowd waved his pudgy hand—surely, that must be Jeffy Owen. Yes, he had dark hair and eyes like Dennis. But the woman standing beside him, midriff distended, feet wide apart—could that be Cora? Dottie reached for Al's arm.

"I see them. The baby's in that carriage—see, Cora's leaning on the handle. Oh, Al. she's sick. She's real sick. I can tell from here."

"I'm Al. We met once in Iowa—good to see you again." The two men shook hands, and Dennis offered Jeffy's hand, too. Al liked the way Dennis met his eyes, and his protective arm around Cora.

"Say hello to Mr. Jensen, Jeffy." The little fellow launched his sturdy torso straight into Al's arms.

"We're getting to know each other right off the bat." Al gave Jeffy a squeeze.

Dennis bent for the suitcases. "What'd you pack in these, Iowa soil and rocks?"

"From the looks of things, California soil is fertile enough already. We probably did bring too much for just a few weeks."

Dennis hoisted the suitcases, biceps bulging under his plaid cotton shirt. He swung close enough to reveal determined dark eyes and afternoon growth along his jawline. Al read stark concern there.

"We hope you'll stay a lot longer than that."

The tears simply wouldn't stop. The sight of Cora's swollen face sent a disturbing warning to Dottie's core. Even her daughter's slim nose was unrecognizable. At the same time, she wept for joy at the sight of little Joy and Jeffy Owen.

She hugged Cora and leaned into Jeffy's wiggly body, safe in Al's arms. "Ooh, it's so good to see you. And Joy—how beautiful!"

"Joy Marie, Mom…after you. Go ahead—take her out if you want to."

"I've never wanted anything more." It had been so long since she'd held a grandchild this young—eight months old. Al stepped closer, so Jeffy could touch Dottie's shoulder.

"Gamma?" Saucer-sized blue eyes embraced her.

"Yes, sweetheart." She took a deep breath. All her anxieties shrank into nothing. No price was too great for this surge of satisfaction, completely surrounded by family.

"Have you eaten?"

"We did—we're fine. Kind of worn out, but the grandkids will energize us. Right, Dot?" Al held out his handkerchief. She couldn't answer, but hoped he recognized her gratitude. "But if you folks planned to eat, that's all right with us. We'll take you out."

Dennis turned to Cora, who clasped his arm tighter. "Let's go straight home."

Relief flooded Dottie, busy with Al's hankie and the baby. She didn't want to go anywhere but home—Cora's paleness told her they'd better get there as fast as they could.

Al's whisper revealed his tenderness. "We're going to be busy, you and I."

It was the perfect thing to say. One part of her wanted to curl up in a rocker with this precious baby girl, another wanted to romp in the sunshine with Jeffy, but something even stronger cautioned her. Cora looked completely worn out. Even talking took a toll on her.

Dennis motioned them across the parking lot. "You don't mind carrying J.O.?"

"Nope. We're going to be buddies." By now, Jeffy perched on Al's shoulders, so Al picked up the smaller bags. Chubby fingers massed his hair into a pile.

"Don't mess up Mr. Al's hair, now." Dennis gave the boy a frown.

"It's all right. Hold on, Jeffy." Al kept a hand on a dimpled ankle, Dottie's smaller bag stacked on her suitcase against his side. He broke into a little jig. "We made it to Californ-i-yay, on the Atchison, Topeka and the Santa Fe."

"Fay! Fay!" Jeffy's perfect echo made Dottie chuckle in spite of her worry.

"Cora sings that song so often, he knows most of the words. He'll grow up sounding like Judy Garland."

Jeffy bunched his knees into Al's cheeks, but Al's grin told her he thoroughly enjoyed his new role. Dottie put Joy back in her carriage and lagged behind with Cora, whose steps lingered on the asphalt. They could still hear the men, but Cora was out of breath. Dennis set down the suitcases for a minute and waited for them.

"How far is it to your place, Cora?"

"About forty-five minutes. I'm so glad Dennis's boss gave him this half day off—our neighbor was willing to come along, but Jeffy is definitely daddy's boy."

"I bet you hate to see him leave for work. You've got your hands more than full." Dottie couldn't miss the quiver of Cora's lower lip. "Do you have good neighbors?"

"Not many close ones—you'll see, Mom. Japanese folks work the fields. They keep to themselves, but when I used to take early morning walks, they were always friendly."

Kimiko's parents' address lay tucked in Dottie's purse—she'd have to look it up later—they must live in the same kind of area. They caught up with the men at a dark red vehicle. Al ran the side of his hand along the back fender.

"You drive a Chevy? Looks like it's got a lot of room."

"Yeah. And it's steel-built—that's what I like—the way people drive out here, you'd think monsters chased them. I want my family to be safe." Dennis opened the tailgate.

"The traffic's almost doubled in the past year. The Army used this make for war transports—not this one, of course, but you'll see plenty of green ones around. This is a '45 model my boss found—got us quite a deal."

"Hmm…this'd make a great mail car, don't you think, Dot? All kinds of room for boxes and odd-shaped parcels." Focused on helping Cora into the front seat, Dottie heard Al lower his voice to Jeffy.

"Gotta get your mommy home so she can rest. Grandma and I will take good care of you and your baby sister. You betcha we will!"

# Chapter Twenty-nine

Cora raised her head from the pillow. "Mom, you're an angel."

"*Pffht.*" With Cora's forehead was still hotter than she'd like it to be, Dottie went to the kitchen to refresh her water glass.

"You've still got a fever—drink."

Cora raised her hand in a mock salute and obeyed.

"I mentioned to Al that we need a new source of milk for Joy, and you'll never guess what. Those neighbors in the peaked straw hats walked by, and he invited them in."

"Two sweet little women?"

"Yes. I was burping Joy on the front porch when Jeffy announced, 'Gamma—lalies come.'"

Dottie eased onto the edge of Cora's bed, and Cora turned on her side.

"I told them we like their vegetables. They seemed to understand. Al asked if they raise goats, too.

"They nodded and smiled, but I wondered if they'd understood. He held his fingers to his temples like horns and made a *Ennhee-hyaha* sound that Jeffy imitated. The women burst into laughter. Jeffy ran to the older woman and clamped his arms around her leg. Tears sprang into her eyes as she bent to pick him up. Who knows—maybe the authorities separated her from her grandchildren during the war."

"I wouldn't be surprised—they stayed in a camp for more than a year. When we moved in, they brought a welcome gift of enough food for a week."

"After a few of Al's pretend head butts with Jeffy and more goat bleats, the women got the idea and said, 'Six goats.'"

"It took a while for them to understand we wanted to buy milk, and Al took Jeffy along to their place. But best of all, Joy took to the milk like a spider to moths."

"I've wondered if she was getting enough. I've been so tired, Mom. But I didn't know what to—" From the living room, Joy cried out.

"I'll get her…Be back in a little while."

A note sat on the kitchen table. "Pounding with Jeffy." Dottie chuckled—Jeffy's favorite pastime of hammering nails could fill hours.

With Joy on her hip, she warmed some milk, her goal was to fill the baby's tummy so thoroughly and cuddle her so tenderly she would barely miss her Mama. When she peeked on the way to the rocking chair, Cora had fallen asleep again.

Joy drank a full bottle, and Dottie let her crawl around the living room until she heard Al and Jeffy outside. Cora called, so she carried the baby into the bedroom. She giggled to see Mama, but rested her head on Cora's shoulder instead of seeking food. Cora kissed the top of her curls.

"The goats' milk?"

"You can relax now."

"You're a miracle worker. I never thought—"

"You've had way too much to think about. A woman's body can only take so much. Now, you rest. And don't worry—Al loves Jeffy—he never tires of dreaming up things to do, and likes nothing better than rocking Joy to sleep."

"Dennis noticed he fixed the door on the shed—all on his own, without a word."

"Um…I'm not surprised."

Cora yawned. "Do you think he'd mind if we called him Grandpa?"

Dottie gathered sleepy Joy in her arms. "Actually, Jeffy's way ahead of you on that one—Al loves hearing him say Gwamps."

Joy giggled and waved at some motion outside the window.

"I'm so glad we're here, Cora. You married well. It's easy to see how much Dennis loves you and the children."

"Dot, look out there, way in the distance." Al pulled back the yellow flowered curtains at a dormer window.

Apart from brief interludes when he brought Jeffy in for food and his afternoon nap, she hadn't seen Al all day. She pulled over a chair and dropped beside him.

He pointed west. "See that faint line of blue, darker than the sky?"

"Is that the Pacific?"

"I'm pretty sure—can you believe we're close enough to see it?"

"I like the sea smell—seems like there's always at least a faint breeze. I haven't worn my sweater since we came, except in the evening."

He perched on the corner of the bed. "You like it here?"

That would be an understatement. Dottie hadn't had much time to process her emotions since they arrived a week ago. The grandchildren, now a part of her very heartbeat, required every smidgen of energy she could muster. Many nights, Al gave her a soothing foot rub after they climbed into bed.

But Cora looked brighter than she had at first. She'd developed terrible itching for some reason, so today Dottie bathed her with soothing calamine lotion.

Al took over Jeffy's care completely, and also manned the wringer washer on the back porch, processing load after load of diapers set to soak in an aluminum bushel basket. He dried them on the clothesline and taught Jeffy to fold them in half and carry them to a shelf near Joy's bed.

The two of them also made regular shopping excursions to replenish Joy's milk supply and pet the goats. In Jeffy's Radio Flyer wagon, they toted home sweet potatoes, carrots, greens, milk, eggs, and honey. To satisfy Cora's enormous appetite, Dottie cooked as much as she had at the boarding house.

"They say feed a cold, starve a fever, but not this time. I think she's been starving, Al."

Cora's compliance the first day when Dottie sent her to bed scared her even more than her skin's pasty hue. This independent, scared-of-nothing daughter collapsed in her room without an argument as soon as Dennis parked the Chevy in the driveway.

So there hadn't been much thought of the ocean, but now, the distant line of blue, practically at their doorstep—reminded her of their location. Who would ever have imagined she'd get to see an ocean?

One night, Dennis drove them to see the sunset. Dottie held the baby while Al jostled Jeffy along the sand. Everyone put a bare foot into the receding tide and searched for shells. The golden-orange orb reflecting on the water's vast expanse added fresh beauty to a time of day she'd always loved. And Cora, even though she and Dennis stayed in the car, seemed stronger after the outing.

Dottie rubbed the back of Al's hand. What a trooper—he knew intuitively what she needed. Besides maintaining the milk supply, he and Jeffy hatched a Christmas plan. They stuck a small scraggly pine into a pail filled with sand, decorated it with ornaments Dennis found for them, and brought it into the house the evening of the twenty-third.

"C'ismas, Gamma!" Al tucked a towel around the tree's base, along with a few small boxes, and Dennis added a string of lights and some more gifts when he came home.

"I haven't done any shopping at all…" Cora looked woebegone when she made her first wobbly trip to the living room. But Al produced the little tractor for Jeffy, and Dennis's boss and wife sent clothes and books for the children.

"Neither have I—this week has gone by so fast."

"It's all right. Having you here is Christmas for us. You must know that by now?"

Dennis's words brought Dottie close to tears which formed again as dusk gradually shaded daylight's last nuggets. She rubbed her head against Al's shoulder. She'd cried more the last month than ever before—but she'd laughed more, too.

He loved taking evening walks together, but probably guessed how much her feet hurt tonight. And he'd grown used to the way she sometimes waited before answering his questions. She liked that—a sign of patience.

"You asked if I like it here."

He cupped her chin in his hand.

"For the record, my answer is yes. In case you haven't already figured that out."

By six thirty when Dennis rattled out of the yard in his work truck, Al had lain awake for over an hour. He didn't make a move lest he wake Dottie. Most days, she would have been over at the house half an hour ago. He tipped his head for a better glimpse of her profile.

She deserved every minute of sleep she could steal, but he knew she wouldn't have things any other way. The train ride hadn't been easy on her, but with the grandbabies, she lit up like the Christmas lights people put on their front porches to celebrate the holiday.

Electricity must be cheaper on the coast than back home. Or maybe folks looked at things differently. After lean war years and constant blackouts, maybe they decided if something brought a little sunshine into your life, you ought to do it. He grew up believing money was to be saved. That mindset tempered his actions as long as he could remember. When people came into the hardware and splurged on a gift for their wives or children, he always eyed them askance.

But his perspective shifted over the past few years. That's why he bought the freezer that now sat in Dot's back porch. He hadn't splurged on Nan, by mutual agreement and necessity. But then, so soon, she passed from this world—all of a sudden, it was too late to give her anything or make her feel special.

Dottie wouldn't be around forever, and neither would he. While they had each other, he wanted to bring her as much happiness as possible. What good did it do to hoard every penny, when spending a little money could make your loved one happy? She twitched in her sleep. The flow of her lips down to her chin entranced him. Full lips—how he loved their touch.

Thinking of kisses propelled his mind to Jeffy, who knew how to kiss. Al reached a finger to his jaw, recalling Jeffy's frequent ministrations. He couldn't get enough of those short bowed legs pummeling toward him, chubby arms wrapping around his neck, and that sweet voice calling him Gwamps.

"What were you thinking about just then?" Dottie called him from his reverie.

"Kissing. And Jeffy."

"In that order?"

"Yep."

She snuggled against him and wrapped his arm around her shoulder. Any minute, they'd hear a baby voice across the way, but he didn't mind. Whatever this new day brought would be good.

Then he remembered—today was December twenty-eighth, Cora's doctor's appointment. He'd never chaperoned anyone to such a thing. Nan delivered Charlie at home with Mrs. Murdock in attendance. A couple of years later, she'd miscarried. Maybe seeing a doctor would have helped, but Nan refused, and never conceived again.

He didn't relish the idea of navigating traffic, but his hands itched to touch the Chevy's steering wheel—that car that weighed more than his truck.

It wasn't often Dottie spent time alone in their expansive room above the garage, but today, Al drove Cora to see her doctor. To give Jeffy a new place to explore, she took him to their apartment, along with Joy, plenty of milk and diapers, a dust rag, and a mop. She accomplished the move in fits and starts, bidding Jeffy to wait at the bottom of the stairs while she deposited Joy upstairs.

He took his mop-watching job seriously, but her heart thumped during the twenty seconds it took to deposit Joy in the middle of the bed and get the toddler in her sights again. At that age, they forgot instructions so quickly and moved like lightning. But he waited where she'd left him, and "helped Gamma" carry the pail, cheeks flushed with pride.

"You can dust the furniture, big boy, while Grandma cleans the floor."

"Big boy. Hep Gamma." His willing smile delighted her. She made a game of having him dust the chairs' low rungs and the footboard's far reaches. Joy, sated with oatmeal and goat's milk, batted her arms and gurgled.

Joy Marie…after her middle name and Cora's. Of course, Marie had been her mother's name. She remembered so little about her mother, but Mildred told her bits and pieces. Marie Colwell liked babies and little children. She had a way with them, Mildred said.

Dennis built a closet in the wide area between two dormer windows on the east side of the room. On the opposite wall, a desk and chair centered two matching windows. Such a nice breeze came from the west, and so far, Dottie hadn't noticed one mosquito or fly, even without screens.

"Can you dust the windowsills, Jeffy?" The petite workman stretched to accomplish the feat and trundled across the room for another rag.

"Gamma—cwean yo house. Cwean yo house!"

"Yes, honey. Won't Grandpa be surprised?"

Extra wide floorboards collected some dust, but not the swirls she fought in Iowa. The width of the boards made the area seem even larger, and so did pale yellow walls and slanting ceilings. Dottie remembered little from their arrival, but she did recall her delight with the color as Dennis guided them to their quarters once she tucked Cora into bed.

"Oh, I'm glad you chose yellow!"

"Cora insisted it's your favorite." Dennis installed a bathroom in the unused fourth of the attic. Everything from shiny chrome fixtures to yellow towels and washcloths was brand spanking new. Cora even hung a perky picture of Shasta daisies, forget-me-nots, and geraniums on the wall.

The space fit Dottie and Al perfectly, down to an extra-long bed to accommodate Al's height. The openness, so different from the cramped, dark rooms back at home, gave a sense of spaciousness and freedom.

Jeffy ran by as Dottie mopped a corner, and she held him close for a few moments before he wriggled away. Joy fell asleep, and after a while, Jeffy toddled toward the bed.

"My big boy getting sleepy? So is Grandma. Shall I tell you a story?"

"Stowy." Jeffy situated himself in the curve of Dottie's arm.

"Once, a Grandma came all the way from Iowa to see a little boy named Jeffy and his baby sister. She brought Grandpa along, too. Grandpa took that little boy to see the goats, they pounded nails together…"

"Poun', poun'." Jeffy's hands made fists and hit the pillow.

"They all worked and played together, until one day, Grandma had to…"

Worn out from helping, Jeffy gave in to the weight of heavy eyelids. An involuntary shudder grazed Dottie's shoulders, though the temperature rose to the high seventies.

She was about to say, *Grandma had to go back home.*

Twelve days gone by, and originally, they'd talked of staying three weeks. But she couldn't even think of leaving. She smoothed her fingers along the bedspread as Jeffy's long, shuddery breath signaled sleep.

She'd asked Cora how Dennis managed the extra-long bed. "He can take care of anything, Mom. His senior officer offered him a job with his construction company even before they shipped home. Captain Kenny, we call him. He called Dennis the best worker he'd ever find. He and his wife stood up with us when we got married, and took us out to eat at a real nice place afterward."

The curtain rose and fell with another small gust. Dottie's sigh matched its movement. Sternville seemed like a dream—she must've lived here forever. Being with Al seemed the same way— as if it had always been her reality.

How could they go home? This Captain and his wife, such wonderful people, did so much for Cora and Dennis, but they couldn't be here to help out until the baby came. Cora hadn't gotten her strength back yet. She probably wouldn't until after the baby arrived. And then, there would be double the diapers.

The faint chatter of Oriental women drifted from the road. Such gentle, tender-eyed people. She couldn't think of one thing she would change about this place…not one. Suddenly, from the recesses of her mind, she supposed from one of her morning devotional readings, words wafted to her.

"I will lead thee and guide thee with mine eye."

She formed a quilt into a semi-circle around the children to make sure they didn't roll off the bed, closed her eyes, and sank into the promise. After all, hadn't God guided Al and her out here, so far from all she'd ever known?

He'd given Al love for her and courage to ask for her hand, changed her heart toward Bonnie Mae, and shown her all of Al's admirable qualities. He'd kept him safe fighting the fires, and provided for all their needs to make the trip.

Like the Pacific breeze, a love as big as that massive ocean— bigger, even—surrounded these precious children and enveloped Dottie like the ratty afghan in her armchair back home. *Back home.* Back home seemed a lifetime ago, an ocean away. Had her boarding house life truly existed?

She'd come to a new place, a lovely place, and she liked it more than she ever dreamed.

# Chapter Thirty

"Thank you so much for bringing me, Al. And knowing Jeffy and Joy are safe with Mom—that takes a load off my shoulders."

"It goes both ways. I think your mother worried more about you back in Iowa than she let on."

"That doesn't surprise me."

Al maneuvered the car around the parking lot outside the doctor's office and turned down a one-way street. "You're doing all right?"

He eased to a stop at a stop sign and waited for a delivery truck to round the corner. Back in traffic, he waited some more. Not far from their turn-off, Cora sniffled.

Dottie would initiate a conversation if she needed to talk, but Nan always wanted him to ask what troubled her. With Cora, maybe things worked differently.

Before their turn, he guided the Chevy to the roadside. When he twisted toward her, she fell into his arms.

"I don't know what I'm going to do! I have to be ever so careful or I might…" her voice disappeared in sobs. The clean smell of her hair inundated Al's senses. "But I just can't let that happen."

She'd told him everything except the facts, but clearly, they scared the daylights out of her. Maybe the doctor thought she might lose the baby.

He handed her his handkerchief and Cora blew her nose. "Wow. I guess I really needed to fall apart. Sorry."

"It's not like I haven't seen you cry before—I often wondered what it'd be like raising girls. You and Millie gave me some idea."

She chuckled. "You remember me as a pigtailed brat, fighting the older kids."

"Nope—I recall a cute blond girl who loved chocolate almost as much as she loved her mother."

"You must've brought me hundreds of those little square candies, one at a time."

"And your mother scolded me for spoiling your dinner. But you turned out just fine, Cora Joy."

Another stream poised to cascade from her eyes. At one time, that would have upset him, but not anymore. Sometimes in the night, when bad memories rose up like phantoms, he wished he could force them away with tears.

"I have to stay still until the birth—that's another month and a half."

"The middle of February? I thought you weren't going to have the baby until March."

"I'm farther along than he thought."

"That's good, right? As I recall, Nan didn't mind her waiting time ending one bit."

"Yes. But…" Cora pressed her hand to her forehead. "To have another baby in the house so soon…I don't know if I can keep up. Maybe…oh, I don't know what we'll do."

Al turned the key in the ignition. "It'll work out, Cora. I'm sure it'll all work out."

Dottie and Al sat on the front porch while Dennis gave Jeffy and Joy their baths and put them to bed. Al waved a new railroad timetable in one hand.

"We'd have sleeping car service direct from San Diego starting on March twenty-seventh, Dot. That might be about the time you'd want to go back—the little one would be six weeks old, if it comes on the doc's schedule."

Dottie shook down a tide of emotion. Al's earnestness only

strengthened her aversion to the idea of leaving. "You would go home now and travel back out for me?"

"I'd do anything to help Cora." A breeze blew the living room curtains out behind them, making the faintest swishing sound. "When Del's children were young, I worked such long hours—missed out on them being babies." He clicked his tongue. "You women are smarter than us. We don't see our chances passing us by.

"After Nan died, I should have made more of an effort to drive to Charlie's, but I fell into a rut. So now, I have a third chance—I love every minute with these little ones. In fact…"

His foot jiggled, sending a vibration along the chair arm. "I've been doing some thinking. Seems as though you really like the Golden State, and so do I. What if…" His voice took on a deeper tenor. "What if we moved out here?"

Dust particles floated in the last shards of sunshine. Down the road a goat bleated, and Mrs. Shoko's rooster, mixed up about day and night, crowed. Did he just propose what Dottie thought he did?

"You mean, for good?"

"What do we have to go back for, really? These little tykes need a Grandma and Grandpa so much."

Two cherub faces danced through her mind, young lives that mattered more than anything in the world—three. Al put her own feelings into words. Yet she hadn't considered the idea seriously—you couldn't take everything that came into your head as a possibility, could you?

Inside the house, Jeffy's squeals and splashes accompanied his daddy's laughter.

From the bedroom corner, Joy giggled with Cora.

"What if I went back this spring at the end of March, when things settle into a routine and Cora gets her strength back? Del can handle things till then."

His sincere eyes shone blue as the ocean. She could tell he'd analyzed this ten ways till Tuesday, since he continued. He must believe his plan would work.

"We could sell your place—already got a couple of farmers in mind—Verne and Vera Brannigan want to move into town when Eric takes over the farm."

Vera Brannigan—they'd been close at one time, but Vera only came into town on Saturday nights for groceries.

"I'd buy a car, maybe one of those wooden station wagons like Merv Planter's 1941 model—remember that?"

Dottie paid little attention to vehicles, but Merv's—as big as Dennis and Cora's reliable Chevy—flashed through her mind. She nodded, but her mind could move only so fast.

"Then, when you can get away for a week or so, we could bring out as much as you'd like, or even ship some by train."

Al drummed his fingertips on his knee. "By then, it would be full springtime in Iowa, maybe summer. Who knows—maybe Del's oldest boy could help us move. Or Millie and Ren might have a hankering to see the new baby and the country, too."

Scenes from the train window buzzed before Dottie like tempting sprites. "Like those people we saw on the way, when the railroad came close to Route Sixty-six?"

"Exactly." Al took her by the shoulders, the lines above his nose deep but his eyes animated with light. "We're not too old to make a change, Dot—we could take a full two weeks, if Millie would stay here with Cora."

The ideas made homes in Dottie's head, but Al plunged ahead. "Those people from Chicago we met on our last night, remember them? You know, the guy who left his plumbing business?"

"Yes—they were tired of the city and sold out. The war scattered their family from coast to coast, he realized this was their time, so they pulled up stakes. I didn't know if they were courageous or foolish."

But now, she pictured what a job it would be to clean out her possessions—more than thirty years' worth. She and Al climbed the stairs to their apartment.

Then, another idea occurred to her—what if she asked Millie

and Alice to tend to all of that? What if she stayed put, and waited for Al to return with their things? Millie would understand.

But what if her house didn't sell? Would they still move? Al pulled her to the top stair to watch the stars come out.

"So, you think it's our time?"

His heart beat against hers. "If it's what you want to do, Dot, then it's our time."

"Have more baby milk?"

"No—that is, yes. We need more." Al got out his wallet to illustrate his explanation. "Mrs. Shoko, you remember my wife, Dot?"

"Wifedot." She held out her hand. "Me Shoko. You Wifedot?"

"Yes. Me Dot."

"Dot?" Her forehead scrunched together.

"Call me Dottie. That would be fine."

"Dot—tie. Ah." Wrinkles curved into a smile. "You like some tea?" She gestured toward the back of the house.

"I would. I love tea."

"Yes?"

"Yes." Dottie made an "mmm" sound and circled her palm on her stomach.

As if by magic, the younger woman who walked with Mrs. Shoko the day they stopped by Cora's house, tiptoed into the room with a tray of steaming cups. She gave a mysterious smile and set the tray on a low table. Taking a sip gave Dottie time to adjust to the shadowy interior. Only a few pieces of straight-lined, low furniture and a straw mat divided one side of the room from the area where they sat on a simple wooden bench.

The younger woman knelt on a pillow near her mother, who waved a hand her way. "This Miyako."

"How good to meet you. You are a daughter?"

Miyako ducked her head with a shy smile.

Dottie couldn't think what else to say, and was relieved when

Al plunged in. "Mrs. Shoko, we need milk, but we need help at our house, too."

"You need…?"

Miyako muttered something to her mother in Japanese and Mrs. Shoko turned back to Al and Dottie.

"Need people?"

"Uh, yes. One people—one person." Al set his cup down and held his arms like a cradle. "New baby comes. You know Jeffy, right?"

Mrs. Shoko giggled. "Um…Mr. Sweet Boy."

"Jeffy has a baby sister, too." Al held up one finger, then a second. "Jeffy and Joy."

Mrs. Shoko nodded.

"But soon his mother will have another baby, and she is sick. One, two, three." He rubbed his abdomen and held up another finger. "And I…" He turned toward Dottie. "I must go back home… travel far."

Mrs. Shoko's brows met. She turned to Miyako for explanation and nodded. "Three? Three Sweet Ones?"

"Yes. But in March, I must go on the train, so Dottie needs someone to watch Jeffy—maybe two hours in the morning and two more in the afternoon, until his father—you know Dennis? Until he comes home from work."

"Dennis…um. Cora sick? Wifedot need three babies…need…?"

Miyako spent an intense two minutes conversing with her mother, and held out her palms. "Little boy, Jeffy—so busy, very happy. You need watcher—every day?"

Al nodded. "Yes, every day. For four hours altogether."

Mrs. Shoko held up four fingers. "This much?" The two women conferred again, and her daughter nodded. "You not worry. We watch."

Dottie held her breath. How could she know for sure Mrs. Shoko understood? "Both of you?"

Miyako held up two fingers. "We come ten o'clock and three o'clock, March. Work in fields early. We take Jeffy play—see goats. Make him tired for nap."

Her smile reassured Dottie this might work. But what if they…
how could she trust that they would keep a close enough watch
on him?

As if she understood Dottie's reservations, Mrs. Shoko tapped
Miyako, who left and returned with a framed photo—a young
mother with a baby and a fine-boned boy on his father's lap. Mrs.
Shoko composed her face.

"My sweet ones. Tokyo." She swiped at her eyes.

Miyako held the picture to her chest. "After camp, my brother
say never trust government again. Take babies home." She gestured
toward the Pacific. "Mother's heart broken—she want to watch
Jeffy. She love."

Dottie set her cup down and put an arm around Mrs. Shoko.
"I'm so sorry about your grandchildren."

Al and Dottie communicated without words. Another grandmother—a very lonely one—exactly what they needed.

A thread of moonlight touched the shiny spot on Dottie's forehead
where she brushed her wave back. Even at night, when he could see
only the outline of her features, he marveled at how pretty she was.

"Oh no." Her groan startled him.

"What is it?"

"I forgot to put that chicken in the Frigidaire. I was being organized, getting it in the roaster for morning, but I think I left it in
the sink."

"I'll go put it away." Al grabbed his robe and walked barefoot
across the cool grass. In this peaceful countryside, a person would
never know those twinkles in the distance signaled the great city
of San Diego. He tried the back screen door—strange. Dennis
usually locked it at night.

In the darkness, he judged the distance to the sink and hit it pretty
close. He felt around with his hand, but no roaster. To be sure, he
eased open the Frigidaire door, and sure enough, the blue enamelware

roasting pan sat on the middle shelf. A floorboard creaked as he crossed the kitchen, and a low voice came from the living room.

"Who's there?"

Like a thief caught in the act, Al peered around the doorframe. Dennis held Joy in the crook of his left arm and Jeffy over his right shoulder. "It's just me. Dottie remembered the chicken—you must've put it away."

"Yeah, about the time Jeffy woke up. Didn't want them to keep Cora from sleeping, so…"

Al sank onto a nearby chair. "Looks like you couldn't get up if you tried."

Dennis grinned. "I've been sleeping with them, so everybody's happy."

"You must be exhausted, with such early mornings."

"We're working way up in Thousand Oaks this week—otherwise, I go closer to seven."

"But you work till six—that's a long day, son."

"Maybe, but we pulled lots longer ones aboard ship."

"Um. I remember those days—never so glad to get onto solid ground."

"Navy?"

"No, infantry, but back and forth across the Atlantic was enough ship life for me. You want me to take one of them so you can get up?"

"No thanks. This is really the best, all alone with them, and Cora sleeping. After we married, I shipped out again. Through the last two years of the war, I dreamed about us having a family. Now my dream's come true."

"And soon, you'll have another."

"Yeah." Dennis sighed. "I hope if we ever have a fourth, he waits a few years, for Cora's sake."

Out in the yard, the wind sent something spinning. "Thank the good Lord for Dottie trying that goat milk."

"Sure hope Cora gets her strength up. I'm—"The younger man's voice broke.

Finally, Al broke the silence. "You awful worried about her?"

"I couldn't bear it if anything…"

"No."

"You and Dottie have been so good. Before you came, we…" He sighed again. "I can't seem to finish a sentence."

Al cleared his throat. "If I were you, I wouldn't want Dottie to leave."

"You…you see that?"

"All I have to do is watch Cora drag herself from the bedroom to the bathroom. She needs a lot of help."

"Would you—I know it must seem like a lot to ask, but would you consider staying on?"

"Dot and I have been talking about selling her house."

"Selling? But you sold yours, didn't you?"

"We did, just before we left. But both of us really like it out here, and we're head over heels for Joy and Jeffy. We'll feel the same about your new baby. If you'll have us, we could stay here till Cora comes into her own again. Later we could find our own place nearby, but for now, we're just fine here."

"Hoah…" Dennis choked on whatever he intended to say.

"We could afford to pay you rent by the month…"

"I can't…you and Dottie are saving our necks. We'd be in a terrible place without you—we were, before Christmas. When Dottie couldn't come, I didn't know what to do. Wish my parents and my sisters lived closer, but they'll never budge from Nebraska.

"Anyway, after that phone call, Cora was so downhearted—I never saw her so discouraged."

"I always wanted to see the west coast, ever since I met up with some Californians in France. We like it here—makes us feel young again, needed."

"You've taken a lot off my mind. I'll sleep better now." Dennis rose from his armchair as easily as if feathers floated in his arms.

Al smoothed his hand over Jeffy's back. "Son, you've got leg muscles I sure don't have any more. Good night, now."

# Chapter Thirty-one

On February fifteenth, a unique impression struck Dottie when she wakened, as though the day were a holiday or something. She puzzled over the feeling, like a bell tolling in the center of her being.

Al managed to escape their room without waking her, so she took advantage of a quiet start to her day. She washed her face and hands, brushed her teeth, ran a comb through her hair, and put on the dress she'd bought at the Wearwithall.

Flowers befitted such a glorious day, with brilliant sunshine already warming the earth. The bright fabric would cheer Cora.

Between the apartment and the house, a strange sound drifted to her, like a bird's cry, or children playing down the road. But no children lived down the road. Her pace quickened with her heart's pounding.

Arms full of baby, Al chased Jeffy toward the back porch. "Brace yourself. Cora's calling for you."

The sight of her daughter writhing on her bed put steel in Dottie's backbone. Today might be the day.

She grasped Cora's wrist. "Are you hurting?"

"Unnnhh."

"How long have you been…?"

"After…Dennis…left." Why not before? With his steady temperament, Dennis could handle an emergency far better than she. But that wasn't how life happened.

She brushed the question into the background, with so many others. Why Tunisia? Why that specific battle? Who found Bill and carried him away? And why Owen, so soon after?

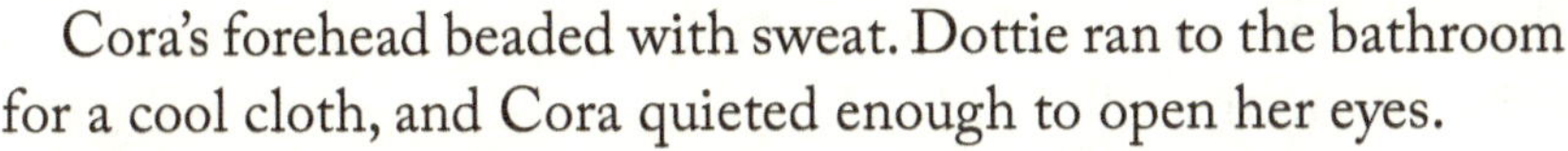

Cora's forehead beaded with sweat. Dottie ran to the bathroom for a cool cloth, and Cora quieted enough to open her eyes.

"Mom?"

"Tell me what's happening."

"I'm so hot…thirsty."

"I'll get you a drink."

The next time Cora opened her eyes, Dottie noticed a yellow tinge. Her breath caught in her throat. That couldn't be good.

"Doctor…I think maybe…"

Cora asking for the doctor was the last thing Dottie would ever expect. Cora's philosophy on childbirth remained simple—women had been doing this for ages, and she'd been through it twice—why bother with a doctor? But Dennis set up her appointment, on advice from Captain Kenny's wife.

Outside the window, Al whizzed by after Jeffy, Joy clutched in his arms. Maybe they should load Cora into the Chevy and drive her to the doctor's office. On the other hand, maybe she'd sleep for a while.

When Cora's head lagged to the side, Dottie consulted Al. Jeffy caught her knees when she reached the front porch, and she whisked him into her arms as Al read her worry.

"What do you think?"

"She's got a fever—she mentioned the doctor. Maybe we ought to call him."

"Can't hurt. His name's Bulow. Want me to look up his number?"

"That would be a big help. Here, let me take sweetie-pie."

"It's been a couple of hours since she ate." Al caught Jeffy with his long arm. "Come with me, buddy. We have something to find for Grandma."

Dottie heated a bottle, and exchanged Joy for the phone.

"On Buena Vista Street—helped to remember that."

Just then Cora let out a yell, and Dottie bit her lip.

"You call, Al. Be sure to mention the fever."

Cora's voice heightened into a scream, and Dottie fled toward the bedroom, panic in her voice. "Oh my. Ask them if we should bring her to the office or the hospital."

The bottom sheet was soaked through. Cora gripped Dottie's hand so hard it hurt. "Com—ing."

Energy shot through Dottie. She yelled for Al. "It's too late. Ask the Doctor to come here, and to hurry."

"If I could use your phone?" Doctor Bulow emerged from Cora's bedroom.

Al pointed to the kitchen and listened as the Doctor turned the dial. This number system made a lot of sense—no one could listen in to your calls.

Quite an improvement over all Sternville's longs and shorts—but then, California seemed ahead in a lot of ways.

Al grabbed the warm bottle, took the children to the big armchair and settled in. The best he could do was keep them fed and happy.

"Yes. Doctor Bulow. Send an ambulance immediately. Six miles north, right on Alameda till you come to the Rancho Bernardo sign. Turn left there—third driveway on your right, a long lane— white frame house. Woman in labor—have them be extra careful. I'll meet them at the emergency entrance."

The phone clicked and he walked back into the living room. "Can you tell me anything?"

"She's dehydrating fast, may need a Caesarean section."

A sliver of fear slid down Al's spine. "You might have to operate?"

The doctor slipped his stethoscope from his neck and opened his black leather bag. "Hard to tell yet. But we don't want to take any chances."

Al rubbed Jeffy's shoulders with his free hand since Joy had learned to hold her bottle. "Jeffy, this is the doctor. He's going to help your mommy."

"Glad you called when you did. Your daughter's a strong girl, but sometimes women need more than their own strength." He glanced at his wristwatch. "I'm going to take off. Is her husband…?"

"He's at work, but I'll try to find him. Where will Cora be?"

"Scripps in La Jolla. The sooner her husband gets there, the better." He donned his hat, and Al noticed a Navy inscription on his bag. So, he'd doctored in the war.

Joy finished her bottle, and Jeffy's sleeping form weighted Al's shoulder. He planted his feet and squirmed from the chair, remembering how easy this maneuver had been for Dennis. He lined a chair and an ottoman along the couch so they wouldn't roll onto the floor. In Cora's bedroom, Dottie bent over the bed.

He hurried to the phone book. Surely, Cora must have written down a number for Captain Kenny. If she hadn't, how on earth would they ever reach Dennis?

"A package came in the mail for you, Dot. Why don't you brew us some tea and come out to the porch?"

"Come, Gamma."

Dottie rubbed her hands down her apron sides, eyeing Jeffy. A package? Who could that be from? She turned a slow circle in the middle of the kitchen.

"The refrigerator's cleaned out, and the oven and floor are scrubbed." Al was right. She couldn't think of anything else to do, not until Cora's sheets dried. Besides, her feet hurt.

Six hours passed since Al talked with Captain Kenny's wife, who offered to drive over to the worksite and send Dennis to the hospital. But he still hadn't called. Work had become Dottie's friend, but a cup of tea sounded wonderful.

She'd polished the kettle until it sparkled, and filled it with fresh water. During the last few days, she'd let things go in the kitchen. Now, she ran her finger along the counter's edge—not a speck. At least she was doing all she could here, so when Cora came home…

While she worked, she prayed like crazy. "Keep her safe, don't let them have to do surgery, please."

She didn't even know which prayers she meant and which she didn't. It scared the dickens out of her to think of them using ether to put her under. What if Cora didn't wake up?

She'd never experienced ether herself, but heard from some women about the process. Wouldn't it be better to have your mind about you as your baby came into this world? Yet doctors kept learning new ways of doing things.

She carried a tray with full teacups, a glass of milk for Jeffy, a teething biscuit for Joy, and some cookies to the porch, where Al kept Jeffy under control. Joy sat at Al's feet, playing with his shoelaces, a slobbery grin on her face. Dottie placed the tray on the table and pushed it back so no tiny fingers could reach it.

"Ah. Tea. Been a long time since we drank a cup together, Dot."

She nodded. "I didn't think I could sit down until we heard from Dennis, but it feels awfully good to get off my feet. Thanks for the idea."

Jeffy charged up the porch steps with a black and white kitten. "Kitty—Shoko."

"Shoko gave you the kitty?" She raised an eyebrow toward Al.

"This morning—she brought it over because he fell in love with it at their place a few days ago. I think she would have stayed to babysit if I'd asked her—she seems so eager to spend time with Jeffy. Hopefully Cora won't mind about the cat."

"Gamma…cookie…"

"It'll have to be a garage cat, with a baby in the house. Jeffy, put the kitty down if you want a cookie. Oh, I should have brought a wet cloth."

"I'll get one, sit still." Al was back in half a minute. Jeffy bent over the kitten, but it toppled off the bottom step and worked its way into the short grass along the porch.

"Come here, buddy—why don't we let kitty explore?" Jeffy climbed into Al's lap for his snack. "Going to open your package?" Al gestured with his chin to a box wrapped in brown paper, shoved partway under the table.

"I suppose so. Who's it from?"

Al let her read the return address for herself. "Why, Bonnie Mae. Wonder what she could've sent?" Jeffy leaped from Al's lap. "Me hep Gamma!"

"Yes. You open it for me, honey."

Occupied for a full five minutes, Jeffy forgot all about his cookie. Al retrieved Joy's rubber teething toy from her dimpled thigh. Dottie leaned her head back in the wicker chair. Rays of sunshine eased her tension. If only Dennis would call and say Cora was all right, this would be a perfect afternoon. Her prayers mounted to heaven, the same request over and over.

Al patted her knee. "I know vain repetition gets us nowhere, but that's all I can manage today."

"Pitty, pitty!" Jeffy pulled some fabric from the box he'd finally pried open, and Dottie helped him spread it wide.

"Why, it's a new apron—I bet Bonnie Mae made it herself. She told me she was going to learn to sew. That girl can do whatever she puts her mind to."

Jeffy handed her an envelope, and she pulled out two hand-written pages. Dottie scanned the first. "She says to tell you hello from George. The men are deep into the afternoon tournaments and have recruited Fred Messerschmidt—Berta's feeling better. Guess Fred hired someone to watch the store in the afternoons. But George says to tell you he's no replacement for you."

Al focused on children and cookies. "Here, Jeffy. Come drink your milk."

"Henrietta's been in the hospital in traction. She fell and broke her leg. Oh, my. I wouldn't wish that on anybody."

"That's too bad. See? If we hadn't come out here, I'd be a miserable man with no one to bake for me." Al wagged his head in mock self-pity.

"And the Langley's daughter's expecting her fourth—the doctor thinks it's twins."

The phone jangled. Dottie stared at Al. "You go." As soon as he hurried through the door, she wished she'd gone herself. Only a couple of minutes passed, but the wait seemed like hours. By the time he appeared, Joy had started to fuss, and Dottie stooped to pick her up. One look at Al's somber face made her grip the chair arm.

"How many babies can you handle?"

"How many? What do you…?"

"Dennis says Cora's worn out, but doing all right. He got there just in time for the birth…the second birth, that is."

"Sec…?"

"Guess twins happen out here in California, too. You have two new grandbabies, Mrs. Jensen."

Speechless, Dottie sank back in the chair and pulled Joy close.

"A boy and a girl. Andrew Albert and Dorothy Marjorie, after the two grandmothers. And they even thought of me." His smile showed genuine pleasure.

"He was serious?"

"Do you think he'd kid about a thing like that?" He reached for Dottie's shoulder. "You all right?"

She nodded. "I think so. But when did you say you plan on going home?"

The stuffy, antiseptic hospital smell faded into the background. Time stopped in the hallway outside a large-windowed nursery. Light pressure from Al's fingers on Dottie's elbow steadied her as a nurse in a starched white cap rolled a metal table toward the viewing window. Side by side, two tiny babies slept under a curved glass enclosure.

Dottie could barely breathe.

Al's sniff, so close to her ear, didn't help matters at all, but at least he stood here beside her. She scrunched closer, if that were possible. Baby Tipton was written on identical hand-lettered signs taped onto the glass above each miniature bundle. Brazen lights glared on newborn patches of skin under blue and pink knitted caps, and noses the size and color of rose blossoms.

The nurse edged her hand under the glass and felt the blanket swathing the pink bundle, then the blue. Were they warm enough? Dottie itched to check them herself. Everything looked so sterile, so steely. But the nurse walked off, so she must be satisfied.

Dottie might have stayed there forever if Dennis hadn't approached—finally, she believed what Al announced earlier: there were two of them. She recognized the *thunk* of work boots on the long linoleum hallway, and Dennis leaned close to the window.

"Doc says even though they're so small, they're doing just fine. They each weighed almost four and a half pounds. They'll keep them here maybe two weeks, and by the time we bring them home, they'll gain some weight."

"He's sure? They look so fragile…"

"Cora feels the same way. But according to Doc they've already proven their mettle—they made it through the delivery. He said—" Dennis's voice broke and his hand smudged the worksite dirt still decorating his cheek. "Sorry."

Al stepped into the circle. "Nothing to be sorry about. You've had quite the day. Cora's doing all right?"

"Yeah. That's the scary part. For a while this morning, Doc was afraid we might…lose…"

"Lose her? Cora?" Dottie's heart rattled against her breastbone.

"It was touch and go there for a while. She had some toxin thing. The swelling was a sign, but Doc thought rest would take care of it. For some reason, when he checked her last month, only one heartbeat showed up. Strange, he said.

"Anyway, they gave her a transfusion—we're the same blood type, and I got here in time for them to use my blood." He held up his right elbow, wrapped in gauze. "Made me feel like at least I did something to help."

Dottie digested his words—a transfusion? "That's an operation? She's really going to be okay?"

"No operation—the babies came fairly easily, Doc said. But she needs a lot of rest now, and they've got her hooked up to a machine to keep her from getting dehydrated again. She can't have company for a couple of days, but Doctor Bulow says he's seen other women through this, and she'll come out like new."

Minty green walls swam before Dottie, but Dennis patted her forearm. "You've had a long day, too. Sorry it took so long to call…" He rubbed his forehead. "Cora looked a lot better when I stopped in a couple minutes ago. They gave her something to sleep."

He turned to his new babies, and Dottie saw how pale and worn out he looked. "Some children at the park across the street can't wait to see you—Shoko and Miyako are watching them for us."

Dennis tore his eyes away. "I could use some hugs."

He took off at a run. Al turned to Dottie. "Want to go back in?"

"No…there's nothing I can do here." They started across the street, those miniature babies and Cora's condition swirling in her brain.

"Dot, you doing okay? You're trembling."

"I can't help it, Al—they almost lost her. The whole thing is too much to…" She needed to hold down her emotions until the children went to sleep.

"You did the right thing. If we hadn't called the doctor, things might have gone much worse."

"But we should have done it yesterday—last week."

"No use second guessing. You did your best."

Dennis walked up with Jeffy on his shoulders. "We're heading home. See you there."

Dottie told herself things were okay now, but her nerves jittered. Al engaged Miyako in a discussion of the weather and vegetables.

Two minutes down the road, Joy fell asleep in Dottie's arms. It was good to be quiet for a while, to rethink everything, with this innocent baby sleeping in her arms. Late sunlight tipped bean and cabbage rows purple, and electric poles cast long shadows across the road—even at this moment fraught with unknowns, California had so much beauty to offer.

# Chapter Thirty-two

Dennis and Jeffy waited on the back steps. Joy wakened and reached for Daddy. He buried his face in her fine hair. When he looked up, he seemed more boy than man. "I went through some things in the war, but this…"

Dottie spun into action. "You're hungry. I'll heat up some stew for you."

He drew the children close. "Thanks. I'll give them their baths. Captain Kenny told me to take tomorrow off. Maybe you folks could use a little break?"

Al cleared his throat. "Would you mind if I drove Dottie down to the ocean? Maybe we could take a picnic." He gave her a questioning look, but she couldn't find her tongue.

"Feel free to use the car. I'll call to check on Cora in the morning, but won't go to the hospital till evening—give her some time to get her strength back. It'll do me good to be here alone with these two."

Al pulled Dottie down on the stairway landing. "Look—just in time for another amazing sunset."

She sank on the top step. The sensation of his warm skin on hers relaxed the tight string drawn between her shoulder blades. Ocean breeze caressed her face. The golden-orange spectacle along the coast and the airy taste of salt mesmerized her.

Long after darkness drained brilliant color from the sky and the breeze picked up, the day's events filed through Dottie's mind,

281

stirring a parade of deep-seated feelings and memories, ending with two newborn human beings, so utterly frail, so helpless. Of all her emotions, the one that surfaced was relief. Al had gone in to see them with her—she hadn't needed to do that alone.

"Thank you for all you did today, especially for going in to see the babies with me tonight."

"Wouldn't have missed it—I thought of Owen—felt as though he ought to be standing there at that nursery window instead of me."

"He wouldn't have gone in."

"What?"

"He was afraid of things like that, Al—hospitals, sickness… newborns. When Millie had her babies, it was weeks before he held them."

Dottie hadn't ever put it into just those words, but memories flooded back—dirty diapers to change and soak and wash, the children sick in the night, that haying accident Owen's brother had in '31 with a dappled horse named Derkin…Owen disappeared that day, unable to take the sight. When his mother took to her deathbed, when Millie had her tonsils removed in fourth grade—he disappeared each time.

Something about the smells, the sickness, the brokenness caused his reaction. She'd never thought much about it—he was what he was. But she knew without a doubt that he never would have entered the hospital today to see his newest grandbabies. The diapers would have rotted in their soak water if she hadn't washed them.

She'd always seen it as her business to tend to household things, and that included anything having to do with feelings—the emotional work of a family. A wave of gratitude deluged her, because Al entered into it all—they could shoulder both joys and burdens together. These grandbabies were his, too—he'd earned them. She snuggled against him, reluctant to move, even to go inside to bed.

Worries roiled in Dottie's mind. Tonight was her chance to sleep, but she couldn't. How would she ever manage when Cora came home, needing so much care? Those delicate babies would take so much work, and Jeffy and Joy required constant watchfulness. After Al went back to Iowa, Shoko and Miyako would help, but communicating would be so difficult.

She knew it didn't pay to borrow trouble, but her thoughts refused to settle down.

Finally, Al reached for her in the darkness and whispered in her ear. "I can hear the wheels turning in your brain. We can't solve it all right now." She knew that, but hearing him say it helped.

"We've got the day off tomorrow, Dot. We'll pack a lunch, walk the beach, maybe even take a dip. How does that sound?"

"Good."

"And I'm giving Del a call in the morning. He can take care of the bank and anything else we need him to do. I'm not leaving here until things calm down—way, way down."

Dottie shifted her position so she could see his eyes in the shadows. "You really think it'll—"

"—be all right?" He smoothed his fingertips from her temples to her jawbone. "I do. We'll wait on selling your house. Maybe later on, Millie can come out to help for a week. Then I could make a quick trip back. We'll see—there's no need to worry about all that right now. We'll take it as it comes."

His kindness lodged in Dottie's throat. She could no longer deny her tears. "You would put all that off for…?"

"For you. You bet. I'll do whatever it takes, Dottie Jensen, because I love you, and that includes your family. Whatever it takes."

Sky the color of robin's eggs, without even a single cloud, met the ocean as far as the eye could see. Al packed the car with Cora's wicker picnic basket, a blanket, a glass jug of water, and even a carafe of hot tea.

Just like their first date—the trip to the river, when he took care of everything.

Dennis had the children out in front of the house, Joy in a perambulator waving her hands and babbling, and Jeffy helping Daddy chop weeds.

"You're sure you don't need me?"

"I would never say that, but I'll get along for the day. I've got a few chores to do around here that'll make Cora happy when she comes home. And Jeffy promised to show me the goats and a whole lot of kitties."

Al strode up the steps and brushed Dottie's shoulder. "Ready? We couldn't have a prettier day."

"That's for sure, and I definitely am ready—after all, you did everything."

He guided her to the car, held the door while she slid into the seat, and gave her a wink. "This is our day—the whole day."

A twinge of guilt stalked her as they drove down the driveway toward the road. Dennis here alone with those two—how would he manage? But he seemed so excited to spend the day with them. Who knew how much of the necessary housework he'd been doing after work before she and Al came?

"Most people must be already at work. Maybe they were still driving home last night when we came back from the hospital—the traffic's so much thinner."

"Or maybe people get out more here in the evenings."

Al had written down the turns he needed to make, and Dottie held the list. The last turn, Jenner Street, led to the beach.

When he handed her the slip of paper, he chortled. "Jenner Street—pretty close to Jensen. It's a sign for us, Dot. We're going to have a wonderful day."

"Okay, turn left here—there it is."

Al turned off the motor. "Let's leave everything in the car." He took her hand, and they stopped to read a wooden sign at the edge of the sand:

By act of the California Legislature, 1931:
Casa Beach,
a gift from Ellen Browning Scripps,
shall be devoted exclusively to public park,
bathing pool for children,
parkway, highway, playground,
and recreational purposes.

"Hey, I should've brought some poles!"

"Maybe next time—Jeffy would love that. I wonder if Ellen Scripps founded the hospital, too, or her husband." She scanned the area. "So, that walkway keeps the biggest waves out? Maybe this would be a good place to bring children to swim."

"Yeah—Dennis suggested we come here. Guess he and Cora made some memories on the seawall walkway."

"Oh, now I remember. It seems so long ago. I was preoccupied with…" Dottie paused. "Anyway, I think when Cora called to tell me Dennis proposed, she mentioned waves crashing into a seawall."

"Well, this must be the place. How about walking down to the pier?"

It wasn't so far, but by the time they came back, Dottie's stomach growled.

"Already? Maybe I didn't bring enough food."

She chuckled. "That growl doesn't mean we have to feed it right away, you know."

"I'll get the chairs, umbrella, and blanket. You rest."

That was one of Al's favorite words, along with *relax*. He repeated it again last night just before she dropped off to sleep. "Cora's going to be fine, and so are the babies. I'm glad they're in good hands, and we can relax—just think of all the nurses staying up tonight to take care of them."

The scene his words painted calmed her. She imagined the nursery where they'd turned down the lights by now and some nurse watching over little Andrew and Dorothy. The babies looked so fragile, she would much rather have that nurse in charge than bear the responsibility.

Now, she recalled tiny babies like Cora's that had survived—the pitifully small infant born to Henrietta Perry's younger sister, grown into a strapping young man. She tried to recall his name. And didn't Ily have a mighty small one, too?

She positioned her striped canvas chair beside Al's, closed her eyes, and let the breeze carry her away. The Pacific Ocean—still, it didn't seem she could actually be here, close enough to touch the water. Al brought a tourism book, but Dottie wanted only to take in the sunshine and do absolutely nothing.

He read her snippets about various locations along the coast. "If we live here forever, we'll never get to all of them."

*If we live here forever.* Forever in California seemed longer than Sternville's forever, for some reason. Maybe because the ocean and beaches stretched so far, they seemed endless, or because the sky angled into the water with nothing between.

Then she thought of all the work ahead of them—it didn't diminish the joy of being involved in her grandbabies' lives. Best of all, she would be doing it with Al. How could she be such a lucky woman?

He burbled away about giant redwoods up north, San Francisco's highlights, and Hollywood. He seemed so content. Her eyelids grew heavy with the rhythm of surf crashing into seawall and gulls overhead calling to their mates. When she woke, a magnificent meal awaited her.

Al had made sandwiches from leftover roast beef, apple slices sprinkled with cinnamon, a bowl of lettuce and parsley from Mrs. Shoko's garden, carrot and celery sticks from the same source, tea, and a box of cookies for dessert. But best of all, he sat there Indian style, with a grin. The glitter of his blue eyes matched that in the distance as waves met the sun.

Dottie stretched her arms wide. "You're treating me like a queen."

He rolled his arm toward the feast. "You deserve it. Come on, enjoy."

She lowered beside him. A big sandwich later, he reached for her hand. "Are you happy, Dot?"

"Oh my—my heart is so full, I don't know how to talk about it. But how about you—I wish I could offer you something besides work. Dirty diapers, running around after Jeffy—and it's going to get far worse."

He squeezed her fingers. "You have no idea what you offer me, Dot. I have everything I need."

They packed away the containers and sipped another slow cup of tea, but Dottie juggled his reply. It wasn't the words so much as the quiver in his voice.

"Race you to the seawall!" Al leaped up and took off, leaving toe marks in the sand. Dottie followed him in a fast walk—no reason to sprain an ankle—this day was supposed to be fun.

Along the seawall again, swinging arms like carefree children, they traced the water's edge. A few people migrated to the beach, most in swimsuits or shorts. Dottie's dress fluttered in the breeze— the liberating sensation eased her nagging squiggle of worry. She picked up conch shells until her hands would hold no more.

"Jeffy would love this, wouldn't he? If we're going to bring him out here, maybe I should buy a swimsuit." She thumped a fist against her hip. "Do you think they'd let me on this beach in one?"

"You've got a good shape. You ought to buy one—we both should." Al's rolled-up pants made his long legs look even thinner.

"I don't know how to swim. I've always wanted to, but my folks were so afraid we'd drown, they never allowed us to attempt it."

"You can still learn. I was lucky to have a pond right on our farm, and we all jumped in after a hard day's work in haying season." Back at the blanket, he pulled her down. "Time for a nap."

When had she ever rested this much during daytime? She couldn't remember, but it felt wonderful. Al fell asleep, and so did she. A seagull's call woke them some time later, and he raised himself onto his elbow, cocking his head at a humming noise.

"Sounds like an airplane." He scanned the east and stood up, shading his eyes. Finally, a black speck came into view. "Over there...see? Must be an airshow or something."

Closer, Dottie recognized a green biplane with something written on the side in yellow. The plane dipped and circled, dipped again. Then, as if headed straight for them, it came near enough for her to read the words, *Wilson's Flying Circus.*

Al's fingers slipped from her hand. His jaw tightened, his stare fixated on the machine, and his shoulders hunched in self-protection.

"You know that kind of airplane?" The sky dancer spun around, came back, and waggled its wings at them. This time, some smaller print showed up: *De Havilland - D H 4.* The pilot, dark goggles holding down a scraggle of curly red hair, waved at them.

Al always answered right away, even if he wasn't sure of his reply. But not this time.

She turned toward him as the plane made another pass. "Al?"

His face crumpled like Jeffy's when he had fallen down and scraped his knee. Startled by the sight of his own blood, it took a few moments for the little fellow to howl. Now, Al looked exactly that way—startled and distraught.

The plane's drone carried him back to the countryside of Northern France. He held his breath. Where was his buddy, John Milford? Major Anders sent them to patrol around their base camp. But John thought he heard something, signaled for Al to wait, and crawled up an incline.

Waiting for the birdcall signal, Al peered from some low bushes. But the sign never came. He waited longer, hoping John would reappear, and tried to figure out what to do if he didn't. Then a low hum, like his older brother's motorcycle turning toward home on a clear Midwestern day, reached his ears.

But an ocean and a war separated him from such pleasant reality—his parents sent word that Al's brother now languished in some makeshift French army hospital. Perspiration rode Al's collar—any moment might give him the same fate, or worse.

He ducked farther into the scraggly growth along a field's border.

No crop this year, that was sure. Unruly rows succumbed to so many tramping boots that it was impossible to tell what grain once grew here.

The *bangity-bang* of his pulse hedged his hearing. The hum increased. A scrape of trees along the field's southern edge invited him to investigate, but he had no idea what that haphazard grove held. Maybe John had arched into it, or maybe it disguised a gaggle of Huns.

When in doubt, wait. This unwritten rule threaded through their makeshift unit, mostly farm boys who wanted nothing more than to make it back to fertile fields and family. In an awkward squat, Al waited, his empty stomach voicing its disapproval.

The drone turned into a buzz. Just beyond the grove, he saw it—a warplane. German or Allied? Sunlight reflected off its body, but when he got a closer look, a relieved sigh shuddered from him. American—a D H - 4 de Havilland, one of the newer makes.

Designed in Great Britain, made in the U.S.A., she carried either bombs or precise photographic equipment that could capture even a footprint on the ground. If she carried bombs, it might mean that grove sequestered enemy troops. Moisture dripped from Al's forehead to sour on his lips.

The buzz transformed into a boisterous roar—no bombs—must be a photography team. But the plane's left wing clipped something. The thwack of metal on wood slashed the air. He couldn't see what the pilot hit—probably a wide poplar branch.

He rose without thinking and heard his own moan as the plane spun around, the landing gear crumpled like a paper wad. A maniacal hiss steeped his senses as she rolled into a ball of wire and metal framing.

He crept forward. Arms flailed as the passenger fought his seatbelt. With no thought of enemies, Al vaulted toward him. There'd be a camera to save, possibly loaded with precious photos of enemy positions.

The soldier struggled in his seat, but something hindered his progress. He reached behind him for his camera, and scrabbling onto the wing, Al grabbed the khaki canvas strap. He reached for the soldier's stubborn buckle, and in what seemed like hours, forced the catch into submission. The photographer peeled his body from the pit, and Al propelled him away from the plane.

Behind them, the hiss ballooned into a roar. Al dropped the camera case and raced back, but the aviator's head hung forward. Must've hit against the windshield in the crash. He launched up the wing, inhaling petrol fumes. *Help me get to him.*

The plane transformed into a torch. Scalding oil scorched the pilot. Hot black splats penetrated Al's olive wool uniform, and intense heat formed a wall around the airplane. Al gasped forward into tunneling, acrid smoke that concealed the screaming man from sight.

But powerful hands grappled at his waist and pulled him backward. Crinkled metal crackled and blistered. Wood splintered, sending ragged pieces from the smoke spire like Fourth of July rockets.

"It's too late. He's a goner." The photographer's breath hit the base of Al's neck, and though he strained to try one more time, his rescuer prevailed. "Stop, man—nothing we can do for him now."

That was the last Al remembered: the sickening stench of burning wool and seared flesh. He woke in a medical tent, where someone told him the photographer had knocked him out and gone for help.

He hadn't let the memory surface—not when he was awake—for almost thirty years. After those first few times at the hardware store where some customer had to call him back from this nightmare, he'd learned how to squelch it. Part of the secret was staying so busy his mind had no opportunity to wander.

The specter still stalked him in the night, though, and he always woke with a desperate hope of saving that pilot. If he only had one more chance, he would run faster, pull harder, and never give up.

Wet sand crumbled between his fingers. Dottie's hand worked under his neck. But an unfamiliar male voice jolted him.

Dottie's tones came through, soothing as silk. "Al, are you all right?" Her hands on his shoulders, soft brown eyes enormous, she leaned so close he smelled lavender. Her breath came in spurts, or was it his own? Sunshine soothed his bare arms, sand gritted between his toes and under his knees, and the sky's blue hurt his eyes.

A strong arm and the scent of Bay Rum pulled him up. "Want me to call an ambulance?"

Dottie squeezed his shoulder. "Al, can you talk to me?" He squeezed her hand and attempted to communicate with his eyes that he would be okay. She turned to the stranger.

"No. No, thank you. I think—I believe he's all right now."

"I'll be right over there if you need me. Those pilots are a menace." The man shuffled off, and Dottie took Al's face in her hands.

Heat scourged the back of his neck and scalp, yet icy prickles covered him as she smoothed her fingers down his arms. Then he buried his face in her shoulder, a child awash with sobs. Moments passed, or was it hours? He stumbled along with her, felt the blanket under his feet.

"Here, drink this."

The rush of coolness on his tongue brought him closer to the beach, to their blanket…to Dottie. The soft fabric of her dress quieted him. Her eyes testified unquestioning acceptance and concern. Even the blanket's coarse filament felt right against his hands.

The worst was over. He only needed to breathe.

She didn't say a word, but simply sat there holding his head, and the longer she did, the more he loved her. He didn't even attempt to hold back the drops that still coursed down his cheeks. Her eyes filled too—he felt at one with her. After a while, she eased her face closer to his.

"You're going to be all right, Al."

Even though he had no idea how to start, he owed her some explanation. The strange thing was, he wanted to tell her—tell her things he'd never breathed to another human being, not even to Nan.

They stared at the tide, whooshing back and forth, a giant's breath. In and out, day after day and year after year, that tide continued, totally reliable. Though the world erupted in war, though millions died, the tide still continued, in and out, day and night. Pastor Langley would liken it to the faithfulness of the Almighty, he supposed.

When he glanced at Dot, her serious expression gave him permission to do whatever he needed—speak or remain silent. Just what he needed. It took a while longer for the words to well in him, another while for him to wrestle them out.

"That plane took me back to France, a long time ago…to a day when I only accomplished half of what I wanted to."

The story resurrected piecemeal, faltering out stiff-legged and halting, like Lazarus coming to life again. But Dot understood, as much as anyone could. Her eyes told him so.

"That's why, when you saw that medal with the purple ribbon that day just before we left…"

He nodded. "Yeah. That brought it all back, too."

"Thank you for telling me."

"I could never talk about it before, but something changed today—I don't understand it at all. But seeing that de Havilland so close, and the pilot, out for a lark…"

"I can't imagine. You must be exhausted."

"Drained, yes. But you know what?" He sat up and lifted her hand to his lips. "Dennis needs us tonight while he goes down to see Cora. I want to get back to our babysitting job. I miss Jeffy."

She shook her head. "Al, you're amazing."

He stood and pulled her up. She bent for the blanket and they folded it together. On the last fold, he brought her into his arms.

"Thanks for listening to me—for being here. Somehow, I think things will get better from now on."

For once, Al fell asleep while they waited for Dennis to get back from the hospital. So did the children, and Dottie sat in the twilight, content to watch the rise and fall of their breathing, the children's so much faster than Al's. He cradled Joy against his chest, and their grandson's husky body covered the area between them on the couch. She fluffed Jeffy's fine hair with her fingers, marveling at the heat rising from his head.

February sixteenth—she thought no day could ever hold as much as yesterday, but then today came. Seeing Al collapse, fixated on his tormenting memory, her heart catapulted into her throat. He fell so suddenly, like a tree axed into submission.

What could she do but kneel beside him and pray? When the bystander offered his help, Al started to return to her. A voice could change things, like the touch of someone you loved. He still couldn't respond, yet his eyes revealed he wanted to.

And then, his story—at the time, she hadn't known what to do with it, like the unneeded decorations Helene sometimes purchased for the boarding house. Walls, shelves, and drawers already over-flowed with unused objects—why did she insist on buying more? But Dottie always found storage room and better yet, when Helene wanted them, remembered where she'd put them.

But this story—where could she put it? Maybe she had no choice in the matter—the scene had already etched its outlines in her consciousness. And maybe because that was true—because it was real to her as an onlooker, with Al the main character, she'd absorbed some of its poison. She hoped so—maybe part of the pain would be lost to him from now on. She was thankful to share it.

Tires scraped the driveway, and the Chevy's lights swirled over the room as Dennis circled the yard. Touching Al's neck, Joy's hair shone silvery in the lamplight. Such a lot of life here on this couch—such an abundance of precious life. The screen door squeaked open, and Dennis walked in.

"You're the only one left standing?"

"Guess so—I had a lot of rest today, and of course, I want to hear everything."

Dennis plopped into an armchair almost too small to contain his bulk. "They're all doing fine." He leaned his head back and released a long breath. "Cora's rallying, still a little pale. But besides everything her body's been through, she's had a shock—two babies instead of one.

"Hard to believe, but they both seem bigger today, or maybe it's that their color looks better. The nurses wheeled them into Cora's room, and we got to hold them."

He stretched his legs out. "That is, Cora did. I decided to wait—they looked so miniature in her hands, I couldn't trust myself to handle them quite yet."

"Hmm…don't know if I'd be ready for that, either."

"Prepare yourself, because I can bring you along tomorrow night—a Grandma gets special privileges, you know."

"Thank you. I'll…we'll see."

Dennis swept his hand over the couch. "Looks like the day wore Al out—or Jeffy did."

"Probably a combination, but it's the best kind of worn out." Dottie surveyed Al's slack jaw, and her voice came out in a whisper.

"An old war memory came back to him today, Dennis. I had no idea he saved someone's life…he's a hero. But another man died, and Al still feels he failed. He's kept that inside all these years. Nan confided that he's always been a fitful sleeper, and now I know why."

A shadow flickered over her son-in-law's features. Maybe he muzzled his own war memories. Dottie waited, but he only stared at Al's sleeping form. "You've found a good man."

"You're right. And you're a good man, too. Cora and I are lucky women." Jeffy stirred, opened his eyes, saw Dennis, and backed off the couch. He bounced across the room into Daddy's arms.

"*Oopfh!*" Dennis did a mock drawback as Jeffy hit his chest. "How's my big boy tonight? You have fun with Gwamps?"

Joy stirred and Dottie touched her back. The little girl's eyelashes fluttered, and her lips curled into a scowl. Soon she would let forth

a hungry wail. But so far, Al stayed asleep—that told Dottie what she wanted to know.

"I'll fix Joy's bottle."

"Thanks. Guess I brought trouble." Dennis cuddled Jeffy in one arm and reached for Dottie with his other hand. "We have our work cut out for us, don't we?"

When Dottie returned with the bottle, Dennis had left to put Jeffy in bed, and Al patted Joy's back. "About time you brought this little girl some food!"

Dennis took the bottle from Dottie on his way back into the living room and grinned. "Here, let me do the honors. You'll have plenty of bottle holding to do in a few days."

Al handed Joy over to him, and Dennis nestled her in the crook of his arm. Then, with a tender sigh, he addressed Al and Dottie. "Thanks for being here. Thanks for everything."

Al twined his fingers in Dottie's. "It's our pleasure. Good night, now."

Under a twinkling halo of stars, the walk from the house to their quarters took on a magical quality. Al's arm so close, the touch of his fingers, the thought of spending the rest of their lives together, surrounded by all these little ones, filled her heart to bursting.

"Thanks for letting me sleep, Dot. I must've needed it."

"We all do from time to time. Remember when I went to sleep that time you massaged my feet?"

"Of course I do. Nothing that important escapes my memory, dear. That night, I felt as though there was hope."

"What do you mean?"

"Hope for me, that you liked me enough to trust me."

Dottie leaned into his arm as they sank on the steps to stargaze. "So what will you do if I fall asleep again, here and now?"

"That's easy. I'll carry you up to bed." He nuzzled her neck. "I'm so glad we're in this together, Dottie Jensen."

# About the Author

Words have always been comfort food for Gail Kittleson. After instructing expository writing and English as a Second Language, she began writing seriously. Intrigued by the World War II era, Gail creates historical fiction from her northern Iowa home and also facilitates writing workshops/retreats.

She and her husband, a retired Army chaplain, enjoy grandchildren and in winter, Arizona's Mogollon Rim Country. You can count on Gail's protagonists to ask honest questions, act with integrity, grow in faith, and face hardships with spunk.

Visit Gail online at:

GailKittleson.com